Praise for Alexander Boldizar

"Alexander Boldizar's brilliantly wild *The Man Who Saw Seconds* is part thriller, part gunfight (hell of a gunfight), part intellectual examination of what we mean we say 'freedom,' and all heart. Absurd, hilarious, and deadly serious, this is the rare novel that is both compulsively readable and philosophically deft. If the thought of Kafka as a chess boxer, or Kundera fighting a polar bear excites you, this is definitely the book for you."

Mark Powell, author of *Hurricane Season*

"There are books on brain physiology, books on anarchist philosophy, books on the nature of time. There are certainly books whose hero is pursued by governments of all stripes, books in which the entire world is at stake. There are books whose body counts put Schwarzenegger movies to shame. But there has never been a book to combine all of these with supreme intelligence, set not in some remote future but an all-too-plausible present. *The Man Who Saw Seconds* is the first."

Aaron Haspel, author of *Everything*

"With Jason Bourne's frenetic pace and The Terminator's body count, *The Man Who Saw Seconds* is at the surface an action-packed thriller. But as I raced through the pages I also delighted in Boldizar's intelligence and humor as—bit by bit—he shows us how male decision cycles and egos can escalate the mayhem. I kept thinking, 'No, he won't,' but then he did, and I was fascinated at every turn. This nail-biting novel left me blinking, reeling and contemplating fear and love, and the horrifying extremes we'll go to for each."

Emma Payne, author of *Technology with Curves*

"*The Man Who Saw Seconds* is wickedly smart, outrageously funny, and unsettling in its accuracy. The satire is pointed, and the action is non-stop. Think: Elmore Leonard meets Nabokov, Michael Crichton meets Vonnegut, Carl Hiaasen meets Joseph Heller. And it has what is probably the best gunfight in literary history. But this book is more than a fast-paced satire. It's a warning for America, for the world, really. And, at its core, it's a poignant love story. *The Man Who Saw Seconds* is destined to be a classic and, with it, Boldizar's place as one of literature's most important satirical writers is assured."

Kevin Winchester, author of *Sunflower Dog*

THE MAN WHO SAW SECONDS

ALEXANDER BOLDIZAR

For Samson, of course. And in memory of Tania—though time gives me hope it's never just memory.

THE MAN WHO SAW SECONDS

"Now he has departed from this strange world a little ahead of me. That means nothing. People like us, who believe in physics, know that the distinction between past, present, and future is only a stubbornly persistent illusion."

—Albert Einstein in a letter to the family of his lifelong friend, Michele Besso, March 1955

"Very specific and personal misfortune awaits those who presume to believe that the future is revealed to them."

—John Kenneth Galbraith in The Great Crash, 1929

"Time flies like an arrow, but fruit flies like a banana."

—Groucho Marx

Chapter 1

"You need to think like a monster," Fish said as he and Preble walked out of the Flea House. "Just a little bit. Just enough to crush the other guy's mind."

"That's always your answer."

Fish's saggy, anarchic face took on a look of mock hurt. "Chess is war."

"For you." This was an old debate that Preble Jefferson found ironic, given their preferred styles. Preble was the current New York state champion in both chessboxing—alternating rounds of chess and boxing—and one-minute bullet chess. Fish played traditional, slow chess. But for Preble, both chess and boxing were fun, social games that helped him train his window. He could never beat his friend at an hour-long game, which Fish insisted was half psychology and all war.

They played every Thursday at the new Flea House in lower Manhattan—the original in Times Square had been turned first into the World Wrestling Federation store and then The Disney Store—and always finished with a game of slow chess, because he couldn't cheat at slow chess the way he could with anything that happened at a faster pace.

Fish raised his hands slightly in surrender. "All I meant was take time to cook your opponent. Whatever that means to your strange brain. You want a lift home?"

"Nah, thanks." The way the subways ran this late he'd need to transfer, but he could never sleep properly on a Thursday night anyway. "It'll give me a chance to replay my mistakes."

Preble walked the two blocks to the subway, then headed underground. The clock behind the empty attendant's booth said 1:58 AM. The one on the platform said 2:09 AM. "Why would you need two clocks if they told the same time, right?" he said to himself aloud. There was no one else on the platform.

The 4 train eventually arrived, as empty as the platform. He walked in and sat down absentmindedly, thinking about Fish's opening. Preble knew it was a Ruy Lopez variation, though he refused to study chess books. He kept his chess to Thursdays, tournaments and boxing rings. When someone asked how he could play at his level without studying, he said he didn't want to turn his brain into a storehouse of useless information. It was true to a certain extent, and offensive enough to other chess players that it cut off any further questions. But Preble's real reason for not studying was a personal sense of ethics, not anything strictly rational: since he already had one big advantage he felt he should counterbalance it with a disadvantage. He liked balance.

The subway stopped and two NYPD officers came in, looking almost like a couple. As the train started up again, they stood talking at the other end of his car. Preble was always happy to see cops making their rounds. He would never need them himself, but when he and Jane had first moved to Williamsburg the neighbourhood had still been rough—they'd moved in just as the very first wave of lawyers and investment bankers had started to drive the artists out to Berlin or Detroit, their financial comfort visible enough to make their building a target of anti-gentrification posters and a few burglaries. The RMPs driving by and the beat cops walking their routes always made Jane feel safer. And for that, Preble was always grateful, a feeling that multiplied exponentially when Kasper was born. It was the reason he'd been a touch irritated by Fish tonight.

Fish's real name was Robert Legmegbetegedettebbeknek. The Hungarian word meant "the sickest," but since that was nearly unpronounceable by anyone other than another Hungarian, since he was only 5'5", and since he styled himself after Bobby Fisher, he'd gone through some nickname drift from Little Fisher to Little Fish to just Fish. Having survived the communists in Hungary as a teenager, Fish's opinion of all authority was low, and when they played he tended to talk politics all game long. He called himself an anarchist, and his favourite topic was tearing down "the machine," or at least, in his words, cracking it a little to let some light in. Fish was also a Leonard Cohen fan.

Preble's own dislike of the government started and ended with the IRS. On some Thursday nights, by the end of the evening, he might find himself vaguely agreeing with Fish that the city was becoming a bit claustrophobic, that Central Park now seemed to have more fenceposts than grass and that there wasn't an unlit alley left anywhere in Manhattan. But that political hangover from the Flea House was flushed out every Friday morning by the knowledge that his family was safe because of the fences that the police built with their "thin blue line." It was no contest, really.

Sort of like their game tonight. Whatever could be said about his politics, Fish could play chess like few others in the Flea House. Preble had responded with the Arkhangelsk Defence because he liked sharp positions, like the chins on the poster he realized he was staring at on the subway wall: three square-jawed passengers—multiethnic Wall Street types, chins bravely raised, ties fluttering back in the wind—held stoically onto subway poles. Bold text reminded riders to *WATCH, RIDE AND REPORT*, with smaller text underneath saying *Report any unusual activities or packages to the nearest police officer*. Preble was used to the *If you see something, say something* message, so much so he didn't notice those anymore, but this one was new. It seemed stolen from Goebbels. Or Stalin. Or Disney.

He smiled to himself at the thought of Goebbels enforcing his copyright, tried to get back to thinking about Arkhangelsk and how it caused him to delay castling, and looked at the two officers just as the male was saying to his partner, "Next time, they want my badge number, know what, I don't care. But I ain't giving the perp my pen. Might stab me in the neck with it. You never know. I'm telling you, don't put yourself out there, 'cause you never know."

The officer noticed Preble watching, and stopped talking as

their eyes locked. Preble wasn't really staring at the officer. He was thinking about the poster and Goebbels and Disney and Fish. Together with the officer's story, they brought one of Fish's favourite sayings, crude and unbidden: *the pen is mightier than the pig.*

Fish used the childish double meaning—pen vs sword and pen as fence, fence as laws—to explain why a self-proclaimed anarchist would become first a lawyer and then a law professor. To Preble this seemed like a recipe for unhappiness, but he knew Fish would consider both the poster and the overheard conversation a gem. But for now, Preble tried to chase his friend out of his head and the smile off his face as he realized he'd been staring and the staring had turned into an accidental contest.

Too late. The cop straightened his belt and walked towards him.

The subway sped up as it went under the East River, bouncing hard, and the big cop had to catch his balance on a pole. The wobbliness clashed with his barrel chest and general size, the muscle-and-fat mass of ex-football players, and it slowed his approach. His partner was small, tiny for a cop, with blond hair in a ponytail. There was a wariness about her, but it was only skin deep, like the premature wrinkles on either side of her mouth—not like Fish's bone-deep, almost Darwinian circumspection. She followed three steps behind her partner, gyroscopically erect in the bouncing car without holding on to anything. Maybe she'd been a gymnast. Preble couldn't help but notice the contrast between the way the two cops moved.

He could see the future, and he could see this was going bad.

It had started when he hit puberty, at first barely noticeable, a half second or so. But with a lifetime of training—chess, boxing, gambling—he'd expanded it to nearly five seconds. With a five-second window he was never surprised by events, except when he became emotional or absentminded or there was a heavy human component. Unfortunately, he was absentminded far too often, and most interactions were with humans. Now he broke eye contact with the large cop but couldn't quite bring himself to stop smiling, even though he knew the cop would take it the wrong way.

Officer L. Paskalakki, according to his name tag, took his time looking at Preble, then at the chess bag on the seat beside him. "Seat hoggery."

"Pardon me, officer?"

"You're taking up two seats." He turned to his partner, R. Gliny. "What was the summons on that? We were doing it a month ago."

"Section 1050.7."

There was nobody else on the subway, at least not in this car. Just Preble, his chess bag, and the two standing cops. Paskalakki didn't stop until he was so close that one of his knees was between Preble's legs. "That's right. Section 1050.7"

His biggest problem was people. Maybe every human mind had the potential for so many near-random decisions—he'd seen Thornton Wilder's *Our Town* in high school and even then had been struck by the line, "Whenever you come near the human race, there's layers and layers of nonsense"—that the sheer amount of information was far higher when dealing with people than with a slot machine or a falling rock. He thought of it in terms of ripples: bigger rocks made bigger ripples, humans more fragmented ones. Now, what came out of Preble's mouth surprised even him. "You've got to be kidding."

Paskalakki shook his head, moving and speaking with deliberate slowness. "You could have answered that in a whole lot of different ways."

Maybe the WATCH, RIDE AND REPORT message of the poster actually did bother him. Maybe he did agree with Fish a little bit or just because it was a Thursday night. Maybe it was because Paskalakki was so close that Preble had to look straight up to talk to him, triggering something that had nothing to do with politics and everything to do with personal space and two men facing each other.

"I could have," he said, forced to crank his neck all the way back in order to maintain eye contact. "But I was just sitting here minding my own business, smiling because of that ugly poster up there, and thinking about a friend who's always complaining that in this city you can get a ticket for sitting on a milk crate or putting on a puppet show visible from the street or climbing a tree or driving a taxi while wearing shorts. If a man in blue has a badge that's too heavy for him, he can always find something."

"Maybe what your friend meant is that acting like an ass isn't going to help the situation. Break the law, and, yeah, I'll bring you into compliance."

If Preble didn't say anything, Paskalakki would just continue to stand there, neither moving to write a ticket nor adding anything for at least five seconds. So he asked, "How much is one ticket, officer?"

"Fifty-seven, ninety."

"Okay, then. I'll take two please."

"What?"

"I'd like to buy two tickets for section 1050.7, please. One for me and one for my bag. Is two enough? I want to make sure I'm obeying the law. So that's $115.80, right? Or should I buy five just to be safe? Safety is important, right?"

Gliny's face cracked. "Are you serious?"

Paskalakki took a step back. Preble could see that in a second the cop would flip the cover off his holster, but as the cop stepped back the physical space cleared Preble's head. Five seconds wasn't enough to get hypothetical answers to personal questions, but maybe Paskalakki was just tired of working the 12 to 8 shift every night, giving bullshit summonses like late-night seat hoggery because that's when the brass could get the numbers—when the trains are crowded people don't take up two seats. Maybe his father was sick or he was battling his wife for custody of his kids during the day while working at night. Maybe a million things, and maybe Preble *was* being an ass. With a twinge of guilt, he reached into his pocket to get his wallet.

Paskalakki flipped the cover off his holster but didn't draw the gun. "Keep your hands where I can see them!" He pointed a finger at the culprit taking up the second seat. "Open the bag."

Preble nodded at the holster. "You're not going to shoot me for being a jerk. Which I apologize for. Let's just do the ticket. You need my ID, right?"

"Open the bag."

"Like I said, I apologize. You're right. Bad manners I picked up in a chess club—"

"Last time. 'Open the bag.'"

Preble sighed and reached to unzip the bag. There was nothing in there except a chess clock (thankfully not ticking!), board, pieces, and a copy of *Liberty Unbound* in which Fish had just published an essay. An anarchist essay in a libertarian magazine. Paskalakki wouldn't care about his reading material—this particular essay was about big corporations being similar to big governments, not anything critical of law or order—there was no reason to refuse to open the bag. Except that the person asking was doing it purely to show who was boss. Preble knew he'd been doing the same thing with the two-ticket bit, treating the cop like a subway attendant, but Paskalakki had the full weight of the United States government backing him. It felt like a violation of an honour code, bringing a gun and a gang into verbal fisticuffs.

Fish always said that if only people with severed heads in their bags claimed their rights, then pretty soon those rights would be gone. Then he'd have to open his bag whenever someone like Paskalakki said so. And soon after, they *would* start examining his reading material.

Preble took his hand off the bag. "I'm sorry, officer. I apologize for being rude earlier. But I also don't consent to a bag search."

"On the subway, you don't have a choice."

"The law is that you can search me as I enter the subway, so long as I have the option of walking away. That option is the only reason the subway search law was found constitutional." He'd had so many conversations about this with Fish and a dozen other aging ornery ex-Soviet émigrés turned libertarians who played chess at the Flea House that Preble felt like a second-hand expert in the Fourth Amendment. It was amazing how much anarchists knew about law. Like vegans who know more about meat and digestion of meat and slaughterhouse procedures and how many acres of feed a cow uses than any normal omnivore—though Fish was more like the vegan who works in a slaughterhouse just so he can really absorb the awfulness.

Preble had never expected to find himself repeating Fish's voice to a cop's face. He was tired, he'd played chess all evening and didn't want to think, and the whole conversation seemed absurd, like he'd jumped into the poster across from him while in the real world cops who were not named Paskalakki continued to maintain the bubble of protection that kept his wife and son safe from all the crackheads, rapists and gangsters. He saw what was coming, a few seconds of it, anyway, but it was like a dream.

Paskalakki was done jumping through hoops. He pulled out his old cocobolo wood baton, the kind still referred to as "n- knock- ers" by the old-timers. It wasn't standard issue for the NYPD, which preferred the unmarkable, collapsible metal batons, but cops had some leeway in choosing equipment, especially if they could show it was inherited from an MOS father or uncle. "Let me tell you something, Adam Henry," Paskalakki said now, his voice slow and cold, like he'd learned at some point in his past that anger didn't have to go hot, that it can come out either hot or cold. "There's more law in Billy here than in all your law books. Now open the bag."

Preble didn't know who Adam Henry was, and he didn't need to be able to see the future in order to know things were going downhill fast. Living in Brooklyn was precognition enough. "I'm sorry, officer," he apologized again, trying to find the right balance in a situation that still didn't seem real. "I'm not going to open the bag, because that would be consenting to an illegal search. I'm not going to physically stop you. But—"

Preble suddenly shut his mouth, because he saw that he'd just gone much further down the wrong road, as though from the whole sentence Officer Paskalakki had somehow only heard "physically stop you," without the negation in front. To Preble, he seemed to have a particularly chaotic decision-making process, and together with everything else, Preble's fatigue and irritation, it shrunk his window. And suddenly it was too late to stop the cascade of events short of letting himself be slapped around.

"We're done talking," Paskalakki said and yanked Preble's shoulder. He lifted him out of his seat and slammed him chest-first into the vertical pole hard enough to knock the wind out of him if he hadn't exhaled, while twisting his left arm behind his back.

Preble wasn't easy to shove. Besides boxing, he'd studied a half-dozen martial arts, always picking clubs that emphasized "aliveness" in sparring, from MMA and BJJ to Dog Brothers and garages filled with street toughs who spent the class punching bags of pennies to toughen their knuckles, then fighting to submis- sion while still wearing street shoes. Being shoved by Paskalakki shifted his mindset into a lifetime of almost-mechanical training reactions. They jumped ahead of the knowledge that fighting back was a bad idea.

As Paskalakki reached for his right arm, Preble stepped into it and slammed his elbow into Paskalakki's own solar plexus. The cop gasped and stepped back.

Behind him Gliny drew her gun. Paskalakki caught his breath and brought Billy swinging.

Preble saw where the swing would go and how his own potential movements would change where both Paskalakki and Gliny aimed. He felt echoes of a giant kick to his left side, knocking the wind out of him without pushing him over, then an intense burn, like someone had shoved a red-hot poker through his ribs that exploded into a hundred burning pieces inside his chest, leaving it hollowed out, a cavity where his heart had been.

He'd lived his death countless times, in millions of potential futures five seconds away—every time a subway arrived or a car drove past, he could not just imagine jumping in front, but experienced that little unlived strand of the future like a chess player who doesn't just think of contingencies and checkmates but plays each of them out and then rewinds. Gunshot deaths were less common, but not new. Here, it was one possibility among countless, all still a few seconds away, from a shot through the heart to a bullet through his hand to making one cop disarm the other. He chose that one.

Preble stepped back and twisted as Paskalakki came at him, just as Gliny lifted her gun and pointed it at Preble's torso. Paskalakki's swing smashed down on her hand, and she dropped her gun with a sound that was half-scream, half-grunt.

Despite the pain, her own training kicked in and she immediately lunged for her gun on the floor with her left hand. At the same moment, Paskalakki tried to smash his club into Preble with an uppercut slash that was all rage. It hit Gliny's throat. Choking, she grabbed for her larynx with her broken hand and pulled the trigger with the other. Preble knew the bullet was going to hit Paskalakki in the thigh, but under the circumstances that seemed better than getting shot himself.

The sound of the gun inside the train was shockingly loud. Paskalakki collapsed on the floor. Preble twisted the gun out of Gliny's hand and pointed it at Paskalakki, who'd just started reaching for his own gun.

"Shit," Preble said, ears still ringing, as he realized he was pointing a gun at an NYPD Officer. They'd both reacted like idiots. But the difference was that Paskalakki was a cop and Preble should have known better.

"Shit, shit, shit!" He was calm now, but too late. He could see consequences before they happened, but those were immediate things, actions. It didn't mean he "thought ahead" in the grown-up sense of the expression, not when he just reacted as he'd now done.

Paskalakki dropped his own gun, then lay down. The subway floor was already covered with blood. Preble took the two guns, and a radio from Paskalakki.

"What's "officer needs medical attention'?" *No, no, no!* Preble cursed himself again. He'd turned an avoidable situation into a monstrous mess. Why hadn't he just taken the ticket and moved his bag?

Gliny gurgled and Paskalakki didn't answer at all. But Preble didn't need an answer. He lived in a fragmented future with infinite monkeys on infinite typewriters eventually authoring Hamlet —when he was calm, anyway, and when the reactions on the other end were fast enough—and he could just take a step backwards, from effect to cause. He clicked the radio on. "Ten thirteen. Two officers down in third car of 4 train currently at Bowling Green station headed to Wall Street. Need urgent medical attention. Repeat, 10-13 at uptown Wall Street 4 train in three minutes."

At that moment, the subway stopped and the car door opened. He dropped the two guns between the subway car and the platform, and started to run.

Then stopped himself. A strong ripple: If he returned to the train, he'd see that officer R. Gliny was drowning in her own throat. She'd probably be dead before the train reached Wall Street.

Preble cursed and jumped back onto the 4 train just as the doors were trying to close.

Chapter 2

When Preble jumped into the car, Paskalakki was on the floor, describing him into the radio: "...blue jeans, white T-shirt, worn brown Brooklyn Industries messenger bag."

He was bleeding too much. The NYPD uses dumdums, hollow-point bullets that explode inside a body, sending shattered fragments through arteries, veins and organs. Dumdums are illegal under international law for military use, against the Geneva Convention, but the NYPD used them anyway. The official reason was to stop the bullet from exiting and hitting innocent bystanders, but what the NYPD liked was that it stopped the bad guys cold. *The bad guys: that would be me*, Preble thought. *Damn.*

Five seconds hadn't been enough. He should have trained harder. If only he'd trained harder.

He half-rolled Paskalakki and took the pen from his breast pocket and a knife from his utility belt. He ripped the ballpoint out with his teeth, cut a slit into the unconscious Gliny's throat, then shoved the pen casing in at an angle that, two seconds later, would lead to a quivering intake of breath.

Paskalakki stopped talking, eyes glassy, unresisting. Preble thought of unbuckling the utility belt but saw that the various police gadgets wouldn't slide off. So he took off his own shirt and tied it around Paskalakki's thigh, above the entry wound. Wall

Street would be full of cops—someone would get Paskalakki to a hospital. And Gliny was unconscious but breathing through her improvised tracheotomy. And Preble was going to have problems.

━━

Ant colonies can exhibit such sophisticated behaviour that early entomologists theorized mechanisms as improbable as telepathic links to explain how an animal as simple as an ant could aggregate to create such complexity. Their language of pheromone trails is only capable of about twenty different signals, and yet they all seem to know where the food is, where the threat is, how to respond, in what numbers, whether to avoid another colony or fight with it, when to forage, build nests or take care of young, where to put their cemetery (furthest point from the colony), where to put their garbage (so as to maximize both distance from the colony and from the cemetery), and so on.

Ants with no forebrain and a language of only twenty pheromonal signals make complex political decisions and solve difficult geometry problems simply by crowding. The sheer number of individual information exchanges creates a quasi-intelligent system of its own. By encouraging random encounters between individuals, paying attention to each other's neighbours, and treating quantity as a quality signifying importance, the ant colony prioritizes tasks and conveys information to individual ants that don't ever have to think of the idea of a colony any more than a cell in a human body has to think about the body. The *inability* to think of the big picture and the simplicity of the language is a key factor to the system. A densely interconnected swarm made up of simple elements creates patterns of sophisticated behaviour, whereas an individual ant capable of thinking about the colony would be as destabilizing—as cancerous—as a suddenly sentient human cell.

Police ten codes serve a similar simplifying function. Besides creating a separation between police and civilians, limiting the types of information that an officer can convey to a dispatcher to roughly one hundred total possibilities allows the information to be aggregated. It allows systemic patterns to emerge. Like forager ants, 39,000 NYPD officers wander the city, seeking random encounters, looking for patterns, paying attention to their environment and their fellow cops. Like the pheromone trails of ants, increased police radio activity on a particular city block will be enough to bring more police to that block. More is different. A uniformed officer who thinks about the city as a whole is not doing his job. One who thinks about his street corner and sends simple data up to the dispatcher is. But the dispatcher is not a commander. She is a filter who aggregates the information that comes to her and responds with predetermined responses that themselves were created by a process of evolution within the system, based on millions of previous cycles. Successful responses survived, unsuccessful ones died out.

When the "officer down" 10-13 call came through to the dispatcher, her procedures were simple. She repeated the call and the location, and every cop in lower Manhattan dropped what he or she was doing—writing summonses, helping homeless shift their cardboard homes out of doorways, chasing kids over subway turnstiles, blogging on NYPD RANT with their RMP Toshiba Toughbooks, eating Pakistani food, bitching about brass, searching an attitudinal teenager for the eleventh time this week just to teach him how things work, or waiting for a street-corner douchebag to make a deal—and drove at full speed to the Wall Street subway station. As soon as the dispatcher repeated the 10-13, an integrated command and control system, adapted from the U.S. military and designed to ensure information integrity, used voice-recognition software to automatically create a log of the 10-13 call as well as its location. Because it was a 10-13, the computer slaved all the NYPD TARU cameras tagged with that location and began silently streaming copies of all footage into a file it created for this incident. At the same time, it created a one-sentence summary that was automatically routed to the precinct captain, and if the precinct captain was off duty, then to the highest-ranking NYPD officer in the bureau—in this case, South Manhattan. And because the Google Maps-derived software tagged the location of the incident inside one of the department's "terror zones," the computer also horizontally disseminated all relevant information—filtered to correspond with how far up the receiving unit was in its own vertical chain of command—to the U.S. military. The individual national guard units at the Wall

Street and Broad Street entrances to the New York Stock Exchange building received the following simple instructions: "NYPD officer down at Wall Street subway station. Possible terrorist attack. Maintain positions. Prepare for live fire authorization." This was followed by an automated code proving the authenticity of the message.

Preble stepped out of the train and had a full second of odd quiet as four cops coming at him from across the platform saw and absorbed the fact that two uniforms lay on the ground in pools of blood. Then everything happened. All four had already drawn their guns, and two fired before he reached them.

But knowing the trajectory of the bullet was a big advantage. To the cops—and to the unblinking TARU video cameras—it looked like he was dodging bullets, but for Preble it was more like playing Twister. While running.

The NYPD training manual says fire three shots and evaluate, then fire three more and so on, but the only cops who follow this are ex-military. The overwhelming majority of police never fire their weapon live, not once throughout their entire career. And when they do, the shooting is like a virus, contagious and panicked. Once bullets start flying most cops keep shooting until their cartridges are empty, sometimes reloading without even being consciously aware of it. Which filled the air with bullets. Preble could duck and weave and contort himself, but he couldn't make himself any skinnier. In a few seconds there would be no room for him.

So he jumped between the cops, who kept tracking and shooting. Two went down, shot by each other, both in the vest. Then another went down, shoulder shattered by a dumdum. Preble ducked under another burst and pulled the last cop's wrist down just as he was about to fire again. The bullet went through his size-12 police-issue black shoe. Shocked by the pain, the cop almost didn't notice Preble twist the gun out of his hand as he fell to the ground.

"Tell them not to use guns."

The officer looked up at him, his face contorted in pain and surprise that Preble was talking to him. And pointing a gun at him. "What?"

There was total silence now in the subway.

"Go on the radio. And tell them that if they come at me with Billy clubs, then their only injuries will be from Billy clubs. But if they shoot at me, they'll end up shooting each other. There's not enough room for me between all the bullets. So tell them not to use guns."

"Tell who?"

"The hundred cops coming here right now."

"Jesus," the cop said, suddenly regaining his senses and noticing the other three cops on the ground. "Get an ambulance."

Preble pulled the radio out and gave it to the cop. He was forty, forty-five, mixed-race, black and Latino. He looked like he smiled a lot under other circumstances. "What's your name?"

The officer, Frank, looked up at Preble, watching him take the unconscious cops' guns with his left hand, moving like a cop himself except that the gun in his right hand was pointed at the ground in front of Frank instead of right at him. Cops were trained to keep a distance—if you see a perp as a human being, you hesitate, and if you hesitate you die. But this situation was backwards. He was at the wrong end of the gun, he was the one who wanted hesitation. "Frank. It's Frank. I live on Staten Island. I have two daughters and a wife."

"I'm not going to shoot you, Frank. I'm not going to shoot anyone. But when cops start shooting at me, they'll end up shooting each other. Like you and your three friends. So just tell them not to shoot, and nobody will get shot. And get your ambulance."

Frank nodded and pressed the button. "Ten-thirteen, four MOS down, request bus Wall Street subway station, north exit. Ten-sixty-one, within earshot. Officer held hostage. Perp, uh, subject says 'don't use guns.'"

The radio was silent for a second before the dispatcher answered, "Please repeat last. Over."

For the first time, Preble pointed the gun directly at Frank. "Say it like I said it."

"Subject says if members come at him with clubs, then he will only hit the members. If they come at him with guns, then subject will shoot them. Correct that, if they come at him with guns, they will end up shooting each other. That's what happened with the four of us. We all, uh, went down from each others' shots. Over."

Captain George Crumb liked the 12-to-8 tour. With the exception of noise complaints, a higher percentage of the calls that came in were real, rather than the quality-of-life crap that the mayor and commissioner, and thus deputy commissioners, inspectors, deputy inspectors and all the rest of the brass had suddenly decided were the new sliced bread of police work. As a captain, he was technically "brass" as well, but he still got to do things other than restructure CompSat numbers down at election time and up at budget time. At 2:30 AM the day after July 4th, technically July 6th already, he was in charge of all of Manhattan south of 14th Street, and he didn't have to think about his own precinct's numbers.

Everyone was tired from the night before, even the animals, and he was just opening a new bag of coffee—he made his own; the medium-roast stuff that sat in the precinct pot baking during the whole tour always gave him heartburn—when the 10-13 came in from what every cop still thought of as "dispatch" despite the monthly memos reminding them that the Public Safety Answering Point must be referred to as *PSAP* in all radio communications, never *dispatch,* so that the computer would understand. He would never understand how the brass could think it easier to retrain 39,000 cops than tell the damned software vendor to get the computer to recognize *dispatch.* But then Captain Crumb had given up on understanding the brass on a number of issues.

He requested live audio and cursed TARU for resisting full integration of its video cameras. He knew the computers automatically took control of all relevant devices, or at least those that the technicians had tagged correctly, but TARU segregated the footage so that it could only be viewed live from a TARU unit, a mobile command unit, or at One Police Plaza, but not in his own precinct. The footage was there, the little yellow file icon was on his computer, but the system wouldn't give him direct access. Meanwhile, a separate set of rules required the night captain to stay at his own precinct despite being responsible for a whole bureau. But audio didn't go through TARU, so he could at least listen live to his cops getting shot, even if he couldn't watch it.

The audio came on just as Frank was requesting a bus. By the time he got to "went down from each others' shots" Crumb was cursing TARU again and yelling at a sergeant to order footage. TARU couldn't just flip a switch, and with only a skeleton crew working, processing the video for vertical dissemination—since he was below deputy inspector, the computer considered it downward even though he was the ranking officer on duty at the moment—would take at least fifteen minutes. A lifetime of a difference from live footage.

Wall Street. How could this happen at Wall Street? The National Guard couldn't leave their posts, but even tonight there was enough firepower around Wall Street to fight off a small invasion. They'd just need a little time to get to the subway.

"This is Captain Crumb," a cigarette-damaged voice said over the radio, cutting off the dispatcher. "What's your name and shield?"

"Hi, George, it's—"

"Name and shield."

"PO Frank Barney, 890034, Transit Two, sir."

"There's a bus on the way. Who's hurt?"

Preble took the radio from Barney. "Sorry, captain, perp here. I don't have time for this. I don't want to hurt anyone. I am not armed. Repeat, I am not armed. Well, at this moment I am, but that's because the two cops who shot each other in the vest are conscious now and Frank here only shot himself in the foot and who knows what kind of ideas he'll get. As soon as I finish handcuffing them, I will throw all the guns away, and when the rest of your cops come after me, I will not be armed. All four of these cops were shot by cop guns. But I figure the way this works is they shoot each other and I get hunted by the whole city. So please, *please* tell them to come after me only with clubs or tasers. A hundred cops with clubs can surely take down one unarmed man."

"What's your name?"

"There's no honour in a gun, captain. Please tell your men that. I don't want this to spiral out of control. British cops don't use guns. Japanese cops don't use guns." He threw the radio onto the subway tracks and handcuffed all four cops, but before he could do anything with their guns, he foresaw two more cops coming down the subway stairs on his side, northbound. Followed by another pair.

He briefly hesitated, thinking maybe he should just give himself up. But the moment they saw four cops on the ground they'd open fire. They wouldn't give a blood-covered, half-naked man time to talk. Better to get out of here and walk into a precinct tomorrow morning, with a lawyer. And a shirt.

He jumped down to the tracks, across to the southbound platform and towards the Trinity Church exit. As he reached the exit, he had to dodge bullets aimed at his back. Two cops were coming down this entrance as well: they were storming all the entrances at once. He ran up the stairs at them, worried about having enough space in the narrow tunnel, but most of the shots went too high even without his ducking. Hitting a moving object with a pistol is difficult under the best circumstances and the stairs made for unusual aim. Preble made it between them without having to move more than an arm out of the way.

But once he was between the two cops, there was so little room it was hard to miss. Whether due to panic or an instinct to track a moving target or the knowledge that dumdums don't travel through a perp, both cops kept shooting and shooting. And there wasn't enough room for Preble to twist.

The cop on his right was left-handed, and after hesitating for a moment—a moment that was visible only within Preble's precog window, not in the "real time" in which the cops lived—Preble slammed the gun hand with his own open hand. Every other scenario played out with Preble getting shot. The outside of the other cop's hip exploded. He screamed and crumpled at the same time, then fell down the stairs. The shooter tried to grab Preble in a rage, but Preble ducked, pushed him after his partner, and kept running.

Pushing a hand was no worse than ducking—or rather, his form of prescient ducking was no better than pushing the hand or pulling the trigger himself for that matter—but it still shook him. Together with the scream, with the blood and pieces of pelvic bone, the push felt far more wrong. Intellectually, morally, he knew that there was no difference. In both cases, he'd put his own life ahead of another's. He'd injured, possibly killed—he didn't think so, but he couldn't see far enough to know for certain. He did it so he could live, but still, it was an awful thing. And he had started it by being a smart ass on the train. He had caused this.

Later.

There would be time for guilt later. Now he had to keep ducking. Definitely keep running. Cops were coming at him from all sides, cars screeching, and a police helicopter was five seconds from shining its light on him. But five seconds was an enormous amount of time in a firefight. He jumped over the Trinity Church fence and ran, weaving between gravestones, bullets and the helicopter light. The small cemetery was apocalyptic with cops. Alexander Hamilton's cenotaph took a half-dozen hits, and Preble thought of the one quote he'd always associated with Hamilton, "Hypocrisy is the first step to virtue," though Jane insisted, and then proved to him, that he had made it up, a double misremembering of La Rouchefoucauld's actual quote that "Hypocrisy is the tribute vice pays to virtue."

She'd once asked him, "How can a man who can see the future make so many mistakes?"

The cemetery was flat, but Rector Street slanted down, so the far fence on Trinity Place was raised off the street by a full storey. If he landed right, he wouldn't break anything. He jumped, then ducked to the left before a National Guard soldier standing at the near corner of the AMEX building—as far as he could go without technically leaving his post—started shooting.

Preble crossed Trinity Place, ran down Rector, right around the corner from an NYPD substation at 104 Washington Street that housed the 1st precinct's Scooter Task Force, the Citywide Homeless Outreach Unit and the Movie and T.V. Unit. Fortunately, all the available cops who'd been at the substation had already met him at Trinity Church and were now behind him, chasing. Bullets rang off the scaffolding in front of 40 Rector, the office of the Civilian Complaint Review Board. Maybe he could file a complaint. For discourtesy.

That's how he felt—offended that they were shooting at him. Not anger or fear, but simply that it was incredibly rude to shoot at someone. He wished they would stop, wished he could grab them and shake them and say, "Stop shooting!"

He ran behind the building as though to follow the pedestrian bridge over the West Side Highway but jumped down instead. The first three cars wouldn't have stopped for him, but the fourth would, and did, when he jumped in front of it. He slapped the hood as hard as he could. A very large man in a *Cuba Libre* baseball cap came out holding a no-jack steering-wheel lock. Preble ducked under a swing, kicked the man in the knee, and twisted the no-jack out of his grip. Holding it like a bat, he asked the man to take off his shirt. Preble took the white dress shirt and cap, then pushed past to the still-running car.

He drove onto Canal Street, then Center, Kenmare and Delancey, but instead of taking the Williamsburg bridge he went under it. It was just a matter of time until the NYPD started connecting dots on their aerial surveillance. Preble pulled under the bridge, put on the oversized dress shirt, and was about to stop another random car when a yellow cab came. This time of night Manhattan was all cabs, drunk people going home. He flagged it down, told the driver to go back to Delancey but westbound. At a red light, he saw another empty yellow cab beside him. Hopefully the cameras saw a sea of yellow. He handed his cabbie a twenty. "Sorry, too much perfume."

He jumped into the other cab.

"What you doing, man?" his new cab driver said with a slight Slavic accent. Preble couldn't place it exactly, and then found the question that would have yielded the right answer, so he never had to ask: Lithuanian.

"The other guy had on too much cologne." While true, the reason he said it was to avoid either of the cab drivers thinking. Maybe having seen too many movies and deciding to call the cops. "Take me to Brooklyn, first exit. You know Peter Luger, the steakhouse?"

The driver sighed. He didn't like driving into Brooklyn. He'd never get a fare back. But he went.

Preble got out at Peter Luger, then walked three blocks east on Broadway—Brooklyn's Broadway, not Manhattan's—to the 24-hour dollar store. He bought an umbrella. It wasn't a great idea if a human watched the surveillance, since it wasn't raining, but Fish always told him the real threat was from face-recognition software, and hopefully software didn't think about rain or not rain. Silently thanking Fish for his paranoia—everyone should have at least one paranoid friend—Preble walked to the waterfront and into his apartment building, ran up six flights of stairs and opened 6A, all with the umbrella pulled unnaturally low, spokes touching his head.

Chapter 3

Preble hung up on Crumb at 2:27 AM on July 6. By 2:29 AM, the captain was explaining to the TARU civilian employee that if he didn't have the video stream on his computer by 2:35 the civilian would be looking for a new job *and* getting three parking tickets a day for the rest of her natural life. Then he called Aviation.

"The 206 is doing sweeps, but we lost him," the lieutenant on the other end said. Normally Aviation was run by an assistant chief. Not tonight. But at least they'd gotten the 10-13 and had tried to get in on the action right away.

"How? You had him on open ground."

"No, we didn't. We never even got the spot on him. No face."

"We'll get a face in ten minutes. I don't suppose 23 was up?" Twenty-three was the most sophisticated helicopter in the NYPD fleet, with infra-red, license plate and face readers. Named after the number of NYPD officers who died on September 11, it was unmarked and circled New York landmarks and lower Manhattan. But it had been up all day and night on the Fourth.

"No. But I'm sending up another 206 now. We'll get the bastard."

He hung up and switched lines. Nineteen cops were on their

way to the hospital. Six from the subway and thirteen more from what sounded like an undisciplined all-directions shoot out in the Trinity Church cemetery. Paskalakki on the subway had almost bled to death, Gliny was breathing through a tube—apparently, the animal had saved her, but he wasn't getting any credit in Crumb's book since he'd put her in that condition in the first place —Miller was leaking spinal fluid from a hole in some sort of spinal sack caused by a piece of his own pelvic bone, and a cop from the Movie unit, Ed Smacks, was in a coma from a headwound he got in the cemetery. The rest were relatively minor. In sheer numbers of wounded, it was the worst night for the NYPD since September 11 and Crumb swore that he was going to nail the son of a bitch who'd done this. No matter what.

TARU also seemed to get it. The video arrived at 2:36 AM, unedited but organized footage from the various surveillance cameras in the subways, platforms, stairwells, and street-levels along Broadway, West Broadway, Rector, and the Trinity cemetery—as one of the few unlit areas in all of Manhattan, the cemetery had three cameras always filming.

Crumb started with the subway a few minutes before the 911 call. He stopped the video at the perp's face, knowing that TARU's computers had already plugged it into the system. He always liked to look at the face. A face could tell you a lot. Especially the mouth part. Detectives who did a lot of interrogations might joke, but Crumb used the face to orient himself, to get a sense of his enemy. To make his own features mimic the perp's, to feel what the perp felt, and think what the perp thought when he made that face.

He was smiling. The perp was smiling before Paskalakki and Gliny walked up to him. Amused, superior, arrogant—no, it wasn't an arrogant smile. It was tired. It didn't fit. People who started blowing away cops didn't smile like that. He let the video move forward and forgot about the smile because he'd never seen anyone move that fast. He'd done a stint as a combat instructor at the academy, and *nobody* moved like that. Good fighters don't think. The brain takes almost a full half-second to react and tell a muscle to move. We don't notice it because the brain then rewrites the memory to feel as if the reaction were instant, but it never is. With training, reaction control moves from the brain to the muscles. It becomes instinctive and almost instant. But with this guy, it wasn't *almost* instant. It was instant. Or even...but no, that wasn't possible.

Crumb called in the desk sergeant. "I want Smith and Wesley here early. Six AM. Tell them they take any DTs they need for this. Anyone. Then I want this picture compared to every professional fighter, soldier, or ex-cop in the city. Everyone. Got it?"

The sergeant got it. With nineteen cops down, nobody had to be told twice, nobody would complain about coming in early and no brass would complain about signing OT slips. Then Crumb watched the rest of the surveillance. Start to end, the whole thing had taken less than ten minutes, though with the multiple angles, there were hours of footage. Crumb watched thirty minutes, repeating the subway, stairwell and cemetery footage. And again. In slow motion. Again.

He called in Lieutenant Gleason, checked the progress of the search—none—and told him to mind the house. He wasn't supposed to leave, but he knew Frank Barney and this just didn't make sense. And it was his job to make things make sense.

Jane never tried to stay up on Thursday nights anymore. After the first year or so she'd resigned herself to the fact that several nights a week her husband would be out "working" late. He insisted that the chess and martial arts were work, training that helped him in Vegas or Atlantic City or one of two dozen international casinos. She didn't really mind, not anymore. It gave her a night alone with Kasper and allowed her career to be "poet." As the old joke goes, when prose writers greet each other, they ask, "How are your sales?" When poets greet each other, they ask, "How's your day job?"

She'd published seven chapbooks of poetry, but they could never have lived on that or on her teaching. And certainly not in a $1.4 million apartment overlooking Manhattan, Montessori school for Kasper, and the ability to be generous to friends and family whenever they wanted to. There's a Chinese proverb that *If you want happiness for an hour—take a nap. For a day—go fishing. For a month—get married. For a year—inherit a fortune. If you want happiness for a lifetime—help someone else.* But helping others was much easier when you have time and money, and whatever it was that Preble did, it bought them a very good life, a happy life. She was able to help out her own mom, who'd raised three kids as a single parent while trying to run a wooden-doll business that cost more money than it made. Her mom was a great sculptor and a terrible businesswoman, and watching her struggle Jane appreciated that every child needs a non-artist parent.

It also made her realize—or rather, not forget—how lucky they were, how comfortable their life was. The only real source of stress was worries about how safe Preble's method of gaining a living was. And the IRS, of course. He never went to the same casino more than once every two years, but he didn't seem to worry otherwise, even taking her and Kasper along whenever he went to some exotic location. He always played the slots and roulette, where he couldn't get accused of card-counting, and always stopped when he'd won $50,000.

Though all his income came from the one-night-a-month trips, he insisted it was a full-time job, divided unequally between arguing with suspicious tax collectors and "training his window" as he called it. But she knew that Preble considered the money secondary, a fringe benefit. Oh, he would always have found a way to provide for his family, but money was not the cause of his obsession with his "window." The obsession was just that, its own thing, almost as important to him as she and Kasper. At the beginning there'd been times she thought of it as a mistress claiming Preble's time, or a sword hanging over all their heads. But now it was more like another member of the family. At worst, like an ugly old armchair some men insist on keeping in the living room.

She woke to Preble squeezing her leg. Still mostly asleep, she asked, "What time is it?"

"A little after three. But I need you to get up."

She blinked the sleep away and saw him sitting on the side of the bed, looking oddly stiff. "Can't it wait till tomorrow? I'm asleep."

"It's important."

Preble got up and turned the light on. The bedroom was mostly books. A four-poster bed and books stacked along all the walls, under and above the windows. As expensive as their apartment was, it was still small. Great views of the city, but just a two-bedroom with no office for either of them and not nearly enough space for all the books they both accumulated. Preble was on a first-name basis with all the used-book sellers along Bedford and most of the ones in the City, and he'd even gotten Fish to help them fight off cops that had confiscated books under pressure from neighbourhood bookstores that didn't want the competition. Books were specifically exempt from the street-vendor laws, but the police confiscated the books anyway and let the vendors go to court and prove it. The books were always returned to those who took it all the way to court, but that took months or years. And then the police repeated the process, until they drove the vendors away and the stores were happy. So when Preble told Fish and Fish filed abuse-of-authority complaints and this stopped, suddenly Preble started receiving books at half price and the vendors went out of their way to find rare editions that he or Jane wanted. There was an old-world integrity about the half-homeless guys who lived with nothing but boxes of books.

It was the only time he'd ever had a confrontation with the police. And though he'd done almost nothing, had never actually even talked to the cops himself, seeing all the books now made him feel like he lived in a safe, warm cocoon that was about to be invaded, one that separated him from society and made him guilty just by virtue of that separation. If you're a troublemaker, it eventually catches up with you.

"Let's go in the kitchen," Preble said. "I'll make coffee."

"Coffee?" Jane stumbled to the bathroom and put a robe on—she looked great even when shocked awake at 3AM—then walked to the living room with its open kitchen, sat on the sofa and closed her eyes. She opened them again when she heard the sounds of Preble making Turkish coffee on the stove. She must have dozed off, because the next time she opened them he was handing her a cup. She shook her head. "I'm going back to sleep after this."

"I doubt it."

She looked at him, more awake now, and took the coffee. "Okay, what's going on?"

"I got into a fight with some cops. First on the subway and then on the platform and in the stairwell—"

"What?"

"A bunch of them got shot, and now the NYPD is after me."

"Not funny." She closed her eyes as though trying to go back to sleep, right there on the sofa. After a few seconds she opened them again looking fully awake and concerned for the first time. Then she listened as he described his evening, not interrupting until he finished. "Do they know who you are? I mean, can they track you down?"

"It's New York City, Jane. There's a camera on every block, and dozens in the subways. They have my face. It's just a matter of time. That's why I was thinking...we need to get out of the country before they put a name to my face. Which means we need to leave today."

"Leave the country? A little fugitive family? Jesus Christ, Preble."

"I'm sorry."

"But you didn't do anything."

"Of course, I did. There's no real difference between what I did and shooting the cops myself."

"Fuck the real difference. I care about the legal difference right now."

"I think that if you're committing a crime and someone gets killed, you're automatically also guilty of murder. Fish once told me that if the two of us rob a store and a cop kills him, I'm guilty of his murder, not the cop."

"Call him." She saw Preble look at the wall clock. "I don't care what time it is."

Preble finished his Turka, distracted. Still pulling grains of coffee off his tongue, he dialled Fish's number. Fish picked up on the second ring.

"You're still awake?"

"Poker on one screen. Porn on the other. Thank you, Al Gore. But that took less than five seconds to say, so you knew it from the moment you thought of asking the question, or even before, so why bother asking? Or, why do I bother answering? Oh, yes, because then you'd only have conversations in you head. Which over time would change the nature of our friendship and thus my responses. So instead, I'm the one talking to myself imagining you talking to yourse—"

"Fish."

"Yeah, hold on. I've got a great hand. And I'm not going to tell you which screen—"

"I need your legal advice."

"At three...oh shit, okay, what happened?"

Preble started to tell him, but Fish cut him off. "I'll be right over."

"Just tell me on the phone."

"Dude, the government already thinks you're laundering money, so even if every phone in America weren't always bugged anyway, which it is, they'd have a tap on you. Specific, old-fashioned wiretaps. With warrants and everything, just so they can feel moral about it. I'm coming over."

Without traffic it took Fish less than twenty minutes to get there. In the meantime, Jane made more coffee. She kept her back to Preble, then pulled a fork out of a drawer, closed one eye and looked through the prongs at him.

"What are you doing?"

"Wondering what you'll look like in jail." She forced herself to smile. "We'll figure this out, right?"

"Fish has spent half his life using the law to fight the law. He'll know what to do."

When Fish walked in the door, instead of saying hello, Jane handed him a coffee. He scowled at the grinds still swirling but didn't make his usual comment about the invention of percolators and espresso machines and other coffee paraphernalia. He was a caffeine addict, and he'd take it with the grains if he had to.

Fish sat on the sofa while Preble repeated the story: a shorter, more fluent version of what he'd told Jane. "So?" Jane interrupted. "If one of these cops dies from their own shots, will they blame it on Preble?"

There was a dead moment as Fish, Jane and Preble all sat in thought, picking coffee bits off their tongue. "That's the felony murder rule," Fish finally said. "If someone dies as a result of your committing a felony, then you're guilty of murder. The question is, were you committing a felony?"

"Resisting arrest?"

"Misdemeanour. Did you ever touch any of the cops? No, stop. If the prosecution were presenting its case, is there any point at which they might allege that you touched a cop?"

"You really think this place is bugged?" Preble asked. He could check, but he was suddenly very tired. "I wouldn't even recognize one if I saw it."

"I'm right here."

Preble nodded, and momentarily felt glad that the only two people in the world who knew about his gift were in the room with him. "Answer fast, okay?"

Then he mentally jumped forward, into a smear of infinite possible futures and all the ripping of walls and smashing of electronics that five seconds allowed. Too much junk was buried in the walls, things that would have taken more than five seconds to dig out, show Fish and get an answer. But given those limitations, there was no near future where Fish said, "Bug."

The whole process was instant because he didn't actually have to imagine ripping out each wall, but it was still exhausting for Preble. For Fish and Jane it was all invisible.

"Assuming any bug is easily accessible," Preble now said, "and you know what you're talking about, then the room is clean."

"I know what I'm talking about when it comes to bugs, so I have to assume whatever I theoretically said in all your alternate futures was as intelligent as it is in real life." In their present world, Fish hadn't answered a single question. "So, might a lying-bastard prosecutor claim you touched a cop?"

"In the stairwell. I shoved a cop's arm forward. Only a few inches, but there was no other way to avoid the bullet. And another on the platform, in the foot."

"Hmm. Self-defence in my book. But probably felony assault on a police officer in theirs."

"That's ridiculous," Jane said.

Fish raised his bushy Brezhnev eyebrows. "You go down to Brownsville or anywhere in the 75th precinct and tell that to all the kids jailed for 'flailing their arms' while being handcuffed. Max sentence twenty-five years for bumping a cop, even if the cop is searching you illegally every day of your entire teenage life. Then they plea out, of course. Don't want to clog the system. That's the thing about the American legal system. The constitution guarantees us the most generous procedural protections of almost any nation, and so we've compensated by passing the most draconian substantive laws of anyone. No other country has RICO, conspiracy, felony murder—"

"Fish—"

"What I'm saying is, that kind of stretch works against inner-city kids with overworked public defenders. It's not going to work against you, if the cop lives." He sighed. "But you better pray that particular cop lives."

"Jesus, I hope they all live. I tried to make sure none of the bullets went into spots that could kill them, but, you know, I can't tell very far ahead. And in most of the cases there was no possible future in which I could've examined where all the pieces went. Why in the name of all that's good and holy do they have to use dumdums?"

"Because only a dumdum would take a job that starts at $23,000 per year in New York Ci—"

Fish stopped himself before Preble had to, noticing Jane. Her mouth had tightened when Fish had started on the flailing arms. She'd started off treating the mess as almost a joke, as though she didn't truly believe it, but Fish was making it real. Now she unexpectedly started to cry, silently, seeing her nest of comfort and complacency dissolve right in front of her eyes. Out of the blue and for absolutely no reason. It was disorienting seeing her family threatened by the same social machinery she depended on to protect Kasper on their way to playgroup, to be snagged in the protective net that allowed her to walk the streets of Williamsburg at night without having to even pay much attention to the people around her, let alone be afraid. She couldn't remember the last time she'd been afraid, not really.

"It'll be okay," Preble said.

She shook her head. "No. It won't. Best case scenario, our life as we know it is over. You'll be fighting this for the next ten years, or we'll be fugitives living in the jungle in Brazil or Borneo with no decent schools for Kasper, or something like that. Worst-case scenario, they put you away for life, alone in a cage. Was it worth it?"

"What?"

"Was it worth it?" Her voice rose, then tensed as she tried to control it so as not to wake Kasper. "Was it worth risking our entire family so you could tell The Man where to shove it?"

"I just looked at the cop the wrong way. Just looked."

"Damned cops," Fish said, trying to help.

Jane ignored him. "You can see the god-damned *future*, Preble. You spend all your time practicing so you can see better. Time you take away from Kasper and me, so you can see better, and you couldn't even see this? Or you didn't want to see?"

"I didn't see. I really didn't see it coming."

"God, Preble, I know you. What was it, two weeks ago we watched that movie, *Vanishing Point*? And you went on how you loved the 'unapologetic' plot? How the man got into all that trouble just because he wanted to drive, to not be harassed, to not be controlled. That there was no *superficial* justification for not stopping when the cop tried to pull him over, just an *existential* one. How many times I've listened to you and Fish talk." Each quoted word came out as evidence of violence, as though the words had stabbed her and she was now simply showing him the wounds.

She turned to Fish. "No, Fish, I've always hated your immaturity when it came to politics, but I don't blame you. I blame my husband." She turned back to Preble. "You chose yourself, your ego, your pride, your honour, over us."

"Jane, I honestly didn't see—"

"Stop. It's too late. Now we need to fix it. Fish, you're the paranoid anarchist lawyer. Two out of three will have to be good enough. What would you do?"

"Two out of three? Oh, I get it, paranoid and lawyer. Well, I guess I'd wait and see. Sounds awful, but I'd wait to see to make sure the cop from stairwell—"

"Miller," Preble said quietly.

"Yeah. You'll make more headlines than a corduroy pillow. If Miller is alive in the morning, I'd turn myself in and spend the next few years in courtrooms. If Miller is dead...If Miller is dead, my...wait, give me some paper. Just in case."

Preble looked around for paper but saw only books. He grabbed a book by Proudhon off the shelf, a gift from Fish actually, and handed it to Fish, who already had a pen in hand. He tore out the second last page and wrote: "Have survivalist cottage on Hudson's Bay in Canada. Mothballed, on over 1000 acres. Cold in winter but has everything you'd need. It's yours." This was followed by an address.

After Preble and Jane had read the note, Fish burnt it in an ashtray, then went home to get the keys. Jane packed. Preble waited for the morning news.

⊏▭⊐

Crumb arrived at the Downtown Medical Center at 3:45 AM and despite his rank he was fought off by the night nurse defending her patient's sleep. He gave up and went to talk to the doctor. Fifteen minutes later he walked into Frank Barney's room, alone. No well-wishing cards yet or flowers or any of the stuff he usually saw in cops' hospital rooms—just the standard cold hospital bed, tray, I.V., and slight smell of disinfectant. Crumb realized it couldn't have been more than an hour since Frank had finished surgery and hoped he wasn't too groggy to talk. But he opened his eyes when Crumb stopped at the side of his bed.

"George." His voice was a bit slurred, but barely so. "What are you doing here?"

"How's your foot?"

"Bunch of shattered metatarsals. Or metacarpals. I can never remember which is which, except the doc says they take forever to heal."

"Tarsals. Just think of carpal tunnel, metacarpals are hands, metatarsals are feet."

"Sure, if you say so. What are you doing here so soon? I thought they kept you captains locked up."

"I saw the video of what happened."

Frank shook his head.

"But I still gotta see a face, talk to a real person. That's why I'm here. I needed to ask you in person."

"I fucked up. I still don't get it, but I guess we all fucked up."

"Yeah, a whole bunch of New York's finest shot each other today. However we spin it, it's not going to look good. But I need to know what kind of fuck up it was. Off the record, Frank. Cousin to cousin." Wife's cousin, but whatever.

Frank pushed himself up higher in the bed. "What are you asking?"

"Like I said, I saw the video. Not just you, but all the guys. I watched it on slow motion, regular speed, slow motion again, forwards, backwards. The perp was reacting before you guys shot. It was a split-second difference, but he wasn't just fast. He knew what was coming."

"What does that mean?"

"I don't know. It looked like a movie, Frank. Choreographed. If one of the guys wasn't you, I'd take the video straight to IAB and let them figure it out. But one of the guys is you. You shot yourself in the foot—"

"I think the guy hit my gun. I don't know. I really don't. It all happened so fast."

"Draft-dodger wound, Frank."

"Hey—"

"And so was every other shot except two freaks of bad luck. Miller chipped a piece of pelvic bone and it somehow went into his spine. And an MOS named Ed Smacks from Movies, of all things, got a grazing shot to the head. Didn't go through his skull, didn't seem to cut any arteries. He walked away from it and collapsed ten minutes later with a brain haemorrhage."

Frank exhaled. "Shit. Will they make it?"

"Too early to say."

"I'm sorry. If I'd just been a little faster. But—"

"Every shot, including those two, looks like it was planned for least damage," Crumb half whispered while squeezing the railing of the hospital bed. "No sane person would accept a plan that called for a grazing skull shot in a running gunfight. But I've got *nineteen* cops down, and except for the two freak injuries, all have about as light a wound as a police bullet can inflict and still take a man out of the action. Nineteen! All going down exactly like the perp said was gonna go down. And then I see a video that looks like it was choreographed by the Beijing Opera."

"Opera?"

"Jackie fucking Chan, okay."

"Are you suggesting that I was in on this with the perp somehow? Cause if you are—"

"I'm not suggesting. I'm asking. The video makes it look choreographed, but you'd have to be both a bad cop and fucking nuts.

And I never thought of you as either, Frank, so I just want to know what the hell is going on."

━━

The National Guard soldier who had fired at Preble on Trinity Place was named John Jones. Like the UFC fighter, just with a different spelling. Despite the authorization codes, he'd hardly believed his order to go live if he saw the shooter, not until he'd heard the familiar popping sounds coming from Trinity cemetery. He'd done a tour of Iraq—only one, thank God—and he knew a firefight when he heard one.

The church sounded like a war zone, though the firing was less controlled. Cops shoot like Iraqis, he thought, then focused on the figure jumping down to the street. He took a bead with a slight lead, the guy was moving fast, and pulled off a burst of three. Then another. And another. And then the perp was around the corner and Jones' orders were clear about not leaving his post. He couldn't believe he'd missed. He'd bagged five *hajis* in Iraq with much harder shots.

He cursed his orders, then radioed in to Lieutenant Jackson. Jackson was waiting for the call, but still in a state of unreality—surely this was some sort of exercise, except she knew it wasn't—that it had happened, that a National Guardsman had opened fire in downtown Manhattan. She punched a preliminary live-fire report into the Homeland Security database that connected the Homeland National Guard units with the rest of the government. She filled out several computer screens of required fields and drop-down menus—her name, ID, unit, location, number of NG personnel involved, their names, IDs, units, were they within their deployment zone, firearms used, number of rounds fired, direction of fire, types of round fired, estimated hits, estimated misses, number of opp-force members, suspected nationality of opp-force, number of rounds fired by opp-force, number of hits, number of misses, number of NG personnel wounded by opp-force fire, number of NG personnel wounded by friendly fire, number of NG personnel injured by other means (e.g., sprained ankles, etc.), civilians killed, civilians wounded, property damaged, other comments, shit there was a lot of paperwork, and the computer did the rest. It automatically requested TARU and low-classification NSA footage of the incident, and forwarded the package to National Guard brass, Homeland Security, and, unbeknownst to Lt. Jackson or nearly anyone else, to the NSA's Total Information Bureau. Military live fire on homeland soil was bound to create a press emergency that would hit all the way up to the White House. And while the people setting up network priorities didn't necessarily think that the actions of a loose soldier should be reason to wake everyone up, careers depended on managing and structuring information before it reached the unwashed masses. Within thirty minutes of Jones' nine shots, all misses, people were getting phone calls in New York, Albany, and Washington.

⸺

When his iPhone rang, Thaddeus Xavier Yagbig—known as "Thad Bigman" by everyone from the president of the United States down to the NSA parking lot security guard—looked at the 4 AM glowing on its flashing face. With a touch of the screen, he went into his personal interface in the NSA database, typed his key in, and tried to shut off the dull but insistent ringtone. But the classification was higher than the phone security protocols would allow, and the thing was requiring confirmation from a secure landline computer. Pain in the ass. He hoped Fifi wouldn't wake up. They'd gone to bed late, and fighting, and he hadn't gotten enough sleep. He walked into the next room, tapped his computer awake, went through the sign-in process, and, sitting nude at his desk, read Lieutenant Jackson's one-paragraph summary.

If it had been a human being on the other end, he would have chewed her head off, but the computer limited the number of possible reactions, and telling it that a cop-killer was an issue for Andrew in Communications wasn't one of them. The fact that the assistant director of the NSA's TI Bureau would be woken in the middle of the night for what was in essence an image management issue rubbed him the wrong way. Too much of the whole "War on Terror" was image management, in his opinion, especially on three hours sleep.

A green second lieutenant fresh out of military academy could tell you that the most common symptom of military stupidity was "fighting the last war." Like checking shoes after the shoe bomber or liquids after the liquid plot, though there wasn't enough explosive in either plan to do more than mess up a pedicure. The point was always to "restore confidence," to look as though the nation's security agencies were on top of the situation. Security theatre. But Bigman was a big, scowling pasty-faced man with a noticeably unbalanced forehead from a skydiving accident two decades earlier that had crushed his left supraorbital ridge, and he didn't care what he looked like. He wanted to fight the bad guys, not *look* like he was fighting the bad guys.

It didn't help that he constantly flew around the country and had to take his shoes off along with the rest of the pukes, taking orders from dropout TSA skells.

Nevertheless, Bigman read to the end of the report. It was hardly a surprise that the National Guardsman had missed—Bigman was an odd mix, but among the mix was a full seven years with the Marines, and he didn't have much respect for the National Guard—but the good lieutenant had seen fit to include a note that thirty-seven cops had emptied their clips at the target and all had missed as well. Nineteen were wounded, two critical. Nineteen? The lieutenant had no business including NYPD incompetence in her report to justify her own, but the sheer numbers were so outrageous that Bigman's interest was finally piqued. He normally woke at five anyway.

The computer had forwarded to him all the TARU video that Captain Crumb had already watched as well as higher-classification footage that didn't show anything different. Like Crumb, he watched the video over and over, squeezing his own testicles until he became conscious of it, irritated by the reminder of last night's argument. Repressing a growing urge to go pee, he called the hospital to find out the exact injuries of the officers involved. Then he called the NYPD and got in a shouting match with a sergeant who insisted that he'd get the number of shots fired when the NYPD was good and ready to share those numbers, and not until then. The bastards were circling the wagons already. Easy to see why. There were only two possibilities: gross incompetence or corrupt cops. Interesting, but not a national security issue.

If he went back to bed, he'd still get twenty minutes before the alarm went off. He thought about it while finally pissing, then went back to his computer and watched the video again. The shootout at the cemetery was too chaotic to be staged. He couldn't imagine a payoff that would justify that sort of risk, not by that many cops. That left only incompetence combined with very bad luck. Sheer crazy coincidence.

Bigman logged out, erased and overwrote his computer traces, turned his alarm off and headed for the shower. But the video nagged at him, beyond his normal distrust of coincidence. Along with the Marine Corps and a respectable number of grey and black ops, always on the intelligence side, his past included a very liberal arts degree from the Great Books program, and ten years with DARPA—the Defence Advanced Research Projects Agency —mostly in its Information Exploitation Office. In college, he had learned the skill of turning his brain half off in the shower to permit a stream-of-consciousness mode of thinking that would link nagging strands together for him: but thinking of nagging, his brain returned to his wife. She was always worried that she'd caught something, cancer, Japanese encephalitis, and last night had been a spectacular new achievement even for her. She was using Rogain to thicken her hair, but last week the store had been out of the women's version. She'd asked the sales clerk if she could use the men's version, and he'd told her, "Sure, if you don't mind growing a beard." It was a joke, she'd taken it as such, bought the Rogain, used it on her head, and gotten a totally unrelated rash on her crotch. Instead of thinking about how damned humid it had been lately, she was suddenly convinced she was growing testicles because she'd used the men's version, and wanted Bigman to take her immediately to the emergency room. In the middle of the night. He'd refused, insisting there was zero probability of Rogain applied to her scalp making a woman grow testicles, and the ridiculous fight had taken more time out of his evening than a trip to the emergency room would have. Standard Pavlovian training, making sure that his lack of compassion cost more than acquiescence, even if what she was requesting was patent nonsense. Mrs. Fifi Kennedy Yagbig—Mrs. Bigman to everyone who knew them both—was better at this sort of thing than any of the guys at Guantanamo, CIA or DARPA. Maybe it was compassion itself. He'd read a memo once that the most effective torturers had the highest "compassion" ratings, and the CIA's calloused psyches failed that test miserably. Maybe he should institute compassion training for all government torturers? It would be hard to do at DARPA, with its "100 geniuses connected by a travel agent" mindset. Too scattered and geeky. Though that description wasn't altogether accurate. He'd been in TI, but he'd seen lots of Tactical and DSO presentations, for example. They were always working on their future-soldier Land Warrior Program. As an information guy who focused on the I in C4ISR systems, he'd even helped with some of their real-time data processing issues—and when it came to the C4ISR, everything aimed towards shorter decisions cycles and instantaneous flexibility. The OODA loop—observe, orient, decide, act—that every military and law enforcement agency worldwide was always trying to tighten. As the manual said, "The measure of command and control effectiveness is simple: either our command and control works faster than the enemy's decision-execution cycle or the enemy will own our command and control." And as with most systemic rules, this one was replicated at every stage of the hierarchy, from the strategic down to the lowest-level tactical. But the closer you got to the ground, the more the real world interfered. Getting a computer to sort out on a video-game level which real-world tactical information was relevant to the individual soldier was an artificial intelligence nightmare, even with machine learning and neural networks. The information had to be instant, reliable, and actionable. There was nothing more actionable than knowing a bullet was coming at you and where it would go, but a cycle short enough to make that knowledge useful was way beyond anything DARPA had envisioned. Predicting bullet vectors was so far in the future that DARPA ignored it as a possibility, focusing instead on weapons, body armour, and a tactical real-time net. Still, he could imagine the shootout at the cemetery as some sort of Tac presentation for a robot soldier. Except the cop-killer had a decision-execution cycle that was less than zero. He was reacting *before* even instant computer reactions would have. And he wasn't shooting back. He'd have attracted less attention by shooting the cops himself than by letting them shoot each other. Maybe. At any rate, this couldn't be a foreign agent. The *a priori* reactions made it impossible. It was either corruption or coincidence.

Improbable, he corrected himself. *Not impossible.*

He towelled off, then went back to his computer and watched the video again, frame by frame. Each time, the guy clearly started his dodge before the trigger was pulled. Corruption, coincidence or something terrifying that left DARPA in its dust. Every time he wanted to settle his mind on coincidence, he hit play again and got unsettled. Finally, he assigned the highest probability to a modified corruption hypothesis—a staged op by some of the cops but not others, then something went wrong.

Still, he woke his secretary and told her to book him on a 7 AM to New York. Only then did he get dressed, still shaking his head at the mind-boggling stupidity of the idea that Rogain could make Fifi grow testicles.

Chapter 4

THE 6 AM NEWS WAS ALL ABOUT THE SHOOTOUT. NINETEEN cops shot. Two in critical condition, no other information. Breaking news at 8 AM that PO Edward Jonathan Smacks had died from head wounds received at the cemetery. No update on Miller. By 9 AM, Miller was out of surgery. He would not only live, but was expected to make a full recovery, creating an ideal news-day of one-third tragedy, one-third relief and one-third manhunt. Preble's night-vision-green face was all over the news as were unconfirmed accounts that thirty-seven cops had emptied their clips without hitting anyone except each other. Even assuming nobody had reloaded, that meant the NYPD had fired over five-hundred rounds. All misses. Already the news was raising questions about police training, which was supposed to have been improved on exactly this issue after the Bell incident. CNN discovered math, and within minutes all the stations except for Fox News were flashing "15 x 37 = 555" on background screens while overpaid anchors carried the three as they explained for those who couldn't read, multiply or follow the numbers. To fill in time between real information bursts, several stations closed the circle with specials on the NYPD's Movie and TV Unit.

Fish warned Preble that the prosecution would still try to tie his felony of bumping Miller to Smack's death: if he hadn't pushed Miller's hand then he'd be dead or arrested, but, either way, stopped. If he'd stopped in the subway, the cops in the cemetery wouldn't have been shooting, and Smacks would still be alive. They'd claim that the chase was one continuous criminal act that included a felony and the details of cause and effect didn't matter. The legal theory was there, so the case would make it to a jury. But the felony itself was just a bump and the whole theory was a stretch, and a good lawyer could convince a jury to frown on cases built from bumps and stretches. On the other hand, the victim was a cop, and in a real courtroom the identity of the victim is the heaviest factor in determining punishment. Fish guessed Preble's odds to be about 50-50 for murder, only a little worse for assault and manslaughter.

"I think...I vote Canada," Preble said, sitting down on the coffee table in their living room. He suddenly didn't feel up to standing. "Jane?"

"I don't want to hide in the Arctic for the rest of my life."

"Fish?" Preble started to ask, but Jane cut him off.

"No, Fish doesn't get a vote on how we live the rest of our lives."

"Of course," Fish said. "But you guys shouldn't vote like that either. Preble, how strongly do you prefer to run?"

Preble shrugged. "60-40 in favor of running."

"Jane?"

Jane looked at Preble. "80-20 in favour of fighting."

"That's 120 vs 80 in favor of staying." Fish blew air through his cheeks, as the consequences sank in. "I'll go with you, of course."

Preble hesitated at this, but in the end the practical need to have a lawyer present outweighed his gut sense that he should do this alone. Last night he'd been reacting; now he could think. They agreed that Kasper would not go to playgroup today, and Jane would keep the TV off, not wanting Kasper to see his father handcuffed or worse.

Whatever else happened, this needed to end with a situation where Kasper still had a father in his life. Everything else was secondary.

Kasper woke earlier than usual and didn't understand why he wasn't being dressed, why all the adults were running around the house ignoring him. He went to the most forbidden spot in the house, Jane's computer, and started to pound on the keyboard.

Preble finally noticed. "What are you doing, Kasper?"

"I'm writing a poem."

"What's it about?"

"I don't know. I can't read."

Preble laughed despite the stress and hugged his son, but Kasper knew he was supposed to get in trouble and seeing that he didn't made him even more anxious. He spent the rest of the morning clinging to Preble, insisting on touching the mole on his neck every three minutes—Preble's mole was his security blanket —and asking about everything that was happening in an attempt to make sense of the morning.

By the time he saw Preble getting dressed, he was barely fighting back tears. "Daddy's going?"

"Yes, Daddy's going."

"No. You're confused. You're not going."

"I'm sorry, Kasper. I'm going. I'll be gone for a few days, then I'll come back."

"We won't sleep here tonight?"

"You and Momma will. I don't know about me. I don't think so. But soon."

Kasper's face broke. In slow motion, his mouth quivered, turned down, then reversed itself as he forced himself to not cry. He suddenly turned hopeful again. "Tomorrow? Tomorrow you'll sleep here?"

"I'll try. Maybe tomorrow, maybe after."

"After tomorrow? Three days?"

"I don't know, sweetie. But when I come back, we'll go swimming, okay?"

"Kasper too? And Daddy too? And Mommy too? And no bear?"

"Just Kasper and Daddy and Mommy. Okay?"

"No, we won't. It's too cold. And the bear will get us."

"No, it won't be too cold yet, and there's no bear. I'll come back soon, and then all three of us will go swimming. Okay?"

"Okay," Kasper said with a sad look that said he felt he'd been tricked somehow.

Preble kissed Jane, then hugged the two of them together in

the open doorway. Jane started to cry. Kasper stopped the hug to look at his mom.

"Mommy's sad?"

"Yes, honey," Jane said, trying to regain control. "Mommy's sad."

Kasper looked on the verge of tears again. "Mommy's not going?"

"No. Mommy's staying here with you."

"Only Daddy's going? And Daddy's never going to sleep here again?"

"Only Daddy's going."

"Me too. I won't sleep here again. With Daddy."

"I'll figure it out. It'll be okay," Preble said to both of them, while Fish waited in the hallway by the elevators. He kissed Kasper one more time, then repeated, "I'll figure it out."

Fish had parked half a block away, a new Volvo with no windshield wipers—Fish swore he received 80 percent fewer parking tickets since he ripped them off, and since he always parked illegally, the sudden drop in tickets was the reason he now had a new Volvo instead of an old Volvo. Or so he claimed—half of Fish's stories seemed on the Bizarro side of reality, but when things got serious he was solid. They passed a dozen people on the way, and with each one Preble wondered whether they'd recognize his face from the news. Nobody did.

As the two of them drove across the Williamsburg bridge, Fish suddenly broke the silence. "Shit, I should have made you guys write down your probabilities in secret. You said 60-40 first, so Jane knew what numbers she needed to make you stay."

"I knew she was going to outvote me. It's fine."

They waited in silence, in morning traffic, waited while the traffic cops on Delancey waved people forward or stop or go around—it was suddenly amazing to Preble just how many cops there were in New York City—and slowly made their way to the First Precinct, downtown, on Ericsson Place.

Fish shuddered noticeably as they paused in front of the blue checkered doors that seemed modelled on Dr. Who's police box Tardis. They went in without exchanging a word and waited at a counter, sniffing the bleach and Lysol and stale coffee smell. The little bank-cashier window for which they waited had three posters: one about gun amnesty, one for CPR—Courtesy, Professionalism, Respect—under which someone had hand-written "The only substitute for CPR is fast reflexes." And a third with a Confucian-sounding "Cooperation can only be reached if we work together." On the nearest wall—the "history wall," the only one without oversized colourful posters—there was a framed sign from 1949 directing people where to go for "Guns, Tear Gas and Religious Meeting Permits," an article about the first police matron, and a chart showing how dozens of different police agencies had gradually merged into the NYPD, from the first consolidations of night watch, city marshals, constabulary, and municipal police in 1845 through the last of the Transit Authority mergers in 1995.

There was one man ahead of them, complaining about a dog. The bored civilian receptionist, severely obese with two rings on each of her fingers and long fake nails painted with varying postcard tropical scenes, was pushing a complaint form at him that he was working hard to ignore in order to keep complaining. Finally, she cut him off.

"That's the form. You wanna make a complaint, you fill out a complaint form. Don't tell me about it, I don't want to know about it, I ain't gonna do anything about it. The form will go to the people who will do something about it. Next."

"Well, you're supposed to do something about it."

"Do I look like a dogcatcher to you, sir? Next."

"No, you're the police. And you're supposed to—"

"God, I miss Brooklyn. Sir, please move along. If you don't, you get OGA."

"What's OGA?"

"Obstructing governmental administration. Now step away from the window." She looked past the man, but not really at Preble. Just towards the room generally, as though eye contact would expose her to personal liability. "Next."

The dog man took half a step back, but then leaned forward. "Do you have a pen?"

"Take it home, fill it out, bring it back. Next."

He looked at the paper and finally shuffled sideways. Preble and Fish walked up to the window.

"One at a time."

"We're together."

"I don't care if you're married, I said one at a time."

"He's my lawyer."

She looked at him for the first time, then squinted.

"I'm here to turn myself in."

"Holy shit." She looked at him again, then turned back to where two cops stood behind a raised counter overlooking the roll-call area. An hour earlier the space had been filled with angry cops sharing information about their injured brothers, but now most were out on the eight-to-four. All were hoping they'd bump into Mr. Preble Jefferson. The only other people in the roll-call area were a big cop in a yellow shirt that said, "Community Affairs" and a smaller cop shaking and sniffing a vest.

The receptionist shouted to the desk, "LT! It's the perp. From last night. The cop-killer. He's here."

Everyone in the room whipped around to look. Even the dog complainant. The community affairs cop was the first to react. He and the vest cop ran up with guns pointed at Preble. The lieutenant leapt over the counter, barely a second behind them. He looked straight out of a movie about Boston Irish cops: short-cropped red hair and thick red moustache. He wore a white shirt, and his shield said, "Fein."

"On the ground, now!" the community affairs cop yelled.

Preble obeyed. The fake-marble floor was cold on an exposed sliver of his belly as his shirt pulled up. Then the community-affairs cop stuck a knee in Preble's lumbar, handcuffed one hand, twisted the cuffs around twice, and handcuffed the other.

Fish had stepped away from Preble when the guns came out, but now he yelled, "Hey, that's illegal."

The vest cop—his shield said, "Arnolds"—pointed his gun at Fish. "You, on the ground."

"I'm his attorney."

"I said, 'On the ground.' Now!"

Preble knew Fish avoided cops, the government, all the tentacled reminders of communist Hungary. There weren't many things that would have made him deliberately put himself into this position. Other than friendship. He swallowed hard but got on the ground.

"Just search him," Lieutenant Fein said. "No cuffs."

Arnolds glared at the lieutenant, then searched Fish roughly. "Douchebag's clean."

Fish stood, straightened his shirt, then repeated to Fein. "You're not allowed to twist the handcuffs like that. It cuts off the circulation. Please recuff him properly."

Preble was still on his belly on the ground, with the community affairs cop still kneeling on his lower spine. The lieutenant hesitated, then said, "Do it. Then take him to a room. Room three." To Arnolds he said, "Get the captain. Actually, never mind. I'll do it."

Four cops ran into the common area, a little late. They were sweaty, three of them in tank tops. They'd been working out after their twelve-to-eight and were still in the house. Now they started crowding Preble as he stood up. One shoved him hard in the chest. "You the Adam Henry?"

"Walk away!" the lieutenant ordered. "I said, 'Walk away!' You want some OT, calm down, get dressed and come back up. But no bullshit. He's go this lawyer here."

"I can hear you," Fish said.

The lieutenant looked at Fish. "He's got his noob lawyer here. What are you, estates and shit? Mortgages? Jesus." He shook his head. "Cop-killer brings a mortgage lawyer."

Eventually, Fish and Preble were put in a little room, and told to sit at a table, backs to the door. The door closed. And they waited. The room smelled of sweat and oatmeal and bleach. It was the same smell as in the lobby but without the coffee, the more chthonic scents winning out, magnified by the sitting and waiting as though designed to bring the most out of the suspect's adrenaline crash, out of the cement room with its lonely metal desk and chairs. Nobody would come into the room for over five seconds. In four dimensions, there was nothing except the concrete-and-metal cage of the room, and the hopeless smell.

"Are you kidding me?" Fish suddenly said, standing up from his chair.

"What?"

Fish squatted at the end of the table, looking back and forth between the two sets of chairs, two for the suspect and his lawyer on one side, and three for the cops on the other side, all bolted to the concrete ground. Then he started to laugh. "The chairs on our side are two inches lower."

Preble couldn't bring himself to laugh but did manage a smile. He was grateful for his friend's presence. And really glad he'd let Fish talk him into coming along. "Hey, Fish?"

"Yeah?"

"What's 'Adam Henry?' They've called me that twice now."

"'Aggressive and hostile.' Also, 'asshole.'"

Lieutenant Fein knocked on the captain's door. He could hear an argument inside between the captain and the fed who'd come into the precinct less than twenty minutes ago.

"Open."

Lieutenant Fein opened the door. "Can I have a second, captain?"

Crumb nodded, but before he could take a step, Bigman interrupted. "Is this about our man from last night?"

Lieutenant Fein ignored him and waited for the captain. Crumb's tour was technically over at eight, but it was his call until he decided to go home or higher brass took him off. Since he was the only one up to speed, and since the political repercussions of this were likely to be bad, nobody had relieved him. Except, sort of, one phone call.

"It's okay, LT. I just got off the phone with the chief. This is still ours, but we're to include Mr. Yagbig—"

"Bigman," Bigman interrupted.

"Uh, yes, include Mr. Bigman in all decisions and defer to his expert opinions. He's here to help."

"Where I come from," Bigman said, "two Marines don't walk down the street without one of them being in charge."

The lieutenant glared at Bigman, barely restraining a direct comment before turning back to Crumb. "Captain, why do I feel like the masseuse just stuck her finger up my ass?"

Bigman smiled. "There's reason to believe the NYPD's been compromised. The cops involved seem to have been working with the subject."

The red lieutenant turned redder. "Son of a bitch, you're investigating us?"

"What did you come in here to tell me, LT?" the captain asked, cutting off the unproductive conversation.

"Yeah. The perp's here. Turned himself in."

Wiry thin, black Captain Crumb and fat splotchy-pale Bigman both jumped up, as though synchronised.

The lieutenant explained Preble's appearance at the station on their way to interview room number three. The captain told Lt. Fein to get a detective to the room, but Bigman said that the two of them would do the questioning.

"I haven't questioned a perp in years," Crumb said.

"I'm sure you haven't forgotten how, captain. And I want all recording devices turned off."

"What?" Then after a moment, he added, "Who do you think this guy is?"

"That's an order."

Crumb repressed a response. The chief had told him rather clearly what "expert advice" from Bigman meant. But the LT had been right. Except for 9/11, the feds never took over an investigation when one of the department's own was killed. Now they seemed to be throwing that interagency courtesy out the door. And it looked like Bigman was going to dirty the evidence, putting the prosecution at risk. This case was making less sense every hour, except as some sort of national security question.

The two of them walked into the interview room. The perp was white, six-one, two hundred pounds, mid-thirties, built like a fighter. There was a look fighters had beyond the cauliflower ears —forward flexion of the hips, shoulders with an exaggerated roundness, shortened lats, hip flexors and pecs—postural imbalances that grow out of long hours in a protective stance. Crumb had boxed for the department team and taught enough fighters that he saw it instantly. It was a form of mutual recognition, except that the man didn't return Crumb's look. He was staring at Bigman as though Bigman were talking to him. Which he wasn't.

Crumb was what they called a "fluid" interrogator. Most cops learned a spiel, a routine, that worked most of the time on most subjects. But that had never been Crumb's style. Instead of starting with "what's your name?" which the Academy taught was supposed to open the perp up by sharing something harmless, but inevitably reinforced the interrogatory nature of the conversation —and the duplicity of the interrogator who almost always knew the name up front—he started with what came naturally. "You two know each other?"

The cop-killer finally looked at Crumb, and noticeably relaxed a notch. "No."

"The LT read you your rights and all that?"

"Yes, thank you, captain."

The room had five chairs, three and two. Now it was two against two, except the way Bigman sat, slightly sideways and facing all three of them made him feel like he was both above and against everyone else. While Preble, Fish and Crumb were clearly shaped by their chairs, Bigman created the impression that his chair wasn't bolted down. He flowed over it. He could pick it up and move it anywhere in the room at will.

Crumb seemed almost chummy by comparison. "You feel you were treated okay out front? Cops can get a little crazy in these sorts of cases."

"All things considered, I've been treated extremely well. Thank—"

Fish interrupted: "My client has explained the situation to me. I'll explain it to you, if you don't mind."

"I'd rather hear it in his own words."

"He'll sign a statement when the time comes. Right now, I'll explain what happened." Fish described what happened in the subway and cemetery, making the whole thing sound like Preble had mouthed off and then, when the cops in the subway went nuts, simply run for his life.

Crumb and Bigman waited patiently until Fish had finished. Then Crumb asked, "So why did he radio in and say if the police kept coming at him, they'd shoot each other? He knew exactly what was going to happen. I'm sure there's a good reason why the whole thing looked planned." Crumb looked at Preble. "He doesn't seem like a psychopath to me."

"He was upset. Two cops on the subway, followed by four on the platform, had just shot each other trying to gun him down. He was not only terrified for his own life, he was concerned for theirs. It doesn't take a genius to know that if cops get hurt while chasing you, you're the one who gets blamed. By the time he radioed, he'd seen NYPD incompetence take down six officers. Six. Every time they started spraying bullets, they seemed to shoot one of their own. On the one hand, he felt like he had a protective angel looking out for him. But on the other, he saw people getting hurt. If the police had come at him more peacefully, like peace officers, he would have allowed himself to be arrested. He said so on the radio, he pleaded with you not to use guns—"

"To some people it sounded more like a threat of an eye for an eye."

"—but they were shooting like some sort of crazed gang. Over five hundred wild rounds. Given the NYPD's history of turning unarmed civilians like Sean Bell and Amadou Diallo into human sprinklers, is it any wonder he fled? The media are already talking about the five hundred misses, about police training and gross negligence, turning downtown into a war zone over one unarmed man who looked at the police the wrong way."

"So is that going to be your defence? Protective angel?"

"Police negligence. Every man and woman on the jury will understand how it feels to run, unarmed, from a rain of five hundred bullets."

Crumb sighed. "It was closer to seven hundred. Several of the officers reloaded."

Fish hesitated, thrown by the captain's generosity. "Ah, thanks."

"That's my dirty little secret. The problem for Mr. Jefferson, however, is the video footage. We have at least one clear incident of your client directing an officer's arm into shooting a fellow officer—"

"He didn't pull the trigger."

"—An officer, I might add, who is now in critical condition and still might not fully recover. That's aggravated assault on a police officer. Just that, you're looking at twenty-five years. Another officer is dead. Your client could be facing the death penalty for this, and if you think a New York jury, a downtown Manhattan jury, is going to let a cop's death go unpunished, you don't know this city, counsellor. This, right now," Crumb poked his finger into the table, "is his one and only chance to prevent that." Again Crumb turned to Preble. "You help me understand what happened, and why it happened, what you were thinking, how it felt when all those cops were shooting at you, and I can help you. It takes about half a second to see you're not a psycho or a criminal, but if you're not, then I need to understand why this happened before I can help. I have a video, I don't need facts or evidence. I just want your side—"

"I agree, captain," Fish interrupted. "About the video. And if it were seven bullets, or even seventy, I might even say you're right. But with seven hundred missed shots, I think that punishment will fall on the PD for its incompetence. An issue that will be dragged through the newspapers and Sunday morning shows for years."

Preble looked at his friend. He'd always known Fish had a professional side that was far more precise and analytic than what came across in Flea House conversations, or when he grabbed on to meandering ideas about windshield wipers or doing away with all government. A frumpy, Crocs-wearing, slightly neurotic anarchist professor who ate breakfast at the same diner every single day for at least a decade, Fish could come across as a bit of a joke to some people. But now, here, everything about how he spoke changed. His words had become chess pieces. Preble had seen a glimpse of it when he'd fought for the Bedford Street book tables. But Fish's sheer presence in the room surprised him—despite his constant criticism of the law, this was truly Fish's calling. Preble felt a surge of gratitude towards his friend.

Crumb had clearly been hoping to pull Preble into the conversation directly. Now he gave up and turned back to Fish. "So your theory is incompetence?"

"Sorry to say so."

"And if the prosecutor moves this to Staten Island? All cop families on Staten Island. And even if he can't, your client will still get the twenty-five. The jury will see it as a compromise. Solomonic justice."

"I'll just keep repeating seven hundred, or 555, or eight hundred or whatever the exact number turns out to be. So long as it ends in 'hundred' it will trump your video. But what are you looking for, captain? You're obviously trying to pull out some sort of confession."

"No confession, just—"

"Asking for my client's 'opinion,' sharing a 'secret,' you're trying to get him to open up. For what? As you said, you have the video. What more do you need?"

Crumb looked at Bigman—who was leaning back in his chair with his wrists clasped and resting on his head, elbows sticking out like wings, a look of mild irritation on his face, perhaps because the front two legs were bolted down and he couldn't put his feet up—then leaned towards Fish. "All of us here know this wasn't incompetence."

"What do you think it was?"

"You tell me," Crumb said. "Tell me without using the word 'coincidence.' Cops hate that word." Again, he turned to Preble. "All I'm asking for is that you tell me what went on in your head. If it makes sense, we'll plea out to—"

The door opened and Lt. Fein came in with a thick blue folder, handed it to Crumb without a word, then left. Crumb skimmed through it for a few minutes, then passed it to Bigman.

Preble's heart jumped. If Bigman had received a copy when he landed, then the feds must be at his house by now. He must have just missed them. Which meant that Jane and Kasper were—well, they hadn't done anything wrong, there's nothing the police could do to them.

"I received a copy when I landed."

Crumb looked offended. "You had a name, and you didn't tell me?"

"I had a name, and I didn't tell you," Bigman answered and lifted an index finger that was short, thick and almost red in its pinkness. The gesture was odd, something one would expect from a schoolteacher, or a Frenchman saying attention.

Crumb took the folder back, a bit flustered, and kept reading. While he did so, nobody talked. Bigman stared at Preble, Preble stared back, and Fish fidgeted. When Crumb finally put the folder down, his tone lost its bedside manner. "Mr. Jefferson, you have a very strange profile. Chess champion. Money launderer. Cop killer."

Fish interrupted again. "My client is lucky. He wins at slots. Bullets miss him. He doesn't launder money and he doesn't shoot cops. The IRS and FBI don't believe in luck, so they've been investigating him for years, but they've come up with exactly nothing. Because there is nothing, other than extraordinary luck. Or, perhaps, like I said earlier, a protective angel. If we start talking about angels, even Fox News will be on our side."

"If he's so lucky, why does he play chess?" Crumb asked. "It seems the one game where luck doesn't help, where every accident is carefully structured."

"A sense of fairness. Like helping the two cops in the subway who had tried to shoot him."

"You done shampooing yourself, counsellor?"

Fish smiled. "I don't need shampoo. My client's clean."

Crumb started to say something about shampoo, then thought better of it. Instead, he said, "You know what the best thing about being a cop is?"

Now it was Fish's turn to bite his lip. "No, captain, I really don't."

"The customer is always wrong. None of us in this room believe in angels or luck, or fairness for that matter, so why don't you try again."

"Juries believe. So does the media. I can already see the headlines: 'The luckiest man alive.' It's a consistent narrative. As is the fact that the NYPD can't control its shooting."

Crumb turned to Preble directly again. Money, casinos, chess. "You were working with some of those cops. We can prove the shootout was choreographed. You should have been a little slower, because several times the video shows you moving out of the way before the trigger was even pulled. That's not luck. That's choreography. I want names, and the only way I can protect you is if I get them now, before IAB realizes what this is and takes it out of my hands. We're on the clock here. But most of all, I want to know what was going on. There must have been an awful lot of money involved. You tell me the whole story, the whole chess strategy, and we'll put you in a witness protection program along with your family. Otherwise, best case scenario for you is twenty-five years. Worst case, IAB—internal affairs—takes this and leaks. The IAB guys are only on two-year rotations and then go back to their precincts, so they always leak. And if you are working with bad cops, that's a death sentence."

Preble spoke for the first time since Fish had interrupted him:

"You give me an ironclad agreement that keeps me with my family, and I'll sign whatever you want."

It was Bigman's patience that undid Preble. Because while Bigman thought, more than five seconds passed. Crumb had time to say, "I don't want anything except for the whole story."

Preble bit his lip, then Bigman said, "Get rid of the lawyer."

"What?" Crumb asked.

"In the immortal words of Groucho Marx," Fish said, glaring at Bigman. "'Why don't you bore a hole in yourself and let the sap run out?'"

"Get rid of this asshole."

"That's just going to make the case—"

"It's no longer that kind of case, captain."

Crumb motioned at the mirror and the door opened. Lt. Fein walked in, but Fish didn't get up. "This is a clear violation of the sixth amendment, it's unconstitutional, and you don't give a shit, do you?"

"Get out," Crumb said quietly.

"What's so extraordinary here that you'd do this?"

Preble realized that although Fish was facing Bigman, he was really speaking to him. He'd heard this spiel many times, though usually it was in the context of Fish claiming that anarchists served a vital function in society. It went like this: since law is just veiled power, the fewer people who believe in the "rule of law," the more transparent the veil, and the more the law has to obey its own rules in order to maintain legitimacy. The more people who believe in the rule of law, the less likely it is to actually exist. But when propaganda isn't enough, the powerful have to actively limit the arbitrary use of power and shrink the number of cases they can treat as extraordinary. Fish was telling Preble that the veil had just been discarded. They were abandoning pretense and going with power, which probably meant that Bigman knew.

Fish finally let the lieutenant pull him out of the room.

"You too, captain," Bigman said, still disconcertingly calm.

"This is my house. You want to call the chief again, do it."

Bigman stared at Crumb for another second, then turned to Preble. "You'd have been okay with one or the other, but roulette and bullet dodging? That's just too much for one man, don't you think?"

"Like Fish said, I've been lucky."

"You feeling lucky now?"

"'Punk.' The line is, 'You feeling lucky now, punk.'"

"Nah. I figure you could take Dirty Harry. Let me introduce myself. I work for the National Security Agency. You could say I'm in the information sector, but what I really do? I study perception. I've devoted the intellectual side of my life to studying the interaction between information and perception, between information and the human brain."

Preble tried to relax, to breathe, maintain eye contact and avoid touching his suddenly itchy cheek. He knew from a lifetime of watching future reactions that cops treat any hand-to-face gesture—whether the itchiness is coincidental or anxiety induced —as a polygraph spike, a shorthand admission of guilt. But the more he tried to not think about touching his cheek, the itchier it got. "And what do you think you perceive here?"

"Did you know, Mr. Jefferson, that the human brain actually sees the future? Constantly. We live in it. It takes nearly a full half-second for the brain to react to unexpected external stimuli. If our brain didn't anticipate the future, we'd always be a half-second behind in our reactions. We'd never be able to catch a baseball. And that would be downright un-American. So the brain predicts where the ball will be a half-second later, then lies to us and makes us think we 'saw' the ball where the brain predicted. In other words, it anticipates the future in order to see the present rather than the past. You following me?"

"Right behind you."

"Really? I thought you'd be a step ahead."

Preble didn't say anything.

"Isn't that the essence of chess? To think one step ahead of your opponent?"

"Not really. I'd say it's the ability to wrap a finite brain around an open system."

"Interesting." Bigman tilted his head. "Especially since a chess board is a closed system, not an open one. Unless you count the players. The thing is, the prediction mechanism of the human brain is perceptual. It's not always right. Move your face towards a checkerboard, a chessboard if you prefer, and the lines seem to bend, because the brain incorrectly predicts how the lines will reshape as they move closer."

Bigman was smart, but Preble was mentally throwing an infinite number of "questions" at him, questions Bigman didn't even imagine because they never happened. And though the bastard was too patient, too slow and niggardly about answering, Preble could piece together the endless possibilities of five-seconds hence to see that Bigman was just wrong enough about the nature of his skill. Unfortunately, most of this was happening outside the five-second window. He had to guide Bigman's opinions by guessing at effects instead of seeing them. Thursday-night chess.

Preble said, "I had a friend who took LSD once then went to a pool hall. He said he kept seeing the balls fly off the table when they didn't."

"Exactly. The brain extrapolated the trajectory, and because of the LSD it couldn't cover up its mistake fast enough."

"So the cops were all on drugs?"

Bigman snorted. "How do you beat the casinos, Mr. Jefferson? Once a month, different casino every month, you always win."

Preble leaned forward and stared into Bigman's grey eyes. He wasn't sure whether it was the fluorescent light in the room reflecting the concrete walls, but they really did look pale slate grey. "Hippomancy."

"What?"

"The neighing of horses. I tried tasseomancy, that's, uh, reading tea leaves, and astrology, but I found hippomancy the most effective. Cephaleonomancy is also good, but it takes hours for each donkey's head to boil, it's hard to find big enough pots, and the donkey-head suppliers in New York City are difficult."

Bigman frowned at Preble's sudden change in tone—LSD and horses and donkeys' heads—but the pool ball analogy stuck. "Distract all you want, nobody wins at roulette. There's no way to cheat unless the dealer's in on it. But roulette you can see the ball, see where it's going, extrapolate and lay your bets when it's already spinning. Blackjack has better odds, but you can't extrapolate what you can't see. Oh, if it were one casino, you might be working with someone on the inside. But twenty-four casinos? Winning fifty grand each time, $600,000 per year, every year?

That's not luck. That's impossible." He smiled. "Stupid, also, not to lose some years."

Bigman didn't seem to know about the slots, just the roulette. Preble's standard approach was to win a small start fund on the slots, then move to the roulette wheel. There was too much time between when the dealer called bets and the time the ball came to a stop, but five seconds combined with years of practice was enough for Preble to get a sense of which portion of the wheel the ball would land on. That had the double benefit of practice, helping Preble extend his window, and of making his win-loss ratio more realistic. The odds of hitting any given number on a balanced wheel are one in 38 (or 37 in European casinos, which have only one zero), with the house paying out 35 times. So the house edge is 5.26 percent in U.S. casinos and 2.70 percent in Europe. When Preble started, he could only tell which half of the wheel the ball would stop in, but that was still the equivalent of playing on a very biased wheel. It effectively made his odds of winning about 1/20. And after years of doing this, he'd narrowed it down to a quadrant, raising his odds to 1/10. With a 35-times payout, over a large number of spins that translated into a player edge of over 40 percent.

Casinos all knew the story of Joseph Jagger, who broke the bank at Monte Carlo in 1873 by hiring people to track numbers on every roulette wheel in Monte Carlo's casinos. Eventually he found a biased wheel that had higher odds of landing on one side. And he cleaned out the casino. Since that was the only way to cheat—since there was no equivalent of card counting—casinos checked their wheels regularly but didn't pay much attention to the players themselves, especially when the numbers weren't too large. Though Bigman was right about the stupidity of never giving himself a bad year, because if Bigman knew about his roulette it meant that the casinos at least suspected him. He'd initially imposed the $600,000 annual limit on himself as a maximum that he'd never reach, but then, they'd always seemed to need money for something. And he wasn't very good at planning a year in advance.

"I'm here because of the shootout. Not my legal gambling."

"They're the same thing. In both cases, play long enough and the house always wins." Bigman forced a smile at his double meaning, knowing that cops referred to their precinct as the house. "Eventually your luck breaks. And yours broke the minute I watched that video footage."

Preble wished he could talk to Fish—though his "extraordinary" comment probably said enough about what Fish thought. If Preble admitted his talent, then Bigman would never let him go. It was better to deny, deny, deny. Bigman already knew, sort of, but maybe nobody would believe him. Or should he make a deal? Cooperate, help them with research, whatever, so long as they didn't keep his family away. Become a prisoner of government research labs, but at least he'd be with Kasper and Jane.

No, then they would want to do tests on Kasper too, see if it was genetic.

Five seconds just wasn't enough to steer thoughts. Conversations didn't go tick-tock, they meandered, jumped around too much. Bigman might react to something Preble had said twenty seconds earlier, a day earlier. He should have trained harder. This whole thing, from the subway on, could have been averted if he'd just trained harder, if he could see hours or even minutes instead of seconds. Or if he just hadn't been tired and irritated. If he hadn't been so stupid and reactive and absentminded.

There was a sort of constant recoil to his skill that made him want to act without thinking, to react to the world rather than thinking about the consequences of his actions. Like lawyers who get drunk out of their minds on Friday nights. Contingency and consequence exhausted him not just mentally, but spiritually—he had noticed before that the more he used his skill, the more the pressure built to let go, to stop thinking and just live in one flattened point of presence. When the whole world is hyperrational, you want to indulge irrationality. To keep yourself sane. But it was his responsibility to control when he released the pressure, and on the subway he'd chosen the worst possible time. He didn't know whether rationally bracketed irrationality even made sense, maybe it wasn't enough to release the steam—but the bottom line was that for a moment of relief he'd destroyed not just his own life, but that of the two people he loved.

Bigman asked, "You know what's going to happen, don't you, Mr. Preble Jefferson?"

"Yes. This case will plead out because the NYPD won't want to drag seven hundred missed shots through the media."

Bigman smiled. "No. This case will be closed. You were shot on the scene or escaping or whatever, and you will die of your injuries. And you'll be disappeared into a hole somewhere."

Crumb couldn't hide his look of surprise but didn't say anything.

"I think you've gone crazy, Mr.—" he stopped himself, realizing Bigman hadn't told him his name.

"Crazy makes one less predictable. Who are you working for?"

"Chresmomancy," Preble said and pointed a finger at Bigman's face. "That's what I'll use from now on. If you'd just give me a pen. Divination by the ravings of lunatics."

"The perfect soldier," Bigman went on, ready to present his theory to Preble, to see how he'd react, while shifting into his shower mode of free-associative inspiration. "Able to extrapolate beyond the half-second delay. How far? Another half second? A full second? No, roulette means at least...what? Ten seconds? How accurate is it? Fascinating. Extraordinary. That's the word your lawyer used. Truly extraordinary. It's some sort of chemical treatment, isn't it. Something like LSD. Do you hallucinate, Mr. Jefferson? There must be an awful lot of noise. How do you cut out the noise?"

Bigman had no idea just how much noise there was, because he assumed Preble's skill really was perceptual. He was starting off with how the brain normally worked. Bigman's theory was Newtonian, based on the historical idea of Laplace's Demon[1]. Except whatever it was Preble's window did for him, it was probably some gap in the laws of physics, not a super-soldier mod to his perception. His brain didn't extrapolate from perceived information in the way that the Demon did. He never actually analyzed contingencies one by one. Instead, he worked backwards from the million partly overlapped, simultaneous effects back to the moment of presence that everyone else lived in, rippling backwards, as though it wasn't that he saw the future, but rather lived in it. More exactly, it was as though the present, infinitely short for everyone else, for him lasted five seconds. He didn't have to mentally test different lines to see where they would lead five seconds hence—though he could—because he could also go backwards from the line he wanted to five seconds ago. He had to consciously pay attention, but when he did, it was instantaneous, a million potential worlds every moment that he funnelled back to a focal point that everyone else called the "present." If he wanted to crack a safe, for example, he didn't have to imagine testing 0001, then 0002, and so on. He just looked at the line where the safe opened, "remembered" the number, then used it. Whatever his perception was, it was fluid, and included missing information, bullets coming from behind, information that was not perceptible in the present—so long as the time was short enough, below the h-bar on Preble's volatile window of time dilation.

"How do I cut the noise?" Preble stalled. "By filtering it through my lawyer. I think I'm done answering until he comes back."

Bigman looked at Preble's handcuffs. "Why did you turn yourself in, anyway?"

Preble didn't answer. No matter where he looked, he didn't see a way out. He wasn't used to feeling trapped like this. Like riding an elevator.

"You know, I could wait to ship you off to your future hole, a place with proper conversation tools, but I'm having a hard time believing there's only one of you. So right now, you're going to tell me exactly who you're working for, with whom, why. Then, when we have lots of time together, you can describe the technical details."

Preble kept silent. Bigman stood up and punched him in the face, connecting hard with Preble's cheekbone.

Captain Crumb stiffened in his chair. He didn't move or say a word, though if his men had done that in front of him they'd lose vacation days. He knew guys in other precincts did it, usually in the spleen or other non-marking areas, but Crumb insisted on due process. You did that sort of thing in alleys, not in the house. Not in his house. But he bit his lip.

"So it's conscious, not instinctive," said Bigman. "I'm looking forward to learning all about it. But you really should have ducked, because you're not going to convince me I'm wrong. First, you're a boxer, and a guy as fat and slow as me would never be able to hit you unless you let me. Second, not many regular people include sesquipedalian fortune-teller words like chresmomancy and cephaleonomancy in their daily vocabulary. Unless you have a special interest in the subject."

"My cheek was itchy," Preble said. "And as for my use of foot-and-a-half-long words, it's because I read books. That's probably —" He forced himself to continue despite Bigman's next sentence, "—in my file."

"And just in case you're thinking of breaking out of here, you should know that we have your wife and son."

He gritted his teeth and asked, "What does that mean?"

"They're going to jail for aiding and abetting a fugitive. Well, the woman is. The child will go to an orphanage."

"My wife's name is Jane, and she talked me into turning myself in."

"It seems that without them, we'd be missing leverage. If you can dodge seven hundred bullets, you can break out of here."

"Leave my family in peace, and I'll leave everyone else in peace."

"Like those cops on the subway? Resting in peace?"

"Fuck off!" Preble started, then calmed himself, started over. "You're right. I should never have lived in a city. I'll leave and stay away from people. It won't happen again. You tell me where to live, with them, and the three of us will stay there." I'm sorry, Jane. I just destroyed your teaching career. Maybe more.

Bigman laughed. Actually laughed. "That's a joke?"

"So what, they're hostages?"

"The United States government doesn't keep hostages. Now, who are you working for, with whom, and why?"

Preble wished he weren't handcuffed, so he could see whether there was a future in which he could hit Bigman hard enough to realign the bastard's crooked forehead. "It's just a skill I have. I was born with it. Nobody else is involved. You give me an ironclad agreement signed by a judge saying that my wife and son will be left alone, and I'll be your guinea pig nine to five, forty hours a week. I get to see them evenings and weekends, and they have a normal life. No government facilities, no contact with you or any other government agent or scientist or whatever. Otherwise, I'll be yours, I'll answer any questions, take any tests, cooperate fully with whatever you want. But first I want an agreement. Signed by the damned president."

"The president of the United States? You think pretty highly of yourself."

"No. You think highly of me. You give me that agreement, and I'll surrender totally. Inside and out. Not until then."

Bigman thought about this. Crumb looked bewildered—the conversation had smashed through mental guardrails of normalcy and experience and left him floating, uncertain in a way he was unaccustomed to. Bigman thought far too long, seemingly in no hurry. He just stared at Preble, leaning back again, elbows again forming wings beside his head, though he unclasped his wrists and started to rub his forehead with both thumbs, fingers interlaced. It brought attention to his lopsided bone structure and gave him a slightly crazed look. "You're stalling," he finally said.

"I'm not stalling. I'm offering you everything you want!"

"An agreement like that would take days. In the meantime, your people get out of the country or do whatever it is they're here to do."

"You—" Preble clenched his jaw shut. It took all of his self-control to keep himself from reacting too early, and he failed.

"Okay, let's be frank. If you don't work with me, I'll hurt them."

Preble just glared back. He'd heard the sentence five seconds before it came. Unfortunately, his out-of-synch reaction made it look like what upset him was Bigman's comments about his "mission" rather than about hurting Preble's family.

Bigman took out his cell phone and dialled a number. Without a greeting, he said, "You on site?"

There was a pause, then he added, "Send the locals home."

Another pause, then Bigman looked at Preble as he talked into the phone. "In one hour start a water treatment. Do it on the child...You heard me...Yes, that's an order."

Preble stared at Bigman. Bigman stared back. Then, slowly, Preble said, "You're going to waterboard my son?"

"That's up to you, Mr. Jefferson. I'm just an instrument of your choices. You have one hour to tell me the who and why."

Crumb had been watching the conversation like a tennis match, becoming more and more puzzled. Now he said, almost as coldly as Preble, "Mr. Bigman, can I speak with you outside please."

"Captain, you may leave if this makes you uncomfortable. But do not interfere."

"The hell I won't interfere. I've given my share of Motorola shampoos, but you don't threaten a three-year-old."

"Captain Crumb, you have no idea what you're dealing with here. You get in my way, and I'll end your career. And your pension. And anything else I need to. Do we understand each other?"

"No. Not the slightest fucking bit."

---

1. * Laplace's Demon: Pierre-Simon Laplace imagined a hypothetical entity who knew the precise location and momentum of every atom in the universe and could thus use Newton's laws to predict the course of all future and past events.

Chapter 5

"MR. BIGMAN," CRUMB REGAINED HIS COMPOSURE. "PLEASE step outside with me and let's discuss this in private." He wasn't sure whether everything Bigman had said was for the benefit of Preble Jefferson, a monstrous but empty threat, or whether he truly intended to waterboard a three-year old. It was an absurd idea. All police departments took shortcuts to help make sure the bad guys were put away, and he assumed that the national security folks took a lot more—still, no U.S. government agency would ever do something that straight-up evil, not to that extent, surely. But every one of Crumb's 19 years of experience on the force reading people's honesty was telling him that Bigman meant what he'd said.

Instead of answering, Bigman dialled a phone number. "I want secure transport with twenty armed men, a doctor, and tranquilizers. Immediately." He closed the phone, then looked at Preble. "You have 58 minutes. The water's not really going to injure little Kasper, but I'm told it traumatizes even grown men for life. They have nightmares about drowning for years, never sleep properly again, can't shower. One man went crazy, gibbering in panic whenever it rained. For years afterwards. I spent two months at Abu Ghraib, another month at Guantanamo. You should have heard the screams and whimpers all night. Otherworldly and interesting. My daughter is an artist and I have to say, I was really tempted to record the noises and give them to her to use as a sound installation. Couldn't do it, of course, what with all the clearances. Yale Art School is far too liberal. I can't imagine what it would do to a child. Physically, he'll be fine, of course."

Without rushing, Crumb stood from his chair and turned. The hell with his pension if he couldn't shave during retirement. He didn't like shaving without a mirror. "That's enough!"

If this escalated any further, Preble thought, Bigman would have to wait outside until his men arrived or until Crumb was removed from his position. This wasn't seeing the future, it was guessing and predicting like anyone else had to. But two problems were often better than one; they could be used to resolve each other. The truth of that saying had kept him alive in the subway.

And he could never convince Bigman that he wasn't involved in some plot against the government, not in time to save Kasper from—

He didn't want to think about it. Thinking about it blinded him, all he saw was red. He just had to prevent it. And in three seconds the door would open as Lt. Fein saw Crumb grab Bigman's tie, and the red tie would come off in his hands. It was a clip-on. The lieutenant liked his captain and didn't want to see him throw away his career. It was time for Preble to gamble.

Bigman started to say he was done with the captain's interference, the captain grabbed the tie, Bigman stiffened, the tie came off, and Preble jumped up at exactly the same moment as Lt. Fein opened the door. Fein was a good cop, with quick reflexes. He came in for his captain, whose back was to Preble, but when he saw the perp lunging he drew down. But he wasn't going to shoot, not here.

Preble kicked the captain in the back of the knees, then rammed his own knee into his head with a silent apology. As the captain fell forward, still holding the tie, Preble wound up for another kick. Bigman shouted "No" just as the lieutenant finally pulled the trigger. Preble twisted. His position wasn't ideal, there had been no way to make it perfect. If Fish hadn't prevented the double-twist on the handcuffs, he'd have had no movement at all. As it was, he had to take a grazing shot through the ass, through a little bit of meat but mostly skin. Not enough to explode the dumdum, which put an inch-long groove into his right asscheek and smashed itself on the handcuff chain hard enough to cut into both his wrists. But the cuffs were broken and the door was open.

The lieutenant realized his mistake, and instead of trying to shoot again, turned for the door. Bigman pulled his own gun out, but at exactly the wrong moment. He might as well have been handing it to Preble. Preble had time to either smash Bigman's face or to just barely make it to the door. Instead of doing either, he remembered something Fish had said about Samuel Johnson, that you couldn't argue with him because if he missed with his pistol he used the butt end to beat you to death. He could see the choice ahead. He could think about it. The rational decision was the door, but it took almost all of Preble's precog window to force himself to do the rational thing.

He slammed into the door with all his weight and the lieutenant, behind it, staggered back. He stood in the doorway. Behind Preble, in the room, the captain lay semiconscious on the ground, with Bigman momentarily at a loss, no gun, no plan and no reactions. In front of him, the lieutenant's training and muscle memory was about to override his knowledge that shooting at Preble was a bad idea. In the doorway, Preble froze again within his window, a precious few seconds that were invisible to the external world because they only existed in his mind, in the little mutation in his brain that was suddenly sending him a nearly overwhelming foreboding that he should shoot Bigman right then and there, just kill him straight up, even if it was murder, even if it meant the lieutenant would shoot him during that wasted half-second. But maybe this wasn't any sort of foresight, just emotion, just an excuse for releasing anger. A primal reaction to the incredible offensiveness of a man who'd just ordered the torture of his son. A man like that should not be. A man like that created instant redness that overwhelmed and twisted his precognition skills. Because he didn't have insights into the far future, didn't have prophetic visions. His window might fluctuate, particularly strong ripples might extend a bit forward of five seconds, but not like this, not hours or days or months. No, this was just hatred, and he wasn't going to give in to hate.

He dodged the bullet and put Bigman's gun to the lieutenant's head. "Give me your gun."

Fein pointed his gun to the floor, then grudgingly handed it to Preble, who put it in his pants just as the six other cops in the precinct came running up the hallway.

"Everybody back off," Preble yelled to the hallway while he slammed the interrogation room shut with his foot. It was a one-way door, so Bigman and Crumb would have to wait for someone to let them out. Then he focused on the six new cops, trying hard to figure out a way to prevent a repeat of the subway. "Everybody, keep calm! Think! Last night, 37 of your friends shot off seven hundred bullets and all missed. If you shoot, you're far more likely to kill the lieutenant here. And if you don't shoot, I don't shoot."

"Drop the gun, now!" the community-affairs cop yelled.

"Please! Just break your pattern for a second, okay? Just think. Standard operating procedure did not work last night, so—"

"I said 'Drop the gun, now!'"

"—just stop and think for a second. Adapt. You never trained for someone who can't get shot." As he talked, Preble advanced on the six cops, lieutenant in front.

"You're bleeding out your ass," Arnolds said, backing up, his voice breaking into an unnatural laugh that was more stress than humour.

"I needed a shot in the ass."

"You need one in the head." But none of the six cops fired. Instead, they backed up into the roll-call area, all with their guns pointed at Preble's head. His body was shielded by the lieutenant. The whole progression moved into the front room, where Fish suddenly jumped up. He'd been left alone, sitting on a bench, as whoever had been staying with him ran towards the first gunshots. Now he looked at the standoff in disbelief. "Jesus, Preble, what are you doing?"

"The guy from the NSA just ordered Kasper waterboarded." Preble didn't let his eyes move to look at Fish, because he saw that if he did, the community-affairs cop would take the shot.

"What? That's nuts."

"Yeah, well, the guy is nuts. I heard him order it. And this asshole in the yellow shirt will pull the trigger the second I move my eyes to look at you, Fish. You think I should just shoot him right now?"

Now he could move his eyes safely. Obviously, community-affairs wouldn't have just been reacting to an impulse. He'd planned out the shot already, thinking he'd found a way around Preble's ability to dodge bullets.

"They're not going to torture a three-year old, Preble. He was just trying to get you to crack."

It was odd to hear Fish say that. There were usually no limits to his cynicism about the government. "No, he meant it all right. And the guy at my house took it as an order."

"Well, it's an illegal order. We'll get an injunction, we'll stop it legally. But you can't win a gun fight against the U.S. government. Not like this."

"Listen to the man," said the lieutenant, twisting to look over his shoulder.

"You were listening to the exchange through the mirror," Preble said to the lieutenant, "though you weren't supposed to. You heard Bigman. I have less than an hour to stop my son from being tortured. You have children, lieutenant? Or let me ask this a different way. If I trusted you, if I surrendered, could you stop the feds from torturing my son?"

The lieutenant swallowed hard and turned to face Preble, who let him. They were exactly the same height, and suddenly the lieutenant wasn't seeing a cop-killer with a gun to his head, but a man with a son. "I could send a squad car."

"You heard Bigman say, 'Get rid of the locals.' Would your men resist?"

The lieutenant hesitated.

"The chief of police ordered your captain to obey Bigman and the NSA. Would your men resist?"

The lieutenant was confused now, thinking, trying to fit an impossible situation into a logical framework. "You're some kind of terrorist threat," he finally said. "If they're willing to go that far, there's obviously a reason. There must be." He turned to the other cops. "Whatever happens, do not let this man out of here. Use whatever force is necessary even if it means you shoot me too."

As short as five seconds is in a conversation, it's an eternity in a gunfight. He'd once read that the entire Amadou Diallo altercation—from the moment the cops pulled up to his front stoop to where they'd misidentified him, chased him up the stairs, and shot him 41 times—had all happened in seven seconds. When you're being shot at, five seconds is a lifetime.

And the roll-call area was too perfect for an ambush. The six cops had found cover in different directions. Three were behind the main C-shaped counter, two had gone into what looked like an office, and one—Arnolds—had tucked himself around a corner where it was only the staggered shape of the room that provided any protection. If Preble moved forward a bit, Arnolds would be exposed.

But he was also the one cop who would land a bullet if Preble tried to simply run out, ducking and weaving as he'd done on the subway. So for the first time, he pointed his gun around the corner and shot first, hitting Arnolds in the forearm of his gunhand. A half second later the five other cops shot back.

Preble was still holding the lieutenant, who was wearing a bulletproof vest. Preble now maneuvered him, and himself, so that any shots that didn't go wide would hit the vest. The LT's chest would be black and blue with bruises, but no holes. Preble fired over the counter and at the office, not to hit but to keep the cops down, then spun the LT behind himself to block one last bullet as he ran out of the police station.

He busted through the blue Tardis door yelling, "Sorry, Fish!"

Once he was through, even with five cops running after him, shooting, even with his ass hurting every step, they had no chance of hitting him. The area was too open, with too many variables. Two were faster runners than Preble, including the community-affairs cop, so he shot them in the legs. Although he truly hoped that the leg shots would not cause long-term harm, he felt oddly glad to be done with the commission-omission weaselling of letting the cops shoot each other, of pretending that he was not responsible. He was. PO Edward Smacks' death was his responsibility, his fault, and the fact that he had only moved out of the way rather than pulling the trigger didn't change that. Shooting the cops directly was at least honest.

The legal system believed there was a difference between act and omission. It believed responsibility was like a bullet. It either hit you or it didn't. And he had tried to work within it. It had seemed like his best chance of preserving his family intact and, well, he couldn't win a fight against all of society. It didn't seem like hypocrisy to use the rules of the system, facts on the ground, even if he disagreed with them. It might even have worked if Bigman hadn't thrown out the rules—but while the system had flexibility at the top, it was hard as a hammer and anvil on the bottom. The government could move in and out using "national security" or other holes, but Preble Jefferson couldn't be half-in half-out. He was an outlaw now, and he could only fight or hide.

Outside the law, he also shed a layer of restraint. He stopped a car, stole it, and drove at a speed made possible only by precognition. Brooklyn, Williamsburg, outside his apartment: the whole block seemed to be in chaos. Black federal SUVs stood around haphazardly, looking like feral machines, ignoring the artificial boundaries society created between lanes, between street and sidewalk and garden. NYPD RMPs had come, been sent home by the feds, and then been radioed back by news that he'd broken out of the police station and was most likely on his way here. For some reason, they hadn't blocked off the bridge. Maybe that sort of economic interruption required higher approvals than could be obtained in the ten minutes that it had taken him to get here from downtown. Outside his building, and probably inside as well, feds in black suits were arguing with New York cops, while an Emergency Services Unit team stood around, unsure where it was getting its orders.

For all the restructuring of command authority that had taken place after 9/11, the fact that a cop in blue had been killed, combined with the lack of any terrorist attack, made the line cops push back against the feds. With a budget of $10 billion, plus a billion in overtime, if the NYPD were a national army it would be the 19th in the world. And unless the chain of command was crystal clear, they were not about to roll over for any federal agency.

Preble could shoot his way in and then out—and leave a massacre behind. If he made his way in quietly, somehow, he still didn't know how he'd get Kasper and Jane out. If he killed everyone, he could probably do it. But that was insane.

He forced himself to calm down, to sit in his car parked two blocks away, staring at the SWAT truck, to think. Then he picked up his phone and ran numbers through his window. Finally, he dialled one.

It took the Assistant Director of the National Security Agency, Information Branch, Thad Bigman, a few minutes to get over the feeling that he had just narrowly avoided death. He wasn't a superstitious man, he considered it bad luck to be superstitious, but there was a moment when Preble Jefferson had stood in the doorway, a look in his eyes that seemed far more articulate than words. In all his time with the military, he'd never had such a moment of clarity. Or probably such a close call.

He shook it off, found the captain talking to the lieutenant, interrupted, "I need a car to take me to the wife and kid."

Crumb was on the verge of telling Bigman to fuck himself. "Is your man really going to do it?"

"Now."

"Alright. I'll drive you myself." I'm not going to let you hurt a three-year old. Consequences be damned. He told the lieutenant to get him a car. Three minutes later Bigman and Crumb were on the road.

"Hello? Who is this?"

"Good morning, Mr. Mayor. This is Ronald Stone, director of the NSA."

"How did you get this number?" It was the mayor's private cell phone, an agreement with his wife and children. Even his aides didn't have it. Even his mistress didn't have it.

"Like I said, I'm the director of the NSA. We have a national security emergency unfolding as we speak, and going through regular channels would take too long. I need you to get the NYPD off the Preble Jefferson case right now. Right now there is a clusterfuck going on in Williamsburg, with my men and your NYPD arguing over turf. I need you to get the NYPD to back off. Get them away from 170 Broadway within five minutes, do you understand Mr. Mayor?"

"I'm sorry, Mr. Stone, but I'm not going to interfere with my chief—"

"Yes, you are, Mr. Mayor. Mr. Jefferson is a black federal

program, and every cop who sees what is going on is one additional security risk. If there is an RMP anywhere in Williamsburg five minutes from now, you will get no financial help from your party for re-election, you will be investigated for corruption, ties to the mob, lobbyists, sex scandals, whatever. We'll dig through everything, and even if we don't find anything, we'll still find something. There is no bottom to this one, you understand? This goes to the White House, and if you screw this up, we will neither forgive nor forget. This is not city politics we're talking about right now. Do you understand, Mr. Mayor?"

"Uh."

"Good. You tell the chief of police that he can leave one ESU truck outside"—he'd almost called it SWAT but heard the mayor say you mean ESU?—"but the ESU guys stay in it. They do not look out their windows, unless they get an explicit call to action. Do I make myself clear? Other than the one ESU truck, not a single cop in Williamsburg. NYPD, FDNY, Port Authority, Transit Authority, vollies, ambulances, I want them all out of the way. I don't want to see a meter maid or dog catcher. My agents will take care of Mr. Preble Jefferson, and the rest of Williamsburg can take care of itself for one hour. And Mr. Mayor?"

"Yes?" His voice was small now.

"You have a lovely wife. And a lovely mistress. Anything goes wrong, and your family is fair game as well. We play full contact."

Preble hung up, with a bad taste in his mouth. He reminded himself that this would save lives. The mayor didn't have time to think, and it would never cross his mind that the phone call had been faked.

———

The mayor dialled his chief of police. The chief was used to getting his way to a rubber-stamp mayor when it came to police issues, but not this time. He'd fire the stubborn son of a bitch if he didn't do what he was told, and the Policeman's Benevolent Association be damned.

———

Preble wished he could pull the same trick with the NSA, but it wouldn't work. It probably wouldn't even have worked with the chief of police. A politician mayor with presidential ambitions was far easier. But there were things the NSA would believe. He dialled the number of the field agent in his home.

"Bones here."

You're the bastard. "Director Stone. Has the Assistant Director called in?"

"What? Uh, yes sir. About fifteen minutes ago, directing me to, uhm, use hard questioning on—"

"That's enough, Agent Bones. Bigman has made a clusterfuck out of this case, and it's going to get political. I want complete radio silence until Bigman shows up at the apartment. Do you understand?"

"Complete radio silence, sir?"

"No cell phones, no radios. Bigman will be there in fifteen minutes. I've just directed the NYPD to back off and give you full authority. You're in charge of the site until Bigman gets there in person, but I don't want a single cell phone, hard-line, anything going off until then. No matter who it's from. Fifteen minutes. And leave the kid alone until the politics get sorted out. That's important."

"Yes, sir!"

"Otherwise, you're in charge, Agent Bones." Tell a man like Agent Bones that he's in charge and he'll swallow everything else that comes with it.

⸻

"You're not going to believe this, sarge," Gonzo said, clicking off the radio.

"Oh, I'll believe just about any old thing."

"We've been ordered to stay inside the truck and not look out the windows."

"That's a new one."

"Just came in direct from the chief."

"I don't work for the chief. I work for ESU," Papi Mike chimed in.

Gonzo ignored him, "And you're not going to believe the rest of it. All RMPs are to leave. Not just the site, all of Williamsburg."

"Somebody hack into the radios?"

"No. Maybe the chief lost his mind, but it's real. The feds are in charge and they're screaming 'national security' at everyone. We're the only PD unit in the area. For emergency support only. And we're supposed to close our eyes until we get orders to open them. Maybe the perp's a little green man and we're not supposed to see his UFO."

The sergeant waved his five-man squad into the back of the truck. Papi Mike gave him the ugly look that his twenty years on the force entitled him to. Then they sat there, staring at the walls. Or, rather, the cabinets. The back of the ESU truck was basically a small bus, with cabinets everywhere—cabinets for guns, for rams, for medicine, for a thousand plastic handcuffs, for almost anything imaginable related to smashing, shooting, and arresting. Sort of like the service area in an airplane where the stewardesses make your coffee, except the drawers were bigger and covered with stickers for the PD, the PBA, the SBA, and, in a step away from the police department and toward the military, the Latin logo used by all SWAT teams: "Robur gregi in lupo, robur lupo in grege." The strength of the wolf is in the pack, the strength of the pack is in the wolf.

Papi Mike finally couldn't take it. "So what happens if we look? Get turned into a pillar of salt?"

"Worse. Find a new job as an airport screener." The sergeant laughed. "I see you with the TSA scrubs, Papi, waving your magic wand."

"Hey, sarge, I can read. That disqualifies me from the TSA."

Gonzo added, without humour, "He actually said anyone who looks would get charges and specs."

"Yeah. The chief can take that up with the PBA. Charges my ass."

"I hear you. Sergeant's Benevolent would chew him a new one too. But orders' orders."

"You ever hear of something like this?"

"Nope. But this is New York City. Like I said, I'll believe just about any—"

The back door of the heavy truck opened and Preble jumped

in with a "Freeze!" shooting at almost the same time as Papi Mike reacted with his own gun. Papi's gun hand exploded. Before Gonzo or the sergeant could move, Preble's gun was pointed at Gonzo's face. The other two cops in the truck were in the middle of suiting up, their guns momentarily inaccessible.

"I really hate shooting people," Preble said, barely recognizing his own voice as it cracked with frustration, turning people into something that sounded more like peep. "Why do you guys always have to shoot first and talk later?"

"We shoot the bad guys," the sergeant said, slowly raising his hands.

"You shoot anyone who's a threat to you. Same as me." And you go for kill shots.

"Yeah, 'xcept we're doing it to protect the city. Why you doing it?"

Preble shook his head. "Just believe me, okay. You don't try to shoot me or my family, and I won't shoot you. Just believe that, and nobody else will get shot. Okay?"

"Don't live long on this job believing perps."

But they didn't really have a choice, and seeing Papi Mike wrapped around his hand made them think twice. Together with the stories from last night, cooperation seemed the best of bad options.

Preble collected weapons and handcuffs, and found some duct tape. ESU had long ago fallen in love with duct tape, and now Preble used it first to tape up Papi Mike's bleeding hand. It would hurt when they took it off, but it also stopped the bleeding. Then he taped their mouths, eyes, ankles, fingers and handcuffs. If somehow they had extra keys that no questions or search would reveal within five seconds, he'd make it hard for them to insert the key into the cuff's keyholes. He hoped none of them had a stuffy nose.

He put on the full gear, took another SWAT suit in a bag, took a heavy shield and all of the weapons. He dumped half the guns on the passenger seat of the ESU truck, hidden from 170 Broadway by the body of the truck, then walked into his apartment building. The two NSA agents wouldn't let him pass with his ESU facemask down, so he pulled it up as he came to them. It still covered his hair and changed the shape of his face, and he didn't see them recognizing him.

"No PD," the heavyset blond on the right said.

"Your Agent Bones wanted one suit delivered."

"How'd he tell you that?" the agent asked, suspicious, given the radio silence.

"The last set of orders were for all RMPs to leave the area, four of the ESU guys to stay in the truck, and me to go up to Agent Bones with a suit, where I'm to wait with him for your assistant director. I was sent in because I have security clearance. Did some time with the NYPD's overseas units. Now I'm delivering pizzas."

The agent didn't like making decisions like this without being able to radio it in. But he said, "I'll go in with you. Danny, you stay here. Eyes peeled."

Danny nodded without a word.

They took the elevator up to the sixth floor, and there Preble made a mistake. He lived in 6A, but he saw that the agent would turn to 6B. Suspecting that he might come, or just as an instinctive precaution, they'd moved Jane and Kasper to the neighbour's apartment. But seeing the agent turn to 6B, he turned there himself, too soon, too eager and emotional in his focus on what was going to happen inside. He caught himself, but too late.

The agent paused, then asked, "How do you know we moved them?"

"I was following you."

"No—"

Preble raised the shield as hard as he could in an uppercut that slammed the agent's chin back and his head into the wall. He sat on the floor unconscious, and Preble moved sideways to avoid three bullets that came through the door. Someone on the other side had looked through the peephole upon hearing the ding of the elevator. Preble fired back to where he knew he'd get a scream and a stop to the shooting, but there was no way to open the door and look in under five seconds. He didn't know how seriously the agent on the other side of the door was hurt.

ESU executed three to six "high-risk" no-knock warrants every day, and they'd developed excellent portable rams for smashing through locks. It wasn't much bigger than a police flashlight, and it was standard gear. So it was in the bag. Preble took it out, placed it on the lock and pressed a button. The lock flew into the living room, the door swung open, and three agents opened fire. But Preble now had options. The walls between the apartment and the hallway were concrete, and the ESU shield was both bulletproof and transparent. He'd put the shield down when knocking the lock out. Now he ducked behind the concrete, rummaged through the bag, decided on a pistol rather than an M-16, and came back out behind the shield. He could shoot their hands now, able to see.

For a moment, with his shield, gun, and window, and with the whole weird flow of the gunfight, he felt invincible. There is something about shooting a person: it's nearly impossible to do the first time, at least consciously, deliberately, but as you do it more and more, it becomes just an action. At least shooting their hands was. Nobody would bleed to death from a hand shot, but it would stop them from shooting back. And his ability to work backwards from a bullseye made him an unmatched marksman. Now, as he was shooting, feeling like he could take on the whole world if necessary, he suddenly realized that if he'd just shot all the cops in the subway and cemetery himself—rather than focusing on legal technicalities by letting them hurt each other—then Ed Smacks would still be alive with only a hand wound.

The thought would probably have paralyzed him except that he fore-heard Kasper's voice and foresaw Jane in the neighbour's bedroom, tied to a chair. The apartment was an exact mirror of his and Jane's, except that the furniture looked like Martha Stewart meets Asian fusion—the Tangs weren't close friends, but they were neighbourly, and over the past couple of years they'd visited each other many times. The circumstances, however, made the apartment feel alien and turned the plush orange carpet and everything on it from hip to grotesque.

Like their own apartment, this one had a large bathroom with a door to the bedroom and another to the hallway. Except that it had too many towels—a towel showroom first and a bathroom second, all either blue or pink, all fluffy, neat and stacked and organized, enough for endless showers to wash off all this blood and lunacy. Bones was sitting in the dry bathtub with Kasper. Both were fully dressed, dry. No torture yet, except the psychological damage of seeing his mother tied up by a bad man in a suit. And being forcibly confined to a bathtub. With a gun to his little head.

Preble's window recoiled from five seconds to almost nothing; all those kitsch towels were absorbing his ability to see, or the bathtub was bouncing it back like bullets. Emotion was interfering, but he didn't need to see very far—Bones was the last agent with functioning hands. Preble had already shot everyone else.

He walked in through the hallway door. Bones kept the gun pointed at Kasper, its barrel touching Kasper's wispy blond hair. Preble struggled to control his anger, his own gun pointed between Bones' eyes. Seeing Kasper like that shrunk his window down to under a second. Even that was fuzzy, uncertain. This was when he needed it most. He had to know, if he shot Bones... To see whether the bastard would have time to pull the trigger. But seeing the two of them in the bathtub like that, Bones terrified and liable to do anything, and Kasper just terrified, crying uncontrollably, Preble couldn't calm himself.

He cursed his own emotional incontinence and stalled. "You're the asshole who was going to waterboard my son."

"I...didn't."

"But you were going to."

"No. I...I'm sure that was all just for your benefit. Bigman wasn't serious. He couldn't have been."

"Why not?" He had to ask. He couldn't see the answer. He couldn't see anything, and time, stalling, might bring it back, forward.

"Nobody's going to torture a little kid."

"Good. So let him go and I'll let you go."

Bones looked nervous, but his hand—and the gun at Kasper's temple—didn't waver. "I can't do that."

"So holding a three-year-old hostage is okay? Where's the line?"

"He's not a hostage."

"Then why are you holding a gun to his head? Is he under arrest?"

"The minute I put this gun down, you'll shoot me."

"Incorrect. If you hurt him, I'll shoot you. Kill you. If you continue to hold the gun to his head, I'll kill you. If you let him go right now, I'll let you walk out of this building. I give you my word of honour."

"I have orders." Bones looked nervous, beyond nervous, his face on the verge of cracking. But his hand and gun were carved out of rock. Kasper was still crying, quietly now.

"What?"

"I do my job, that's it. You want to be pissed at someone, be pissed at Bigman. Or yourself."

Preble realized they were both stalling. He for his window, Bones for reinforcements. "Your job? Holding a gun to a child's head?" This wasn't calming. He needed ice, not heat. "Is that why you went into law enforcement?"

"Fuck you. If I put a gun to your kid's head, it keeps a million other kids safe. Normal kids. So fuck you, and yeah, I do the hard shit, so put your gun down or I'll do it right now."

Normal kids. Preble's heart froze. His jaw suddenly hurt. He had to consciously make himself breathe, to lift his lead-heavy solar plexus with his lungs. The NSA, the government, the United States of America were going to treat Kasper not as a child but as Preble's genetic material. To be tested. No matter what Preble himself did, no matter how thoroughly he surrendered, he could never buy Kasper a normal life.

Preble said, more to himself or the gods than to Bones, "He's a 3-year-old child."

"I don't own that." Bones shook his head, his own jaw clenched. "But I do what I have to do."

"Daddy help you!" Kasper said suddenly, struggling to control his crying enough to get the words out. As though he'd had enough of listening to the conversation and wanted out of the bathtub. He hadn't confused me and you in nearly six months, but now all his will was focused on trying to understand. Understand what was going on, why his mother was tied up and the bad man was hurting him and his father just stood there talking to the bad man instead of helping.

"It'll be okay, pumpkin. Daddy's here."

"Daddy's here?" he sobbed. "Kasper's not crying." Preble and Jane had tried to teach Kasper that if he wanted something he should ask for it without crying.

He thinks I'm not helping him because he's crying! The thought didn't help Preble calm himself.

"It wasn't my decision." Bones kept talking, hadn't stopped, his voice layered under that of Preble and Kasper, his tone and words jumping oddly between grandiosity and fear. One minute he seemed to expect compliance, and the next he was almost pleading for his life. "I would never choose that as...as a tactic. But you've got to understand, you can't just say 'no' to an order. Everything would break down if people started saying 'no.' It would all fall apart. Everything would fall apart. So just put your gun down and nothing will happen to your kid."

"What?" Preble had lost track of his conversation with Bones, except for the muzzle of the gun, which Bones kept pressed just above Kasper's ear. A little round anchor, the centre of the universe, it tied Preble to Bones and put the conversation so far out into the fish-eye-lens periphery as to be distorted. Agent Bones shouldn't be here. He shouldn't *be*.

"I said, put your gun down now!"

"Be quiet. I'm talking to my son." Then he turned to Kasper, "Yes, Daddy's here now. Daddy will help soon. You can cry if you want, it's okay, Kasper."

"I can cry? It's okay?" Then another idea came to Kasper and he did stop crying, though his eyes were still red. "Mommy's stuck?"

"Mommy's okay. She's just sitting in the chair."

"Put the gun down and your boy won't get hurt."

"No, Mommy's stuck. The bad guy stuck her."

"Pumpkin, you remember when we were painting, and you knocked the paint over and it went everywhere and it made your hands and feet red?"

"And I had to wash it?"

"Don't even think about it! Try anything, and my last spasm will blow his brains out."

"Yes, Kasper. Now you're going to get some red paint on you again, and then we'll wash it. Mommy and Daddy and Kasper will wash the paint from you. Is that okay?"

"I'm not kidding, motherfucker! I'll blow his head right off! All over the fucking tiles!"

Preble was calm now. Ice. Giant endless arctic sheets of ice.

Those two-mile tabs of floating ice. Ten-mile tabs. Tabs big enough to get their own names. "You won't be scared from the red paint, will you Kasper?"

"Daddy will wash it! And Mommy too."

"And the bad man will go away." Preble pulled the trigger and Bones' brains and blood splattered the back wall of the neighbour's bath. A few flecks hit Kasper, but there was no spasm, no second shot. Preble pulled Kasper out of the bathtub and took him to the sink to start washing, keeping him looking away from the tub.

"And Mommy too!"

Preble wiped Kasper's face, hugged him fiercely for a full ten seconds, then carried him into the bedroom. He wanted to tell him what a brave boy he was, what a thoughtful boy to worry about Jane instead of crying about himself, but he couldn't get a sound out without his own voice breaking. The last thing Kasper needed right now was to have his world further shaken up by seeing his father start sobbing. Jane was sitting in a chair, gagged and bound, eyes wide and tears streaming down her cheeks, but without a noise. Preble cut her free.

"Is he dead?"

Preble nodded, not trusting himself to speak.

"Good," she said, looking directly at Preble before moving to hug Kasper.

This was a different Jane than Preble had ever seen. She'd always been strong, but gentle. Before Kasper had been born, they'd had a house with a backyard and grape vines that the raccoons raided every September, just as the grapes were at their sweetest. They woke him up late at night, so he'd run out back with a stick, usually naked, while Jane stuck her head out the window and yelled, "Don't hurt them!"

He marvelled for another second at how much change 24 hours could bring, then joined her and Kasper in a hug.

Chapter 6

As Crumb drove Bigman to Williamsburg, both worked their phones against each other. Crumb knew he was outranked and Bigman didn't want to waste time looking for a new ride, so they sat in the same car going to the same location and tried to ignore each other's conversations. Bigman tried a half-dozen times to reach Bones, who wasn't answering. Nobody at the site was, so he called the Cube at Fort Meade. Meanwhile, Crumb shouted into his phone at his real boss, the assistant chief. "Mill, that's a crazy order and you know it. Clear out of Williamsburg?"

"Talked to the chief myself, George. This comes from One Police Plaza. It's political."

Crumb swerved around an overweight auxiliary on Delancey who saw his lights and was trying to stop traffic to let him through. "It stinks, that's all. I'm not hurting kids, I don't care if this guy is some freak military experiment. And if he is, let's just follow him, OJ style. Slow, calm, don't engage. You know if we pull out, the military guys are going to go nuts, right? In the middle of Brooklyn."

"George, I'm probably not cleared to hear that. But it explains some things. The feds are all over this and they want us out of the way. And we're going to get out of the way."

Crumb looked at Bigman beside him, yelling into his own

phone, then back at the snarled traffic trying to get on the bridge. Then to the assistant chief, "The people running this are idiots. They're just pissing the guy off. You saw what he could do last night, unarmed. He's still trying—"

"George, enough! Your orders are to drive the assistant director of the NSA to the site, and then go home and sleep. And if the bastard tells you to kiss his ass until it shines, you ask, 'How many watts?'"

"Percent."

"What?"

"Albedo is measured in percentages."

"Why the hell do you know that, George? You need to learn that sometimes it's better to not know."

▭

The elevator light was on the European-style "G." Not that he considered it as an option. He hated elevators even under normal circumstances, the way they froze time in a box, claustrophobic in four dimensions. The only person he'd ever told about his fear of elevators was Jane, and he was normally able to ride them with just a slight discomfort. Now the thought of stepping into one made him feel physically ill in his stomach, like vertigo or extreme hunger, bringing back a lifetime of recurring nightmares of dying in an airless elevator that was going deep into the ground.

They made it down one set of stairs.

At the fifth-floor landing, the door opened a crack and a grenade came out. Preble was waiting for it, caught it, and dropped it down the centre of the stairwell. It exploded with a surprisingly soft crack, followed by screams on the ground floor. A head peaked through the small window in the doorway. It was reinforced with wire mesh, but not bulletproof. Preble put a bullet into the agent's head.

"Oh my God," Jane gasped, but only after the shot. The whole game of grenade catch had been too quick and nonchalant to trigger a reaction. But Preble was struggling to stay calm.

▭

After Bones, they had dressed Jane in an oversized SWAT uniform, with Kasper in a too-small Ergo carrier on her front like a koala. Then they'd run through their own apartment, discordantly bright in the wash of clean gold light shining in through the windows. Direct sunlight extended from the balcony a couple of yards into the living room, but reflected light glinting off the HSBC dome across the street reached through the entire living room and down the hallway. The end of the hallway leading to their bedrooms and bathroom seemed night black in contrast, creating a three-part progression from double-bright sunshine to indirect light to darkness.

They had minutes to shed their double-bright life, to decide what few items to take from an accumulation of memories, relationships, accomplishments, things done together, gifts from friends and family—left behind in favor of items that could be turned into cash, only what could fit inside the ESU uniforms. Mostly just each other.

For the dead agent to have known they weren't ESU, he must have seen Kasper's blond head sticking out of Jane's uniform. And he'd still thrown the grenade. "There were two of them. Another one's behind the door."

"Leave him," Jane pleaded.

"Then we'll have someone at our back." He didn't need to kill this second guy. Not in the immediate way he'd needed to kill Bones to protect Kasper. But they were the ones writing the rules, throwing grenades at kids. At Kasper. Why should he keep limiting his response?

"What's he doing?"

"Cowering in fear."

"Then leave him."

Preble hesitated. "Now he's talking on his radio. I guess the radio silence is done. Which means we're out of time."

"Please, leave him!"

Preble knocked on the window with the barrel of the gun. "Mr. Federal Agent. You can live if you leave that door closed and stay behind it. If you open it, I will shoot you in the head. Not your hand, not your leg, but your head. Do you understand? Answer me."

"I understand." The voice, used to giving orders, sounded like tin.

"Good. And stay off the radio." In a future where he looked, Preble could see that the agent was terrified. "Actually, open the door a crack and push your radio through. You can keep your gun."

The fact that Preble didn't care whether the agent kept the gun scared the man far more than if he'd taken it. The door opened a sliver, and the earpiece radio came through. Preble put it in his ear.

"We're going down?" Kasper suddenly said, with a voice that was now more curiosity than fear, and suddenly Preble was glad that he'd listened to Jane, and not killed the second man behind the door. If she hadn't been with him, he would have.

"Yes, pumpkin, we're going down," Jane whispered.

"And the bad guys can't stop us?"

"Nobody can stop us," Preble said.

⌑

"The one thing we cannot do, absolutely cannot do, is let this man go free," NSA Director Ronald Stone explained to the president of the United States. "Ideally, of course, we would catch him and figure out where this threat is coming from. Most importantly, whether there are others or could be others. It could just be a freak skill that this particular individual has, as he claimed in the interrogation. He's received no additional support from the outside since this started, and he's had over eight hours to get it, so I'm starting to lean towards the theory that he doesn't have outside support."

"Then he's not a threat," said the president. "Is he?"

"Sir," Stone drew himself up, though nobody on the conference call—a sort of truncated Principals' Committee made up of Assistant Director of the CIA James Grill, FBI Director Steve Guther, and the president's chief of staff, Mickie Fred—could see it. "Whether he's alone or not, Assistant Director Bigman and I both believe Mr. Preble Jefferson poses a far greater threat than this nation has ever faced before."

"I find that hard to believe. He's lived among us in peace for thirty years."

"A ticking bomb isn't a problem either, until it blows up. It seems that this all started because a police officer looked at him the 'wrong way.' A man who can see the future is not used to any, any, external restraints. Things don't happen to him; he structures things. He chooses what happens to him. He is absolute master of his destiny. He is completely free, the ultimate spoiled child. Put aside campaign rhetoric for a second, Mr. President. A society of truly free individuals is impossible. It's anarchy. You have to leave people with some freedoms, of course, in the same way that allowing prisoners to re-arrange their furniture drastically lowers prison riots—"

The president frowned into his phone, wondering suddenly about Director Stone's description of his men cornering the terrorist. The NSA was just supposed to gather information. Why had nobody ever told him that it had its own black-ops troops? But this wasn't the time for that conversation. "This is off point—"

"With all due respect, Mr. President, it's relevant to understanding the damage that Mr. Jefferson could cause. You need to understand the limits of your own power in order to appreciate how dangerous someone without limits can be."

"I heard this on the eve of my inauguration, Ronald. I don't need to hear it again." He'd sat through a series of speeches, awkwardly idealistic in their cynicism, when he'd first come into office, down to the same metaphors. At the time the nearly overwhelming idea that he, John Grape, was really going to be the most powerful man on the planet had made him patient, and even eager, to listen to lectures about how powerless he really was. From everyone except his VP, Garland O'Reilly, who was constantly pushing for a more powerful executive. Though Garland also seemed convinced that the voters had gotten the ballot flipped, that he should be president because he was older and had come up through the CIA.

"With all due respect, you do, Mr. President. You are the most powerful individual in the world, and yet your every action is constrained by other people, institutions, reality, nature, accidents. Laws still apply to you, both natural and man-made. Now think of Mr. Preble Jefferson. None of his actions are constrained, except to the extent he chooses them to be because of his attachments to his family and so on. Society cannot function with unconstrained people. If he chooses to, he could walk into the White House tomorrow and execute you, and all your Secret Service staff couldn't stop him. Or he could simply use that threat to change your behaviour, my behaviour, anyone's. As the president, you only have access to certain levers of power, with millions of other levers acting as checks and balances, both domestic and international. But through you, Mr. Preble Jefferson could decide the policy of the United States. He could do the same thing to the leaders of Russia, China, to the CEOs of the biggest multinationals, as he did with the mayor of New York. He could wield any and every lever of world society."

"But you can't know that he would want to. Maybe he really would just go and live in peace with his family."

"I'm sorry, sir, but you don't run a country on trust. Eventually, something would happen that would push him to fight us. Or some other nation would get its hands on his family and use them to control him. Don't imagine that the Russians and Chinese aren't watching this unfold. What if this is a learned skill, and he teaches others? What if it's genetic, his children inherit it, and in a few generations we have a class of totally ungovernable super-terrorists loose within our borders? Completely autonomous individuals, reproducing like cancer cells, immune to any societal antibodies. But I don't think we have to wait that long. I think he's already at war with us, and our only chance is to finish it before he realizes just how much potential he has to harm us."

Grape was stopped by Stone's absolutist tone. The man seemed so certain of the risk, and he'd been calculating risk on the nation's behalf for a very long time. "You really think it's that bad?"

"I think it's far worse than I can articulate, Mr. President. One definition of intelligence is the ability to predict the future. To take the environmental cues together with memory and extrapolate the future. It's the only definition I know that captures all forms of intelligence. And in that sense, Mr. Preble Jefferson is a qualitative leap above the rest of humanity. When you called, I was just getting a briefing from our neuroscientists. We should have his medical records within the hour and then we'll know more, but our people already have some theories. I'll spare you the details, but basically the normal human brain, the neocortex is a stack of six layers that aggregate information and send feedback expectations, predictions, back to the senses. As we look out at an ocean of constantly shifting patterns, all parts of our brains try to predict what their next experience will be. If I say 'Fee fye foe' you think, before I say it, 'fum,' and that thought is sent to your ears so that if I then actually say 'fun' you will nevertheless hear 'fum.' When you take a step, your brain predicts where the floor is, and so long as it is where you expect it, you don't even notice it. The entire neocortex is a probabilistic pattern-prediction machine—"

"Slow down. You said you'd spare the details."

"Yes. Mr. President, reptiles don't have a neocortex. They just react to stimuli. Mammals other than humans have a three-layer neocortex. They can aggregate, and thus predict, patterns up to a certain point. Turns out, the ability to predict patterns proved to be an evolutionary advantage. Humans have six layers. We suspect that Mr. Preble Jefferson has seven or more."

"So what does that mean?"

"My guess is that he has a deeper cortical hierarchy and can thus see higher-order patterns. It also means that if we don't stop him, the rest of us could end up like the Neanderthals."

President Grape didn't answer for a few seconds. Everyone else on the call knew not to interrupt. "So how can we stop him? I mean, if he can get to any world leader, anyone?"

"He's not used to an aggressive posture yet, but he's learning fast. We have a short window of opportunity. If we don't catch him in that time frame, then we'll have to restructure our institutions. No important decision to be made by one person. Minimum two out of three vote on anything to do with catching Mr. Jefferson. Maybe more broadly. I'm sorry, Mr. President, but it may mean temporarily giving up some authority. What we really need is to make all decisions in a sort of board of directors. So if any one or two of us is compromised, the group will still come to the right decision. I suggest the people on this conference call, plus CIA Director Frankfurter and my Assistant Director Bigman. If we have two from the CIA, we need two from the NSA, since the nature of this threat is information based.

"I'm not sure about Bigman," said the FBI director, his first words on the call. "I know he and the Vice President go way back, but the man is a loose cannon. He's the reason—"

"Yes, but he's also brilliant. He's the one who figured out—"

"Whoa, wait a minute!" the president yelled as everyone talked over each other. "You're not going to restructure the United States government on this conference call."

"No, sir. I'm only talking about creating a subcommittee for the hard decisions that will go into neutralizing Mr. Jefferson."

"You're talking about a politburo!"

"A board of directors' subcommittee, sir."

"Enough. What's the address you want to blow up?"

"170 Broadway in Williamsburg."

"Can't you wait until he's not in major city?"

"Not if you want to spin it as a terrorist attack. And it's Brooklyn's Broadway, not Manhattan."

"Fine, bomb the goddamned building. The whole block. You have my authorization for that. As big a bomb as you want short of a nuke. Just get rid of this problem before it makes us screw ourselves up totally. But no politburo."

Chapter 7

Preble was grateful for the concrete-panel construction of the building. It allowed him to place Jane and Kasper out of the line of fire without having to leave them one floor up. He placed the ESU transparent shield in front of him, as he prepared to open the door to the ground-floor landing.

"Hey, NSA guys!" he yelled. "I know you think you have me trapped. But you only have me cornered. I can get out of this, but only if I shoot to kill. I am not a terrorist. I'm not an agent of a foreign government. I'm just a guy who wants to be left alone. I want my family left alone. If you leave the building now, the worst that could happen is you lose your job. A job with a boss who lies to you. If you stay, you will die. And it won't be for the country, because I'm not a threat to it. You have thirty seconds to leave the building."

There was silence from the lobby. An odd silence, as though every one of the twenty soldiers pointing their guns at the stairwell were thinking the same thing, that the speech was exactly backwards, that the government should be warning the nutjob to give up or be killed, not nutjob warning the government.

Instead of thirty seconds, Preble waited a full minute. Thirty seconds extra was all that he was willing to give them now. His civilization buffer was getting squeezed, like a cushion with all the stuffing falling out of it. That's the image that went unbidden through his mind as he opened the door.

⸻

After 9/11, Homeland Security put a Black Hawk helicopter on standby at La Guardia, armed with laser-guided missiles that could service both air-to-air and air-to-surface targets. Heat- and radar-guided weapons made no sense above New York City. It took only three phone calls and five minutes for the president's order to bomb 170 Broadway to reach the base, but the fast-track approval that had been established after 9/11 was only for shooting down civilian airliners. It took an extra fifteen minutes to verify that the president really wanted to bomb a gentrified condo in Williamsburg, then another three to get the helicopter up.

⸻

The NSA soldiers opened fire. All of them were ex-military—Navy Seals, Green Berets, Rangers, Delta Force—on permanent loan to the NSA, and they shot at the ESU shield only long enough to be sure it was bulletproof. Then they started shooting at the edges, keeping Preble from sticking his gun out to shoot. A few even tried to shoot behind him, hoping to hit a metal railing that would bounce a bullet, something, into Preble's back. It was as though he suddenly found himself in a snow globe, with white paint chips flying in all directions off the steel stairwell door and concrete walls.

But paint chips couldn't cut through his ESU gear. And the shield, together with knowing what was coming, was too big an advantage. Slowly, systematically, he took the openings he had, poking just his gun out and taking a shot every few seconds. With each shot, there was one fewer man-in-a-black-suit shooting at him. Kasper and Jane were behind him, around the corner, terrified, and he was done with aiming at hands.

Then someone shouted, "Hose it!" and five grenades came flying towards the stairwell. They were too good, too synchronized, so the grenades all flew at the same time.

Preble closed the door. The grenades bounced off, in different directions but all back into the foyer. They exploded. There was no fireball, just a gray transformation of all the wooden furniture in the foyer and the two sets of glass doors into a meat-shredding maelstrom of splinters, glass, and grenade fragments that ripped everyone inside into a gory spray. Preble was protected by both the door and the ESU shield, Jane and Kasper were safe around the concrete corner. The metal door flew off all its hinges except one, above Preble, mangled and harsh, its white paint blasted off from the side that faced the world. He held onto the shield, then advanced.

⸻

Bigman and Crumb arrived at 170 Broadway just in time to get caught in the crossfire, saved from the grenade blast by the handicapped ramp. The ground floor and foyer were a half basement fronted by a sunken areaway, with a ramp for baby strollers and the handicapped that ran parallel to the façade of the building. Glass flew over their heads, but the edge and angle of the four-foot depression blocked the mincing bits. They scrambled back to the cover of the ESU truck. Bigman tried to reach his men inside the building while Crumb called in a Level Four mobilization. He didn't care if he got fired for going against orders, he had to get more men here. And a Level Four would bring in every cop in the five boroughs of New York City.

Bigman gave up on the radio and started shouting at the four men he still had left outside. "Don't try to hit the guy. Just pin him down!"

He turned to the ESU sergeant. "You have grenades? And launchers?"

"Yes."

"I want one grenade every fifteen seconds shot into that foyer. From a distance, not all at once. Just pump one in every fifteen seconds, doesn't matter if you see anything in there or not. We don't care about hitting him, just want to make sure he doesn't have an opening. Do you understand me?"

Crumb interrupted, "Some of your men might still be alive in there."

"Stay out of this, captain."

"Sir, I don't have enough grenades for that. We carry three each, plus a reload. That's thirty total. At fifteen seconds per..."

"That buys us more than seven minutes," Bigman cut the sergeant off. He didn't like the math at all. "It's got to be—."

"Sergeant, you will not shoot grenades at a woman and child," Crumb ordered.

"No, sir. I will not." The sergeant looked relieved, then twitched as they heard gunshots. All three peeked out around the ESU truck and stared in disbelief as Preble walked calmly out of the destroyed foyer. Holding the transparent shield like some sort of Greek warrior sacking Troy, he executed the last four NSA guys. They were shooting at him the whole time, but it still looked like an execution. They had no chance.

Papi Mike unwrapped a piece of chewing gum with his good hand and put it in his mouth. "I guess it won't keep him in there."

"He'll have to go back to get them. We just have to hold him for a few more minutes," Bigman almost pleaded.

"And then what?"

As though in answer, Bigman looked up and west. He saw the speck that he'd been waiting for.

"Ah shit." Papi Mike said.

"Officer, your orders are to fall back as far as you can while still maintaining a field of fire. But hold this man here at all costs." He picked up the phone to warn his own men, then realized he didn't have any left. Then he turned and started to run down Broadway.

Crumb ran after him, yelling, "Are you serious? I've got half the force on their way here! How far is the blast radius?"

He hesitated between taking the time to catch Bigman and stopping his men from arriving. He tried to do both, running and yelling into his radio for the dispatcher to keep all units five blocks away. As he ran around the corner of Bedford, he almost ran into Bigman.

"Stay off the radio!" Bigman panted.

"I'm not going to let my men—"

"You dumb son of a bitch. You don't realize what's at stake here."

Staring at Bigman's face, Crumb continued to shout into the radio for the NYPD to stay five blocks away from 170 Broadway.

Bigman looked like he wanted to take a swing, and Crumb prayed that he would.

They heard more gunfire. Both looked down Broadway and saw Preble get in the ESU truck and drive it up to the handicapped ramp. Then he jumped out, still with his shield, and ran back into the building.

Bigman called Ronald Stone. Stone picked up after the first ring.

"Patch me through to the helicopter! He's out of the building. We need to shoot the SWAT truck!"

In the distance they could see Preble with someone else in an ESU suit run into the truck while shooting at Papi Mike's team. Crumb could just make out a little tuft of baby blond hair at chest level.

"Blackhawk pilot, this is NSA Assistant Director Bigman. Change of targets. You are to shoot the SWAT truck in front of the building, do you understand?"

"This is Hotel Two-Six, who is this?"

"NSA Assistant Director Thaddeus Yagbig. Hotel Two-Six, you are ordered to change targets. Shoot the SWAT truck in front of the building."

"Copy but unable to comply, sir. I cannot change targets without new live-fire authorization from Bushmaster Two."

"Listen to me, pilot. The package has moved out of the building and into the SWAT truck. You are to take out that truck now. I don't have time to figure out who your ground control is."

"I'll confirm with Bushmaster Two. Please hold. Over."

"Execute first, then confirm!"

"I'm unable to comply with that order, sir. Please hold. Over."

Crumb was relieved. He'd been fighting a desire to handcuff Bigman on the spot and to hell with everything else. Because it would mean one little kid wouldn't get blown to bits in thirty seconds. But what if Bigman was right, if saving that one child meant thousands of others would die? He didn't have the intel, and it wasn't his call. The government was certainly treating this as a National Security emergency on par with 9/11. If they had shot down those planes, killed three hundred to save three thousand. Still, he couldn't stand by and watch a psychopath issue orders that would kill a child. He just couldn't.

Now the decision would be made by someone other than Bigman, and he was sure nobody else would approve it.

Someone did, in less than a minute. Everyone was patched into the pilot's line, from "Bushmaster Two" (operational ground control for New York City air security) up to the president. Someone had even grudgingly told the director of Homeland Security. The SWAT truck was already moving well away from the building when the pilot acknowledged the change in targets. He'd been flying with his targeting system on, weapons live, everything ready. When the revised order came into his computer, he made sure of his shot, exhaled and released.

It was close enough that Crumb and Bigman saw it shoot from the helicopter. There was a flash of flame and a little bit of black smoke and a pop that sounded like a firecracker that echoed off the buildings a couple of times. The pop seemed far too weak for a smart missile that could adjust its course for the movements of its target, gauge target speed and continually recalculate projections of where the target would be at impact.

But it didn't take into account obstacles. When the truck disappeared under the Williamsburg bridge, the missile just missed the *Welcome to Brooklyn. You name it, we got it* sign and hit a post on the bridge. There was a split second where the missile looked like it had simply disintegrated without exploding, followed by a yellow-white blossom of fire that ballooned in every direction except down. One spur of the fireball shot north towards Preble's home like an accusing finger as the rest turned into a black cloud of roiling debris. The *Welcome to Brooklyn* sign sailed towards them, a giant green kite flying at what seemed like a leisurely float after the missile and fireball.

Bigman watched the sign fly through the air and Crumb punched him in the face as hard as he could.

———

A pop-up box appeared on Analyst Hsien's computer, and she clicked on it to listen as she had done in one way or another every day of her twenty years with the People's External Information Bureau, now at the Chung Hom Kok signals intelligence HQ in Hong Kong. After twenty years of twelve-hour shifts, the headphones were as much part of her body map as her ears, though they had also caused a permanent ringing in her head that made it hard for her to sleep at night. The doctor said there was nothing she could do other than stop using telephones, earphones or any other electrophonic system—a suggestion that almost made her arrest the doctor before she realized that he didn't know how important her job was.

China's kitchen-sink approach to spying had yielded tremendous results. It traditionally preferred live assets—translation bureaus in Hawaii that took contracts from the NSA, moles who lived as U.S. citizens for a generation before activating, and, of course, the Ministry of Trade and Economic Co-operation (MOFTEC). Those live assets had brought back high-tech SIGINT capability and the know-how to supplement the live assets with China's own form of Eschelon spy software and, increasingly, Trojans and worms that pulled information directly from enemy computers. But signals intelligence was still the foundation of all snooping, and, ironically, the Chinese had received most of their capabilities from the NSA directly and openly. First through Project P415—an NSA cooperation with the UK, China and New Zealand to ensure that every communication on the planet was monitored by someone, with parts of the globe assigned to each participating agency—and then through a joint project between the Chinese Communist Party and the NSA to limit internet anonymity.

Chinese wetware assets were far superior, and their electronic snooping was now at parity with that of the NSA. They had their own Zircon spy satellites, total information systems, and an Eschelon-style (actually Eschelon exactly) smart software named Harmony. Harmony didn't just track the use of keywords like "bomb" and "missile," it had a finely calibrated sense of frequency and one of the best AI minds in the world. The enemy could use code phrases as much as they wanted, but keywords revealed little compared to sudden spikes in specific types of communications, ganglions of information that tied certain agencies in certain ways.

Now, this algorithm decided that a human analyst needed to listen to what was happening in New York City and directed Analyst Hsien to click on her pop-up box.

Only some of the alphabet-soup agencies in the U.S.

encrypted their communications. CIA, DIA and NSA were pretty good, the FBI's encryption was from the early 1990s and could be cracked by a twelve-year-old, the NYPD pretended, and the ATB, Port Authority and the other police-level agencies without the NYPD's delusions of becoming platforms for the international projection of law and order didn't even bother. It took Analyst Hsien less than one minute of listening to hit a key that ordered the computer to monitor all associated communications and to pass the whole problem up the line. Then she continued to listen as the Americans shot at each other.

General Klurglur, Information Chief of FSB's Foreign Directorate, hung up the old-fashioned rotary phone that sat on his desk. He liked the heavy cradle, the thick handle he could squeeze in anger without crushing or tuck under his chin without it getting lost in his beard, but he also liked all the little functions hidden within its primitive exterior—like a built-in polygraph, recorder, automatic GPS call tracer, and so on. All very handy when his wife called to say she was at the hairdresser and would be home late, but not much more useful than a regular phone for real work. His web of computers and human analysts was supposed to connect the million-dollar phone to every datum of information that could be accessed by Mother Russia—but they had missed the activity in New York. It was from CNN that he'd learned the Americans had fired a missile in the middle of Brooklyn in order to stop some highly dangerous terrorist. Along with unconfirmed reports that it was the same man who earlier had sent nineteen police officers to the hospital. Which, of course, made no sense at all. The NYPD had more police and SWAT units than all the regular police forces of Russia put together, and nobody was that dangerous. If there were an election coming up, he'd assume it was a political stunt, but the American presidential election was nearly three years away and this was too big for mid-terms. Something was going on.

And then the phone call from a monitoring station in Siberia. The Soviet Union had always eavesdropped on the U.S., but like the Chinese, they preferred human intelligence. The Soviet

Union had been very good at wetware and hardware—tank-level hard, not silicon-chip hard. Not so good with software. Modern Russia had changed that, but old habits died hard. For nearly fifty years the Chinese had tested the Soviets on their shared border, sending over a unit or two every few years just to see how aggressively the Russians would react. Siberia had room, it had resources, and China made sure that Russia knew she had to defend it. And China was as difficult to infiltrate with human assets as the United States was easy. So first the Soviet Union and then Russia had focused on developing a deep signals intelligence net over their southern border and beyond.

What that net now picked up was that the Chinese were interested in Brooklyn. Klurglur had expected their Propaganda Ministry to pick up on it, and of course the political levels had to be prepared in case the "terrorist" was accused of having embarrassing connections or the incident could be used by the hybrid programs dedicated to increasing internal U.S. political tensions, but the Siberia station had traced communications going all the way up to Chi Mak, the head of Chinese Military Intelligence. The quantity and direction of traffic tied to the Americans bombing themselves was far beyond what propaganda or simple political contingency planning would have called for.

Klurglur poured himself two-fingers of Glengoyne 21 year— not vodka—and let his mind wander briefly to a week he'd spent in New York. He liked Williamsburg, and recognized the location of the attack. What was that place with the excellent coffee? The Verb Café. Not true at all that the Americans can't make coffee. They've learned how to make a good cup of coffee. The Chinese have learned high-tech snooping. What has Mother Russia learned? How to make people fight themselves?

He googled the address that was bombed. Residential. Although the media focused on bombing the bridge, Klurglur's analysts had picked up the original target—a man named Preble Jefferson—from the Chinese. Then he grabbed the phone and called the deputy secretary. "I want assets on the ground in New York. In Williamsburg, Brooklyn. Set them up as artists, living off a trust fund. Tell them to sit at the Verb Café. It's a few blocks from the Williamsburg Bridge." Klurglur already had a reputation for near-omniscience, but it never hurt to burnish it. He remembered people playing chess at the Verb, and Jefferson was a chess player. "Sit, play chess, talk to people, find out everything about everyone who lived there. I want a dossier on Mr. Preble Jefferson, on everyone who lives there, on every friend and relative we can find. Get the embassy in on it. The humint can supplement as they go. Don't burn any moles. You can send Russian passports with proper visas, just do it fast."

"What kind of artists?" the deputy secretary asked, interested. He'd gone to art school before joining the KGB, before it became the FSB. A very long time ago he'd thought he'd become Kandinsky or Malevich.

"What? I don't know. I don't care. Just don't send anyone who paints. Tell them to melt plastic into abstract creatures. Give our man a cover, say, two years in a Soviet mental asylum to avoid going to Afghanistan. Took chemicals to drive himself insane, got out of war, became an artist, won a Fulbright, whatever—a cover that lets him act a little crazy. Someone aggressive."

"'The more frightening the world becomes, the more art becomes abstract.'"

"What?"

"Vassily Kandinsky, General. Just a quote."

Chapter 8

It was the loudest sound Preble had ever heard, a short but massive cracking sound above that buckled all their joints, jellied their backbones, and snapped all four axels of the SWAT truck just as Preble was trying to shove the brake pedal through the floor with his foot. They were directly under the Williamsburg Bridge. Preble and Jane climbed out, blinking through white and tears as though they'd both just been smashed in the nose by a baseball, Kasper still tucked into Jane's jumpsuit. Despite the shielding of the bridge and the armoured truck, the concussion left all three dazed and half-deaf, wobbling inside as though in an earthquake that just wouldn't stop, complete with hot flashes and blood pounding in their skulls. When Preble handed Jane a shield and told her to hold it above her head it was like someone else talking and he wasn't quite sure she'd heard him. When he took another shield, gripped Jane's hand, and they ran out of the truck, his limbs felt disconnected. Movies are full of explosions, but being in one was very different, as though the concussion had pushed his soul out of his body. Odd how soft her hand felt in his own mechanical claw. He was touching it for the first time and his fingers were asleep.

It was only when Kasper suddenly started to cry, almost mad, saying, "That was too loud, Daddy!" that he snapped out of it, or his mind snapped back into it, or whatever—he saw red. Another burst of livid anger that the assholes would launch missiles at a three-year-old. At his son. It was irrational to keep getting angry at this, they'd proven it over and over now. But each time it happened, it set off a small war in his own mind, a struggle to control the urge to just huddle around Kasper and lash out, kill everyone in sight, to go postal, or biblical, or whatever it took to stop all the assholes trying to hurt them.

"Daddy!"

He noticed unidentifiable metal bits had fallen down from the bridge between the Brooklyn-bound lane and the subway rails, but the devastation on either side of the bridge was much worse. The bridge went East-West, they'd come from the south, and there he could see five different crumpled cars burning, sending distinct waves of heat towards them. To the north there was a single truck blocking the road on its side. It had either been thrown off the Manhattan-bound side, or across it and off.

They ran up the bicycle path, still a bit disassociated. Their muscles, especially their thighs, had somehow been actually bruised by the concussion. It hurt to run, but there was no time to think about the weirdness because a teenager came barrelling down at them on a black Rockhopper mountain bike, obviously terrified that the bridge would collapse and doing his best to get down as fast as he could. He was bleeding from the right arm. The explosion must have slammed him against something, but his bicycle still worked.

Preble pressed Jane and Kasper to the side and used the ESU shield to knock the teenager off his bike. It hit too hard, and the teenager crumpled backwards as the bike reared up and flipped.

"Get on," he told Jane, picking up the bike. He avoided looking back at the body of the boy, maybe seventeen, but did check the window—where the boy lay flat on his back, bleeding from his mouth and nose, blood trickling down his neck onto a black T-shirt with the single word Motormouth in Gothic white letters. He still had a pulse. He hoped he hadn't just killed his first innocent person.

What am I talking about? Dozens of drivers and passengers on the bridge. Right here. All innocent. But more than worrying about the boy on the bike, more than all the people on the bridge, Preble worried that Jane would want to stop and help. Preble's sense of empathy wasn't egalitarian. They'd had arguments about this, enough so that Preble had forced himself to look closely at his own values. For Jane, a human being was a human being, the end, and her empathy was reactive, based on who needed help the most in the moment, often to the extent of forgetting not just herself but her family. For Preble, it was different. His own emotional commitment to others was highly structured, concentric rings of tribalism that centered on Kasper and expanded out to Jane, then himself, Fish, close friends, other friends, children generally, underdogs generally, strangers whom he respected for some specific reason, women who were attractive or intelligent though he found this one embarrassing to admit, people with roughly similar values, women generally, and then very last, all other adult males. Regardless of these categories—which Jane had once forced him to articulate, and thus create, during an argument, though the reality was much more fluid than the word boxes made it sound. What Jane had difficulty accepting was that he found the millions starving in some distant part of the world to be an intellectual problem that needed to be solved, not an emotional one. The concentric circles of his emotions weren't based on an idea of right and wrong—they were just how he was built intuitively. He felt a slash of guilt for hitting the boy in the Motormouth shirt, a tear in some internal fabric, but if stopping to help him would put Kasper at risk, then he would not stop to help.

But this time Jane seemed to feel the same way. Perhaps because of what she'd seen in the bathtub, or the concussion from the bomb that still hadn't fully let their minds and bodies reintegrate. He suspected all three of them had actual concussions from the blast. She dropped her shield, took the bike without a word, jumped on, and although it was uphill, biked at the same speed as Preble at full run. When she slowed, he grabbed the back of the seat with his free hand and pushed, running. It took three minutes to get to where the bike path rose above the roadway.

Ahead of them, the bridge was covered. Behind them, it was a disaster area, with cars sprawled crazily, many of them burning. A few people around the edges in suddenly stopped cars were climbing out, some running, others standing like pillars of salt. A few were trying to get others out of cars. Lots of dead innocents.

No police had arrived yet: the Brooklyn-bound lane was a giant screaming traffic jam. The Manhattan-bound side was empty, blocked by wreckage.

"Oh my God," Jane said. Although the carnage was three blocks behind them now, a scent of burning plastic, rubber and hair was starting to poison the air where they stood. Preble was grateful that Jane had a very weak sense of smell—he'd always thought that was weird for a poet, he somehow associated poetry with scent—and that Kasper had inherited this lack in a more magnified form. He had no sense of smell at all, and, for the first time, Preble was really glad of this. Glad Kasper would never know that smell.

"Keep going!" he said, starting to run out of breath. They continued up, finally reaching a point where the bicycle path was no longer surrounded by cages on all sides. There was still a metal mesh on the outside edge to prevent jumpers, but they could climb down onto the subway tracks that were between and above the car lanes. From there, they had the option of jumping to either lane. Brooklyn-bound had jammed up faster than they'd run. They were still below the crest of the bridge, but Preble suspected it was standing traffic all the way to Delancey Street in Manhattan. The Manhattan-bound side was empty except for two police motorcycles that were just now coming in from Manhattan.

Preble hesitated between options—every second counted now —then jumped onto the empty road and waved down the cops. They had to slow down just ahead of him anyway, where a twisted *Leaving Brooklyn. Oy Vey!* sign was sprawled across the bridge. They signalled to each other, then one of the cops continued to the mangle of burning cars. The other pulled over to Preble.

"ESU?"

"No," Preble answered and smashed the ESU shield into the cop's face, then caught the motorbike before it fell. The uppercut had knocked the cop unconscious. Preble's mind flashed to an image of the teen wearing the Motormouth shirt, laying there, and he thought he could smell the burning flesh again—

I'm losing my mind...

Jane climbed down and without a word got on the back of the bike, behind Preble. She held him tightly, with Kasper squished between them. He regained his focus.

"Momma! Momma! We can't go! I don't have my helmet!" Kasper said from inside Jane's ESU jumper. They spent a couple of months every year in Bali, where they drove around like this, the three of them. Kasper had been riding since before his first birthday. They all associated squeezing onto a motorbike with happy times, long leisurely vacations, weaving along mountain roads with terraced ricefields on either side, passing everything from seven-year-old girls driving their four-year-old sisters on motorbikes too big for their feet to touch the ground, while texting with one hand, to giant Javanese diesels carrying a thousand chickens and spewing black clouds of exhaust, to skinny old men driving a horse and buggy while talking on a cell phone. Now, with the empty bridge and the *Leaving Brooklyn. Oy Vey!* sign directly in front of them and half the city after them, it created a dissociated sense of placelessness, almost a vertigo.

"I don't have my helmet!" Kasper yelled again, this time near crying.

"You don't need your helmet today," Jane answered him.

"Yes, I do need my helmet today!"

"You're a big boy now," Preble said, searching desperately for some logic to make Kasper accept that they didn't have a helmet for him. "Helmets are for little babies."

"Daddy's wearing a helmet."

"Daddy wants to look like a cop, Kasper. Like a police," Jane said.

"Momma is not wearing a helmet?"

"No, you and I aren't wearing a helmet. Only Daddy because he's in the front. In Bali you have to wear a helmet, but not in New York."

"Not in New York?" Kasper asked, and accepted the statement that was exactly backwards.

It helped when Preble started the bike. The low earthquake rumble of the 1200cc police motorcycle was so different from the high pitch of the racing-modified no-battery Suzuki T4 125cc (with pistons manually expanded to 175cc, open carburetor and handmade racing muffler) two-stroke dirt bike he drove in Bali, that the feeling ebbed a bit. Preble wedged his shield between his belly and the handlebars. He'd once carried three mattresses on his motorbike, and he'd seen Balinese carrying far more. He worried that the wind would catch it and flip it in his face, but then he remembered that he'd know before it happened.

With that reassurance, he raced at full speed into Manhattan.

"Did we get him? I don't think we got him!" Bigman yelled into the phone. A bruise was starting to form on his left cheekbone. Crumb's career was finished, but there had been nothing Bigman could do about him alone, at this moment, here on the street. You don't argue with cops on the street—that was as true for him as it was for the lowliest civilian. You comply on the street and then destroy them in office buildings, courtrooms, environments built of paper and computers, not concrete and guns. So he had taken the punch and walked away.

"Uh, negative, sir. The missile hit the bridge," the pilot answered.

"Has the target come out the other side?"

"Negative. I don't think he could. There's what looks like a refrigeration truck blocking the road on that side, and the south side is completely clogged."

"You see that truck come out, you shoot it. You see the two targets come out, you shoot them. They're wearing ESU gear."

"Copy that, sir. But it'll be swarming with ESU in five minutes. How do I tell the difference?"

"For the next five minutes, you see anyone in gear, you shoot them. Out." Bigman turned to Crumb, not quite able to restrain himself. "You understand that this is your last shift ever as a police officer?"

Crumb looked at Bigman, then radioed in, warning all ESU to change out of their gear before going near the bridge.

Everyone was following the bombing of the Williamsburg Bridge on their own screens, from the president down. The conversation was instant, though dispersed across the White House, Pentagon, Langley, Cheyenne Mountain, and Fort Meade. If there was an American "center" to the operation, it was the latter, NSA headquarters, gathering, sorting, filtering and sending out what it considered to be the most relevant images on a near real-time basis based on computers with Preble's face programmed into face-recognition software. Human beings were overseeing the footage, to catch things the computer missed. The computer wouldn't have cared about seeing a motorcycle cop knocked off his bike by someone in ESU gear. A human would notice.

But the Williamsburg bridge was covered at that point, so the knocking wasn't caught on the three satellites looking down at the chase or by the helicopter that had shot the missile, or the three others that were on their way. And it wasn't caught by the primary security cameras pointed outwards from the covered portion, monitoring the license plates of all the cars coming onto the bridge. There were secondary low-res Port Authority cameras all along the bridge, but none of them were being monitored by human beings—because neither the computers nor the NSA nor anyone else in the monitoring room was aware yet of the fact that the bicycle path over the Williamsburg Bridge had two exits on the Brooklyn side, one of which was on Driggs Street directly under the bridge, under the impact point, beside the abandoned ESU truck. NSA agents didn't ride bicycles.

The FDNY arrived and started trying to put out the fire. The NYPD arrived by the hundreds but couldn't get past all the burning cars to see if Preble Jefferson was still under the bridge. They had the entire perimeter covered, a long narrow strip under the burning bridge, cut off by the water to the West, by the belly of the bridge to the East, and by an army of cops lined along the south and north sides. But Bigman didn't know exactly where Jefferson was, and that meant he was blind. So he was working the phone. It was his radar, his sonar, his only sense left, moving from helicopter pilots to the mayor to his boss.

"Ronald, I am tired of every agency moron in this city telling me they can't take orders without authorization from their own little chief. Oh, and I want Captain Crumb arrested at the earliest possible opportunity."

"You're cutting against the grain here. We've got automated procedures—"

"Not for this, we don't."

Bigman heard his boss' voice shift to the weasel tone he usually reserved for Congressional subcommittees. "This is exactly the type of situation where we should take ourselves out of the picture, open a contingency folder and apply—"

"You have a folder for Laplace's Demon?"

"Who?"

"Never mind. We're wasting time, and time is not on our side here. Tell the president to get on the phone and start calling every relevant agency to tell them I'm in charge here. Start with the mayor. Make sure he shuts down all traffic into and out of Manhattan. All the boroughs. Every bridge and tunnel. And I don't want Port Authority telling me to fill out forms in triplicate."

"From what I'm seeing, he's somewhere under the Williamsburg."

"He is. But what if he's not? I like redundancies."

"That's a massive disruption you're talking about."

"We just shot a bridge."

"Alright. It'll take at least fifteen minutes to clear the Jersey access points."

"But you can shut the entry points within five. I don't care how long it takes to empty them, just so no new traffic can come in. If you have to prioritize, start with the Holland Tunnel, then work north."

"What makes you think he'll use the Tunnel? If I were fleeing Brooklyn I'd go through Staten Island into Jersey. Last thing I'd want to do is go crosstown."

"That's because you're thinking, not driving. People running from the cops almost never turn left. Look at bank-robber getaway-car statistics."

"Seems that logic breaks down once he's on a highway, Thad, but I'm not going to argue with you. What about Eastbound?

What if he tries to get out to Long Island? Much easier than trying to cut across Manhattan."

"Then he'd end up depending on a boat. I don't think our man would like the idea of being trapped at sea on a boat. It cuts away his natural advantage. But get the Coast Guard out there just in case."

Preble was a bit shocked to see that nobody was following them. He wished he'd gotten the other cop's helmet too, though he didn't want to knock any more people down. He couldn't shake Motor-mouth. And between his cop bike, helmet, Jane's ESU gear, Kasper invisibly squished between them, and the burning bridge behind them, nobody gave them a second look. The whole city was either stopped or on fast forward, and wearing police gear justified fast forward. He drove towards the Holland Tunnel as fast as he could weave through traffic, helped out by the auxiliary traffic cops that stood on every corner along Delancey and Kenmare. The radio stations must have already been on the story, because New York City drivers were going out of their way to get out of his way. Even on Canal Street. He made it to the Holland Tunnel in seven minutes, wondering if there was some sort of record.

NYPD cars were already sitting perpendicular across the entrance of the tunnel. Preble slowed down, prepared with a nonexplanation about "ESU emergency," but they just waved him through without really looking. The cops had gotten only embry-onic instructions: shut down all traffic, which to them meant all civilian traffic. War mode was simple: good guys against bad guys, and he was wearing good-guy gear.

They reached the Jersey side before the last of the tunnel stragglers. At about the same time that the cop whose bike they were riding was waking up, Preble pulled over an older-model plain white van. He handcuffed and gagged the driver in the back —it smelled like carpet cleaning chemicals—hid the police bike behind a pillar and started off northbound. A minute later the cops knew he'd stolen a PD bike, and computers interfaced with cameras to retrace his route through Manhattan, the tunnel, and into New Jersey. They knew roughly in which stretch the motor-bike had disappeared, but Preble had chosen well—a long, busy and slow road under the Pulaski Skyway that was made invisible from the air by a web of covered and multilevel roadways, with stop-and-go traffic. There was just no way to tell which car had taken too long to exit. And this part of New Jersey was such a tangled knot of highways, with traffic from all over the U.S. headed to New York blending with traffic bypassing the city for elsewhere in the Northeast, that even a hundred individual road-blocks wouldn't cover all the possible exit routes. By the time Preble was on the 78 West, there were a dozen helicopters in the air searching, with no idea of what they were looking for.

He drove west, past the 80-380 split, took the driver out and handcuffed him to a tree in the forest. It was in an isolated spot—they needed time—so Preble gave him a bottle of water and tied him in such a way that he'd be able to drink. Then he went to the nearest strip mall with a Bank of America branch. They told him that to withdraw more than $10,000, they'd need 72 hours prior notice, particularly since it wasn't his home branch. Then Preble and Jane went to all the ATMs in the mall, withdrawing what they could.

He had long ago negotiated high limits with his banks, because gambling was still a cash business. For the same reason, he had more bank cards than recommended by credit rating agen-cies, and Jane had her own set. This was their last chance to access their money, and even this was risky. If the NSA had already put traces on his cards, cops would be here within minutes, but he was betting on things having moved too fast. He hadn't become a fugi-tive until an hour ago, and they were still focusing on a chase rather than a search. Finally, there was a jewellery store in the mall, tucked in behind a Thai restaurant that made him realize he hadn't eaten all day. He used a debit card to buy thirteen one-ounce gold coins (all that the jeweller had), as well as the most expensive diamond-studded necklace in the shop. It was the fastest sale the jewellery-store clerk had ever made.

There was no doubt that the whole thing would be traced—what counted was how long that trace took. They jumped in the car, drove west another mile, just out of town, and stopped in an empty lot. There Preble tore through the van, their clothing and all their other possessions, removing RFID chips from nearly twenty percent of them—again, it was only thanks to Fish that he even knew companies put these things into their products, even things like jeans and shoes, let alone how they looked. They had no cell phones or GPS devices, and he hoped the age of the van meant it didn't have a satellite tag, since he couldn't find anything in it. That left their passports, driver's licenses and credit cards, each of which had an RFID chip beaming their location to anyone who knew to listen to that radio frequency. Fish said the range of passive RFID chips was currently 15 meters, but the readers were always improving. Who knows what the U.S. government had, or where he might walk within 15 meters of a reader.

Microwaving—Fish said five seconds fried any chip—hammering or piercing the chip would disable it. He didn't have a microwave, so he used the SWAT ram, careful to smash the chip and not the magnetic strip on his cards. Then, for insurance, though it made him feel like a bit of a loon, he re-wrapped all their IDs and cards in aluminium foil.

With all the little bits of government, corporate and institutional Big Brother smashed, they doubled back east to the 380, then drove north to the Thousand Islands—a collection of 1800 islands and 3000 shoals, most privately owned, each with a boat.

Crossing into Canada was easy. The geography here had caused both governments endless headaches since at least the time of the Fenian raids in 1866, through Prohibition, American marijuana laws and Canadian customs agents trying to stop cheap cigarettes. Both sides patrolled the islands, but there were just too many tiny islands and too many private boats. And here, unlike the open ocean, five seconds made a difference.

They drove along the shore until they found a house built on top of two garages: one for cars coming from land, the other opened to the water like a happy squatting face, with a door exactly centered, windows above and on either side, a porch for a moustache, and a giant gaping mouth of a water garage that held a speedboat and a key on a hook. With nobody home, it was simple to break in, leave the car a few blocks away at a public boat launch, then steal the speedboat, binoculars, an extra Jerry of gas, and a 30-30 Winchester.

They crossed at an angle, weaving between islands and

avoiding line of sight with other boats or anything that looked like it had an antenna on it. On the American side, these tended to be skeletal metal towers. On the Canadian side, they were red-and-white mini lighthouses, much easier to see at a distance. They climbed out in Canada, without incident, then tried to send the boat back towards the US, hoping—without the certainty of his window—that it would beach itself back on American soil.

They stole a little Nissan Versa from a driveway, drove to Toronto, sold the necklace at a pawn shop for $3000 and the sovereigns at a jewellery store for nearly their real value, then walked up and down a long-term parking lot while Preble waited for a key to pop into his head five seconds hence. It took a while, but eventually he found one placed in the wheel mount of a Jeep Cherokee, well hidden unless you knew where to look—someone had left the pickup there for someone else or had been hiding it there or just had a bad habit of leaving their keys with the truck. At any rate, it was transportation that nobody would report for a while.

They drove to Winnipeg. Every town they passed, Preble struggled to fight off the temptation to buy more sovereigns, more necklaces. He considered cutting up his cards and throwing them away like some sort of addict who knows he can't trust himself, but he didn't. He could trust himself. The problem was that they had only about $40,000 in cash with which to start a completely new life. Far too little. With access to all their savings, they could have found quiet passage to a third-world country and lived in anonymity, breathing the humid air of tropical corruption. They wouldn't go to Bali, of course, because their history there was traceable, non-random, but they'd been pulled over by Indonesian cops often enough to know that two dollars into a pocket solved almost any problem, human to human, without computers, names, records or any other mineralized traces. With real money, they could have lived in any one of three dozen countries where this sort of small-scale, democratized corruption is a way of life. With $40,000, they could only go to Fish's cottage. Illiquidity took away random choices, and without randomness they'd be far easier to catch.

He had a moment of sympathy for all the low-income fugitives in the world. All life was easier with money, but life outside the system far more so. In-system passage to a third-world country might cost a thousand dollars. Doing it illegally would be fifty times that.

Instead of jewellery stores, they stopped at gas stations and hardware stores. He filled the back of the pickup with water, coffee, Jerry cans of gas, flour, yeast, oatmeal, matches, boots, assorted camping gear, a portable shortwave, batteries, and clothes for Kasper, including heavy snowsuits. He smashed more RFID chips. Most of what they needed would surely be available in Churchill, if it wasn't stocked at Fish's cottage, but it would probably be far more expensive. And once they arrived, he wanted to attract as little attention as possible.

They drove through Winnipeg in the middle of the night, and Preble stopped just long enough to break into a small pharmacy and steal medical supplies that would require prescriptions—various antibiotics, inhalable steroids for Kasper, birth control pills for Jane, frostbite cream. Neither of them knew enough about pharmaceuticals to predict what they'd need with any intelligence, so they tried to piece together any prescription they remembered for Kasper, Jane or himself, plus anything they could think of for living in the cold North. As fugitives, they could only go to a doctor anonymously, which meant they'd never be able to get a prescription. Another advantage of third-world countries: drugs without guilds.

It wasn't until he was almost finished robbing the pharmacy that it occurred to him he could get money this way as well. Enough money to travel to South America or Africa or Southeast Asia. He knew all the bank vault combinations in the world, after all. The thought was enough to stop him in his tracks.

"Jane?"

"Yes?" she looked up from the prescription cupboard she was searching.

"I could rob a bank. Get enough money to go anywhere."

"You want to be a criminal?"

He started laughing. The first laugh since New York.

"I mean, I know," she shrugged, a pill bottle in each hand. "But it seems different."

She was right. Despite suddenly discovering sympathy for fugitives, however, he didn't want to become a criminal, at least not yet. Shooting back at people who were shooting at him, stealing motorcycles and cars to get away, even medicine for future illness, all those didn't feel criminal regardless of what the law said. It was silly, he knew, since "criminal" was defined by exactly those technicalities, but something in him resisted such an enormous shift in morality. He would steal necessities, but not luxuries. He couldn't shake his memory of the kid in the Motor-mouth shirt because that act had crossed some invisible line inside himself. He didn't want to repeat that.

Rationally, he knew that robbing a bank to take his family to Brazil was no different than stealing a getaway car. And a part of him insisted that that's exactly what he should do—when he and Jane had argued about her reactive empathy, or about his concentric circles, they'd both accused the other of selfishness. Preble's point had been that giving something to a stranger that she had promised to Kasper was putting her own emotional gratification ahead of their son. Jane thought this was a crazy way to see the world. And yet now his choosing not to rob banks was the exact same thing. He was putting his morality, his squeamishness, ahead of his family. Morally, perhaps it was correct, but ethically, it was selfish. He should do everything necessary to get them to a country where they could disappear in anonymity, where medicine is sold as goods without a doctor as a middleman, where computers don't tie your life into a picture for someone else to paint. He could think about it all this way, but he couldn't quite do it. Not in the calm of the evening without bullets or explosions.

Perhaps it was just a question of how far in the future the need existed. A bullet, family held hostage, car, medicine: those were all immediate problems that needed to be solved. Imminent threats. Robbing a bank was a far longer-term idea. Until a hundred years ago there had still been a concept of "necessity" in the common law—a man could trespass in order to save himself from a storm and such—but the concept had been chipped away by Congress and the courts, so that now stealing a million dollars from shareholders was more lightly punished than stealing a loaf of bread.

But Preble was already a fugitive. He no longer had to obey laws out of fear or coercion. He was willing to break synthetic laws drafted by politicians, but there was still something in him that wanted to hold on to the old laws that had evolved over hundreds of years. Not some sort of quasi-religious "natural law," but laws that had grown out of customs and traditions and ways of minimizing people hurting each other. A stick or a billy club, a criminal's gun or a policeman's gun, both sides violated other people's lives.

"Besides," Jane interrupted his thoughts. "Wouldn't bank vaults have cameras and cops coming within minutes? I don't want to go through that again."

He nodded. He didn't either.

"We have a plan. Let's stick with it. At least for now."

"Okay. For now. Thank you." It was a relief that she agreed. If Fish's cottage didn't work out, he'd steal what he had to, just as the idea of Kasper not having antibiotics when he needed them far outweighed any other considerations. He'd rob Fort Knox if he had to. But he wasn't there yet.

His train of thought as he drove through the night, while Jane and Kasper slept, made him think of Fish again, all these thoughts reminded him of Thursday nights—the look of astonishment on Fish's face in the police station as he watched Preble shoot his way out. Fish hadn't done anything illegal, he should be okay. But from what Preble had seen of Bigman, he knew his friend would have problems. Simply because he was Preble's friend.

There were real risks in going to Fish's family cottage. It wasn't legally in Fish's name, but there was a connection, and that was dangerous. They'd question him for sure, but Fish was a lawyer so they'd control themselves—they wouldn't dare torture an American attorney on U.S. soil, would they? One who published on a regular basis, who was a professor at a respected university. And as long as they didn't torture Fish, the cottage should be safe. Nothing else, maybe not even that, would make his friend talk.

They'd see Preble had a history of vacationing in warm, developing countries, no connections to Canada, and everything in his profile would send signals that he was more likely to run south than north.

They continued up the 6. And then north for a very long time on a dirt highway with no name, past tens of thousands of little perfectly round lakes and ground that alternated between orange, white and green. Surreal lakes and colours passing by endlessly on a road that didn't bend, just cut north, two thousand kilometres north of any other humanity, with nothing to do but drive and think. North of anyone who could chase them or hurt them or get hurt by him.

Part 2

Chapter 9

THE MAN HAD TWO THALAMI. HE'D GONE TO A DOCTOR TEN years ago and paid for extensive fMRI tests. He'd taken all the records, but he couldn't take Dr. Sweeney. The government could.

Dr. Sweeney was both a clinical and a research neurologist, and he would have given up several minor processes in exchange for a copy of that fMRI—no case of a double-thalamus had ever been recorded in the literature—but Jefferson had paid out of pocket and before taking the tests had presented Dr. Sweeney with a bulletproof contract about keeping all documentation, including doctor's notes. He'd said he didn't want to become a case study, and he never explained to the good doctor what symptoms had prompted him to come in for the tests.

"What does the thalamus do, doctor?" Bigman asked, though he'd had a half dozen DARPA neuroscientists working on Mr. Preble Jefferson since they'd lost track of him a week ago. His last known location was a jewelry shop in Blakeslee, Pennsylvania, just off Highway 80. The 80 went west directly to Cheyenne Mountain, Colorado. It continued into Utah and Nevada, land where a man might think he could still disappear, but the fact that the highway went straight to NORAD and Strategic Air Command worried Bigman. It might be a coincidence, of course.

Heading out from New York City, you might start with the 80 regardless of where you wanted to end up, including Mexico or Canada. There were good reasons why criminals always fled to Mexico, though today they'd be wiser to keep going south, at least to Nicaragua. But it was Cheyenne Mountain's location smack in the middle of the 80 that kept Bigman from sleeping at night.

Bigman was back at Fort Meade, outside Washington. He'd had the doctor flown in from New York. Now the two of them sat facing each other in overstuffed chairs over a coffee table in Bigman's office. He used this setup when he wanted his visitor to feel comfortable. Which was almost never—he couldn't remember the last time he'd sat here. He wanted Dr. Sweeney to relax and think rather than just obey, but he knew that no matter what he did, his visitors were never truly comfortable. He felt a mild sense of professional payback: he'd been referred to a cardiologist a few years back after a routine EKG test, followed by a NIMBI EKG, had both come back with what turned out, after far too many other tests including a CT angiogram, to be false positives. Sitting across from the cardiologist, he'd started to experience chest pain symptoms. When he'd told this to the cardiologist, the doctor had smiled and said, "Everybody who sits in that chair suddenly gets chest pains."

"The thalamus is the brain's sensory gate," Dr. Sweeney answered, having his own chest pains. The whole office had a looming feel to it, and even the big, padded chair made the doctor feel like he could at any moment get sucked in and disappeared. "Think of it as a relay station. It takes sensory information—sights, sounds, touch—and decides which part of the brain to send them to for processing. The only exception is smell, which is directed through the olfactory bulb. It also plays a key role in motor control, and in regulating consciousness and perception. But to be honest, there's still a lot we don't know about the thalamus."

"And a double thalamus. How could that change things?"

"That's speculative and would depend on how they interact. He might have heightened sensory perception or dual perception allowing two separate streams of consciousness. Maybe improved processing speed, greater emotional intensity, more complex sleep and conscious states, or even entirely novel states of consciousness. But these are guesses."

Talking about the brain, his field of expertise, relaxed Sweeney somewhat. He continued, "Originally, we thought the thalamus only regulated wakefulness and awareness and acted as a relay to the neocortex. When you're asleep, the thalamus shuts off the communication between your perceptions and your brain, so you're not woken up by every sound. But over the last twenty years, it's become clear that it does more. The thalamus is a double-bulb—in Mr. Jefferson's case, he has four bulbs—and they have connections to all parts of the cortex. Any information that goes from one part of the cortex to another actually sends a second stream that travels through the thalamus. Explaining this is complicated, because it requires you to understand how the brain works."

"Assume I don't."

The doctor nodded, certain that the NSA man must have some idea. "You know that the cortex is structurally identical in all its regions? Vision, hearing, motor function, all have the exact same structure. The brain sends a constant stream of input from the senses up through the cortical hierarchy and another constant stream down with the names of patterns that it recognizes, which in turn shape the interpretation of the sensory inputs. The two check off against each other. Perhaps you can't make out a handwritten letter by itself but have no problem understanding it if you see the whole word. Or can't make out a word but understand it in the context of a sentence. That's the feedback coming back down from the higher cortical regions to the lower sensory ones. To free itself up for other tasks, the brain pushes the names of recognized patterns down the hierarchy as far as it can. That's learning. I learned what a face is when I was a child, so when I see yours the lowest levels of my cortical hierarchy no longer send up information on angles and shadows and such, but just send up the idea of 'face.' After meeting you, the lowest levels don't even say 'face,' they say 'NSA Director Bigman.' Most of what we 'see' is actually generated by our internal memory model, with just enough reality coming through to trigger the appropriate pattern. All stage magicians use this fact, for example, and it's the reason that crazy people and those with low IQs are harder for a magician to fool than smart people—their internal model is faulty, and so their brains actually see the magician's fake thumb instead of dismissing it as a thumb. Anyway, if there is nothing wrong with the picture, then the secondary stream through the thalamus doesn't seem to do anything. But if there is a real mistake, something unexpected, the thalamus can cut off the feedback going back down to the senses. Say you had a big boil right on the end of your nose. Then my thalamus would cut off the downward message saying 'face.' I would see the shape and lines from scratch, send them up the hierarchy until the higher regions found a name, a pattern that works called 'boil,' and send this information back down to my $V1$ region, uh, that's vision one, which would confirm, yes, it's a face with a boil, or Bigman grew a beard, or whatever."

Bigman liked to hear problems framed by many different people. Each came with a slightly different angle, and he had long ago learned that the best way to solve a problem was to rephrase it. And Dr. Sweeney was fluent at framing problems in a way patients could understand, which made him easier to talk to than the DARPA guys. "So the thalamus short-circuits the pattern and forces the brain to look at additional detail?"

"Yes. It's a gate, but it's a two-way gate. Our entire brain is one big stereotype-verifying machine. We learn, we make stereotypes so that we can predict what will happen, we send the stereotyped information back down to our senses, we verify to see if it fits. If it doesn't fit, the thalamus kicks in, forcing conflicting information through. It's a sort of disconfirmation organ that falsifies predictions or models or stereotypes, or whatever you want to call them. Neuroscientists call them 'invariant representations.'"

"So someone without stereotypes would be, what, a Zen monk?" Bigman prodded, wanting to set up a specific background in the conversation, a vector, before he arrived with his central questions. Questions that might help him defend against Jefferson in the event that he made it to Cheyenne. Every interaction was a choice between exploitation and exploration, and he'd learned long ago that investing in the latter usually paid off in terms of the former.

"No, he'd be nonsentient. Actually, not even that, because even the simplest bacteria have patterns codified in their DNA memory telling them that a nutrient gradient implies more food in the direction of the gradient, and so forth. No stereotypes means no intelligence. All life has some intelligence. So, someone without any invariant representations at all is dead. Or a computer. It's why artificial intelligence failed so dismally before neural networks and large language models. Because it was difficult to get a computer to stereotype."

"How about seeing the future, doctor?"

Bigman had asked this without a pause, and he'd expected the doctor to be thrown by the question. But he wasn't. "That's exactly what I'm talking about. Predicting the future is the essence of intelligence, at every level. It's all predictive processing. The bacterium predicts the future by comparing the nutrient gradient in which it's swimming with its DNA-encoded memory that moving up the gradient means more food. Knowing there will be more food higher up the gradient is prediction. It's seeing—"

"I'm not talking about memory-prediction models. I'm talking about seeing where the roulette ball will land."

The doctor shook his head. "Impossible."

"Why?"

"Too many variables. But more than that. Once you move predictive processing into a sort of dynamic Bayesian filtering, trying to predict the trajectories in the moment, it all comes through a Feynman path integration formulation—."

"Slow down. And skip the jargon."

"Newton's laws state that a particle follows a predictable path that minimizes its action or energy. But in quantum mechanics, things are probabilistic. A particle doesn't just take one path from point A to point B, but rather takes every conceivable path simultaneously. Each of these paths has a certain amplitude related to its probability, and these amplitudes can interfere with each other, or even cancel each other out, like waves on a pond. When you add all these interfering amplitudes for all possible paths, you get a single path.

"So, for the roulette ball—in a Newtonian world once the ball is spun with a certain force and direction, its path and final resting place would be predictable if you could accurately measure all the variables, which you probably couldn't. But in Feynman's quantum world, it's different. When the ball is spun, it doesn't just follow one path around the roulette wheel. Instead, it simultaneously takes every possible path. It might loop around the wheel three times and land on red 16. Or it might make five loops and land on black 22. It might even take a path that pops off the wheel, tours around the casino, visits the buffet, dips into the swimming pool, then comes back to finally land on green oo. Every single one of these paths, and infinitely more, are taken by the ball simultaneously.

"Each path has an associated 'amplitude,' which is related to the probability of the ball following that path. The paths that behave most like the ones we'd expect in the classical world, where the ball simply loops around the wheel a few times and lands on a number, have the highest amplitudes, while the crazier paths through the buffet have incredibly low amplitudes. The mathematical sum over all paths, including their interference with each other, gives the final result. And the square of this resulting amplitude gives the probability of the ball landing in a particular pocket. But since the real-world ball trajectory is determined by an infinite number of quantum probabilities, to predict the future you'd have to focus on the higher-probability paths. Leave out the buffet path. Your predictive errors would grow to unmanageable proportions within seconds."

Bigman leaned in. "How many seconds?"

The doctor shrugged. "I don't know. Very few."

"What if I told you to take as a given that Mr. Preble Jefferson can see into the future. At least a few seconds. Is there any mechanism by which a double-thalamus could account for that?"

"It just seems...highly unlikely," the doctor said, then stuck the pen he'd been fiddling with in his mouth. He'd started sweating as Bigman's intensity had ramped up and the conversation drifted into science fiction. "We don't really understand the thalamus. And, of course, I never did a biopsy of Jefferson's. For all I know it's a brain tumour that looks identical to a thalamus in shape and has no functionality at all. Though that's unlikely, because he also had extraordinarily high levels of orexin."

"Orexin?"

"The thalamus basically has an on and an off position, like a light switch. On when you're awake, off when you're asleep. The neurotransmitter that turns the thalamus 'on' is orexin. An insomnia patient, for example, can't turn the thalamus 'off.' A narcoleptic is stuck halfway between on and off. Jefferson had extremely high levels of orexin. But as I said, we still don't understand all the oddities about the human thalamus. We're still not sure how communication happens within the thalamus, but predicting even three seconds into the future would require sifting through millions of probabilities, which means you'd have to be working at computer speeds."

Bigman tried to lean back. When he couldn't, he remembered why he never used these chairs. "We held our own against computers at games like chess and go for a long time, at a millionth of their speed, by sorting relevance and patterns."

"Yes, but the way we do that is through internal models, sometimes called active inference or Karl Friston's free energy principle. Prediction is not just a question of computer-like accuracy. From an evolutionary perspective, you actually want some uncertainty in order to maintain greater flexibility to adapt to incoming information. The greater the accuracy of your predictions, the more complex your model has to be, and the lower its entropy or flexibility. Everyone understands the concept of accuracy when it comes to predictions, but the heart of intelligence is predicting in a minimally complex way. Or call it maximally compressed. The free energy principle, which seems to underlie all intelligence—maybe all self-organizing systems—equally weights both accuracy and complexity. You can think of complexity in terms of data compression. That's why we could match computers for a while despite our far lower processing speed."

"You're losing me. Is this physics now, or neuroscience?"

"It's where physics and neuroscience meet. At the level of neurology, prediction is thinking about what the brain does when making sense of data. At the level of physics, it combines the dynamics of Feynman's path integration with time and even consciousness—the Markov blankets that separate me from not me, or Preble Jefferson from the external world he's integrating and changing through his actions."

Bigman sighed. "I'm not even going to ask what a Markov blanket is."

"It's the subset of variables—"

"No! Stop."

"At any rate, the compression part of the model is necessary to prevent us from going trippy with all the noise. Jefferson would have to deal with that noise somehow."

"I was led to believe that noise can bring stimuli that would otherwise be below the threshold of perception above it."

"Well...yes, that's true," the doctor said, at first grudgingly, but then warming up to the idea. "The human brain incorporates that principle. If you think of a phenomenon as a fluctuating line, the noise creates a band around it, and though the pattern of the line might not cross the threshold of perception, the edges of the noise-band might. Which allows us to see a pattern that is below our sensory threshold. That's intuition. But anyway, it's the job of the neocortex to aggregate the patterns, not the thalamus. Regardless of how many he has."

"Did any of your tests show how many cortical levels he had?"

"What?"

"Did he have six cortical layers? Or more?"

"You'd have to cut into the brain to find that out. But the neuronal-layer model can be a bit misleading. The brain is far more interconnected. Still, if his thalamus is letting through that much more information than a normal brain, and has been since before he was born, then it would make sense that his neocortex would also adapt. If it didn't, he would go insane or maybe develop a form of fatal familial insomnia."

"Fatal insomnia?"

"It's a genetic disorder of the thalamus that rips it up with tiny holes and prevents it from ever shutting off. Once it starts, the patient loses the ability to sleep. They inevitably die from lack of sleep. Now I wish I had tested him for prion proteins. He refused to let me do a genetic test on him. But I wonder if the double thal-amus could be a protective adaptation to PrNP genetic anomaly... That's the gene that causes fatal familial insomnia."

"You're saying Preble Jefferson developed superpowers thanks to a cure for insomnia?"

"A genetic adaptation, not a cure."

"So you think it's genetic? Would his son inherit it?"

"These are all guesses. Normal fatal familial insomnia is genetic, but who knows about Mr. Jefferson. Still, it's a hell of an adaptation, if that's what it is. Especially if he has, metaphorically speaking, more than six neocortical layers as a result. Paleontolo-gists are always arguing what sort of adaptation is big enough to qualify as a 'new species,' but I'd say this would qualify."

Bigman smiled his pasty smile. "That's interesting. A double thalamus is okay, but a seventh layer makes him non-human?"

"You see double organs from time to time. Evolutionary blips and mutations that usually turn out to be dead ends. But, no, if a double thalamus could lead to completely novel states of consciousness, then, yeah, that's a different species in my book. Additional cortical layers would just...hmm...put it this way, one sublayer is enough to differentiate humans from monkeys. Three layers is the difference between humans and dogs."

"Yes, it would leave the rest of us behind. That's precisely the concern some of us have. Could additional layers help deal with all the noise? With the millions of possibilities?"

"Additional layers should allow him to see higher-order patterns."

"Would it make him more intelligent?"

"Einstein's brain had unusual patterns of sulci, uh, grooves, in the mathematical and spatial reasoning regions, it had 15% more surface area than an average brain, and it had more glia support cells per neuron, but he didn't have additional cortical layers."

"So what do you mean by higher-order patterns?"

The doctor searched for an example. When he finally answered, it was in a hesitant tone, unsure. "A dog can learn that a whistle means food is coming. A human can learn that and also see that he's being manipulated by the trainer, probably for some future reason, and can build possibilities of what that reason might be."

"Sounds more intelligent to me."

"It's a better predictive model, with a single explanation that covers all the training sessions. Higher accuracy, lower complexity, less free energy."

Bigman leaned back in his fat chair to the extent he could, moving his intense, anaerobic bubble off the doctor. "I've been told some pretty strange things by our scientists since I first saw a video of Mr. Preble Jefferson dodging bullets. I have physicists telling me time doesn't exist objectively, that it's just a subjective manifestation of how our brains work, and that all of spacetime is just one block. Meanwhile, neuroscientists are telling me that all the invariant representations are both spatial and temporal, that even vision has a temporal element as our eyes make a dozen saccades every second, that touch is meaningless without movement, which again requires time, and that even taste and smell, which turn out to be the same sense—out of which our entire brains evolved—depend on molecular vibrations, and vibrations depend on time. Our brains couldn't make patterns without four dimensions. And I'm not sure whether the physicists and neuroscientists are contradicting each other or agreeing that our brains create the illusion of time. And this would all be fine material for Ph.D. candidates in several fields, with, pardon the expression, lots of time to spare. Except that I have an alien on the loose who can see the future and I don't know how to stop him."

Before Bigman finished, Dr. Sweeney knew what his next words would be: "We're back to model error. There will always be error."

"Go on."

"Even in the Newtonian world, I might have a perfect grasp of the laws of physics, perfect aim, all the regular variables covered, and so on, but if a gust of wind suddenly blows while I'm shooting my arrow at the apple on your head, I'll miss. It's why we can't predict weather more than three days out—"

"If he can see three days out we're doomed."

"—despite an army of supercomputers trying. No matter how detailed a picture he has of any situation, he can't cover all the variables. And in the quantum view, he can't cover the path through the buffet. The inevitable consequence of lowering complexity is errors that compound. That's why we can't truly predict things like the weather or the stock market."

"Have you heard of Laplace's Demon, doctor?"

"Yes, but that's a theoretical construct. Unless he's the Demon, he can't hold an infinite number of variables in his head."

"My point was going to be that Laplace's Demon has been proven impossible on this basis. I've been told that using the minimum amount of time you need to move data across the Planck length, at the speed of light, there's a limit to the computational power of the universe. I forget what the number is, something like 10^{120} bits, but anything needing more than that many bits can't be computed in the fifteen billion years or so that the universe has existed so far."

"Hmm." The doctor thought about this. "That sounds like

disproving God. An omniscient God who obeys the laws of physics, at any rate."

"Not a practical tangent, doctor."

"Yes. But your point is that it disproves omniscience, right? Which means he has to simplify, so in effect he's engaging in active inference. Modeling. Which means he leaves things out, he rounds off. Throw something weird enough at him, and he won't be able to predict it. That's my prediction."

Bigman sat still, without moving, without saying anything, long enough that the doctor thought he was expected to say something more and had no idea what else to add. Finally, Bigman unfroze. "Our model. Not his model. There is something wrong with our model. Some of those cops in the cemetery were shooting at him from behind. Mr. Preble Jefferson would see that gust of wind. I'm certain of it. Maybe he is the Demon, more or less. 10^{120} bits is an unimaginably large amount of information. Maybe I should be talking more with physicists and less with neuroscientists." Bigman was now talking more to himself than to the doctor.

"Laplace's Demon was based on Newtonian physics," the doctor said, glad that his approach to neuroscience was on the boundary of physics. Though he never had enough time to read everything he wanted. "Back to Feynman's path, even without the computational limit, a theoretical know-it-all demon couldn't predict atomic-scale interactions, which means there'd be some error terms, and those errors would expand geometrically for any prediction."

"It would still give him a few accurate seconds, at least."

"Did you say your physicists are telling you time doesn't exist?"

Bigman looked up at the doctor. His preference for cross-pollination tipped the scale over his lack of time. And truth was, as the trail got cold during this past week Bigman had found himself with far more time and far less movement than he was used to. More time and less movement. Is that possible?

"The philosophers tell me that the definition of a second is circular because it's based on the oscillations of the cesium-133 atom, which is movement at a certain frequency, with frequency defined as the number of cycles per second. My physicists say that most laws of physics would work equally well if time ran backward, that Einstein destroyed the notion of Newton's absolute time that flows on its own clock, and that something called the Wheeler-DeWitt equation reconciles quantum theory with general relativity but it only works if we take the counterintuitive step of saying time doesn't exist."

The doctor shrugged. "Well, intuition and common sense are usually wrong in science. It's counterintuitive to say the world is spinning at tens of thousands of kilometres per hour. Or that the Earth goes around the Sun. Or that my grandparents were monkeys. But then why do we experience it? Time, I mean. What is ticking away when the clock ticks?"

"You still have it backwards, doctor. The clock pendulum has motion and energy flow towards entropy, and time is simply a human-created marker of the location of the pendulum. The clock is not measuring time. Our concept of time is a way to talk about where the clock is. Time measures the clock, not the other way around."

"So—"

"What we experience as time is our brain's way of sorting motion in the universe."

"Ah, yes, I get it! It's possible that time itself is a consequence of consciousness, which in turn is a consequence of predictive coding. The dynamics of self-organization require predictions, which leads to a separation of a self that becomes a dynamic variable in those predictions, which creates an evolutionary advantage to higher-order models that include consciousness, which in turn feeds back a sensory perception of time as an efficient aspect of that model."

"That fits what the DARPA physicists tell me. That space and time exist as quanta, discrete fragments that can present as waves. And waves have the odd property that an infinite quantity of them can exist in the same spot. All the quanta of the universe might be piled on in a single dimensionless point. All the quanta of the universe living on top of one another in a sort of unified block without being immersed in either space or time but still interfering with each other."

"Now you lost me."

"Yeah, me too. Angels dancing on the head of a pin. I either take the physicists on faith or believe my own experience that I woke up before I had breakfast, not the other way around."

The doctor shrugged. "I don't really understand most of the tools I use to cure my patients. But I understand the mechanism by which the quack cures are separated from the effective ones. And that mechanism is tested a thousand times a day, so I largely trust it. That's not faith. It's circumstantial proof and, outside of math, all proofs are circumstantial."

"Don't get me wrong," Bigman said. "I trust the physicists, but I just don't care about the ultimate nature of time and reality. Except insofar as it helps me understand and catch Mr. Preble Jefferson. But in this case it matters. I need to know if he can predict things that come at him from behind. If he can predict the gust of wind that blows only when the arrow is half-way to the apple. That determines what tactics will work on him. But he clearly does have some limits. I'm convinced he can't see days into the future, or we never would have found out about him. Whatever his precognition, it's a matter of seconds, or, at most, minutes. Not hours and not days. Probably not even minutes. So let's assume for a moment that the whole universe is sitting on one point, at least in terms of time, and that it's only our brains and our clocks that are creating the illusion of time because they can't otherwise organize all the motion in a 3D universe. And let's further assume then Mr. Preble Jefferson can see through this illusion, can see the vectors of any motion or Feynman probability paths that intersect with his senses in a way that is not dependent on time. Then my question becomes, why is Mr. Preble Jefferson limited to a few seconds?"

The doctor didn't have anything to say. "I don't know."

Bigman picked up his coffee mug. It had an old picture of Dick Cheney on it. "I'm told that if I drop this on the floor and break it, the mug will never jump back on the table and fix itself— not because of Apollo's arrow of time, but because of the second law of thermodynamics, that everything moves towards entropy. Or, alternatively, if time is not a dimension we travel in the way we travel in space, but rather simply a marker of motion, then the idea of going 'backwards in time' would require negative motion, which is nonsense. You can't have negative motion. At any rate, in terms of pure information, knowledge, there is nothing theoretically preventing someone like Mr. Jefferson from seeing the past, present and future of this cup if at any point in his life he crosses paths with it."

"But how does the information get to him?" the doctor asked. "We get information through our senses, which means photons, chemicals, and so on. If that information doesn't arrive until later, or, uhm, elsewhere in the 3D universe, then how does it get to him?"

"Presumably that information is present within the object itself," Bigman said, with a hint of wonder in his voice that the doctor hadn't heard until now. "When we see a ball rolling, we see its motion in space, where it's coming from and where it's going, we see its colour, and other characteristics. If time isn't physical, just a sensory problem for regular humans, then presumably someone with the right sensory apparatus or states of consciousness can see its motion in time as well as we can see its motion in space or its colour. But if time is merely a way of describing where the cup moves and Mr. Jefferson's peculiar vision isn't blinkered to the infinitely thin now like the rest of us, then what is it that causes him to be blinkered a few seconds out? What is the nature of his horizon? Is it in the nature of his skill, in the nature of the universe, or just a question of capacity, of his brain's ability to process all that information? And, more importantly, how do we manipulate that horizon—"

"Does the present have a Markov blanket or does it leak like a hurricane?" Sweeney interrupted, speaking to himself, in awe at his own question. Which Bigman didn't pause for.

"Are there variables that increase or decrease his precognition? A weapon or context that could shut it down completely? Basically, how do we stop him? The physicists can't answer the questions that matter."

"Try the weatherman."

"What weatherman?"

"Meteorologists devote their entire lives to failing in their attempts to predict the future. They might have some more-practical insights."

"Thank you doctor. You can go home."

The doctor got up from his chair. He started to reach out to shake Bigman's hand, then changed his mind when it occurred to him that Bigman probably wouldn't want to. Still, when he got to the door, he turned back, his curiosity overcoming his urge to go outside and quickly breathe fresh air. "Can I ask? Why do you care? I mean, he's gone. Maybe he'll stay gone."

Bigman looked momentarily sad, the last expression that the doctor was expecting. "Like you said, he's a different species. And we cannot live side by side with the sort of chaos he represents. They are like matter and antimatter. He would never truly stay gone and he could never be subsumed into the whole—an explosion was always inevitable. It was just a matter of time. Good day, doctor."

Once the doctor had left, Bigman took a few seconds to close his eyes and rub his face. Then he asked his secretary to connect him to Hammond de Koek, the chairman of the joint chiefs. De Koek had bristled at the idea of a "subcommittee" or a "board of directors," but he was a military man. He couldn't deny the need for a contingency plan if Jefferson ever got control over the president of the United States.

Chapter 10

THEY ARRIVED IN CHURCHILL, MANITOBA, ON JULY 14, JUST before the start of winter, after an eight-day drive past a million little lakes. At one point they'd tried counting. Kasper gave up after twenty because he wasn't sure of bigger numbers. Jane kept going for a dozen more, then started from one again for Kasper's sake. But Preble, somewhat neurotically, counted for nearly two hours. You couldn't really tell from the road where one lake ended and the next started, of course, but as best as he could see from the road, they passed over two hundred lakes in two hours just on their one little dirt road: the sliver of northern Manitoba that they chanced to see, their one-dimensional vector directly north.

In Churchill, they stayed at the Lazy Bear Lodge, relieved that the security-and-credit-card mindset of the South hadn't reached this far north. Cash was good here, no ID necessary. Then they searched for someone who could take them to Fish's land. It was five hours by boat up the Churchill River, completely inaccessible by car.

Preble hesitated for a long time thinking about what to do with the Jeep Cherokee with Toronto plates. It was a great little truck. The Cherokee was from about 1990, completely mechanical, no computers, just metal parts that moved other metal parts. If it broke down, he could fix it, which wasn't something he could say for any modern car. And living up here without a car seemed unwise. He wished he could buy it from the owner somehow, but he couldn't, and a stolen car from Toronto was a bad idea. He couldn't even rent an ATV and have Jane follow him, because an ATV rental would ask for a credit card or some other ID that might leave a trace.

He left Jane, Kasper and all their supplies at the Lazy Bear, and drove early in the morning along old logging roads to one of the million lakes. He removed the plates, buried them in a two-foot hole, then pushed the pickup into the lake. The process left him cold and depressed. He'd given up his home, his books, his laptop and every other object he owned, not to mention all his friends, his entire social world. He'd done it all without crashing. It had all been too fast, too reactive. And on the drive up, he'd had Kasper and Jane to think about, preparations and plans and the future to focus on. But testing the depth of the water with a thin dead tree, manoeuvring the truck to its edge and then physically pushing it in brought the whole depressing reality of the past week together. He was the one who was pushing his world under-water, into the cold. Then he had a ten-mile walk back.

Five miles out of Churchill, an old Inuit in a Toyota pickup picked him up, then laughed at him. "City boy, eh?"

"Yeah," Preble answered. "How can you tell?"

"Michelin Man. Michelin Man means you've been up here less than a month."

Preble flipped down the vanity mirror in the passenger seat and looked at his face. He looked like he'd gained forty pounds. "Is it from the blackflies?"

"Nah, blackflies just hurt. And you never get used to those. It's the mosquitoes. Enough of them bite you, you get an allergic reaction. And then you get immunity. After a month, they don't even itch. Or so I'm told. Never bothered me. Blackflies bother me."

They drove in silence into Churchill, where the man took Preble straight to the Lazy Bear Lodge. Without Preble ever having given him the name. Churchill was worrisomely small. "Name's Taget. Shiatie Taget. You ever want to see the narwhal, I do boat trips." Shiatie handed him a card.

"Nice to meet you, Shiatie. Thanks for the lift." And for not asking questions, he added silently. Kasper and Jane were in the lodge restaurant, a room straight out of a movie about Alaska or the Yukon, complete with all-pine tables and chairs, rounded log-cabin walls, and a bearskin splayed out above the entrance, surrounded by snowshoes. They were eating caribou and mashed potatoes.

"Daddy! I'm eating Rudolph the Red-Nosed Reindeer!"

"Hi, Kasper." Preble noticed that Kasper and Jane were looking puffy as well, from all the bites. "Does it taste good?"

"Yes." Kasper nodded. "I like it. Caribou is reindeer, daddy!"

Preble kissed Jane. She said, "Nice walk?"

He laughed. "I found out why we're getting so suddenly fat."

"Oh?"

"Mosquito bites. We're just swollen."

"Are we going to unswell?"

"Apparently, yes. And after we do, the mosquito bites won't itch."

"See, everything's good for something."

The waitress came, a chubby matter-of-fact Inuit girl, and he ordered caribou as well.

"Daddy, who's that?" Kasper asked when the plate came but didn't wait for an answer. "Is it Donner or Blitzen? It's Blitzen." And he nodded happily, carefully making sure he kept his mouth closed while chewing so he wouldn't make the smacking sound.

The next morning Preble phoned Shiatie. He hadn't asked in the car because he didn't want anything tying him to the Cherokee, even remotely, but he reconsidered over morning coffee. Shiatie picked them up at eleven, helped Preble load up all their supplies, and took them upriver to Fish's family cottage.

Fish's whole family had come from Hungary together to Canada. Fish had gone on to New York, while his father had wanted nothing to do with people. He wanted to cut trees, catch fish, shoot caribou. And his wife, Fish's mother, had put up with it for ten years. Then one late spring day she announced that she was moving to Toronto, or Ottawa, or even Winnipeg. Somewhere with people, and sunlight even in wintertime. Fish's father didn't argue, and on the day she left, he started to transform their house into a seasonal cottage. He spent the rest of the spring and early summer setting up stores. He stocked up on basics like kerosene and benzene, winterized the house, put the boat and snowmobile into the shed, and shut everything down tight. Then flew after his wife. He never came back, though Fish came once every two or three years to check on things, swap out the gas and other semi-perishables, and have time to himself while plotting whatever anarchist revolutions he plotted, which he then turned into articles and lectures and survivalist manifestos.

When Preble, Jane and Kasper arrived, the house instantly felt Fish-like. It was made of rounded pine logs with heavy tent material stretched on the inside, except in some places where the tent material was on the outside. Where it was on the outside, ropes had been used to stretch it and tie it to logs, and two-by-fours were attached with complicated rope loops to flatten the tent material without using nails or otherwise puncturing holes in it. Most of the walls—there were nine, since the house was built in a C-shape rather than the traditional square or rectangle—had a window. The windows were all triple-paned, with frames of wooden planks, painted red, and roll-up canvas blinds.

Aside from the windows, nearly all the wall space was covered by books, so many books that Preble wondered whether they served a dual function as additional insulation. They were heavy on nonfiction—particularly warfare, chess, game theory, survival, plant and mushroom manuals, and anything else even remotely related to strategy, as well as the sorts of old chemistry books that had long been pulled from libraries because they described in detail how to make bombs, poisonous gasses and other nasty stuff. But they also included the classics of literature and countless miscellaneous other topics, from economics to self-help. With the knowledge in Fish's library, you could rebuild most of civilization from scratch.

There was a door on either end of the C, one with its border painted red, the other just varnished pine. The roof was covered by foot-thick sod with wild grasses growing on it, which gave the whole house a Hobbit feel. Or Icelandic Viking. One outside wall was painted green, one triangular fitting was blue and the rest of the cottage was just varnished pine, unpainted. It really did look like the sort of house that would be owned by an anarchist professor with an environmentalist green-roof streak, one who insisted on giving free rein not just to individuals but all the way down to every stray impulse and conflicting aesthetic preference within. If Walt Whitman contained multitudes, Fish not only contained them but allowed each one to choose a different colour.

The whole sat in a meadow surrounded by tall pine trees, which were cleared all the way to the river, about fifty meters away. A creek ran behind the house.

Inside, the cottage felt forebodingly dark until they rolled up the canvas blinds. Then it was just musty, but with a remarkable amount of light. One half of the C-shape was a living area— kitchen, living room, two bedrooms, bathroom, and regular closet space. The other half was a mini-warehouse of necessities, fuel, conserves, a dozen guns ranging from a 0.22 to a 0.454 magnum rifle that could knock your shoulder off, each double-sealed in its own plastic bags, fishing rods, hooks, battery kits, matches, ammunition, boots, enormous parkas, oil, triple-sealed sugar, flour, an enormous quantity of vacuum-dried food that seemed to come straight from NASA, just mix water, and what must have been sixty blankets. Blankets enough to crush a grown man. Outside, next to the house, were eight fifty-gallon gasoline drums. The house seemed built to last through a war or the Zombie Apocalypse, and Preble had no doubt that that was exactly the frame of mind that had gone into preparing it.

It occurred to Preble yet again how lucky he was to have a friend like Fish. He'd always known it, but it wasn't until the shit had hit the fan that the knowledge became a solid thing. Fish could be oddly positive for an anarchist (at least, Preble suspected that most were negative; he didn't know any others), and he'd always said that there was a good side to the increasing authoritarianism of the U.S. government. He claimed human beings become more human, have better friendships, act out their extremes of good and evil, and are generally far less superficial when they live under dictatorships. Preble considered it absurd to think of the United States as a dictatorship—he knew that Fish used hyperbole to ring a warning bell and was never quite sure to what extent Fish believed his own words—but he agreed that pressure forged real friendships. Without pressure, what you had was a body to play chess with, but rarely real friendship.

"I need to go pee-pee, daddy!" Kasper cut into Preble's thoughts.

They went to the bathroom, Kasper used it, and they discovered that the septic system was broken. Preble had no idea how to fix pipes. Despite being able to see into the future, in New York City a toilet that wouldn't stop running flummoxed him. He felt about plumbing, electricity, and clearing the chimney the way someone who has never used a computer for more than email feels about mounting virtual drives. It's in the realm of theoretical possibility as something that could be learned over time with much pain if absolutely necessary, but better left to other people.

With the cold here, he suspected plumbing would be a regular problem. Churchill and its plumbers were five hours away. So he learned. He found the broken pipe, thankful that it was a broken pipe and not a full septic tank, and fixed it. He cleared the chimney. He checked for cracks and exposed spaces around pipes, windows and doors, he caulked and added insulation—Kasper insisted on a detailed explanation of how inflation, as he called it, keeps the house warm—wherever he could imagine heat escaping when January came. He cleaned the engine on the boat and got it in the water and running smoothly. He learned to fish and hunt caribou. He made a few trips to Churchill, mostly for information about how to prepare for winter, but also for more unusual things. Since Churchill's number one tourist attraction was polar bears, the general store carried everything imaginable to do with polar bears, including military-grade perimeter defences for people who wanted to sleep in the bush without a rotating guard. The tourist information about polar bears had a split personality. One-half cute: don't bother them and they won't bother you—postcards with furry pictures, a law that required the first two cartridges to be blanks, another law limited the total number to three. One-half scary: warnings about how polar bears are the only land animal known to track and hunt human beings, how they can move so quietly that they can sneak up on even the most neurotic birds, then pounce with 2,000 lbs of muscle, tooth and claw, and printed instructions at every store, restaurant, and hotel about how to remove the plug on your shotgun so that it holds more than the legal limit, along with jokes by everyone, including the police and park wardens, about how only a southerner would be stupid enough to go into the bush with only three cartridges in their shotgun, two of them blanks. Making the bears scary—Churchill residents referred to this as their "constitutional right to arm bears"—increased their tourist appeal as much as making them cute did, so nobody had a problem with doing both.

The polar bears suited Preble just fine. It meant ammunition was easy to buy and, just as importantly, that he was able to set up a large motion-detecting perimeter with slaved cameras all around their new home without attracting attention even when he bought five perimeter-defence systems at once. The store clerk's only response was a matter of fact, "You set the perimeter too wide, you'll get no sleep."

Preble didn't believe that Bigman and the American government would ever give up, and broken sleep was a small price to pay. With his precognition, he'd see intruders five seconds before they walked into his home and made themselves visible to him. With the perimeter fence set at a hundred meters around the house, he'd see intruders five seconds before they got a hundred meters away. He wanted as many layers of protection as possible: within arm's reach, within the C-shape of the house, within his five-second window, within the perimeter fence. Outside of that, there was the area around Churchill, then the protections of Canada. As gentle as Canadian culture was, as lacking in military and walls and hard barriers, it made up through the sheer power of the land. With the exception of Hudson's Bay, where its sovereignty only reached twelve miles before it hit international waters, the country extended for thousands of miles in every direction. And even the Bay was surrounded on all sides by an endless expanse of cold and land inhabited only by the Inuit, reaching into what seemed like forever.

The clerk was right about waking up whenever anything bigger than an Arctic fox wandered through the sensors. Some nights it didn't happen at all, other nights he woke a dozen times, but he didn't have to actually get up. He had the monitors set up beside the bed, so that he could just check to see if there was a future in which he did look and see that the trespasser was a human being. Nine times out of ten that was enough, and after a month or so he trained himself to do it without actually waking up in the present. And anyway, it wasn't a bad thing to know if there was a polar bear around, especially when the toilet broke down.

When he had the infrastructure of their home set up, Preble

started fishing and hunting in earnest. He took Kasper with him, initially over Jane's objections. She didn't want Preble going out on the water, or into town by boat, or generally doing anything that might undo the miracle of them having somehow escaped. Somewhere on the long drive north, counting lakes, she had pulled her husband and her son close, and as the nearly unbelievable unlikelihood of them still being together sank in she became terrified of risking it. They had used up all their miracle credits, and now they should stay inside the cottage.

She and Preble had met in their last year of high school, when Preble's family had moved to New York City. He'd had a crush on her that had completely short-circuited his window. She had asked him to the prom twice, indirectly, but he'd been more a nervous teenage boy than a future-seeing psychic. She'd asked him whether he wanted to ask her something. He'd looked surprised, said no and walked away. The next day, she asked him whether he was going to the prom. He answered that he had nobody to go with and again walked away. She took that as disinterest and left him alone. It was only because they had both gone to the prom separately, with friends, that they had ended up together.

After they'd married and he'd shared his secret, she teased him at times about how oblivious he'd been at the start. But she was glad of it. She wasn't sure they could have started a relationship if his window hadn't shut down during emotional moments. At least initially. She couldn't tell her friends about Preble's precognition, but she could imagine what they'd say, particularly her poet friends. The perfect man, able to foresee what she needed and avoid making mistakes, avoid saying or doing the wrong thing. And sure, there were some advantages to knowing how she'd react —in bed, for one—but there was also a death in knowing things. Or at least a dampening. No surprise, no spontaneity, no mystery.

It felt frustratingly disarming sometimes, like he'd robbed her of her charm not just as a woman but as a human being. As they'd settled into their relationship and his window no longer closed the moment he saw or smelled her (he'd later told her it was her scent that had disconnected him), his ability to predict the future made her predictable. A woman's compass within a relationship is supposed to have a touch of strangeness, otherness, it wasn't always supposed to make complete sense to her husband. Worse, she started to feel that she was losing herself. Anything she did or said would be little more than a response, and a late one at that. She felt like she lost agency, like she could never initiate anything, was always trailing behind him by five seconds and thus slightly unnecessary.

They'd gone through a rough patch when she'd grown to absolutely hate it, peaking while she was doing her MFA in upstate New York. He'd moved with her and supported her through school, since his "work" wasn't tied to NYC anyway and he didn't attend university, though he read voraciously. She'd nearly had an affair on him just out of a sense of claustrophobia, but she'd known he would know instantly, because there was always some possible future where she said the wrong thing and he figured it out. He wasn't a mind reader, but sometimes it felt awfully close.

And his attempts to fix it just made everything worse, as he started trying to pretend he didn't foresee some of her reactions in order to avoid hurting her feelings. She'd started fearing that familiarity would breed contempt, and instead it bred a messy mix of insecurity and claustrophobia in her and dishonesty in him.

The worst was that it was not her. She'd been raised by a poor single mom who'd been too busy to helicopter parent. From the time she was in grade 5 and her brother in grade 3, they'd had no babysitters. They couldn't get into their house until their mom got home from work, so they'd terrorized the neighbourhood, built forts, played street hockey, and generally grown up far more free-range than would be legal these days. She had little patience for the sort of paranoid parenting that had stunted an increasing percentage of her students at NYU. She valued strength and independence and hated seeing herself constantly thrown off balance by Preble's five-second advantage.

Instead of an affair, she found an outlet by building more of her life outside Preble. While still upstate, she joined the local search and rescue team. She loved climbing and nature, and SAR gave those hobbies a practical purpose. After her MFA and her second book, she started teaching part-time at NYU and that helped even more. And after Kasper was born, that claustrophobia was replaced by simple lack of time. She still remembered the feeling, but as though it had belonged to someone else's life.

Aside from making Preble promise never to fake it—never to

fake surprise or ignorance—she'd settled back into her natural pragmatism, though with a great deal more maternal exhaustion and suburban complacency as Preble's gambling made them increasingly financially comfortable. Their lives became more compartmentalized, but happily so. He had his external life in chess and boxing and training his window, and she had her poetry and teaching and writing groups. They were not two halves of a whole. They were two independent people who added a great deal to each other's lives by being together, including an amazing son. With time, she'd learned how to work around his precognition. She never grew to like it. But by the time Preble's subway ride had blown everything up, their relationship had been in a really good place.

In the North, it had to change again. First through a few weeks of maternal terror and nightmares, then with a return to a harder edge. They needed to hunt and fish, and Kasper needed to learn these skills if this was to be where he was going to grow up. It wasn't without fear—the water was so cold that his little body would freeze long before he'd drown. But falling in was always preventable with a five-second lead, and Preble wouldn't let anything happen to him. And she knew he had his own paternal terrors that insisted he keep Kasper close.

The North also focused Preble. While Jane had always had a practical core despite being a poet and poetry professor, Preble tended to live in his head. Even his lifelong drive to expand his precog window had always had a gamelike quality, lacking urgency. Until now. Now that skill was his best hope for keeping Jane and Kasper safe.

He knew it was only a matter of time before some satellite snapped a picture just as he was looking up at the sky and a message would arrive on Bigman's computer. To Preble, the idea that "the world is shrinking," had always seemed like a positive, vaguely multicultural thing. Not anymore. Now it felt like people had shrunk a vast and beautiful planet down to a prison cell small enough to be watched with one eye.

His only real defence, besides a hat, was his window. But he'd long ago moved far into diminishing returns. The future beyond five seconds simply would not yield itself to him, and here there was long-term survival to think about. Food, heat, and mechanical means of seeing the future—things he could do together with Kasper and Jane. So he took Kasper fishing and hunting, and helped Jane salt the fish and build a small greenhouse. With the exception of things that could be fixed in under five seconds, she was more mechanically skilled than he was. She designed the greenhouse and fixed the motors. He helped by telling her whether the motor would turn over or not, but mainly by lifting heavy things.

Kasper was in kid heaven—hunting and fishing with Preble, gardening with Jane, and all of them reading together at night—and Preble discovered just how much fun conversations with his son were. Even the endless "why" questions.

"Why does it rain, Daddy?"

"To make the trees grow."

"Then why does it rain on the roof?"

So they tested the roof's load-bearing capacity and found that, like everything from Fish, it was overdesigned. Jane expanded the green roof, which made Kasper happy and helped camouflage the house from aerial views.

When the snow came in October, the three of them fixed the snowmobile together: the 1985 Ski-Doo Tundra started almost magically after they put in a new battery and changed the oil. The track was frayed, so Preble went and bought a new one in Churchill. The river would soon be frozen, and then this would be their only transportation.

October and November were fun. Snowmobile rides, ice fishing, snowmen and snow forts, and there was even a good hill without too many trees for tobogganing. Preble took an old unused mattress from storage and wrapped it in plastic sheeting—among all the other things, Fish or his father had stocked endless rolls of tent material and plastic sheeting because these could be turned into additional layers of insulation if needed—and then tied a string to it like a pair of reins. The plastic-covered mattress was the best toboggan Preble had ever seen. It was nearly frictionless and accelerated at a frightening rate, and it made for its own padding when they crashed into a rock or a stump or a tree. Kasper made a rule that they had to toboggan at least once a day, and Jane often joined them.

By Christmas, however, they had to start breaking Kasper's

rule. There were days when it was just too cold to go outside. The only consolation was the northern lights, which turned the sky into a giant Omnimax performance. It was music, theatre, dance, and Hollywood movie all in one, but by February they rarely watched. Kasper got them through February. Kasper, and the C shape of the house. They were tired of being locked in together, but the storage end of the house also had a side room with privacy. They could retreat to opposite ends. Even the fact of having their own doors was a psychological relief, though neither felt the urge to go out into the cold. But just the fact that they could, without passing by each other, was like a partial release valve on the cabin fever. Preble marvelled at the foresight of Fish's father. Surely, he had built the house in the summer, and yet he had seen six months into a future that seemed impossible in the present—that you could love someone completely and yet still be driven mad by the prospect of having to brush past the weird psychological triggers that grew out of being locked in one space for months on end.

The architecture helped, but they were still locked in one cabin. Jane felt the cabin fever rise and worried it would turn into a relapse of her MFA days, but it didn't. This was a more natural, more mutual sense of stepping on each other's toes. It didn't have the same sense of having her identity sucked into Preble's five-second window. She wrote poems about snow, space and time, but more and more about family, then about what a family means in the wild versus what it meant in civilization. What was a family—a man, woman and child—who stood outside the bounds of society?

She asked Preble about Fish's theories, something she had never been interested in before. She asked not from a political stance but from an aesthetic one. They often found themselves discussing Fish, and his ideas, by candlelight, late into the night. If the house had been a spaceship, it would have Fish's voice and thoughts and personality. It was like they were living inside him, and meandering conversations like "if the house were a spaceship" were their version of Netflix in the evenings.

She started a new book of poems with the working title, "(Un)bounded," but it wasn't about politics or the social contract as much as it was about the bonds of family. If they kept going north, further into the wild, would there be fewer and fewer external laws and stronger and stronger family bonds in a delicate balance, surrounded by nothing but snow?

But even as she wrote poems about escaping further north, north forever away from all human society, she also revived conversations about helping humanity as a whole—conversations they hadn't had since Preble had first told Jane about his window. At the time, she had been excited about all the possibilities, going so far as to research what sorts of diseases would benefit from being able to see a few seconds into the future. She had been shocked by how much it could help. "Malaria, AIDS, even sleeping sickness all defend themselves against the immune system by shifting their protein shells," she had explained. "The shells are like doors with locks. The immune system fights back by randomly shifting its keys hoping one will fit. To get through the armour, the antibody has to find a design that fits perfectly, and the whole immune battle is basically a race to see who can shift faster. Finding a vaccine is a matter of finding a compound that triggers all the shells at once. Malaria has something like sixty shifting protein shells, and the search for a vaccine is a question of figuring out which compound will trigger all sixty so that the immune system can learn how to counteract all of them. And the research method is nearly random, just like the immune system, testing tens of thousands of compounds in tens of thousands of Petri dishes in the hope that one will work. That's why Big Pharma R&D is so expensive. But you could choose the right code every time, first guess, right?"

"Yes, if the reaction is fast enough," he'd told her back then. "But research labs are controlled environments where 'guessing' right would instantly attract a lot of scrutiny. Maybe if I had my own lab, I could hide it, but those are tens of millions of dollars. I need to earn that money first, and I can't do it too suddenly."

Jane had understood but couldn't fully hide her disappointment at how parochial his focus seemed, that he hadn't pursued anything directed towards humanity as a whole. Until Kasper was born. Then she'd come to agree with keeping a low profile and had stopped reminding him how much good he could do. But now, in the Canadian cabin, she brought it up again. The world knew now, so if they could figure out how to make peace, he wouldn't need to hide anymore. "Or maybe we can build a lab here in the cabin?"

At first Preble had laughed at the idea. He had a hard time thinking beyond making it through each day without the U.S. government showing up at his doorstep. But as the winter dragged on, the idea seemed less and less crazy. If they were to spend winter after winter here, they'd need something to do, something positive, something beyond running and hiding. Maybe it would take ten years to accumulate all the materials to build a lab, but it was a good goal. And if he cured cancer and AIDS and malaria, maybe the world would stop seeing him as a threat.

By March the days were longer, the brittle insane cold snaps of minus 50 and minus 60 stopped, and they could take snowmobile rides into Churchill. First for fresh fruit and vegetables, but Preble also looked for medical or lab supply stores. The Churchill Health Centre was a good modern hospital, but it had no research facility. The most important thing, though, was that they had held off the worst cabin-fever month, February, and now could take weekends enjoying the "big city." They even started up the tobogganing again.

In April, the ice melted. Preble started taking Kasper fishing again, and Jane's writing moved more to their environment. But poems that started about hunting and fishing and the cycle of life and death quickly became haunted by a subtext of all the people they'd killed in their escape from New York—zombie bodies underneath every line of her poetry, limbs revealed by the melting snow—then, influenced by their conversations, started drifting into Solomonic territory, the horrible idea that real power is the power to not take life. These felt like intrusions, strains of rot that didn't belong in a northern landscape.

With the boys gone all day and it still being too early to garden except in the greenhouse, she decided to take up landscaping. It was tangible, real and physically exhausting. She could make the writing-landscaping process a two-way street. She started to gradually shape their enormous front "lawn" into small rolling hills with about five feet between peak and trough. With the ground full of rocks and head-sized boulders, it was exercise and meditation and a project that, like the lab, would take a decade to complete.

Kasper loved helping her, because it was his job to catch the worms for their next day's fishing and helping her dig meant he was helping both parents at once. He'd put them in their worm jar, then check on them throughout the evening, yelling, "Look, daddy, the worms are wiggling!"

In the morning he carefully carried the worm jar, while Preble packed the fishing poles, tackle box, gasoline, fishing maps, net, club and shotgun in their aluminium boat with its Yamaha outboard engine. Jane insisted Kasper use a lifejacket, though Preble thought of lifejackets as something a boy wears when his mother can't swim. Kasper could easily swim for ten minutes; any longer than that and swimming wouldn't matter this far north. Still, he agreed for Jane's sake, and even wore one himself.

They went south on the giant river, upstream, finding little bays and eddies where the fish went to school, while Kasper worked on his backlog of questions that had accumulated since the previous night, and Preble tried his best to answer each one. "The arctic char swim upstream to spoon, Daddy? And then they go to school? When will I go to school? Will the bad guys try to catch me when I go to school?"

"Are you a fish?"

"Noooo! I'm not a fish. I'm a people."

They weren't very good fishermen, they didn't get up at dawn, they talked nonstop, but they still caught dozens of char that swam in from Hudson's Bay and, when they wanted to, Manitoba sturgeon. Churchill River was one of the few places where the sturgeon populations weren't stressed—though the old timers in Churchill said that in Junes long past you could walk across the river on the backs of these giant prehistoric-looking fish—and they always fed in the same troughs at the bottom, which made them easy to catch. Some were enormous: they lived over a hundred years and kept growing their whole lives. The record in Churchill was a 15-foot, 400-pound monster. And though they never saw anything that size, they did catch sixty, seventy, eighty pounders. There was nothing that excited Kasper as much as watching a long fight between his dad and the spine-ridged monsters, and Preble frequently found himself fishing for sturgeon even though he wanted char simply because of Kasper's excited "Dinosaur fish! Dinosaur fish! We're going to fight the dinosaur fish!"

One time, Preble had to let one go, along with his fishing pole, because Kasper started to jump up and down in the boat, so excited that a few seconds later he would have fallen out.

They caught their biggest fish one day in early May. It took nearly an hour to pull in—there was nothing else in the world that would have kept Kasper's attention for a straight hour—and Preble guessed it was their first dinosaur to break a hundred pounds. When they finally wore it down, he had second thoughts about putting the flailing giant in the same boat as Kasper. The shotgun was "regulation" loaded for polar bear—stupid or not, he was determined to be the most squeaky-clean citizen on the continent —so he discharged the warning cartridges into the river and then shot the sturgeon in the head.

"You shot it, daddy? You didn't club it?"

It worried Preble a little that Kasper liked the clubbing part. Normally, Preble pulled the fish into the boat, clubbed it, and then Kasper took his own little club and clubbed it too. But he saw the fish as a monster and learned the clubbing from Preble. And it was a fact of life that if you wanted to eat a fish you had to kill it first. So instead of trying to take away Kasper's enthusiasm for clubbing the dead fish, he read him Hemingway's Old Man and the Sea—Fish's walls of books included all the great man-against-nature books ever written—and taught him to thank the fish after he clubbed them. It was a little weird seeing his four-year-old clubbing a dead dinosaur fish in the head and then saying, "Thank you fish for giving us your meat to eat." But Kasper Jaspers Jefferson could never be a city boy, and since Preble didn't know how to raise a son in the wild, he leaned on Hemingway, London, Coleridge, Melville, and the rest to help him out.

"No, I didn't club it. It's too big. It could have hit you with its tail."

"It wouldn't hit me with its tail, daddy. I would club it."

"This one's too big, Kasper. This is a shotgun-sized fish."

"I'm big too!"

"Yup, you are." As he spoke, Preble tried to pull the fish into the boat, but it tilted dangerously. "And this fish is too big to pull into the boat."

"It's so big?"

"Yes, we'll have to take it to shore." He took some rope, stuck it through the gills of the sturgeon and out the mouth, and tied it to the front of the boat. Then he tied the tail to the back. The thing was nearly the length of the boat. He motored to the shore, with the sturgeon staining the water from the hole in its skull. Preble aimed for a rocky clearing. Behind it was endless pine forest.

When they reached the shore, Kasper said, "Daddy? I know a word that starts with A."

Preble smiled up at him, just as the boat reached the shore. He cut the engine. "Oh? What's the word?"

"Asshole."

"There's no such word. It doesn't exist."

"That's funny."

"What's funny?" Preble asked, a bit confused by the sudden turn.

"The asshole exists but the word doesn't."

"Where did you hear that word?"

Kasper looked down at the bottom of the boat. "You said it to the bad man. In the bathtub. And then his brain went out of his head and a little bit went on me and you washed it. And now you're going to cut the fish in the asshole and its brain is in the water." He looked at the shore. "I want to get out!"

"Ah, okay, but don't go anywhere." Preble felt whiplashed by Kasper's sudden mention of the bad man in the bathtub, his whole sudden shift. There were odd moments when Kasper sounded preternaturally grown up, and other times when he sounded like a baby. He hadn't ever brought up the episode with Agent Bones before, but then he changed so quickly to the fish that Preble had no idea what to say. Instead, he said, "Stay close to Daddy and the dinosaur fish."

"Are there snakes?"

"No snakes."

"But there are bears." Kasper made his bear face, head hunched, lips trying to snarl, eyes and shoulders and arms up like claws, a monster. "I'll be a good bear and I'll punch the bad bear when he comes."

"The bear won't hurt you if you stay close."

"He'll squish Daddy."

"Remember, Kasper, why do animals bite people?"

Kasper thought about this for a long time. Finally, he said, "Because of helicopters?"

Preble laughed. "Usually only when they're protecting their children. The bear won't hurt you if you stay close. Okay?"

"Okay. But he'll hurt you a little bit." Kasper nodded to himself as he said this, lips tight and little eyebrows raised at the inevitability of it all.

Preble had intended to just use the shore to lift the fish into the boat, but now that he compared the sizes of the fish and the boat he decided that the fish was too big. It was still only 10 AM, he had lots of time. He paused a second before sticking the knife into its anus, or vent as the fishing books called it, regretting lying to Kasper. Of course, assholes existed. They were all over the place and they carried their names with them. Then he slit the fish up to the lower jaw. It stunk. He scooped out the guts with his hands, gagging at the smell, then pulled the gills clear. Poor Jane, all those fish he'd brought home for her to prepare. But then she couldn't really smell them. Lacking a sense of smell had some definite benefits, something he'd first noticed when Kasper had gone from breast milk to solid food, and then during potty training. Kasper was a great kid, the best, even all their friends-with-their-own-kids said so...had said so, past tense, when they still had a community...but he'd taken forever to potty train. Because he didn't mind the poop, he didn't have a sense of smell or disgust, and so he'd just run around, continue playing, not noticing his diaper was full.

Would he grow up here in the woods, with no friends his age? Jane could write, but with a readership of two. Kasper without friends, both their lives irrevocably stunted because of his ego on a subway? He'd read everything there was on the nature of time—but he couldn't rewind it, not far enough.

Preble tried to focus on the guts and gills. He dropped them in the water and moved a few feet over to wash his hands and breathe some clean air and settle his stomach and his heart. He turned back and had a split-second of panic as his brain refused to put together what was wrong. Kasper was gone. He'd been squatting beside Preble, watching him gut the fish, and now he wasn't there. Then Preble's blood froze as he heard his son scream five seconds in the future.

He sprinted into the forest and reached Kasper two seconds before the polar bear. The thing was enormous, its white fur dirty from the forest and bones showing, old and hungry. The ice floes had been gone for over a month, and with them went the bear's ability to hunt seal. The smell of sturgeon guts that had nearly made Preble gag must have been sweet salvation to the bear.

A man had no chance against a polar bear, even an old and hungry one. Maybe especially against an old and hungry one. When Preble was 17 and still figuring out all the possibilities of his precog window, he'd signed up to fight in a sportsman show against a 700-pound, 7-foot-7-inch brown bear. It had been declawed and detoothed, before such sporting events had been banned, but still, it had been no contest. The bear took all comers, window or not.

The man who had gone before Preble had been a bear of a man himself, and the bear had knocked him out of the ring with one lazy swat. He was carried out on a stretcher with a broken leg, then it was Preble's turn. The bear reared up, and 17-year-old Preble froze. There was not a single thing he could do that would work. He tried anyway, tried a double-leg takedown only to find what he already knew, that the two legs were too far apart. He switched to a single leg on an oak tree, unmoveable. With every ounce of strength, just strength, no precog window whatsoever, he managed to stand back up. He tried a hip throw, and found the bear had no neck to grab onto. He grabbed the ears and found the bear too long to throw. The whole thing felt like a trap, an elevator, seeing that no matter what he did, nothing would work, like fate, the way people sometimes talked about fate, determined in a way he rarely experienced. He'd only escaped without injuries because the referee/trainer saw that Preble had managed to annoy the bear and had stopped the match.

And that had been a declawed, detoothed, circus-trained brown bear. A koala compared to a polar bear. He'd gone on to wrestle camels in Turkey and kangaroos in Australia and wild horses in Spain, but the declawed brown bear remained the only hopelessly closed fight Preble had ever been in: a memory that cut in as he saw the dirty-white monster charging at Kasper. Probably for no other reason than that two humans were between it and the smelly sturgeon. The shotgun that Preble carried for exactly this situation was in the boat, discharged and far away. He was still holding the fish knife, but the bear had five-inch claws and two thousand pounds of muscle and bone that couldn't be ducked like a bullet.

Preble collided with the bear three meters ahead of Kasper. The last thing the bear had expected was for something to dive at him, and the impact came a second before his pounce, so the bear had been simply running. As he dove at the bear, Preble feinted with his knife at the bear's eyes, just enough to make him raise his maw, then, barely in time—threading a needle in time—pulled the knife down and through the bear's throat, trying to ram it into its braincase from the bottom as the bear bowled him over like a Mac truck sucking down a cyclist, crushing Preble's ribs. A polar bear's skull can deflect medium-calibre rifle rounds, but from the bottom it's vulnerable. Unfortunately, Preble's knife wasn't long enough to reach the brain. He knew it wouldn't work, but had to try, forced to try things he already knew wouldn't work because nothing would. This was the only way forward that didn't involve the bear crashing into Kasper. The knife didn't reach the brain, but it was enough to make the bear snap its face down in mid-charge so hard it rammed into the ground. It didn't reach Kasper.

The collapse had turned the bear's face into a ram, with nearly the entire weight of the bear slamming into the ground. It was lucky for Preble—he would have been dead on the spot other-wise from the sheer weight—that the face-first impact into the ground absorbed most of its momentum. It also stunned the bear. Preble was completely covered by it, momentarily inaccessible to its claws or teeth, but he could still make out Kasper screaming, "Daddy!"

Kasper had seen his father disappear under a mass of dirty white fur a meter in front of him. Instead of running away, he started to hit the bear on the head with his bare hands.

Though Kasper's hits were nothing—Mike Tyson's punch would have been nothing—they were close enough to its eyes to get the bear's attention. It lifted up its face and hit Kasper with its snout, too unbalanced to get its teeth up and snap. Kasper was so light that the hit lifted him off the ground and sent him sprawling several feet back. But as the bear shifted, it created room for Preble to move his arm. He could see Kasper fly back, an orange ball of lifejacket with a blond tuft of hair on top, his little face overwhelmed by incomprehension.

Preble screamed in rage, his precog window completely shut. Things had happened during his adult life that narrowed the window. When he'd seen the NSA agent with his gun to Kasper's head, the window had been down to a half second. But, since the end of puberty, it had never been fully shut like it was now. When he needed it most. He couldn't see the future, he couldn't see what would happen to Kasper or the bear. He couldn't see anything except for the bear's throat directly above his face, so he stabbed and stabbed and stabbed while the bear howled and instead of attacking tried to stand up to distance itself from the sharp knife. That gave Preble more room for his arm, and one of the stabs must have cut through an artery but in a weird way because the neck didn't start gushing blood like you'd expect if the carotid was cut, and so he kept stabbing and stabbing. But that was a trick of perception and adrenaline, because when he later climbed out from under the dead bear he realized he was completely covered in blood.

The world was different. He was blind. Everything came at him suddenly as though it were made of jagged-edged glass shards that dropped and cut without warning. The world was painfully sharp, without the smoothness that his precog window normally gave it. The bear's body blocked his view of Kasper, though he could hear him sobbing. Preble finally got out, on the wrong side, nearly tripping as he ran around the bear, gasping through what felt like a fractured rib, to where Kasper was hitting the dead bear on the side of the head while sobbing uncontrollably.

Then Kasper looked up uncertainly and, still crying, said, "Daddy?"

Preble tried to answer but coughed instead, with an explosion of pain in his ribs. Finally, he managed to say, "Daddy's okay. Are you okay?"

"Daddy's okay?"

"Yes. Are you okay?"

"I'm okay. Daddy's not sick?"

Preble kneeled down and hugged Kasper through the pain, feeling the lifejacket against his chest and silently thanking Jane over and over for insisting on the jacket.

"It's a bad bear, Daddy!" Kasper finally stopped crying as he said this. Preble just hugged him, then pulled him away to make sure everything was okay, no broken bones, no cuts. He couldn't believe his eyes.

"Thank God!"

"It's a bad bear!" Kasper repeated.

Preble took as deep a breath as his ribs would allow. "It's a dead bear."

"The bad bear is dead?"

"Yes, the bear is dead. He was just hungry."

"He's a bad bear!" Kasper insisted. "He tried to bite Daddy!"

"Yes, and so we had to kill him. So he wouldn't bite us. But he's not bad. He's beautiful and he's dangerous. So we have to be careful and respect him and sometimes we have to fight and kill him. But he's not a bad bear. He's just a bear."

Kasper started to cry again. "No, he's a bad bear! He tried to kill Daddy!"

"He can't kill me. I'm too strong. And I will always protect you. I'm stronger than any bear or bad man or monster, and—"

"Stronger than the helicopter?"

"I'll always protect you, Kasper. You never have to be scared of anything, okay? The bear made a mistake trying to bite us, but he's not bad. This is his forest too. We have to share it with him."

"But he didn't share."

"No, he made a mistake. I make mistakes too. Sometimes big mistakes. You make mistakes too, right?"

"Mommy doesn't make mistakes?"

Preble laughed but cut it short instantly as his ribs hurt. "No, Mommy doesn't make mistakes."

"If I make a mistake, you will kill me?"

"What? No, of course not! I love you. I don't love the bear. And I only killed him so that he wouldn't hurt us."

"You love me?"

"Yes. More than anything."

"And you love Mommy?"

"Yes. The three of us are a family."

"My family is you and Mommy?"

"Yes. And my family is you and Mommy. And Mommy's family is you and me. My first job is always to protect you.

That's the most important job of every daddy, to protect his son."

"Daughter too?"

"Yes, for sure. But I only have a son. You. So you never have to be scared of bad men with guns or bears who make mistakes, or anything, okay? Even if it looks scary, you don't have to be scared, okay?"

"And the bear is not family?"

"No. The bear is not family. He's not bad, but we had to stop him."

"What's bad, Daddy?"

"What?"

"What's bad?"

"Bad is...I don't know."

"You do know. Tell me. What's bad?"

"The man in the bathtub with the gun. He was bad."

"Why was he bad?"

"Because...because he was afraid. And being afraid made him do bad things."

"Is bad being afraid?"

"No. Yes." Preble had no idea what to say. He wasn't prepared for a philosophical conversation, but Kasper seemed to need it, asking each question with a disconcerting intensity, as if life depended on the answer. He felt he owed Kasper an answer. Or at least a real attempt at an answer. "Being afraid turns people bad. Yes...you're right, Kasper. Bad is being afraid."

"I was afraid. Am I bad?"

"No, you weren't so afraid. Your fear was smaller than your love. You punched the bear when the bear was on top of me. I used a simple word because you're little. I should have said 'Bad is being fearful.' Fearful means your afraidness is bigger than every-thing else. And you weren't being fearful. You were very, very brave, Kasper. The bravest boy in the whole world."

"I want to go home."

"Me too."

"Hold my hand, Daddy." Kasper held up his hand for Preble to take while they walked together to the boat. He looked like he was thinking deeply, and when they got to the boat he added, "Daddy?"

"Yes, Kasper."

"I used my knuckles."

"What?"

Kasper took his hand out of Preble's and showed him a little fist. "I used my knuckles. To punch the bad bear."

Chapter 11

PREBLE DROPPED KASPER OFF AT HOME—AFTER SURVIVING A winter of minus sixty huddled in the cottage, it was unambiguously their home now—and told Jane he was going back to skin the bear. Kasper broke into a sudden spasm of tears, crying that Preble couldn't go. He almost never cried like a standard toddler, with full wailing screams, but now he clung to Preble's neck with all the strength in his little arms, face completely red, crying beyond language with only fragmented sobs of "No, no, no! Daddy stay here. Daddy can't go! Daddy can't go!"

Jane shook off some of the bewildered look she still had from being told they'd been attacked by a polar bear but were mostly okay. "I thought you said you had broken ribs."

"I think they're just fractured. Or maybe it's the intercostal cartilage. At any rate, they're not pushing into my lungs. A doctor would give me aspirin and tell me to rest." He shifted Kasper to his left arm, trying to avoid wincing in pain at his ribs, and pushed the hair back from his eyes. "Kasper, shhh. You're fine now. We're home."

"So take some aspirin and rest for God's sake!" She tried to take Kasper from Preble, but he wouldn't let go.

"No, Daddy, Daddy can't go!"

"Jane, we have no income. That pelt is worth over a thousand dollars."

"We have money."

"Not really. Whatever we had in New York is gone. It burned up just as much as if we'd had it under a mattress when the missile hit the apartment. We try to use a credit card or an ATM just once, and we're done. We need that cash."

He kissed them both, and gently unwrapped Kasper's hands from his neck—Kasper was screaming, insisting that Preble not leave, when he was able to force words out between the emotion that was overwhelming him, incoherent words about bears and bad men and the cold ice and Daddy not having a nose.

"Yes, you punched the bear in the nose."

"No. Daddy doesn't have a nose. Daddy's fearful. Don't go!"

Despite his bravery, Kasper felt like he'd almost lost his father, and didn't want to let him go so soon. Preble tried to explain that he had to go, but he'd be back soon, and the bear was dead already, but after twenty minutes he gave up, gently wiped the hair from Kasper's red eyes again and the snot from his still baby-chubby cheeks, kissed him on the nose, and walked out of the door. Behind him Kasper insisted he wanted to watch Daddy leave and say bye-bye, so Jane went with him and they waved as Preble climbed back into the boat, trying to take deep breaths despite the pain in his chest which was not all caused by his ribs. He waved back until they became tiny, then disappeared behind trees as the river turned right.

He was grateful to see the bear was still there, untouched. It took him four exhausting hours just to take the skin off, his shotgun beside him, loaded in case something else smelled all the blood. No warning shots this time. He didn't try to prepare the skin in any way, didn't even have salt with him. He tried to remove as much of the fat and flesh from the hide as he could, but it was a sloppy job. And he didn't do anything with the meat. Polar bear liver had always been toxic due to too much vitamin A—an adult human could tolerate about 10,000 units of vitamin A, while a pound of polar bear liver had over 9 million units—but even the rest of the meat was risky these days, too high up the food chain. With a growing sense that he wanted to hurry home, he dumped the meat and organs in the water to pay back the fish, laid the skin in the boat, stumbled in after it, and pointed the boat homeward. His entire body ached, exhausted to his bones.

With relief, he rounded the corner of the river, the final bend before he could see their home, imagining that Jane and Kasper would be in the exact same position they'd been when he left, waving hello this time instead of bye. For some reason, he had missed them terribly these past few hours skinning the bear. It was irrational, he'd spent far longer away from them, but the trauma of the bear fight had rubbed all his nerves and fears raw again. Along with the anticipation, he felt a sense of near panic in his urgency to get back to his family. He pushed the boat as fast as it would go.

He just wanted to be home. Even if they weren't standing in the same position—which of course they wouldn't be, that would make no sense—he knew that even the sight of their C-shaped house would feel like a salve. Except that when he came around the corner, the first thing he saw was a big orange helicopter on their front lawn.

Chapter 12

THE CONTINGENCY PLANNING GROUP NEVER MET, EITHER IN person or over the phone. Bigman simply reached out over the course of the winter, one by one, building the spokes of a potential wheel that would probably never roll anywhere. He'd started with the vice president. They'd been friends since law school and even though they now rarely socialized, they had helped each other throughout their careers. Bigman provided information, when needed, and Garland O'Reilly provided political cover, when needed. They liked each other, but even more importantly, they understood each other. When John Grape named O'Reilly as his VP, he and Bigman had cut down the golf games and social visits with their wives without ever having to discuss it. They both understood that their friendship had more value outside the limelight.

"Garland, I need a White House sign off on some politically tricky contingency plans. You saw what Jefferson did with the mayor of New York. He can get to any one person, including—"

"Yeah, I don't want to hear details. You really think group decisions are less vulnerable?"

"Yes. First, he won't even know who's on the committee."

"Don't call it that. The president said no committees."

Bigman smiled on his end of the phone. "Jefferson won't know in whom decision-making power will vest. And it's much harder to manipulate or blackmail multiple people at once. There's a sanity check."

"These plans will never be used, you understand, right? But I agree they need to be built, just in case. And quietly."

"Just in case, and quietly."

"And don't tell me who's on the non-committee either. Not until it's needed."

Bigman followed up with CIA Director Felix Frankfurter and Assistant Director James Grill. Knowing that the vice president was on board made it easier for them to agree, so long as it was kept as a contingency plan. Then he called FBI Director Steve Guther, who was typically legalistic. "You'd need the whole cabinet on board if you want to do this under the 25th Amendment."

"Being a hostage or similarly compromised is a form of incapacity, but it's temporary. We're not talking about permanently removing the president, so it's a different standard."

"You're still talking about giving executive authority to another body."

"We're just trying to prepare for a threat. Any shift in chains of command would be temporary. We can work within the shadow of the 25th without actually invoking it. When Reagan was shot, then-VP Bush took over without actually invoking the 25th. We're just preparing plans for something similar, so we're not flying by the seat of our pants if something happens. The nature of the threat means we can't vest the power in person, so it has to go to a group."

The CIA director paused before asking, "Why not Congress then?"

"If the president is a hostage then we're in a war footing, and you want to give the decision to 435 House members and 100 Senators who can't agree on anything?"

"At least Jefferson couldn't hold that many members hostage."

"They hold each other hostage. All I'm saying is that we need to wargame this and prepare plans. That's all this is."

"But why you? I still don't understand why an AD of the NSA is putting this together."

"Jefferson is an information problem and I'm the point man on that problem. But this is not 'me' organizing it any more than if the vice president's secretary called you."

"Hah. Secretaries are the highest power in a bureaucracy."

"Do you want to be on the body or not?"

"Yes."

The only person who said no was the chairman of the joint chiefs, Hammond de Koek.

"I'm surprised at you, Ham," Bigman told the old general. "I figured if anyone understands the importance of contingency planning it would be you."

"I do understand. But the end result would mean I go outside my chain of command."

"We need you. We have the White House on board. We have the NSA and the CIA and even the FBI. But this could easily turn into a military threat, and we need you."

"These are two separate issues. One is creating a plan for a nightmare. That's necessary, and I'm glad we're doing it. The second is putting my ass on a seat that takes power unlawfully from the elected president of the United States. Get permission from President Grape, and I'm in. Otherwise, count me out."

"Do you have a better suggestion? If Jefferson takes the president hostage?"

"The VP."

"And who makes the decision to transfer power to the VP if the president is still alive, talking, but doing Jefferson's bidding? Assume Jefferson also controls one other person to prevent the cabinet invoking the 25th?"

De Koek was quiet so long Bigman started to wonder whether he'd hung up. "No," he finally said. "I don't have a better suggestion."

"I understand your hesitation, Ham. But the vice president was elected and we were all confirmed by elected members of the Senate. If Jefferson takes control of the president, is that an elected government? Doesn't that scare the shit out of you?"

"It does. Even more than you do. Which is why I'm going to pretend this call never happened. But I'm also not going to cowboy. I have a chain of command."

Bigman hung up, regretting the call. He should have gone straight to the vice-chairman of the joint chiefs, General Ythane.

He'd worked with Ythane for years when she ran the U.S. Strategic Command, which was DARPA's contact point for all their C4ISR research. She was not only highly competent, but far less rigid than Hammond. Ironic given their age difference, but she was a lot more old school when it came to the value of military flexibility than her boss. Where Hammond was a bureaucrat, Ythane was a throwback to Patton or McArthur. And at the moment she held both positions, since a new USSTRATCOM commander hadn't yet been named—but there was no telling how long that would last.

Bigman hadn't called her first because she was three steps down. If the noncommittee was going to be able to react adequately, it needed the military on board. But the secretary of defense was a political hack whom Bigman hadn't even considered bringing on board, and Hammond was proving just how rigid the modern military had become. At least he'd agreed to keep one eye closed.

Bigman dialled Ythane's number. If she agreed, maybe he could nudge the right people to delay any replacement for the USSTRATCOM position. With both hats, she'd have the ability to project a lot more power.

Chapter 13

THE THROTTLE WAS ALREADY FULLY OPEN AND PREBLE HAD to force himself not to twist it right off as he helplessly watched men in military camouflage run in and out of his house. He saw it five seconds forward, but that made no difference with the miserable distance the boat could cover in that time. Two of them dragged Jane, who was trying to get to Kasper. Kasper was fighting as hard as he could against a huge man who held him like a sack of potatoes under his armpit. Preble couldn't hear anything over the hundred meters he still had to cover, a football field, over the sound of his boat engine at full throttle. He gripped his shotgun with one hand and strangled the throttle with the other, willing it to go faster.

The boat slammed into the shore at full speed, launching Preble at a run towards the helicopter just as it was taking off. He would have broken Olympic long jump records, landed running without even noticing his ribs, but he still had fifty meters to cross and the helicopter quickly climbed too high. He couldn't jump, he couldn't fly. His only option was the shotgun in his hand. If he'd had a rifle he could at least aim, shoot the pilot, but with a shotgun he had only seconds before the helicopter was out of range. His options were terrible, and a helicopter took longer than five seconds to crash.

Awful to gamble with the two lives that were his world. The sum total of his universe was being lifted up by ugly orange metal, outside his sphere of protection in the belly of the chopper. It wasn't going to explode, so he shot the gas tank full of holes. The helicopter started raining gasoline, but not enough to make it land. Soldiers shot back down at him, bullets that he dodged absent-mindedly as he ran at full sprint after the helicopter. He couldn't see Kasper, but Jane somehow made it to the wide-open side. Her left arm was free and she raised it towards Preble in a defeated half-wave gesture, as though pleading for help and saying goodbye at the same time. He didn't see Kasper at all.

Soon they were out of sight, blocked by the trees. From the waving to the trees, it felt like a perverse, twisted replay of his departure that morning. He could still hear the helicopter, so he kept running until he fell to his knees, gasping for breath, unable to fill his lungs or shake the image of his little boy held by the soldier like he wasn't even human, and that's when he realized what was odd about the helicopter. It had an American flag, but it was orange. Military helicopters weren't orange. Icebreakers were. It had flown north towards Churchill, not south.

Of course, they were too far from the American border for a helicopter, but they could have a ship in Hudson's Bay, an icebreaker that wouldn't attract attention. Maybe they had been waiting off shore for a while, watching from satellites until he was separated from Kasper and Jane. The bear skin, he realized, was the first time in weeks that he'd been that far away from Kasper.

It was all speculation, guesses not foreknowledge, but it was all he had. And if they were on a ship, he couldn't get to them on foot. He'd lost the helicopter.

He forced himself to stand, to run back to the house. The soldiers had left the front door wide open, which was probably a good thing because he was shaking so hard he couldn't have put a key into the keyhole. He grabbed ammunition and the .454 and jumped back in the boat.

It was a long ride to Churchill, time enough to come up with every horrible possibility. Shooting the helicopter was a desperate move, but to see clearly he had to cut out the emotion. It blurred everything just when he most needed clarity. Doctors don't operate on family. Lawyers don't represent themselves. He needed to turn off, play this like a chess game, coldly, monstrously, the way Fish had always pushed him to play. This really was war. Losing Kasper or Jane was a game-ender—he prayed the helicopter didn't run out of fuel over water—but to get them back he had to separate himself, become something else.

When he got to Churchill he forced himself to go to the marina, to refuel, buy an extra fuel tank, and see if there were any American ships in. There weren't. The gas station attendant, bundled in a modern version of a traditional Inuit sealskin parka and mitts the size of boots so he could stand handling the gas on the water for hours on end, said he'd heard a chopper on and off a few hours ago—the grey water could bounce sounds almost from Greenland—but hadn't seen one.

Preble searched. He pushed his little boat out past the twelve-mile zone, as best he could guess from a combination of time and boat speed. He had no GPS, no electronic equipment of any kind, not even a cell phone. Under normal conditions it would have been a stupid thing to do in his little boat, though the water was dead flat because of all the icebergs that had recently floated into the bay. Some were the size of small islands, several miles long, and each promised to hide an American warship behind it.

He tried to keep his search organized. He planned to look first in one heading for four hours, roughly paralleling the shore as it turned west then north, then return and follow the coast east, trying to stay twelve miles out, though with no real way of gauging distance to the shore. But he couldn't stick to his plan. Every ice-island that promised to hide a ship became a race around the corner followed by slate-grey water reflecting a slate-grey sky, more icebergs, emptiness that hit him a few seconds before he turned the corner.

If only his window were longer—how much ground he could cover mentally if he could see a day ahead instead of five seconds! If he could see just an hour, he'd have seen the helicopter. He lost track of which icebergs he'd already looked behind and which were new, they all looked new, each angle different, they calved, sometimes they flipped over right in front of him. All it took was a small piece falling off and the iceberg turned upside down, top became bottom, up became down, good became bad, with a giant roar and splash like the end of the world. It sent waves out that were dampened by all the other icebergs, and within minutes everything was back to normal, flat cold and grey, calving towards entropy, and if you came upon the iceberg now, you'd think up had always been down and the calved portion had always been separate.

If it had been summer, the night wouldn't have come. He could have kept looking, but it was only May and around 11 PM the sun set drunkenly, crooked and sideways but eventually slid below the horizon. The icebergs seemed to get louder when it did, but their whiteness gave him enough light. The sea was black, covered with white rumblers that floated peacefully until they suddenly exploded in immense self-shredding violence.

Shortly after night fell, Preble ran out of gas. He was half-frozen. He had cold-weather gear on—fishing is a lot of motionless sitting on near-frozen water—but even a survival suit would have been hard-pressed to keep him warm this long in the middle of Hudson's Bay. Shaking, he wrapped himself in the uncured polar-bear skin, fur on the inside Inuit-style for maximum warmth. At least the cold prevented it from stinking as he sat hunched forward around himself, wearing a monstrous polar-bear skin with chunks of flesh and fat still sticking to it.

He'd never been to a church in his life except as a tourist looking at architecture or culture or history, but now—dressed like a nightmare demon—he tried praying for real. Whatever chance that there is a God, he would take it: please save Kasper and Jane. Kasper deserves a life. He's such a smart little boy. Loving. And brave. He tried to fight off the bear with his hands. With his knuckles. The forty-pound boy, almost still a baby, punching with his soft little hands at a two-thousand-pound monster. And I had just promised to always protect him. Just a few hours before breaking my promise. I promised him. I promised. Preble touched the bear's head, where he knew Kasper's hands had hit it and for the first time in his adult life he started to cry. He could feel the tears freezing on his nose. Then he passed out, knowing he had broken the most important promise of his life and that he was now the monster.

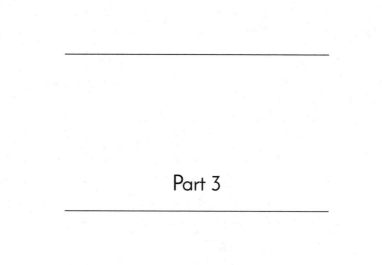

Part 3

Chapter 14

PREBLE WOKE UP TO A ROUND FACE HE RECOGNIZED, WASN'T
sure from where. He was delirious. The man was wrapping him in
blankets. He took Preble's gloves off and rubbed grease into his
hands, caribou fat he'd later learn. Behind him were six astronauts
in red spacesuits.

"Frostbite," the man said and Preble finally recognized him. It
was Shiatie Taget, who'd boated them to Fish's house when they'd
first arrived in Churchill. He ran narwhal and whale-watching
expeditions. Which explained the tourists in survival suits. "Nose
you lose, hands you keep. Feet?"

"Feet I keep."

"Let me check."

"Good boots. Where's my son?"

Then he passed out again.

Chapter 15

WHEN HE WOKE UP, EVERYTHING WAS WHITE. IT STARTLED
him, until his eyes began to discriminate between the open white
curtains, white bed sheets, white walls, white gauze on his hands
and face, white nurse in white in the corner of the room. This far
north, white was the colour of death. You'd figure the hospital
would come up with something better than white. With that
thought came Churchill General Hospital and that he hadn't
found Kasper and Jane.

The nurse noticed he was awake and came with a clipboard.
She had freckles and reddish eyebrows to break the white. She
said, "You're awake."

"Did they find...are Kasper and Jane Jefferson here?"

"Drunk ATV? Southerner, fifty years old?"

"What?"

"The only other admission today was an ATV accident. Guy
flipped, got stuck under it with the thing running and the wheel
up against his leg. Ate the flesh down to the bone." She nodded as
though the gruesomeness proved the richness and mystery of life.

"No."

"Well, we have you here as a John Doe. Shiatie brought you
in. He said your name was your business, not his to give out. He's

a funny guy. Most of them are. But now that we're awake, can we get your real name? And your health card."

Preble sat up in bed. Nothing hurt. "I've got to go."

"Oh, but you can't." She looked down at her chart. "Your fingers are okay. They'll just be a bit numb for a couple of months, but then the feeling will come back. But your nose, uhm, maybe the doctor should tell you."

"I'm sorry, miss, but I really don't care." He tried to swing his legs off the bed and felt something tug on his penis. He flipped back the bed sheet and saw it was a catheter. "How long have I been here?"

"Nearly two days."

He slumped. "No."

"You—"

"No, no, no!" He let himself fall back onto the bed, unable to fight off the despair of what those two days meant. If the chopper had fallen into the sea—because he'd shot it—then they were dead.

He couldn't think that way. He remembered the massive ice islands. The big ones were stable enough for a helicopter landing. But that thought triggered his imagination in more unwelcome ways, the helicopter landing, Jane and Kasper out on the iceberg waiting to be rescued and it calved and flipped and suddenly they were just gone. No, the big ones were miles long, calving couldn't change their centre of gravity so easily. And any pilot flying an orange helicopter out here would know something about ice. It was an icebreaker helicopter. He fought to get the image of them on the flipping berg out of his head. Horrible. No, worst case scenario, they landed on ice and the ship had come to pick them up. Which meant they could be anywhere. Some secret CIA prison, a concrete cave in Guantanamo Bay, a hole in Cheyenne Mountain. How could he ever track them?

"Are you okay?" the nurse asked, genuinely worried.

"No." Preble struggled to get control over himself, to talk to the nurse. "But I guess I have time for you to tell me what's wrong with me. I assume my nose is gone."

"Ah, yes. For the moment. It, uhm, couldn't be saved. The operation...was only to save your life, prevent gangrene, infection and so on. We'll schedule you for plastic surgery to reconstruct your face. You'll look almost normal."

"Can you do that this— Is it morning?"

"Oh, yes, it's morning." She looked at her watch. "It's 7:15AM. But we don't have a reconstructive surgeon in Churchill. We'll have to fly you to Winnipeg. It will be within the month. You'll probably still lose your sense of smell, but aesthetically it will be very similar to a real nose. They use a bit of your pelvis for the cartilage, and some fat from your derriere. But you don't need to tell people that. They're very good these days."

"Assface." He looked at the nurse's name tag. "Thanks, Glenda. Where are my clothes?"

"They're in the basket at the foot of your bed, but you can't leave."

Preble pulled the IV out of his left wrist, then the catheter out of his penis and started to get dressed in front of the nurse, who couldn't decide what to do. Finally, she went to the wall phone and called someone.

A male doctor, older, with wild white hair—more white— came in just as Preble was struggling to zip his pants. He hadn't taken the bandages off his fingers, and he was having trouble with the zipper. "You really should stay," the doctor said.

Preble lifted his hands up. "How long do these need to stay wrapped?"

The doctor shrugged. "If you can fight with the zipper like that, you can probably take them off now. Just sit down for five more minutes, okay?"

Dr. Winger, according to his name tag, unwrapped Preble's hands, squeezing the ends of his fingers. They were a pasty white, like he'd spent three weeks in the bath. On his left pinky he couldn't really feel anything past the last knuckle. On his right hand only the tips of the fingers were numb. "They'll be fine," the doctor said. "Just don't let them get cold again. Even the slightest exposure over the next three to six months could be bad. If I were you, I'd get your plastic surgery and then go take a long holiday in Florida."

"Washington, D.C."

"Warm enough. But your face." The doctor shook his head. "You have a big hole where you nose used to be."

"It's really not a priority."

The doctor gave him a small smile. Preble had the feeling that frostbite surgeons quickly became expert psychologists. "It's not just—"

"It feels right."

"I have to say, I've broken the bad news about lost noses to several dozen people over the course of my career up here, and this is the first time I've heard that. But it's not just aesthetics. It means no mucous membranes, no filter, no warming mechanism for the air entering your sinus cavity. Your olfactory sense is gone, probably for good, which will affect your taste buds as well. Plastic surgery won't fix that, but it will—"

"I'm keeping the hole. How do I prevent infection?"

"I can also recommend a psychiatrist who deals with these issues."

"Infection, doctor. Focus, please."

The doctor raised an eyebrow, hesitated, then shrugged. "Keep gauze on for two weeks, change it every day. I'll give you an antibiotic cream to put on each day. And again, I would get the hell out of this cold. Go south, young man."

"Thank you, doctor. I'll pay by credit card."

"You're not a Manitoba resident?"

"I'm a refugee from the United States. I was hiding up here."

"It's tough to hide with no nose. There is a prosthetics company that makes excellent nose prosthetics in Montreal. They can match almost any face. And I believe there is also one in Houston, Texas, if you prefer made in America. I'll look up the info for you."

"Thanks. But I'm done hiding."

He took the antibiotic cream, extra gauze and information, then went to Churchill's only car dealership, where he bought a Toyota pickup. He made one last trip to Fish's cottage—it was Fish's cottage again, not home, another home gone. Then he drove south.

His credit card had worked at both the hospital and car dealership. He threw out the aluminium in his wallet. If they wanted to know where he was, he'd let them know. If they wanted a war, he would give them a war.

Chapter 16

Halfway between Churchill and Winnipeg, a Predator drone shot a missile at him. He managed to swerve out of the way. Five hours later, a second Predator took out his truck, but he jumped out in time. He walked. Twenty minutes later, a man driving south picked him up. His name was Timothy, driving a Ford King Ranch. He'd passed the blown-out Toyota and asked if it was Preble's. Preble explained that the engine had overheated and caught fire, blowing up the pickup and burning his face. Surprisingly, Timothy didn't wonder how he'd managed to get such professional bandages on the road.

After a couple of hours Preble offered to drive and was grateful that the man agreed. If he hadn't, Preble would have had to steal the King Ranch from him. Five seconds wasn't enough time if you were in the passenger seat.

Just before dusk, an A-10 tried to bomb them.

As he drove and swerved, with the Predators and A-10s shooting and bombing, Preble realized that he was seeing further than five seconds now. It wasn't the same crisp clarity as he had for the five-second window, it was more along the lines of intuition, but it was proving right with each swerve and acceleration and sudden turn, with the cold murderous rage matched by a driving speed that would have killed anyone who hadn't memorized the road or the future.

Maybe it was the cold that let him see further, like the winter air in Churchill. The true cold—emptied of all moisture—was clear, crisp. People who'd never walked through -40 couldn't appreciate how much the heat and humidity beveled the world, made it soft and without edges. The cold gave clarity.

But he knew that wasn't the reason for his expanded window. If it were, he'd have foreseen the helicopter. He'd done a lot of research into the structure of the brain over the years, and his best guess was that he could see further because he'd lost his sense of smell.

Previously, like the old saying goes, he couldn't see for his own nose.

The sense of smell is old and primitive. So old that our entire brain may have evolved out of our olfactory bulb. Unlike the other senses, which go through a series of stations like the thalamus, the olfactory bulb is only two synapses away from the hippocampus. The nose is the only place where our brain makes direct contact with the world. The eyes are an extension of the brain, extruding from the vault of our skull, but even they're protected by a lens. Olfaction both touches the world and has a direct path to the old reptilian brain. It's why olfactory memories can be so strong.

But by losing his nose, Preble had not only cut that anchor tying him down to our evolutionary past. He'd not only cut out the sensory interference. He'd also expanded the area of neocortex real estate available for processing the future. When a sense stops working, the neurons in that region of the neocortex start to atrophy until the other senses take it over. Smell and taste have dedicated areas of the neocortex. When those areas aren't being used, the other senses take them over, which is why a blind person can hear so much more acutely.

This was all new. His brain would probably take years to fully adjust, and the future beyond five seconds was too complex to see crisply. But something new was happening.

It occurred to him that he should cut out his tongue. Neurologically, taste and smell are branches of the same sense, and the difference between five and ten seconds might determine whether he saved his family or not.

But he still needed to interact with people in order to find Karl and Jane. As much as he might want to turn into the angry monster from hell—relentless, without speech, with a gaping hole in his face—he couldn't. He needed society, its answers to his questions. He had to kill his taste buds without losing the ability to communicate.

Which also meant the Churchill doctor was right. He needed a nose. Or, better yet, several.

So with bombs raining from the sky, with the Ford Grand Ranch periodically flying off the ground, with Timothy quietly terrified in the passenger seat wondering whether the face-bandaged hitchhiker he'd picked up was some sort of bin Laden-level terrorist, Preble took out his fish-gutting knife and began to scrape his tongue.

But he stopped after two scrapes. He was acting crazy. He wanted a life at the end of this, a life with Kasper and Jane. There was hopelessness to his single-point focus, to a man with no nose scraping off his bloody tongue, and he needed to maintain hope. There was a light at the end of this somewhere—he would find a way out for all three of them.

The A-10 eventually ran out of missiles, and no more came. Maybe they were too close to Winnipeg now, maybe some other reason. Whatever it was, the bombs stopped. In Winnipeg, Preble dropped Timothy off in front of a police station so he could register his vehicle stolen, then drove on towards Montreal.

He became increasingly puzzled by the fact that nobody was trying to stop him. No Canadian police pulled him over, either for stealing the car or just to ask politely why the Americans were bombing him. He wondered about it simply because he had to think about something other than Kasper or the iron taste of blood in his mouth over the long hours of the drive, but it didn't really matter. What mattered was that he was finally free to act.

Chapter 17

LONG BEFORE PREBLE REACHED WINNIPEG, THE WINNIPEG
Free Press, Toronto Globe and Mail, New York Times, CBC and
BBC had received Canadian satellite images of American bombs
falling on Canadian soil from a Liberal member of Parliament
who knew this could bring down the Conservative government.
The government, equally livid at the United States for bombing
without asking and at the press for covering the story, tried to pass
it off as a NATO military exercise. But since the road they'd
bombed was the only land connection between Churchill and the
South, this explanation managed to upset everyone: the Liberals
and NDP, who disliked Canada's too-close relationship with the
U.S.; the Inuit and other First Nations, who had been arguing for
decades that the Qualuunat government didn't care about the Far
North; the Greens, who didn't like green things to be blown up;
the Westerners, who didn't like to be bombed without bombing
back; the separatist Block Quebecois, who stated that it was
shameful to stay within a country that lets itself be bombed by
neighbours and let's have another referendum; and even a
majority of their own Conservative backbenchers, who saw the
willingness of another country to nonchalantly blow up parts of
Canada as being the last straw of a too-long-neglected military.

By the time Preble crossed into Ontario, the government had

admitted that the U.S. had simply violated Canadian sovereignty in order to take out an American terrorist making his way down to the States. But coming after the false NATO explanation, this was no longer good enough. The Canadian prime minister phoned the American president and told him that the next military plane that came into Canadian air space without permission would be shot down and damn the consequences, news services around the world were replaying the satellite images and making comparisons to Russia invading Ukraine, and nearly every nation on the planet was condemning the United States for unilaterally bombing its peaceful northern neighbour. Suddenly people in Tennessee knew where Manitoba was, and a preacher in Knoxville pulled out Paul Rodriguez's line about war being God's way of teaching Americans geography.

The Conservative government was still struggling to fight off a no-confidence motion in Parliament when Preble drove into Montreal in search of a nose. Montreal had a whole underground city, perpetually warm, and unlike Toronto or New York, it didn't have a police-state camera mindset. Given the bombing, he assumed he'd been under constant satellite surveillance since Churchill. Montreal's underground city might be his best bet of shaking that, and some new noses might help keep it that way.

The prosthetics lab was in a two-storey walk up across the street from Montreal General Hospital, but Preble first drove downtown and parked next to the Royal Victoria Hospital. He entered the underground city at the Bonaventure metro station and walked out at Gare Centrale, where he could catch a taxi under a covered roof with a scarf wrapped around his face, like half the people walking through the still-cold Montreal spring.

At the lab, he had himself fitted for seventeen different self-adhering noses. Each style was named after a famous person and cost nearly a thousand dollars due to his rush request, though he received a 30 percent discount on noses number two through five, and 50 percent on noses six and up. He knew his cards would still work—the government wanted him to keep using them so they could track him—but he used cash here. With seventeen noses and various hats and scarves to keep off spy satellites, they could no longer rely on face-recognition software to follow his movements, but if they knew which noses he had bought then it might make things easier for the computers.

He wasn't sure how sophisticated the facial recognition software was. Cities like New York had CCTV cameras on every block, every ATM machine, every traffic light, but he hoped that now those millions of hours of CCTV footage would have to be watched by human beings, not computers, at least until they got confirmed images of him wearing all seventeen.

It took the lab the entire day to manufacture the noses. It was already dark by the time he took another taxi back to the underground city, wearing a "Julius Caesar" on his face—sharp, overlong, perfectly straight, it was probably the nose that most matched his original—and sixteen others in his fanny pack. The nurse had wanted to put his ass on his face; instead he put his noses on his ass.

The underground city was crowded with early evening shoppers. He wandered around, first to a costume store for wigs, moustaches and beards, and then to think of his next step: how to cross the border back into the United States. He had napped in the waiting room of the prosthetics lab through most of his wait, but he was still sleep deprived, so he stopped for a coffee when he saw the big blue letters of the Tunnel Espresso Bar near the McGill metro. He paid for a double espresso and sat down to think. An older lady got up from the table next to him and moved to the counter to wait in line, examining the vitrine full of baked goods. She took her purse with her, but her phone was in her jacket, on the back of her chair, and she wouldn't notice.

Walking out of the Espresso Bar with the lady's phone, he googled, "Where is the easiest place to cross the U.S. border illegally?" The first result was a Quora article with a link to an RCMP report stating that the border crossing at Saint-Bernard-de-Lacolle was the easiest. The report was on illegal crossings from the United States into Canada, but Saint-Bernard-de-Lacolle was conveniently close to Montreal. And the U.S. Customs and Border Patrol didn't publish similarly helpful reports going the other way.

He found his car and drove to Saint-Bernard-de-Lacolle. There was a safari park and zoo on Roxham Road, less than a kilometer from the border. Roxham Road had once crossed the border, but someone had blocked it with a two-foot mound of dirt and two "No Entry" signs that looked like repurposed "One Way" road signs. A pedestrian or a motorbike could still cross unhindered. On the Canadian side, someone had erected a makeshift refugee welcome tent filled with blankets and food. It seemed like most of the people here really were moving from the U.S. into Canada rather than the other way around.

It all seemed too easy, so Preble avoided the road. He parked his car at the safari park and walked through the forest, paralleling the road. About fifteen minutes in, he stumbled onto an Arabic-looking man walking through the forest in the other direction, U.S. to Canada, followed closely behind by a woman in a black burka. In the forest at night, with only a narrow slit for her eyes, she was nearly invisible. And completely unidentifiable, which made him kick himself.

It was Roxam Road rather than the Rubicon and his nose was hidden by the scarf wrapping his whole face, but it still felt good to be crossing back into the United States, wearing a Julius Caesar. He thought he could understand a little how Caesar must have felt when he brought the 13th legion across the river against the explicit instructions of the Senate, to launch the Roman civil war.

"The die is cast," he said out loud, both to himself as a grim joke and to let the Arabic couple know he was there. They'd been trying to walk as quietly as possible and hadn't seen him yet. The man nearly jumped out of his skin, and the woman's eyes opened almost comically wide. Amazing how expressive eyes could be when that's all you could see. They ran, the woman's burka snagging on branches before they disappeared into the dark.

No, he thought to himself, the die had been cast long ago.

Chapter 18

A HOLE IN HIS FACE, DRIVING YET ANOTHER STOLEN CAR, Preble returned to New York City and looked for Fish. Presuming Fish's home would be watched, maybe even the Flea House, Preble went to the G-Spot. Despite being an anarchist, or perhaps because of it, Fish loved routine. He was one of those guys who had to sit at the same table in the same restaurant—the Green Spot Diner, though nobody called it that—every morning for breakfast and had been noticeably shaken when his regular waitress had taken six months of maternity leave. Preble had been with him the second morning with the new waitress and had seen how hard Fish had had to control himself in order to accept the disorder in his universe caused by the fact that he actually had to order. Fish was happy to give a 100% tip every time, he was happy to chat with the waitress about anything other than the menu, he always said, "Thank you" and "Please" and such, but he wanted the food to appear magically without his ordering, and he wanted his ten refills of coffee without asking. He thought it wasn't unreasonable given that he'd eaten the same breakfast—two scrambled eggs, home fries, toast, salad, and ten cups of coffee—every day for years. Besides nearly ruining his life, the police-station-with-Preble morning was the first G-Spot breakfast he had missed in four years.

Fish was also punctual. He walked into the G-Spot at exactly 8:00 AM, slightly shuffling in a loose yellow T-shirt that said "Tap-water" on it, unzipped hoodie, and what his friends called his "crotch pants"—pants that had been baggy five years ago and now sagged in the middle in a way that made him look like he had elephantitis. And, of course, Crocs. He made it within ten feet of the table before he noticed Preble, then stared, blinked, and said, "You've got one of those uncles, don't you?"

"What?"

"You know how uncles are always stealing your nose. When you're a kid." Fish put his thumb through his fingers. Preble was wearing a J. Edgar Hoover flat low pug.

"The only thing I remember about my uncle is that he drove really slow. Caused accidents wherever he went."

"But his own driving record was perfect, right?" Fish smiled, but instead of pulling up a chair, he examined the table critically. "I, uh, don't like to sit with my back to the door."

"I understand why." Preble moved over one chair so Fish could sit in his regular seat. Talking with Fish felt disorienting in its ease, like he had slipped back into his normal life, before the orange helicopter.

"They all learn in cop school that routine kills love, life, and the mark," Fish was saying, taking his hoodie off and draping it on a free chair. "But my routine bites back: death-by-boredom to the bastards. They sometimes follow me here, but always wait out front in a car. Still, you never know. If they were smart, they'd get one of their own working here as a waitress."

"Is that why you were always so weird when your regular waitress was out?"

Fish shrugged. "Fewer questions if people just think I'm neurotic."

There were no customers except for the two of them. Only their waitress, a black-haired, pale-skinned woman who was so thin that looking at her made Preble want to skip breakfast and double-down on coffee. "Is—"

"No, that's Flo. She's been here longer than I."

"A waitress named Flo?"

Fish laughed. "Some things are just meant to be. Like strippers named Chastity."

Fish's laugh pulled Preble back. He didn't want to be comfortable, or human. He had no right to be. It would just interfere with getting Kasper and Jane back. Still, a look in Fish's eyes made him ask, "You okay?"

Flo interrupted with coffee and two small ceramic containers of milk for Fish, then took Preble's order. While she did so, Fish poured all of one milk into the coffee, then drank the whole cup like he was chugging beer. Flo refilled the coffee, took the empty container, and walked back to the kitchen. Fish took a small sip of the new cup, then said, "Now I am. When you left, they took me in. No due process, no rights, no laws. They even went to the Flea House and questioned everyone who'd ever played with you. Everyone thought they were nuts, an army of suits storming a chess club and asking about how you played chess, how many moves you could see ahead, that sort of thing. You know how chess geeks are. They were like, 'If he killed some cops, why do you care how he plays chess? Does not compute.' And they were disappeared for a week or two. I was disappeared for three months."

Preble flinched. "Sorry."

"Nah. It was good for me. I'd been paranoid for so long without anything happening that I'd started to think maybe I was paranoid. Even paranoids can get complacent."

"I used to think you were just nuts."

"Everyone did. Not anymore."

"No. Not anymore."

"Like I said, the interrogations were good for me. People are friendlier. Water's not, but I'm working on that. Interesting insights into the Spanish Inquisition and such. They invented it, did you know? Waterboarding. And missing that many breakfasts probably wasn't healthy. Where's Kasper and Jane?"

Preble saw the sentence coming, but it still hit him. Through half-clenched teeth, he told Fish about Churchill.

"Jeez, Preble. I don't know what to say. But I want you to know that I didn't talk. I was going to. I had it all planned out. I knew everybody breaks eventually, so I told myself that the cottage would be the thirteenth place I'd tell them about. I don't know why thirteenth, it seemed like the highest number I could conceivably handle. I just decided on a baker's dozen, and each time I told myself that I was one closer to being able to tell them, it helped me focus and put a purpose on the torture sessions, and by then they wouldn't even believe me. It's an old lawyer's discovery trick. When you have to hand over the smoking gun memo, you drown it in ten thousand other memos. They stopped after ten. Only ten sessions, ten false leads. So I never told them. I was going to, though."

"Thank you, Fish."

Fish shrugged awkwardly. "You have a plan?"

Preble shook his head. "I can't think of anything other than finding the tallest tree and shaking it. Go to the White House, hold the president by the ankles and shake until he tells me where they are. Rip up the NSA, track down Thaddeus Bigman, eventually someone will know. It's your plan, really. You always told me to think like a monster, just a little bit. But it's not going to be just a little bit."

Fish scratched his nose, then looked at Preble as though caught. The fake nose was making him conscious of his own, and that made it itch. "The NSC has something called the Principals' Committee. It's chaired by the assistant to the president for national security and includes all the 'assistants' and 'deputies' who are the real power in this country. The secretary of defense is too public, but the deputy secretary of defense can do whatever he wants. You want a tree to shake, shake the Principals' Committee."

"The president's easier to find. Big white house, public address."

"Public war. And the president probably doesn't know anything."

"He'll know how to find Bigman."

Fish finished his coffee and waited for Flo to refill his cup and bring more milk. At the same time she brought Preble a coffee. When she left, Fish continued, "You know, you're not fighting one man here. You're fighting a whole system, and in a system the people are replaceable. They're a resource like gasoline or metal or coffee. You make this into a public war of you against society, and you'll lose. You're a criminal, a virus in the system, and once you're on the radar the evolutionary programming doesn't allow for the possibility of failure. You can hide and the system goes into passive search mode. But if you fight head on, it will all just escalate until either you are destroyed or the whole of society is destroyed. People like Bigman and all the cops you'll have to kill in the process are society's immune system. An immune system doesn't stop. It might fail to recognize a virus or it might fight so hard it kills the body, but once it's on it'll never just let go."

"I tried going off the radar. I tried surrendering."

Fish drained his cup again. "I'll help you. Under a few conditions."

"It's going to mean fighting."

"I'm an old man. If I wait much longer, I'll never get my punch in."

"Have you ever hit anyone in your life?"

Fish looked at his empty cup, annoyed that it was empty. "I'm a rational guy, Preble, and punching people is rarely worth it. If I punch society, I'll only make it more oppressive. A weak virus only strengthens the immune system. That's basically what a vaccine is. If you want to break down a body from the outside, you can do it in three ways. One: overwhelm it with something really powerful. Two: weaken its defences by giving it nothing to fight against, like washing all germs away, for a generation. Or three: use a targeted disease that makes the immune system go into over-drive, burn itself into an auto-immune disease and destroy the body itself. The third is sort of what Al-Qaeda tried with 9-11 or what we did with some of the covid lockdowns."

Flo brought breakfast, and a refill. She was an excellent wait-ress, knew when and how to be invisible—her skinniness helped—but still the sudden silence was awkward. Again, Fish waited until she'd left. "Once you get Kasper and Jane out, the only way to keep them safe is to change the system drastically."

"First, I need to get them back. I can't think about—"

"You can't pick your current moves without an endgame in mind, so bear with me. Our society will always hunt you because it's stuck on autopilot. It's automated in the same way an immune system is automated. Or a machine or cancer, all growth and connectivity with very little intelligence or responsibility. You can't just attack it. Again like an immune system, society is anti-fragile. The more you attack it, the stronger it gets. You need to shift it sideways into something that will leave all three of you alone."

Preble thought about his long-term prospects for living in peace with his family. He had no stake in society anymore, functioning or not. When he got them back, if Kasper and Jane were here, safe beside him, then he would face the long-term problem with a lot more clarity. But Fish's presence was pulling him back, and maybe he was right. Eventually he'd have to find a solution that let Kasper grow up into an adult in safety. He hadn't allowed himself to think much about them, except as a driving purpose. Not emotionally like this. He'd never been good at long-term anything, but he had a slow-chess grandmaster offering his help. "I wonder where they are."

"I wish I knew." Then, after a long pause, he added, "You're my best friend, Preble, and I love Kasper and Jane. I'll do everything I can to help you. But I can't lie to myself. Helping you means that a lot of people will get hurt. No, I shouldn't say 'hurt.' I should say 'die.' How many people will die to get them back? A dozen? Two dozen, before it's over? More? You're mad with grief, I get that, but I can't join you there. If I sign on, I'll share the responsibility as much as you. I can't do it just to trade two dozen lives for two. I can only do it if I think there's a good chance it will build a better world."

"Build whatever you want. But you need to know that I'm doing this for one reason only. Save Kasper and Jane. Everything else, and I mean everything and everyone, is secondary."

"I know."

"I play along with your thought experiment and then we move on to figuring out how to save them?"

"Yes. Saving them is the priority, but then you help me as well."

"Okay. So how? You've said you can't defeat a system. You can only take out individuals, and anyone can be replaced—"

"Yes, but you're Mister Potato Head." Fish made a gesture of pulling his own nose on and off.

"What does that mean?" Preble snorted in irritation that turned into an introspection of how the air flowed through his false nose.

"It means you can be an equal to the system. A fair fight. Mr. Potato Head isn't a normal individual. You can replace every part in a Mr. Potato Head, and he's still Mr. Potato Head. The original required a real potato for the central torso, and you could replace that potato every day, and yet Mr. Potato Head's identity wouldn't change. In a pinch, he can even use a tortilla and still remain Mr. Potato Head. That's the essence of a system."

"The United States is a potato head. I'm still just one person."

Fish spoke slowly, with pauses, fleshing out ideas as he spoke. "You need to get out of the category of individual, criminal, and into that of a state, even an enemy nation. Do you have nukes?"

"What, no?"

"I mean, is there any weird time trick you can do that would get you control over someone's nuclear arsenal?"

"No."

"Too bad. Nukes always seem to get a category shift. But maybe you can still apply the MAD process to individuals. The key is not to take out any individuals, just threaten to. If you remove someone, they just get replaced. But if you threaten to and your threat is credible and you target the right people, the right societal pressure points, then you can change the system."

Preble sighed. "Into what? A dictatorship, where the dictator promises to leave my family alone? I can't image that's what you want."

"No, no, no." Fish shook his head vigorously. "A dictator would always feel threatened by you. Centralized power can't tolerate alternate power centres. I'm talking about change into a democracy. We'll make this a free country."

This was a Fish conversation that Preble had gotten quite good at avoiding, especially over beers after chess. "This is a free country, so long as you don't, well, break the law."

"Yeah, and how did you break the law?"

"I took up two seats—" Realizing that sounded ridiculous, he switched tacks. "Anyway, as you've said, I'm not the standard case."

"Nobody's the standard case in Brownsville or Bed-Stuy or East New York or any other high-crime low-empowerment neighbourhood. What we the people have is a minimal, once-every-four-years type of power, while nearly everything in our lives is controlled by others. And yet, because of the vote, we persuade ourselves that we are free. No large election has ever been swayed by one vote. That individual act of voting makes little rational sense, except as a symbol. And as a symbol, what are we really doing? Handing over our personal sovereignty to a representative we know is lying to us. Even as a symbol, what it symbolizes is self-delusion and an abdication of personal sovereignty. Two hundred years ago, that made sense for the simple reason that there was no better alternative. But with the internet, today you could easily have direct democracy."

Now Preble interrupted. "Unless we go back to the stone age, there would still be people with information and power who would keep hunting me."

"You still don't get it. It's not really people hunting you. It's an automated machine, and that machine is what I want to break. Sure, Bigman might have triggered the machine's focus on you, but he's a cog in a system that sees you as a disease increasing in threat level. The machine doesn't care about your unique skills, it doesn't care whether you're innocent or guilty or whether coexistence is possible. You simply fit into the category 'threat,' which means you are to be neutralized. If you were a country, the decision would be channelled differently, and it would end at a human being, who would decide whether to attack or negotiate. But as an American citizen, you've entered an automated system. The information that matters is simply that the number of signals it's getting about you is increasing, which means your threat level is increasing, to which a proper response is to send more resources to fight you. The machine acts through people, but it was all automated. It's that automation that I want to destroy. And without it, you and Jane and Kasper will be free to live as you like, where you like."

"How?"

Fish nodded, earnest and emphatic now. "We take away all legal rights for institutions or corporations or collectives, including the right to contract. If nonhuman entities can't sign enforceable contracts, if we limit all bundling of rights, then power stays diffused and can't turn into a monolith. Adam Smith's assumption of atomistic markets becomes true again, and all the beautiful original justifications of capitalism will actually apply to the reality of the system. And here's the kicker. The diffusion of power will limit your ability to influence it. In other words, this is a natural adaptive mechanism for a society threatened by someone with your abilities. It will defeat you in a way no dictator ever could, because there won't be any pressure points you can squeeze."

"That's a hell of a manifesto, Fish. But how am I supposed to make all these changes?"

"Initially, Preble Jefferson will have to hang over the heads of all the entrenched interests, over the system as a whole. And the more the system changes, the less power you'll have."

"You want me to become the Boogeyman?"

"The sword of Damocles."

"I don't really want to hang over anybody's head. Not spend a lifetime like that."

"I've thought of that. It's funny some of the things you think of when they wrap your face with cellophane upside down with just a little hole for your mouth, and then pour water in that hole. Your involvement would be temporary, as a kickstart. Institutions and entities will always accumulate power, so we'll create one to take over your functions. An anti-DARPA. An agency whose task will be to continuously prevent the accumulation of power within any institution."

"Vanguard of the proletariat?"

Fish slammed his coffee cup down. "The exact opposite! Its function will not be to build a new future. I'm not stupid, I know every attempt at a utopia turns into a dystopia."

"But a government institution whose job will be to attack the government?"

"Not just government. I'm an anarchist, not a libertarian. No, the Department of Doubt will attack all institutions, any collective ganglion of power. Including especially corporations, which are already an extension of government power since they couldn't exist without a government-maintained legal fiction. You know how Ivan Illych said that all institutions end up working directly against the ends for which they were created? How schools stop kids from thinking, and so on? Well, the Department of Doubt will act as a second-order immune system that limits institutional growth and stabilizes the diffused system."

"And what's to prevent this department from taking over the government?"

"Its power must be purely negative. It can't do or build or create anything, not an institution and not some narcissist's ego. It can only tear down institutions, including periodically itself. It can only destroy."

Preble half frowned and half laughed. "A purely negative institution. No offence, Fish, but only a paranoid anarchist would come up with that—"

"Every creative act requires destruction. By trying to build institutions that we want to last a thousand years, we create massive cycles of destruction and creation. It took us a hundred years to accept that preventing forest fires only creates much bigger fires, that forests need to periodically burn. The world is inherently paradoxical. Time massages out paradoxes by turning them into cycles, but if you build paradox into your system then you don't need the cycles so much because there's no build-up. At the very least, the cycles are gentler. It's an idea intuited by voters even in our form of democracy who vote for abstract change, for disruptors rather than policy. That change is a destruction of established power centres, and it's the change much more than the actual policies that kept the country staggering forward. At least until the power learned to hop lightly from party to party. But that's the key of why democracy works as well as it does—not because it reflects the will of the people, which it doesn't, but because it periodically destroys power centers. And with no power centers, there'd be nobody coming after you."

Preble thought about it, then shook his head. "People will still see me as a threat."

"The desire for safety stands against every great and noble enterprise."

"What?"

"A quote from Tacitus. Never mind. The point is, you're not a direct threat." Fish paused, realizing in irritation that his coffee cup was empty again. "You're an abstract threat. Joe down the street won't see you as a threat until the media arm of the machine tells him to. We've all become automated. It's that automation that I want to destroy. And without it, you and Jane and Kasper will be free to live as you like, where you like."

Preble finished his eggs and looked up to see Flo two steps away with a refill for his coffee. She really was the perfect wait-ress. When she left, he said, "Okay. I don't have better ideas. Your cottage in Churchill was about as out of the way as Afghanistan, and it wasn't good enough. So let's save my family, and then we can change the world to whatever you want."

———

"They what?" Klurglur squint-frowned at his best quant analyst. Ilya Eduardovich Kasparov was no relation to the chess grandmaster, but he was better than any computer at drawing meaning out of communication maps. Anyone else, and Klurglur would assume the analyst had been staring too long at the sounds of silence.

"We don't know what was said, but we do know that there was an unusual volume of directed traffic between the NSA and NORAD's Strategic Nuclear Forces Command. And before you ask, no, it wasn't just the normal satellite imagery contact. That's a completely different set of cables. This was specific to the SNFC. These normally only talk during nuclear exercises, and during such exercises there is a lot of ancillary electronic traffic. Basically, when there's an exercise, much of the North American Strategic nuclear grid lights up. This was different. A series of calls from the NSA cube at Fort Meade to Cheyenne Mountain, most likely at the director or assistant director level."

"And the White House?"

"No spikes. But they get so much traffic from all over the country that it's harder to pull out unusual activity."

Klurglur shook his head again at the implications. "Are you telling me that someone at the NSA was trying to get NORAD to nuke Mr. Preble Jefferson in Canada?"

"No, sir. I'm saying there is an unusual spike in communications between the NSA and NORAD."

"And the White House doesn't know about it?"

"I have a much lower degree of confidence in that speculation. It would be fair to say that the White House was not central to the communications traffic."

Klurglur had dismissed the first several reports of intercepted communications indicating that the Americans thought Jefferson could see the future. It was ridiculous. He had initially assumed it was some strange police excuse for incompetence that had turned political, but the American government's seeming obsession with Jefferson made no sense under any normal scenario. It went far beyond just the biggest manhunt in the country's history, to a massive investment of resources. That now apparently included NORAD. Either the Americans really believed he could see the future, or the Americans were working to create the idea that they believed it. They'd bombed Canada, for God's sake. Nobody bombs Canada.

"Could Jefferson be an alien?" Klurglur asked. "A little green man? Not like our boys. A real one. From..." He pointed to the ceiling, not wanting to hear how ridiculous the question would sound.

Kasparov shrugged. "Maybe the Americans have just watched too many of their own movies. But yes, that's how they're behaving. We did intercept one communication where the White House seemed to be talking about him as a 'threat to our species.' And there were several others where they talk about him as though he were not human. But he has a family."

"Yes. Focus on the family. Any news on that?"

"Still nothing. If anybody knows, they're keeping it quiet."

"What about his friend? The Hungarian?"

"I don't know. The last report I read about him was that the Americans had let him go. Nothing since."

Klurglur sighed. He couldn't risk assuming his enemies were insane. He'd seen satellite footage of the road that the Americans bombed and a report on all naval activity in Hudson's Bay. As odd as it might be, the alien hypothesis made the most sense to him. An alien who could see the future? But with a human family and human friends? He picked up the phone and called the head of the FSB. "I want to talk to the Hungarian. Jefferson's friend. I want to talk to him."

President John Grape had let the NSA run with its operations against Preble Jefferson until the angry phone call from the Canadian prime minister. He and the prime minister had always been on very good terms, and suddenly a man the president thought of as a friend, one constitutionally incapable of getting angry about anything, was not just angry but threatening, a roaring mouse. The problem was that Canada had the doomsday device—they could cut off oil. Most Americans didn't know it, but Canada exported more oil to the U.S. than Saudi Arabia and the rest of the Middle East put together. Oh, they would never do it, and they knew that a real trade war with the U.S. would collapse their economy, but if they became irrational enough to turn off the spigot then the U.S. would also be crippled. The markets knew this, and the rest of the world had overreacted to the bombing, which emboldened the Canadians and put Grape on the defensive. His normal modus operandi when dealing with Canada was to not think about it; if he had to think about it, it included the words "cold front" or, if it had to be political, then "America's backyard." It seemed absurd to have the Europeans and Chinese and Russians and 52 out of the 53 countries in the former British Commonwealth telling him he was out of line. Even the prime minister of Vanuatu had phoned, threatening a Security Council resolution against the United States of America. Grape had pointed out that the U.S. would veto any ridiculous resolutions, and where the hell was Vanuatu anyway? Only Nigeria supported him, apparently because the Canadians had pushed the Commonwealth to temporarily suspend Nigeria's membership over human rights issues sometime in the 1990s and the Nigerians still weren't over it. But other than pissing off Nigeria, the Canadians had spent a hundred years building their reputation as international nice guys. People forgot that the Canadians could afford their free health care and education and international aid programs because they had nearly no military—they knew they could never fight off America, and if anyone else invaded, America would fight the war for them.

John Grape was as angry at the Canadians as they were at him. He couldn't believe the stupidity of anyone who would publicize the bombing, but it was done and the markets had tanked. Oil shot up by $50 a barrel and the Dow Jones lost 1,100 points in one day, triggering the circuit breaker in trading. And then, instead of just foreign leaders screaming at him, he had every major CEO saying that he was jeopardizing a fragile economic recovery with unhinged military stunts.

President Grape had personally called off the bombing after receiving the first phone call from Canada, and he was still shell-shocked by how hard it had been. He'd had to remind Hammond de Koek, his chairman of the joint chiefs, that under the constitution he was the commander-in-chief. The CJC had actually responded with, "Save that for the election, Mr. President. This is a situation."

His struggle to control his own administration improved after the stock market's reaction, as the K-Street lobbyists started showing up with appointments nobody remembered making at offices throughout the political apparatus. The bombing had created a negative feedback loop, and suddenly everyone agreed that it was time to stop bombing neighbours and how did the NSA get the authority to bomb people anyway? Weren't they just a signals intelligence agency?

⊏⊐

Thaddeus Bigman was unhappy as he waited for the chairman of the joint chiefs' secretary to put him through to Hammond de Koek. De Koek picked up the phone with, "The president didn't approve it."

"We had the bastard out in the open, Ham."

"The president didn't approve it."

"On whose advice?"

"Milton's. The entire State Department thought we were nuts. And frankly I think they're right."

"You should have gone through the vice president. It was Empty-Assfuck Manitoba."

"We're not going to drop the first nuke since Nagasaki on our closest ally. We're just not."

"That was just an opening position. You back down to carpet bombing, napalm, whatever it takes to turn a half-mile radius of permafrost into molten rock and end this problem. You don't go after a guy who can see the future with pin-point smart bombs."

"SAC got nervous, dumped this on the working group. End of story. They wanted to minimize political collateral. The only thing they approved was low-collateral ordnance. But that was as far as we could go with the White House involved. People do use that road. Not many, but enough."

Bigman didn't get angry beyond gripping the phone slightly harder. What he wanted to say was, If you want a job making decisions for the health of the nation, then stop thinking like an individual ant and start thinking like the queen. If you want to defeat cancer you don't worry about killing a few healthy cells. If you can't do that, you don't belong in the Pentagon or State Department or White House.

But what he said was, "They couldn't shift to a systemic perspective. They need to be fired."

"That's POTUS you're talking about."

"You're not a lieutenant, Ham. You're brass. So act like it. You don't ask POTUS the wrong questions and you don't get the wrong answers—"

"POTUS called me."

Bigman ignored the defense. "The Canadians lost their mind and went to the press with this. You think they would have gone to the press if you'd done it properly? They wouldn't have dared. But one 'smart' bomb—"

"Twelve. We fired twelve."

"So instead of using clusterbombs, you created a clusterfuck."

"Fuck you, Thad."

"You shot just enough of a load to bring the media in but not enough to solve the problem. And now instead of watching Mr. Preble Jefferson die in melting permafrost, you and I and the NSA and the White House will all be going through a nightmare of melting political allegiances as everyone dives for cover."

It wasn't until Bigman hung up that de Koek remembered he'd wanted to ask what Bigman had done with Jefferson's wife and kid. But he wasn't in the mood for calling back.

Fish left Preble at the G-Spot, drove home, took a cab to a subway station, changed subways three times, took another cab to another subway station, two more stops, and one more cab to the Chelsea gallery where his girlfriend of twenty years—he refused to marry, because that would have brought the law into their love—worked. He borrowed her car and handed her his own keys. "I'm going to do something illegal, so I need windshield wipers."

Rita handed him the keys to her Toyota Yaris with a kiss, then shouted after him, "It better not rain while you're gone!"

"Nobody hates the rain more than I do. I'll see you in a couple of days."

Fish and Preble met up at again an internet café in Baltimore. Neither one had been stopped, though Fish hadn't really expected they'd make it through the Holland Tunnel, let alone New Jersey or Maryland or anywhere near the NSA's private exit off the Baltimore-Washington Parkway labelled, "NSA Employees Only."

At the internet café they'd discussed their options and found a sort of middle way, between bullet chess and slow style. Thanks to Thaddeus Bigman's cultured telephone manners—he answered the phone "Bigman speaking"—it was easy for Preble to work backward to pick out the number. He didn't have to actually call. Once he had the number, they hacked into the Police Assistance and Warrant Department at Verizon to get the cell phone's location. That hack was as Al Jones, senior attorney in Verizon's Legal Department, whose redeeming virtue was his short name. As Fish kept stressing, Big Brother's eyes are systemic and disaggregated. Bigman's phone was in his office on the eleventh floor of NSA Building Two in Fort Meade, and if Preble were to call it, he'd answer it in less than five seconds.

"How'll you get into the building?" Fish asked.

"It doesn't matter."

"Sure it does. The more time you give them to get troops in, the more likely you'll end up springing the trap on yourself. Get a job."

So Preble went into the NSA site and gave himself a job interview. Unlike their sensitive systems, their Human Resources Department was externally accessible. It thought he was Beth Thompson, director of HR, logging in from home to book an interview for Preble Jefferson, entry-level tech support, security clearance pending, etc., etc. Even the NSA had problems with printer-drivers.

The computer insisted that he select at least one non-HR interviewer. He didn't feel like trying to figure out who would be appropriate for tech support, so he gave Preble Jefferson an interview at 3:00PM today with Thaddeus Bigman, assistant director of the National Security Agency.

Fish disapproved of Preble using his real name and of cutting corners on choosing the job interviewer. "What happens if this pops up on Bigman's calendar? Or if the security guard recognizes your name?"

"The name has to match my ID, and I don't have time for a fake ID. It's one now. The appointment's for three. I'll be in there by two. Outlook usually pops up notices fifteen minutes before the appointment. It'll be fine. Besides, he's the one I want to talk to."

Fish shook his head at the sloppiness of it. "You can't count on things going exactly as you plan. And what about security?"

Good fake IDs would cost a day or two, and Preble wasn't feeling patient. Not with Bigman—meaning Kasper and Jane—this close. They'd discussed waiting until 6:00PM, or whenever he went home, but Preble wasn't willing to wait. He had no idea how Bigman would leave—he might take the helicopter, for all he knew. And there was also a real tactical advantage in speed, in acting while the government was still off-balance from the Manitoba bombing backlash. Still, that was hardly what motivated Preble. "I'm sorry, Fish, I know you're right. But Bigman is right there."

They got back into their separate cars and drove south. Fish continued past the private NSA off-ramp without a wave to Preble, who took the ramp to an enormous parking lot, 18,000 parking spaces, with a giant glass square in the middle.

Chapter 19

PREBLE KNEW THAT THERE WAS ALSO A GLASS RECTANGLE behind the square, but from his approach angle it looked like a big dark cube in the middle of empty flatness, with thousands of parked cars pointing towards the cube in supplication. Appropriately, the precursor to the NSA had been called the "Black Chamber." Preble had seen pictures of the Kaaba at Mecca, and the two seemed like sister locations, same inspiration.

Before he could pray, however, he had to stop at security. With thousands of employees coming in and out every day, security at this point couldn't be draconian. The young soldier at the gate checked Preble's ID and typed into his computer to ensure Preble was expected, while two others swept the car for bombs. As he waited, Preble almost regretted not listening to Fish. It wouldn't take much for the computer to tell the guard that "Preble Jefferson" was not only on the visitor's list, but also the most wanted man on the continent right now. Or the man might recognize the name from the news. But the software itself was simply for clearing visitors against a pre-approved list, and if there was a criminal or terrorist on the pre-approved list then that was the problem of whoever made the list. The NSA often dealt with people whose names shouldn't be popping up anywhere, and nobody wanted the guard at the gate making those sorts of judgement calls. He was specifically taught to only check the list and check for bombs. The man was integrated into the software, not the other way around. He waved Preble through with instructions on where the visitors' parking was.

Preble parked the car and climbed out. It was a sunny day, and the thousands of cars in the lot all looked freshly washed, the air light with negative ions. Sunshine glinted everywhere, slivers bouncing off windshields, off the cube, each a little laser papercut to the eyes. Micro-cuts. They get you with a million micro-cuts. He wasn't even sure what the thought meant, let alone why he thought of it. Something Fish would have said.

He was thinking of his own government as "they." Of his own country as the enemy.

Whatever vestiges of his former self Fish had pulled back out from him, the cube of the NSA building cut off—though now he could see the second, rectangular building.

It was the enemy.

He'd had lots of opponents in his old life, but never an enemy. An opponent is a partner, indispensable for improving your chess or fighting skills. An enemy is different. With an enemy there is no fairness, no rules, only winning and losing.

He walked through the front door. There was a security desk and a massive metal detector on one side, three times larger than anything he'd ever seen at an airport. Employees walked in and out by showing badges and placing their hands on a fingerprint scanner. One security guard's job seemed to be just to wipe the scanner after each person with a disposable wipe. Preble thought of the 18,000 parking spaces around the complex and felt sorry for the old man—he looked medieval French, with a pudding-bowl haircut and heavy drooping moustache—as he repeated the same movement over and over like a robot. A machine accumulating several garbage cans full of used wipes behind him every single day.

"Visitor?" asked another security guard, this one a woman with military-cropped hair.

"Job interview. Jefferson. It was originally scheduled for 2PM, but I just got a call saying it's been postponed to 3PM. I was told to wait in the cafeteria."

The guard checked the computer. "Says here 3PM. You're too early."

"I know. They just called me and changed it."

"Who called you?"

"Someone from Human Resources. A Beth Thompson's assistant."

"Hold on." The guard pressed a button. "I have an interview here, says he was postponed to 3PM. Says he was told to wait in the cafeteria... Assistant Director Yagbig... He can't go in unescorted... Okay, I'll send him up."

The guard hung up the phone, then turned to Preble. "ID."

Preble handed over his driver's license.

The guard typed something into her computer, typing painfully slowly. Finally, she looked up at Preble and pointed to a chairless space between the windows and the security desk. "Wait for an escort."

Preble did so, wondering whether the absence of chairs implied that this was not regular procedure. Should he be sprinting upstairs instead of waiting? But less than a minute later a burly red-headed soldier, late twenties, walked up to the female guard, who gestured at Preble. The soldier nodded at Preble. "Follow me."

He escorted Preble to the elevator. Despite the cold fist that had been gripping his chest since he'd walked up to the cube building, stepping into the elevator made his heart race. He watched the guard first press the button for the tenth floor and then a small fingerprint scanner. Preble guessed there was no cafeteria on the eleventh and wondered why they hadn't just made the buttons themselves into fingerprint readers. The separate verification procedure made the process of riding the elevator feel solemn, important. Everything here caused echoes of Fish's charge that the system was "all growth and connectivity but no intelligence."

With a relief, the doors opened on the tenth floor. He hated elevators.

Without a word, the guard walked Preble to the cafeteria, told him to wait until he returned, and left.

There was nobody in the cafeteria except a middle-aged woman at the cash register, her hair up in a net, and another, slightly younger, stacking a sandwich cart. The two of them ignored Preble, talking to each other in a rapid-fire Eastern European language. Croat, maybe.

Preble bought a coffee and a blueberry muffin. It somehow seemed less suspicious than just coffee—bad guys don't eat blueberry muffins. Then he walked out of the cafeteria into a hallway of closed office doors, past a semi-open area of cubicles and back to the central elevator corridor, open on both ends. He'd expected to be captured by now, but the closer he could get to Bigman before he was, the less time there'd be for reinforcements and complicated decisions. He walked to the elevators and pressed the up button, hesitating. He'd love to make it onto Bigman's floor before he got caught, although he couldn't quite see far enough forward to make sure the doors would open on him again.

The red-headed guard came half-running around the corner, clearly tense, his mouth a straight flat line. He was the first person with the right fingerprints to arrive. "You were told to wait in the cafeteria!"

"Yes. I didn't listen."

"Huh? Why not?"

"Because I'm the bad guy," Preble said, feeling distant from the exchange, muffled by a memory. Kasper loved to role-play "the good guy" or "the bad guy," and it always came with an announcement of who was who. As he said the words, Preble heard Kasper saying them as he'd said them hundreds of times. I'm the bad guy. You're the good guy. Let's fight. Or vice versa.

"What?" the guard asked, not quite breaking Preble's absent spell.

"I'm the bad guy. You're the good guy. Let's fight." When the guard didn't react, he added, "The guy who can see the future. The person that the whole NSA is looking for."

"You still gotta wait in the cafeteria."

"The guy on the news. The guy Bigman wants to catch." With an almost-careless motion, he yanked the guard's earpiece radio off.

"Holy shit!" The guard pulled his gun out at exactly the same moment as Preble dropped his muffin, grabbed the gun, twisted, kicked the guard's knee and took the gun away.

DING, the elevator arrived. "I dropped my muffin."

They made it to the eleventh floor with the guard's finger-print. The door opened, and the two of them stepped out. As they did, Preble let his attention wander to the new floor as he took a big sip of coffee. The time-to-go sort of big sip you take before leaving the rest of your coffee on the table. The elevator landing was identical to the one below it, but that didn't stop him from looking to the left, to where the cubicles would be. The guard saw Preble distracted and with a big ham-hock of a hand knocked the gun out of Preble's grasp, then threw Preble across the landing. It sent coffee spraying against the beige wall. Seemingly before Preble could recover, the guard had his gun back and pointed at Preble.

Preble smiled.

With the other hand the guard picked up his earpiece off the tile floor and yelled, "Code blue, code blue. I have Preble Jefferson! The guy from the news. From New York. Code blue!"

Code blue. The NSA were the world's leaders in code making and breaking—couldn't they come up with something more original than "code blue?" Maybe it wasn't for him. Or was that just in a hospital? He'd read somewhere that if you can hear a code blue in a hospital, then it isn't for you.

———

Thaddeus Yagbig was irritated, but there was nothing he could do about it. He'd have to call Kiki—Katherine Anne, but she insisted on Kiki—and apologize, or at least let her know that she'd been right, that her new boyfriend did not, in fact, have a criminal record. She'd brought him over for dinner last night, and when the escargot-in-mushroom-caps appetizer was served the boyfriend had reached for a spoon. Okay, so maybe he wasn't familiar with an escargot fork or maybe he didn't think it was necessary since the escargot were deshelled, but any normal person would still have reached for a fork. Not a spoon. If you were freshly out of jail, that's when you reached for a spoon.

So Bigman had asked. The boy had denied. Kiki had become furious that he'd embarrassed both her and the boy. And so what if he was wrong? It had just been a question, "Did you recently get out of jail?" The answer, really, was, "No, I simply have poor table manners." There was no reason to apologize, except Bigman had pushed it too far afterwards. His wife and daughter both complained that he always pushed things too far. So he would call and apologize, tell his daughter she was right, that the boy was merely a monkey and not a criminal. Except that Kiki would be angry a second time over the fact that he'd run a check.

He buzzed his secretary, "Mary-Lee, get me my daughter on the phone."

"Right away. But sir? I just got a message that security has captured Mr. Preble Jefferson in the building."

"What? Where?"

His cell phone started vibrating on his desk. Ronald Stone. He let it ring. Between his secretary and his boss, there was no contest.

"At the elevators. On this floor. He's being held by security."

"Put me through to whoever has him." He put Mary-Lee on speakerphone and picked up his cell. "Ron?"

"You heard?"

"Yeah, but I don't believe it. Hold on."

A young military voice came in on the speakerphone. "Sir? Sergeant Greg Wales here. I have the package."

"You and what army?"

Ronald Stone interrupted, "The boy's ex-Seal. And I just ordered a team in. As soon as they're here, I want you to figure out what the hell is going on."

"Sergeant, you hold him right there." Bigman turned the speaker phone off. If a single soldier had captured Jefferson, that meant Jefferson had wanted to be captured. "Ron, you and I need to get the hell out of this building right now."

"What? No way, Thad. Wait till the team arrives if you want, but I'm going to meet this man face to face, and I want you there to figure out once and for all what is going on."

"I had a whole team in Williamsburg. Jefferson was cornered and he wasn't angry yet. This is a trap."

"We're in the middle of God-damned Fort Meade, we have the guy, and we still don't know what his deal is. All your theories are just that, theories. We have no idea what the fuck is going on. You've been running this on your own, you have the most experi-

ence with him, and you're God-damned going to question him.
That's an order."

Bigman hesitated for only a second. Ronald Stone had never
served and this wasn't the military. But Stone was a forty-year
veteran of Washington political wars, so he knew the game.
"When's the team getting here?"

"Five minutes."

"All right. I'll see you at the elevators in six." He hung up his
cell. He didn't know what Jefferson's plan was, but it was always a
good fallback rule that when you know the enemy wants something, don't allow it. Even if you can't figure out the full plan.
There was no way he was going to the elevators.

He clicked the speaker phone back on, wondering whom
Sergeant Greg Wales had pissed off to get detailed to security.
Though it could also be some sort of minor permanent injury, like
turning forty. "Sergeant?"

"Yes, sir."

"You still have the package?"

"Yes, sir."

"A team is coming up from Fort Meade in five to back you up.
Just hold the package there until they do."

"Yes, sir."

He flipped to his secretary. "Is there a helicopter on the pad
upstairs?"

"Ah, let me check...yes, there is."

"Make sure a pilot is waiting. That helicopter is mine.
Nobody takes that chopper, understand? And not a word."

"Yes, sir."

━━━

"Can I put my hands down?" Preble asked Sergeant Wales.

"Shut up."

"I'll put them back up when Assistant Director Bigman gets
here."

"I said, 'Shut up.'"

Preble waited in the middle of the elevator lobby, with
Sergeant Wales pointing a gun at him. Wales was tense, but not
visibly frightened. Like everyone else, he'd heard the stories of

Preble ducking bullets, but like all elite soldiers he believed that cops, reserves, and regular army were as liable to shoot themselves as the enemy. What worried Wales was that he knew a few of the guys on the team that Jefferson had taken out in Williamsburg. Those had been no "civvies with a badge." He'd transferred to security voluntarily for the unambitious reason that he wanted to be in the same city as his wife and kids. They made him too old to be getting shot at.

A door at the end of the elevator lobby opened and a team in armour poured in, shields and helmets and body vests and guns making them look like insects running an intrusion exercise. The team spread out as much as they could in the lobby, keeping to one side to avoid a crossfire. If the shooting started, only the package and Sergeant Wales would be dead. This didn't make Wales feel better. He backed up slowly, gun still on Preble Jefferson, while his back itched knowing there were twenty guns pointed through it. It didn't help hearing the team's heavy breathing—running up eleven flights of stairs in armour was hard work no matter how fit you were—and he exhaled his own sigh of relief when he was finally behind the now-friendly guns.

"Now what?" Preble asked, putting down his hands.

"Keep your hands up!" yelled the team leader, a Lieutenant Gaffrey, automatically taking control of the situation from Sergeant Wales.

"What difference could it possibly make whether my hands are up or down?"

"I said, 'Put your fucking hands up!'"

"And I said, 'No.' If you want to start shooting, start shooting. But don't tell me what to do."

The lieutenant was used to telling people what to do, and now didn't know himself how to react. He touched his earpiece, "Captain, we have the package secured."

"Hold him there," the earpiece replied. Preble would have heard it if he'd jumped at the lieutenant and grabbed it. "Director Stone and AD Bigman are coming to you. Take your orders directly from them."

"Copy that. Make sure they come through the east entrance."

"Will do. Out."

Then they waited, skin crawling with momentum that had no

outlet. The team had drilled this sort of thing dozens and dozens of times, but it was always dynamic, fast, full of tension, action and reaction. If someone didn't comply, you took him down. You didn't just stand there staring at each other while the target refused to raise his hands.

It took three minutes before Ronald Stone's bald head peeked around the corner into the elevator landing. He'd have a hard time walking through the twenty-one men squeezed into its east end. A straight-up violation of the U.S. Marine Corps' Manual's single most pithy instruction: "Don't bunch up!"

Stone took a deep breath and walked forward. "Mr. Preble Jefferson, I presume?"

"Yes. Where are my wife and son?"

"We'll have to ask Thad about that." He turned to Lieutenant Gaffrey. "Where is the AD?"

Preble swore a second before Lieutenant Gaffrey touched his earpiece. "He's on the helipad."

Stone could guess why Bigman was leaving and it sent a cold chill through him. He'd increasingly suspected that Bigman was a problem. The man was the single smartest person Stone knew, but he was also a sociopath. A paranoid computer that was starting to go haywire. But Stone couldn't figure out how running made sense now, with Preble unarmed and surrounded by a team. There simply wouldn't be space for a body to fit between all the bullets. "Lieutenant, I want two more teams up here right now."

"Sir? There's no need. And no room."

"That's an ord—!"

DING. The elevator doors opened. Despite themselves, the team had been listening to the conversation. Their training included a lot of things, but not trying to maintain sniper reactions while listening to an unarmed, coldly relaxed target chatting with their frightened boss. Preble's calm was infectious, and it cost some of the crack shots on the team a quarter-second of reaction time when the elevator doors opened. A few reacted quickly enough, but not all twenty, and there was a path empty of bullets through which Preble could dive over the sandwich cart and into the Croat sandwich lady coming for her afternoon-snack tour through the eleventh floor.

With the whole team on the east side of the hallway, the

inside of the elevator was out of the path of any bullets. But the sandwich lady was already halfway out, pulling the cart behind her. Preble yanked her face backwards, out of the way, as a bullet that would have shattered her eye bounced off the corner. Then he hopped on the cart, slipping predictably on a greasy mayo sandwich, knocked open the emergency trapdoor in the ceiling of the elevator, and pushed himself up as he shoved the cart with his feet into the first soldier who made it around the corner of the elevator. The Croat sandwich woman was flat on the floor, looking like this wasn't the first time she'd been around a hail of bullets.

Standing on top of the elevator box, Preble pulled the 12th, and top, floor doors apart and ran toward the staircase. As a fire-safety measure, the stair doors weren't fingerprint coded, though they did set off alarms everywhere. Alarms on top of alarms hardly mattered.

He made it to the helipad in time to see Bigman's lopsided face staring out at him. The helicopter was already too high to throw anything. He had no gun. He vomited a dry heave, totally unexpected. He hadn't even seen it coming with his window as the memory of the helicopter in Churchill blended with his present. Different helicopters but the same helplessness. He stood on top of the NSA cube, watching the shrinking helicopter surrounded by 18,000 shiny parked cars. He wanted his family back. For the first time the possibility that he really might never see Kasper and Jane again sank in. Might never come home again to have Kasper run out screaming "Daddy's home! Daddy's home!" eyes wide, arms stretched for a hug, a tiny gold flower bud opening for sunshine.

The thought stabbed in and finished the transformation.

Chapter 20

THE FIRST SOLDIER MAKING HIS WAY OUT OF THE DOOR TO the helipad was like a morning alarm after a too-short night of sleep. For the first few seconds and their millions and millions of passing alternate futures he ignored it. But then the way your arm might turn the alarm off without your mind ever quite waking up, his body reacted, on autopilot. Something similar had happened after the concussion of the bomb on the Williamsburg bridge, but this was more extreme. He moved to the door, grabbed a gun as the soldier came through it in the moment of time that was the present for everyone except Preble, twisted, punched, took the gun, executed the soldier, and the next one, and the one after him. Everything worked efficiently, a lifetime of training his body to react on instinct, something pulled out of the primordial past directed by a machine-like mind that processed the future with five or six or eight seconds of lead time his window now gave him. The only thing missing was the present now that he had no nose and damaged taste buds and an overwhelming arctic cold freezing everything except for a tiny disconnected core that had shrunk down to memories of Kasper asking, "Where is my blue car? The police car?" and then his voice excited, excited like nobody else he'd ever known in the world, "There it is!! Daddy, I found it! You play chest against the bad guys? That's your job? And Mommy's job is a writer. So she knows what's right? Do you know what's right? Daddy, I'm finished! Completely finished! Come wipe my butt! The poop's nenormonous!"

By the time he had a gun, extra ammunition and a shield, nothing could stop him. Three teams of elite commandos from Fort Meade died in the hallways of the NSA cube while Preble daydreamed about Kasper and Jane. And so did the few who came out of their cubicles and tried to stop him, though by a sense that seemed almost psychic, the overwhelming majority, thousands of unarmed NSA employees, stayed in their cubicles and just watched him walk by. When he asked which way Ronald Stone had gone, they pointed silently.

Someone had belatedly shut down the elevators, and Stone had been cut off by the fighting in the stairwell. Preble found him in a toilet stall on the tenth floor. He looked at Preble wide-eyed, not so much out of fear as shock. As though he'd suddenly realized that he'd actually been right when he'd told the president that Preble was a different species, not human. They stared at each other for a few seconds, Preble in the door of the stall, careless about his back exposed as only he could be, and Stone sitting on the toilet, fully dressed in expensive Italian shoes and a well-tailored suit, maybe Armani, and a red tie. Preble wasn't very good with fashion.

He continued to stare at the suddenly small Stone for a few seconds before either spoke, though Preble couldn't be quite sure about time passing anymore. Finally, he said, "About a month before I fucked up on that subway, Jane, that's my wife, tried to explain to our son Kasper where her brother had gone. Kasper wanted to talk to his uncle, and Jane explained that he'd joined a Buddhist monastery and was in retreat, studying at the monastery and couldn't talk on the phone and so on. Kasper listened to the whole thing. He didn't say a word, but he looked more and more worried. Then, when Jane finished, he asked, in that earnest confusion that he gets all the time, 'Why does uncle Edgy'—his name's Edward, but he goes by Edgy—'Why does uncle Edgy want to be a monster?'"

Stone looked bewildered.

"You see, Kasper thought a monastery was where the monsters lived, and uncle Edgy was learning how to be a monster."

Stone inhaled as though to say something, but Preble knew that there was nothing there. No thought behind it. Not as though he had something and changed his mind, but rather just an impulse telling him to speak that was stopped by the fact he had nothing to say. There was no possible future where words would have come out instead of empty air. "I don't know where they are. I really don't."

"You make monsters here, Mr. Ronald Stone. May I call you Ronald? Ron? You make monsters, Ron. And even if we fix everything. If you give me back my family, and if we go live on a little island somewhere where you, Bigman, the NSA, the United States, the United Nations, where nobody will try to hurt us ever again, Kasper Jefferson will always have a monster for a father. Jane will have a monster for a husband. If she wants to make love to her husband, she'll have to let a monster inside her. You know how many people I've killed since I met Thaddeus Bigman? I've lost count. That's how you know you're a monster. When you can't even count. Before him, I'd killed one. Not intentionally and not technically, but I still caused it. That man who died in the Trinity cemetery, Officer Edward Jonathan Smacks. Maybe his nephews called him Edgy as well. I caused Officer Edgy's death by fighting with Paskalakki and Gliny. In the subway. I was a good person who had caused a very bad thing to happen. Who had done a very bad thing. A thing that would have stayed with me for the rest of my life. For which I never really could have atoned, but it would have been my job to try, because I still would have been a basically good person. My friend Fish used to say that the law should be lenient because good people do bad things sometimes. But that's not my category now, is it? I'm no longer a good person doing bad things. I've walked through the door of your monastery. But each step was mine, mine alone, and if I need to I will continue to own each step as I turn this whole fucking planet into a monastery. Do you understand me? Except for one thing. No, two. Kasper and Jane. You give them back to me, and I'll lock up the monster. I can lock him up. You can't. The entire military might of the United States of America can't. The more you try, the more you feed the monster and the bigger he gets. So, you accept that the only thing in your control is to give me back the keys and then you let me lock him up. Not because you trust me but because no other method will work."

During Preble's speech Stone sat on the toilet, stared, and listened as only a man who knows his life depends on what he's being told will listen. But by the end, he wasn't just a man frightened of death. He had calmed down. He was one of the few NSA directors to have never served in the military, having joined the CIA straight out of law school, worked his way up through its legal department, followed by twenty years in politics first as a state senator, then twelve years representing the great state of Oklahoma in Washington, and then, three years ago, when he should have retired, should have moved into philanthropy, he'd gone back to government service. And that's what it was, despite the money and the influence and maneuvering and all the rest at which he was very good, his whole life had been one of service to his country. But the service had been blurred by those other things, and now, with Preble Jefferson staring down at him, it was as though the fog was burned clear. There was a chance that this man really could destroy his nation—Thad certainly seemed to think so—and Stone believed him even while he realized he'd completely lost trust in his assistant director. Thad seemed to have lost his mind as much as Preble Jefferson had.

He also believed Jefferson would cease being a threat if they just left him alone. But how many people would have to agree with that assessment before it would be followed? How do you turn a ship this size around?

All it took was one agency head to go the other way. One deputy director. If the president himself gave Preble amnesty, someone would leak it to the press. President pardons man who killed a hundred cops. The American people would never accept it, elections would shift, agencies would find legal loopholes around the presidential pardons and even if they didn't, black ops would get organized, police departments would organize their own institutional revenge. Getting the Jeffersons out of the country would help, but not completely. Maybe if they got them out to a military base, a very disciplined military base, run by a friendly nation. The Falklands, maybe. That just might work. A million logistical details to solve, but it might work.

"I believe you," Stone said, nodding for emphasis. "I really do.

And once we're out the other end of this, I think we can get you out of country, set you up with protection. An open prison where nobody can get in or out on an island somewhere. With your family. I'm thinking a British base in the Falklands or South Sandwich Islands. But I don't know where they are. Where Kasper and Jane are. These things are always on a need-to-know basis, but in this case it's extreme because Bigman knew you could get to anyone."

"But you are his direct boss?"

"Technically, yes. But I'm political. He's career. That makes things complicated."

"He's the 'deputy,'" Preble said, remembering Fish's comment about the deputies on the Principals' Committee.

"Yes. Plus he's been friends with the vice president since their college days, so he's always had more leeway than anyone else at the agency."

"Try."

Stone looked at Preble, then pulled his cell phone from his pocket. He dialled and waited. His career was over anyway, and he just might save his country with a final sacrifice. One for which he was far more likely to get jail time than a medal, but then, that's what made it a sacrifice. "Thad? It's Ron."

"How's things, Ron?"

"Where are you?"

"In transit. You?"

Preble snorted in surprise that even the NSA called their building "the Cube."

Ron grimaced into his phone. He had no doubt that Bigman knew his teams had lost control. "Still at the Cube. Listen, I think we need to pivot here."

There was a long pause before Bigman answered. Long enough that Stone suspected Bigman was talking to someone else. "You sound odd, Ron."

"Head cold."

"Yeah, germs attack where they know you're weakest. Maybe you should just hand the phone over to Mr. Jefferson so I can talk to him directly. Cut out the middleman and all that."

"Don't be an ass, Thad. You were right tactically about leaving the building, but wrong strategically through this whole mess. Just tell the guy where his family is. We'll stick them in a Brit base in South Sandwich where nobody else can get to them and pretend Mr. Preble Jefferson doesn't exist."

Another pause. "And he'll just happily stay there on a little island within ball-freezing distance of Antarctica so long as he has his wife and kid? Sure, for how long? And how long before the Chinese or Russians get to South Sandwich. Take a big bite. Or the Brits themselves, for that matter. They're an ally, but you don't give an ally the doomsday weapon. Not when you can't control it yourself."

"And your approach is what? Make sure that the doomsday weapon goes to war against us?"

"So long as we have the wife and kid, Mr. Weapon can't shoot at us. Not really. You're not on speaker phone, but I'm guessing he's right there listening in the future. It gives me a headache just to imagine all the things he can do. And of all those things, with all those powers, he can't get Kasper and Jane back, can he? He can't stop the helicopter. I saw his face. I saw him throw up as he looked me in the eyes. I can't see the future, but I'm pretty good at knowing what makes people tick, and my message to Mr. Preble Jefferson, if you're listening, is to turn yourself in. When you're chained up in a secure facility, with time-delay manacles on your wrists and ankles, then I'll bring your family to you. Not until then."

Stone blanched as he listened to Bigman and watched Preble watching him. Whatever else he could say about Thaddeus Bigman, the man had the best nose in the business. He'd guessed right about Preble not needing to hold the phone in order to hear what was happening—Stone could see it in his face. For a second, he wondered whether Preble would agree to Bigman's terms, such as they were. He wondered what he would do in Preble's situation. But then he knew Bigman too well: he couldn't imagine trusting him. "Listen, Thad. This is an order. Tell me the location of the family now."

"You keep using that word. We're not the military."

"I'm still your boss."

"This phone isn't secure, Ron."

"I'll give you any authentication code you want. Where's the family?"

"You've been compromised, Ron. Enthusiastically so, it seems. At any rate, you're relieved of your position. You'll find that the Cube is locked down."

"On whose authority?"

"SOP enemy infiltration."

"You shut down the whole God-damned Cube you lose signals capability worldwide! You can't do that."

"For a few hours. And everything's backed up."

"And you're going to run it from where? Cheyenne?"

Bigman grunted. "That was not necessary. I'm going to get off the phone now, Ron, because I like you. I've always liked you. And if you keep talking, you're going to talk yourself into a treason charge, and I'd hate to see that. Give my regards to Mr. Jefferson."

The phone went dead.

Without looking at Preble, Ronald Stone dialled the White House, the president's chief of staff. The phone rang too long before Mickie Fred picked it up.

"Ronnie, are you okay?"

"I'm fine. I need to talk to POTUS."

"I can't do that. And you know why."

"Damn it, Mickie, Thad's out of control."

"Yes, and you're under control. We'll try to get you out safe, Ronnie. Now, I've got to hang up on you. I wasn't supposed to pick that up in the first place, but I owed you that much."

"That was you on the other line with Thad?"

"It was POTUS. I'm here with him."

"Thad's going to take us all off a cliff."

"Thad has nothing to do with it. It's procedure, you know that. You helped make it. Now I really have to go. Take care, Ronnie."

And the phone went dead again.

Chapter 21

BIGMAN TOOK THE CALL FROM MICKIE FRED ON THE FIRST ring as his plane taxied on the runway. He was furious about Stone telling Jefferson that his next stop was Cheyenne Mountain, and his "Bigman speaking" sounded like an order to a firing squad.

"You were right," Mickie said.

"I'll call you in five hours."

"We don't have five hours. If Jefferson is at the Cube, we need some serious firepower to go in."

"Will POTUS authorize flattening Fort Meade?"

"Nothing crazy, but the place is a military base."

"Go for it. Someone might get lucky. While you're at it, you might want to call Hammond de Koek and General Lefflen, he's the base commander at Meade, and tell them there's a good chance Jefferson will try to get out using the tunnels."

"You have tunnels?"

"Everybody has tunnels, Mickie. Ron knows about ours, and he's probably told Jefferson, so whoever is running the op should know to plug them. Lefflen didn't have access to the schematics, but the files will open up for him as soon as the infiltration protocol goes through. Which should have happened already. If it hasn't, tell him to call me."

Bigman looked up as the government plane took off. The lone stewardess was sitting on a backward-facing chair, looking at him like she wanted to tell him to turn his cell phone off, as if this were a commercial flight where everyone was too stupid to know that cell phones were on completely different frequencies than airport communications. One of those grandfathered nonsense rules that all the sheep obeyed, like the shoes. Lucky for her, she didn't dare. She was striking, tall, long-necked—

Mickie Fred was still telling him that they'd get Jefferson.

Bigman cut him off. "No, you won't. Not until you send something that can flatten a square mile. Which you will eventually. But until then, we play anyway."

There was a pause before Mickie Fred added, "POTUS has a press conference in the Rose Garden tomorrow."

"I see no reason to cancel it, do you, Mickie?"

Another pause. This one was long, with a lifetime of difficult decisions. "Uh, I guess I'll just add extra security."

"You do that." Bigman hung up and nibbled on his lower lip absently, trying to gauge whether Vice President O'Reilly would have nuked Manitoba. Probably not, he had to admit to himself, but he'd certainly do it sooner than John Grape.

He dialled Garland O'Reilly.

"Thad."

"Garland. How are you?"

"You tell me."

"We have him pinned in Fort Meade for the time being. I just talked to Mickie and he said it's unlikely POTUS will allow us to deal with it seriously."

"Hah. You want to bomb it, don't you?"

"A saturation bombing campaign, a mile perimeter that we tighten inwards either with cluster bombs or napalm."

"You know how many residences there are on that base, Thad? How many geeks we have living there. Bright minds who we can't just sacrifice for your pet project. How much equipment? Just the semiconductors, supercomputers, cryptography labs and chip plant are in the hundreds of billions, and that's not including all the off-the-books stuff that you know more about than I do. You guys have single-handedly almost burned out the entire Maryland electricity grid several times. You think we'll just write you a check for new equipment?"

"'You guys?' Weren't you in the NSA during the '06 burnout?"

"Your memory is failing you, Thad. I got out the year before. '06 was my brief stint in the private sector."

"Look, Garland, Jefferson is not my 'pet project.' He's a risk and an opportunity, though granted, an unusually large one of both. But the reason I'm calling you is to plan for the possibility that without the required sacrifices he might get away. If he does, it would be wise for you not to be in the same location as the president. Just want to make sure you're not going to be at the White House tomorrow, sir."

"You're not cancelling?"

"It's not up to me and would send the wrong message. Mickie will increase security."

"After all these years, you still manage to frighten me sometimes, Thad."

"We're all just doing our jobs. All of us."

O'Reilly snorted. "Including John?"

"Especially the president. He has the hardest job of all. But in case something happens to him, we do need an alternate power center. Preferably one that is more effective."

"How many years have you been planning this?"

"Until last year, I never imagined something like this. But it's my job to make contingency plans and turn disasters into opportunities. I know you agree."

"I'm not agreeing to anything until I see how this plays out. But, yeah, I guess I would write a check for new equipment. If it comes to that."

Stone did tell Preble about the tunnels, but Preble decided against them. Too many ways to get trapped in a tunnel, too much like an elevator. But Fort Meade was the fourth largest military base in the country, and the largest employer in the State of Maryland. Even if the majority of the 40,000 employees were support personnel for the NSA, many of them had some military training.

Besides the live-response teams that had already gone into the cube, there were about a thousand active-combat personnel on site, with nearly half in a position to be armed and deployable within forty minutes of the alarm.

When Preble Jefferson walked out of the Cube, the first thing that hit him was the awful wailing of the base alarm, followed by bullets from the earliest soldiers who had formed a perimeter around the front doors. The fourth and last response team had been sent to the tunnels, but more and more soldiers were running to the enormous NSA parking lot in scattershot fashion. To Preble, the whole mobilization looked chaotic, as though the base had never practiced for this. Nobody seemed to have expected three of the four rapid-response teams to be killed during peacetime. This was American soil, after all.

Still, at least some of the officers were organizing the new arrivals into manageable chunks, screaming about goat ropes, clusterfucks and hairballs in between shouting at people to shoot Preble Jefferson. His latest SWAT shield, picked up from one of the response teams, stopped everything it needed to stop, but it was just a matter of time before someone brought in Bradleys, missiles or a .50 cal. There was a low concrete barrier around the front door of the Cube, a final security redundancy in case a truck bomb made it onto the base, which allowed line-of-sight into the parking lot. About two dozen soldiers were using the barrier as cover, with just their eyes, helmets and guns peeking over the top. Behind it, Preble could see an immense arc of soldiers beginning to form. Nearly a full semicircle, 180 degrees of bullets that would come at him if he made it past the barrier.

He wanted to leave. He shot every head that peeked over the barrier, then everyone on his right, dropping the M-16 and picking up a new one whenever he ran out of bullets. Then he ran, his shield to the left blocking bullets from that side. Soon, no bullets came from the right. Nobody from the left ran to cover the right side. They shot at him through a sense of shock, knowing instinctively that the right side was a death zone, and thanking their raw blind luck for being on Jefferson's shield side, even as they continued to fire.

That fifty-fifty division, harsh as a coin, stunned every person in the NSA parking lot, and, as the various streams of footage were viewed in Washington and Cheyenne Mountain and Beijing and Moscow, everyone who watched. It wasn't just the fact that Jefferson shot and killed nearly two hundred soldiers who were trained, armed and ready. Soldiers, not cops. It was the fact that he hadn't killed the ones standing on his left side. The cold open possibility implied by the fact that he hadn't bothered to kill the rest left a sense of terror in decision-makers around the world. A handful of advisors pointed out that it made sense, that Jefferson was killing the minimum he needed in order to achieve his objectives. But the politicians who saw the footage around the world reacted on an emotional level, not an intellectual one. Killing everyone would have been war. Killing no one would have been human and decent and proper. Shooting every which way and in the process killing half would have been understandable, a defeat at the hands of a particularly tough enemy, but still human. But killing every single man and woman on the right side and leaving everyone alive on the left was too much like a machine. There was something evil in the geometry.

The advantage of the shock effect was that once he broke through the perimeter, the soldiers didn't follow him. They'd heard nothing about Laplace's Demon or foreign supersoldiers, and nothing had prepared them for what they saw. It was too unreal, too much like a movie. They guarded the perimeter their NCOs had quickly formed with courage and determination, but once Preble got through they didn't move, they didn't chase him as he ran to the Land Rover he'd parked at the outer ring of the parking lot. The only exceptions were two helicopters, which Preble shot down as soon as they were within range.

Klurglur always had a satellite over Washington, and, by satellite geography, Fort Meade was Washington. Now he sat at Moscow Sigint Command, a clearing centre for all signals intelligence information that made its way through Russian wires, lenses and microphones. In a nod to Hollywood, the central video room was the size of a small warehouse with hundreds of computer screens, nearly half of them actively watching footage from around the world. Nothing this open would have existed in the days of the

Soviet Union—but where the KGB had spent half its time fragmenting and dividing information, its successor, the FSB, had learned the value of transactive memory, of having all the people monitoring information talk to each other, know each other, eat together, and put pieces of puzzles together. Mostly this was news and other public information, of course, not source-sensitive stuff, but satellite feed could be easily put through onto any of the monitors.

Now the whole room sat watching a satellite view of the NSA parking lot. Seen from directly above, the whole thing had the look of an early generation video game, if slightly surreal in the way the human shape became visible only when someone sprawled out on the ground: from the satellite's perspective, one head was turning all the heads on his right into people.

Apparently, the NYPD and NSA were not insane. The Americans had truly created a super-soldier, lost control and kidnapped his family for leverage. It brought to mind one of Klurglur's favourite Winston Churchill quotes about Russia: "In Russia a man is called reactionary if he objects to having his property stolen and his wife and children murdered." It was nice to see that the Americans were finally catching up. But no amount of satellite footage or other intel gave a hint of where the family was.

Until he'd seen this footage, Klurglur had mostly been thinking of ways to make the Jefferson problem bigger. If the Americans had a thorn in their foot, it would be nice to push it in a bit deeper. But seeing the way Jefferson cut through several hundred soldiers at Fort Meade, Klurglur understood that he'd been seeing the whole thing through far too small a lens. An army of Jeffersons would be terrifying. The perfect soldier or an unstoppable assassin.

This time Russia had no Rosenbergs, no Ring of Five in Cambridge, no moles inside the Manhattan Project. Klurglur dialled the number he'd been given for Jefferson's friend.

"Hello? Who is this?"

"Am I speaking to Robert Legmegbetegedettebbeknek?"

"You called me. You introduce yourself first."

"Mikhail Alexandrovich Klurglur, chief of FSB's Foreign Directorate."

"The head of the KGB?"

"FSB now, but yes."

"Jesus Christ. What do you want?"

"Nothing. Just to give you my direct number."

"Why?"

"Things seem to be escalating. You may need, what do they call it in the American TV shows, a lifeline? If you need to call, then call. That's all."

"1956. That's all I have to say to you."

"That was a long time ago—" He stopped, because Fish had hung up. 1956, the year the Soviet Union had invaded Hungary. But the man now had his number.

———

Preble drove onto the Baltimore-Washington Parkway and passed by Fish sitting in his Yaris under a bridge overpass, a half kilometre past the NSA on-ramp. They'd agreed on that as a backup, with secondary and tertiary meets in Washington, DC, and Baltimore. Now Preble honked and saw Fish pull out, several cars behind him. He kept expecting helicopters, roadblocks, missiles, something. But nothing came.

They met up at Old Glory on M Street, their secondary meeting location and one of the few "power restaurants" in Washington that didn't require a reservation. Informal, noisy, but so popular with lobbyists that it was unlikely to be bugged. Preble had years ago resigned himself to the idea that Fish was an endless storehouse of odd information—he said paranoiacs loved data because the more data they had, the more patterns they could pull out. The difference between healthy paranoia and unhealthy was that most ambiguous of things: reality. At any rate, if Fish's storehouse of data included unbugged restaurants in Washington, all the better.

A heavy middle-aged man who looked more like a senator than a waiter came to take their order. Fish asked for sardines.

The waiter shook his head. "I get people ordering things that are not on the menu all the time, but that's the first time anyone's ordered sardines in here. Would you like some onion and garlic with them?"

"My friend just wants to blend in today," Preble said, irritated but trying not to show it. "Be inconspicuous. He's paranoid about excess attention."

The waiter smiled. "That would be 90 percent of our customers. The other 10 are tourists."

"I just have sardines on the brain," Fish explained. "The big fish have mercury and all sorts of other toxins, and if nobody orders the little ones they're just used to feed the salmon farms. I guess I'll take the Creole fried catfish wrap."

"Environment," the waiter said, without a smirk. "Got it."

Preble ordered the pulled smoked pork though he doubted he could stomach a bite of anything, and the waiter left. When he did, Fish continued, "I always imagine sardines crawling into those sad little cans, locking themselves in, and leaving the key outside."

"You still have the six crazy locks on your apartment?" Preble didn't want to think about Fort Meade anymore, though he'd already given Fish a terse summary of what had happened. Long before Preble had made Fish's paranoia real, Fish had installed six bolt locks on his front door, three of which turned clockwise and three counterclockwise, so that if any burglar, even one with government-issued tools, picked his way in, he'd always be locking three of them.

"That's not why I'm thinking about sardines. I get goofy when I'm stressed."

"You think I should give myself up?"

Fish shook his head, then rubbed his face slowly, hard. "No. No, I don't. I just...this is getting out of control."

"You want out?"

"We're in now, and the only way out is through. It's just...so many people. So many families. Children suddenly without fathers."

Preble bit his lip, staring at all the Americana on the walls and hanging from the ceiling. Flags, lamps, paintings, badges, rear-ends of cars, even a life-sized Elvis playing a guitar. "No," he finally said. "I can't think like that anymore. I'm not looking for right and wrong or other people's families or anything other than Kasper and Jane. All those people I've hurt, if they need to find their revenge or do what they need to do, I will understand and deserve it. Like the bear, only a child would judge the bear.

"Breaking study shows killing hundreds cures fundamental attribution error."

"What?"

"Nothing. I told you I get goofy when I'm stressed."

"I'm sorry, Fish."

"Don't apologize to me!" Fish seemed suddenly angry. "I'm making my own moral choice here too. I'm helping you." Just as suddenly, he deflated, then looked around to make sure nobody was close, that nobody was talking on a cell phone while looking at them. "I can't believe they just gave up."

"They didn't give up. They were in shock. And Bigman had transferred all information capability out of the Cube to Cheyenne Mountain or wherever else they—"

"Probably the C.I.A.'s Counterterrorism Center at Langley."

"I guess they were blind for a few hours, didn't want to get the local police in. Their knee-jerk response is probably to try and keep it secret, which means no local cops. It's impossible, of course. In an hour it'll all have leaked out. By now maybe. But the idea that the military wasn't enough, not even in the middle of Fort Meade...They always think the military can solve things if they get out of hand."

Fish shifted weight, making his wooden chair creak in complaint. "You sound like me."

"I've been running from them for nearly a year now."

There was a long pause that wasn't interrupted by either of them. Not by food. Only by a number of cell phones ringing in the restaurant. Finally, Fish said, "I wonder what else is going on behind the scenes."

"What do you mean?"

"Nothing, really. I just know these sorts of people never want to let a crisis go to waste. Every crisis is an opportunity for someone, and you've created a massive crisis. Means massive opportunities, means manoeuvring. Look how many people are talking on cell phones right now in this restaurant." He moved his head left to right in a gesture that would have been at home in New Delhi and would've been funny on Fish under other circumstances. "At least 20 percent. You think it's always that high? Maybe, but I doubt it. I just wish we knew who was moving where, maybe we could use it."

"Well, I'm pretty sure Bigman's moving to Cheyenne Mountain, Colorado."

Fish nodded. "Safest place in the world from you. Layers of doors, long elevator rides underground."

"I hate elevators."

"All way over five seconds."

"You don't have an army of anarchists somewhere in your back pocket? Ready to go?"

Fish smiled. "Anarchists are a bitch to organize."

"As I see it, that only leaves me with one place to go. And it's nearby."

"Shake the president?"

Chapter 22

THE WHITE HOUSE PROHIBITED EVERYTHING: PURSES, BAGS of any kind, food and beverages, baby strollers, cameras, any sort of recording device, cigarettes, any and all grooming items, anything with a point, including pens and pencils; and they didn't allow tours. Most of the time. Occasionally pre-approved groups of background-checked individuals who did not have any of the offending items could enter, guided by uniformed National Park Service rangers. These groups gathered at the corner of 15th and E Streets, where a big sign gave a comprehensive list of the prohibited items that looked like a thesaurus entry for "stuff." A disclaimer added, "Please note that no storage facilities are available on or around the complex. Individuals who arrive with prohibited items will not be permitted to enter the White House."

"Powers derived from the consent of the governed," Fish mumbled.

Preble had wanted to arrive at the corner with a hockey-goalie bag filled with guns, ammunition and the SWAT shield from the cube. It looked like it had survived two wars and six Indonesian riots and begged to be used again. The gear included a vest, and given how many guns were likely to be on the White House roof, that felt reassuring.

But Fish had convinced him that a combat vest wouldn't stop

the sniper rounds that would be coming at him from all the "ant hills" around the White House—basically every tall building within a ten-block radius. "I love the idea of you going in combat gear," Fish had said over a pecan pie while they'd been planning their assault, as Preble marvelled that he could eat dessert. Preble had eaten exactly one bite of his pulled pork. "Before 9/11, seeing a man dressed for Armageddon on a city street would have attracted everyone's attention. Now it's somehow become normal. The only person who might make a comment is an occasional tourist from Minnesota saying, 'Thank you.' And if you went all geared up, the city cops would assume you answer to a higher authority. They'd became courteous, professional and respectful. I hate the idea that you can walk down the street armed to the teeth so long as you wear the right colours, and love the idea of using the security obsessions to undermine security. But it won't work on the Secret Service."

"I could go in with just defensive gear. Unarmed. I want the shield."

"You still wouldn't get within five blocks. Besides the snipers, Secret Service has walkers on all those streets as well as floaters in cars examining everyone who looks the slightest bit off. Your gear is from the Fort Meade rapid reaction team. It doesn't belong. Even if you got DC SWAT's equipment, no SWAT guy walks alone down the street all geared-up, not here, and even a whole SWAT team wouldn't get anywhere close to the White House without some serious pre-clearance."

"I could arrange that with a few tricky phone calls."

"And Secret Service will still stop you. These are the last guys in the country who continue to use old-fashioned human methods. They don't have the thickness of a police department or a military organization, they rely on computers as little as possible and avoid anything that can be made predictable. They want to recognize each face they let anywhere near the president, and the more armoured-up you look, from a hat on down, the longer they'll scrutinize you. And they'll see right through you. First of all, you don't know how to walk."

"Wha— Oh."

"Yeah. You could fake any particular movement so that it wouldn't trigger a reaction, but any sniper or walker watching you would just accumulate a gradual sense of something being wrong about you. What does that gear weigh? Forty pounds, not including the guns? Guys who spend twelve hours a day wearing that shit walk differently. And while an NYPD cop might not spot that difference, the Secret Service will. The advantage of wearing the gear in New York is that nobody looked at your face. They saw the uniform and their brains stopped working. The Secret Service is not going to be overwhelmed by any symbol of authority. They're going to be looking at your eyes and at the way you move. And they'll have several blocks of white space during which to make that evaluation. You'll be in a firefight by the time you hit H Street, and sure, you can take them all on, but the first thing any bodyguard does is move the VIP out of the attack area. If you want to have any chance of reaching the president, you need to move the moment of recognition to at least the White House perimeter. Otherwise, you'll end up killing a lot of good people doing their job, and it will be for nothing."

Fish looked angry. He clearly hated the idea of what their plans would cost, and the more people died, the more he hated it. Preble, the one actually doing all the killing, had become numbed. His own dad, who'd been a sort of small-town Hemingway, ex-special forces turned journalist, had once warned him not to travel to countries that had just finished a war because once you rupture the taboo against killing, life becomes cheap. Seeing it from the inside, it really was like a sort of rupture. Every person he'd killed since that subway ride had killed a little bit of him. The numbness that increased his window was deadly as bullets to his soul and to whatever relationship he would have with Kasper and Jane when this was over. But there was a hierarchy of needs here, and Kasper having a life free from government experiments came first. Soft things like souls and strangers didn't come close.

Terrorists don't wear shorts, Fish said, so Preble dressed in cotton shorts and a tight white T-shirt. No bags, no coat, nothing that looked like it could hide a weapon, not even a hat to suggest the desire to disguise himself. Despite his window, he felt naked, with a nagging sense that the Nixon nose on his face was upside down, or glaringly obvious in some other way. He'd never worn it before, so it shouldn't be in any of the computer databases. Still, it didn't feel like much of a shield to hide behind.

As it turned out, Fish was right. The snipers and walkers and floaters focused their attention on people with bags, because bags could contain weapons or bombs, and on people with hats or beards or other things that could be used to try and fool all the face-recognition security cameras lining the streets. There was a moderate amount of regular civilian traffic on the roads around the White House, and so the Secret Service did end up having to follow a system of sorts. They focused on what their instincts and experience told them were potentially high-threat individuals, and let the cameras deal with the rest. A Nixon nose could still fool a computer; it was too good to be noticeable at a distance, and too unusual to be a standard target of extra attention the way a hat, beard or sunglasses were.

The shorts, white shirt and Nixon got him unmolested as far as the White House checkpoint at 17th Street and State Place. It was the entrance used by most staffers and was closer to the Rose Garden than coming from the east. The checkpoint itself was a small concrete block of a booth, with wrap-around body scanners and metal detectors to pass through. Objects through the right scanner, people into the centre, and security staff on the left, where the path was clear.

Two very alert Parks Service uniforms stood inside, and two heavily armed guards—dressed the way Preble had wanted to dress—stood just outside. Invisible in the background, somewhere behind the buildings and trees, he could just make out the amplified sounds of the president's speech. He was recounting a trip, when he was just a governor, a tour of the Eiffel Tower that he'd taken with the mayor of Paris. "When I first saw that magnificent structure I was awed by it," President John Grape was saying. "Struck by its magnificence. Finally, I asked the mayor, 'Mr. Mayor, how many barrels a day does she give?'"

There was a pause for laughter.

"Well, I never was able to convince folks to let me drill in the middle of Washington, so today we're doing the next best thing. A major step towards independence from foreign oil supplies, towards—"

"Who are you?" The guard was around fifty, with a policeman's moustache and a lantern jaw, one of those people whose face morphs over the decades to take on the stereotyped look of his job. His partner at the metal and chemical detector belt—present despite the rule of no stuff, presumably for journalists wanting to bring in dangerous items like pens and notebooks—was much younger.

"Press. For the speech."

His eyebrows slowly climbed up his forehead as he looked Preble up and down, pausing briefly at his naked legs. "The speech has started, nobody comes in or out. And you're at the wrong gate. And there's a dress code." Without taking his eyes off Preble's face, he stuck his hand out. "ID and clearance papers."

But then, without waiting for Preble's papers, despite his generally low opinion of the media, despite dealing with brain-dead tourists trying to come in day in and day out with prohibited items, and despite the fact that Preble's dress completely ruled out any sort of attack, the older guard suddenly reached for his sidearm. He had no idea why. His palm just got itchy, and he'd been in protection long enough that when his palm got itchy he pulled his gun and tried to figure out why later. His partner reacted almost in unison, triggered by his partner's reaction but with almost no lag time. It was as though they were on some wireless network together. The two guards might be dressed in Parks Service uniforms, but they were clearly Secret Service.

Preble was impressed, especially since this was probably where they hung Secret Service guys who were too grey or too green to serve as the immediate bodyguard. But Preble could tap into their network, or at least act as though he had. As the two guns came out, he stepped through the narrow security corridor, realizing as he did that there was a button the younger guard could have pushed that would have slammed a metal door down on it. But he'd reacted with his gun first.

The rest was almost routine. A remnant within him still hated the thought, hated the fact that it was true, and hated most of all the fact that he was able to think about it while making sure the two guards shot each other. That taking the older one's gun and putting bullets through the faces of the two armoured guards running in wasn't something terrifying, wasn't even sufficient to take up all his attention. The speech had stopped in mid-sentence as the bullets rang out, just pops really but also loud as a gong: the "moment of recognition." Security protocols were triggered, the president was mobbed by bodies in black suits and a few fake reporters pulled out their secret service firearms and screamed for the real reporters and foreign dignitaries to get on the ground, NOW!, both to make sure the shooter wasn't one of them and to get a clear line of sight.

Preble was on a clock now, but he took the time to rip the shirt off one of the armoured guards, then take his vest, earpiece and M16. Too bad they didn't have shields. Meanwhile, sophisticated triangulation equipment on the roof of the White House pinpointed the location of the shooting as the guardhouse. The information travelled by computer to Secret Service Command in the basement of the White House, by voice to every human member of the Secret Service present, including snipers on the roofs of each wing and each "ant hill" in the area, and—in a weird bit of security planning that seemed almost a joke or someone's brilliant idea that if a thought is clichéd enough it becomes unpredictable again—inside a tree just off the front lawn. And then by computer to Washington PD, which always had a unit on standby for White House emergencies.

Within seconds, Preble was the focal point of a lens of sniper muzzles with a radius of half a kilometer. More than two dozen of the best marksmen in the United States waited for him to step out of the hardened little guardhouse that was giving him temporary shelter. Preble didn't know where the snipers were until they shot at him—his wasn't the sort of plan that would work for anyone else —but then he knew it long before they pulled the trigger. He didn't need to actually put his head outside the guardhouse and, unlike the snipers, he didn't have to aim. He just recognized the future possibility that put each bullet in a place that stopped all movement from the sniper—someone should have told them to wait and hide for ten seconds between shots no matter what, that would have messed up his aim, but nobody had. They were too far for him to know whether he'd killed them or just knocked them out, but either way, they always stopped shooting. Preble unloaded a magazine from the M16 this way, 30 rounds, put another in, then ran at full sprint up State Place NW, and around the corner of the Oval Office, with the South Lawn on his right, toward the Rose Garden. As he ran, holding the vest doubled in his left hand and the M16 in his right, he disabled fourteen more snipers who hadn't been within his field of fire from the guard-house. He also wrecked the barrel of the sniper hiding inside the tree. The tree, it would have turned out had he wasted a shot on it, was bullet-proof.

There was pandemonium in the Rose Garden. The president was invisible behind a wall of black-suited bodies, a virus attacked by Armani-wearing antibody homunculi, a forty-legged bullet-proof fusion of black-tailored humanity that was ushering the president back into the White House. But forty legs make for slow walking, even with practice, and Preble made it around the corner before they'd pushed the president out of the garden and back through the doors.

The Secret Service already knew he was coming, and the moment he rounded the corner the side of the forty-legged monster that was facing him started shooting, without slowing their speed-shuffle through the Rose Garden doors. At least three of the Secret Service guys had Uzi machine guns. Preble blocked the broadside of bullets with the vest—unlike the SWAT shield, it rattled his whole arm—while shooting four fake reporters who were also trying to put holes in him. Several of the other people in the crowd were clearly not reporters or diplomats either. The real guests were all flat on the ground holding their heads. Inter-spersed between them were men squatting like sprinters or line-backers trying to find a balance between shrinking their profile and making themselves ready to pounce. But they weren't shooting at him, so he ignored them.

He cut off eighteen legs from the forty-legged monster before it made it through the doors, but it wasn't enough. He shot at the glass doors in frustration, knowing they were bulletproof and that he had nothing on him that could smash through them. The White House looked fragile, but even its glass doors were built like Fort Knox.

Then he almost couldn't believe his own window as he foresaw three heavily armoured HMMWV Avengers come around the corner, each with two giant missile pods on awkwardly tall air-defence turrets in the back. Fish had told him there was a Marine instant-reaction team stationed in the White House, he'd told him about the roofs and tunnels, about the walkers on the sidewalk and the floaters in cars on the Avenue, but he'd said nothing about armoured vehicles with missile pods. Where the hell did they keep these things? Under the White House swimming pool that for some otherwise unknowable reason the Secret Service kept photoshopping out from Google Earth?

Then Preble realized what he was looking at. Although the White House had a full Patriot battery built into the roof among its forest of antennae, this was extra mobile protection for shooting down airplanes. The 9/11 terrorists had used airplanes, so of course everyone planned for the next attack to include airplanes. The missiles probably couldn't shoot at him—at any rate, they wouldn't in the foreseeable future. But the things also had an M3P machine gun, basically a modified M2 with hundreds of .50 cal rounds that could cut through anything short of an engine block. His improvised shield would be like trying to stop bullets with a pillowcase.

And ducking was no fun either. At 550 rounds per minute, they didn't puncture the air, they sliced it. Or they would. He had two options: wait for them to come around the corner and start shooting, and then run into the White House through the shattered doors, or use the time he had to cut the distance so he'd be almost on top of them when they came. He didn't like the idea of pinning himself against the doors until they were ready to shoot, but if he timed it just right he might get them to shoot the doors and then get in under their rounds.

The Marines driving the Avengers were very good with Stingers. They were linked to a Forward Area Air Defense Command, Control, Communications and Intelligence (FAAD C3I) system that covered a two-hundred-mile zone around Washington, D.C., with external radar tracks and messages passed directly to the fire unit to alert and cue the gunner. With their slew-to-cue subsystem, the gunner could select a FAAD C3I-reported target for engagement from a display on their HTU, then press a button to initiate an automatic cab movement to azimuth.

But airplanes, cruise missiles, unmanned aerial vehicles and helicopters all fly above the horizon. The fire-and-forget Stingers were useless against an individual. Not only couldn't they aim that low or that close, but their computers decided that a single human being didn't make sense as a target and refused to engage.

If the gunner insisted, the Stingers would refocus on the building behind Preble.

The .50 cal could shoot downwards and its target didn't have to "make sense" to the computer, but neither the drivers nor the gunners had practiced aiming below the horizon since before their assignment to WART, the White House Anti-Aircraft Avenger Reaction Team. Their symbol was a fist raised to the air, their motto was *The sky is falling*, and when members of other units wanted to make fun of them in a bar they just rubbed their necks. WART's response was that if it's beneath the horizon, it's beneath them. Their lives revolved around azimuth, elevation, and zenith.

They hadn't trained for fighting infantry, but they were still Marines, they could still shoot. And their armour was heavy enough to stop Preble's M16.

He ran forward, just far enough away when the first Avenger came around the corner that it took the shot and ripped a stream of holes in the Rose Garden glass doors. Then the Marine driver made a mistake. He instinctively aimed the vehicle directly at Preble, and as he did so, Preble realized that the Avenger had a huge design flaw: a broad no-fire zone directly forward. The cab where the driver and passenger sat blocked the gun, and when the gunner turned the turret forward the computer disabled the M3P. Not used to running the Avenger against individual human targets, the driver didn't understand why the gunner had stopped firing. Even the gunner lost nearly a full second before he realized what was happening and yelled "Turn, turn!"

By then Preble had placed a dozen rounds onto the same point on the windshield—he had to stop one of the ricochets with his vest—and got through with the thirteenth. It ripped the driver's left cheekbone off and opened his face. The windshield didn't shatter, it just spiderwebbed around a hole the size of a coin. The second and third Avengers were coming around the corner, and they were at an angle where they could shoot, while the first Avenger started to accelerate from the dead driver's foot. Preble hopped up on the hood, his face suddenly inches from the wide-eyed passenger who was trying to grab the steering wheel but couldn't get the driver's foot off the gas and couldn't see where he was going because Preble was blocking the view. At the same time, the Marines in the second two Avengers decided that duty trumped friendship and started blasting the car on which Preble was hitching a ride. A .50 cal could go through the HMMWV's armour, but Preble had the entire anti-aircraft turret and the armoured cab providing protection, while the second and third Avengers couldn't drive directly after the first without putting it into their no-fire zone. Despite how much it was helping him, Preble was awed by the stupidity of the design, and sitting on the hood barrelling into the Rose Garden doors he imagined the committee meeting where the industry expert insisted that this was an air-defence platform so why did it need a .50 cal and the military guy saying all combat vehicles must have a .50 cal, with the compromise being a .50 cal that couldn't shoot forward.

Preble wondered whether something was wrong with him. He'd always been absentminded, but not like this. Not while playing chess or fighting. Those things had always focused him, put him in the zone, the flow, living fully in the infinite nows of five seconds hence. But lately whenever he was in the middle of combat his mind clicked over into autopilot, then drifted. It was fast, rational, with heightened perception, a window that seemed much longer than ever before. He couldn't measure it, the other part, the one that would be doing the measuring, was broken—but it might be as long as ten seconds. After a lifetime of fighting to get to five, now he could just jump to ten? And the other part thought about the weirdest shit. If he were daydreaming about Kasper and Jane—and he did have long spells of that, did that at nearly every moment except in combat—it would at least make some emotional sense. But in combat he thought about committees, while the Avenger crashed through the bullet-riddled Rose Garden doors. Despite all the .50 cal holes, they didn't shatter. They just popped off, into the hallway, and the Avenger reared like a horse when the turret hit the ceiling.

Preble was flung forward off the hood and into the wall on the other side of the wide hallway. But he'd expected it, cushioned the landing, and hit first the wall and then the ground running in the direction the Secret Service had taken the president.

It wasn't hard to tell which way he'd gone. With the forty-legged black-suited monster he'd been close enough to place his bullets, and he had put each one into an eye socket. But he hadn't paid attention to what those bullets would do afterwards, and several had clearly exited and wounded multiple other Secret Service personnel. There was a clear trail of blood that Preble now followed at a full run.

White House security, once inside, was wholly dependent on the Secret Service. The planners had expected madmen and terrorists, not an army. If an army invaded Washington, they'd have enough warning to get the president on Air Force One. It was inconceivable that anything short of two or three heavy platoons could make it past the Secret Service so fast that they wouldn't have time to move the package, and so the White House didn't have self-sealing doors. It had a hard shell, but, once inside, it was soft.

The only exception to this was the underground command bunker, designed for a surprise boomer attack. An ICBM would take hours to reach the United States, but a submarine-launched nuke could hit the White House within five to ten minutes of launch. The protocol was tight. One minute to evaluate the threat, ninety seconds to get the president's attention, one minute to get him from either the bedroom or the Oval Office to the elevator, thirty seconds in the high-speed elevator, thirty seconds to seal the doors, and thirty seconds as buffer. In reality, if the Russians really launched a surprise nuke from close enough along the Atlantic seaboard—if, say, they somehow managed the unlikely feat of sneaking a boomer into Washington Harbor—nobody expected that the president would survive. If he were anywhere other than his bedroom, for example, it would take too long to reach the elevator. From the door of the Rose Garden, you'd need an additional forty-five seconds. But it was the job of the Secret Service to think within a situation, and the unstoppable madman chasing the president was feeling more and more like a loose nuke. Taking POTUS into the bunker was the plan that seemed to make the most sense.

Unfortunately, the plan counted on the president moving at what amounted to a full sprint for a 65-year-old healthy adult. By insisting on forming a constant full-body shield—not necessary with a nuke—the Secret Service couldn't move at much more than an awkward jog. They left several men behind to slow Preble down, but they didn't even make him break his stride. He reached the president just as the elevator doors were opening.

He wondered what it was about elevators lately. Maybe all of our weaknesses are attracted to us, or we're attracted to our weaknesses. A sort of magnetic force—if Superman and kryptonite are on the same planet, eventually they will find each other, and then they'll keep finding each other over and over. A dynamic similar to the way institutions always promote managers to the level of their maximum incompetence: once you reach a position you can't handle, you stop getting promoted. And so you stay there, in the most inappropriate job possible for your skill set. He killed four more guards at a sprint and dove into the elevator—the one place least suited to his skill set—just as the doors were closing. He slammed into a secret serviceman who fell back into the president. The four other guards in the elevator hesitated, trained never to shoot in the direction of the VIP in case of an accident. Only one took the shot. Preble squirmed, it missed, went through the suit of the guard under Preble without touching flesh, nicked the edge of the president's shoe, ricocheted off the floor, the wall, and flew back out the still open door. Amazingly, it hit no one.

In the meantime, the guard whom Preble had tackled was trying to get his arm around Preble's neck in a choke hold, with the both of them laying on top of the president. Preble saw that with all the ricochets, there was a way he could shoot all four guards with two bullets. Instead, he put the gun against the president's head. "Stop!"

Check. Everyone stopped. The elevator door closed, hit a foot, and opened again.

President John Grape lay on the floor of the elevator. He was unhurt, but he'd been treated like a discounted sack of potatoes by his bodyguards for the last two minutes, and it had sapped something out of his bones. With his gun still to the president's temple, Preble sat down on the floor beside him. The four guards stood inside the elevator, each with a pistol aimed at Preble's head.

"Come on," Preble said. "Enough already. You can't shoot me. And even if you could, I'd take the president with me. Put your guns down, move your, uh, friend...out of the door, and press the down button. Let's all go down."

The Secret Service didn't move. They didn't have a solution, so they kept their guns pointed. Finally, John Grape sat up a little straighter and said, "Do what he says."

A ripple of hesitation went through the Secret Service, but nobody lowered his gun.

"Can I come?"

Preble, the president, and two out of the four Secret Service guards looked out of the elevator. One of the reporters—one of the reporters who'd gone into a combat crouch when the bullets started flying, but who didn't have a gun—was standing there, arms raised.

"Who are you?" Preble asked.

"Russian security."

Grape looked accusingly at Preble, as though this was proof Bigman had been right.

"We're sort of busy right now," Preble answered.

"Whatever the two of you are about to decide in the basement is going to impact the security of the world. Russia has a stake in that. I will come."

"Do you know where my family is?"

"We do have satellite images of the American operation in Hudson's Bay that took them. We can offer you any help—"

One of the Secret Service guards shifted targets from Preble to the Russian. The moment the gun was pointed at him the Russian's face twisted, with a sneer and lightbulb eyes, as though struggling to restrain an urge to berserk. Preble had had so many people point guns at him recently that he empathized. It really was offensive.

"Get in. I need peace from all of you assholes."

Chapter 23

ALTHOUGH THE ELEVATOR WAS AN EXTRA-WIDE, THE RIDE TO the bunker was uncomfortable. The Secret Service insisted on keeping their guns pointed, three at Preble, one at the Russian. Preble reminded them that if they tried to shoot him, he'd know it before they did, then tucked his gun into his belt. President Grape told them to put their own guns away, but they had their own rules for this sort of thing, and when it came to the president's safety, they didn't always listen. POTUS could fire them later, but they weren't going to relax when he was sharing an elevator with a madman who had already killed hundreds.

Jane had done a lot of spelunking when she and Preble had first met, and she would talk about having to exhale to fit through particularly tight caves—the guys she was with would send her in to explore offshoots because she was the smallest in the group. She loved it, though to Preble it sounded terrifying. He missed her suddenly and fought to suppress the surge of emotion.

He didn't have claustrophobia generally. Just elevators. Apparently, it was quite common, and considered difficult to treat because the normal process of incrementally exposing the patient to the phobic situation for long enough for the fear to go away isn't possible. An elevator ride doesn't last long enough for the patient to calm down. In Preble's case, the ride was too long. Thirty seconds with almost no new information—a mix between Jane's caves, jumping blindly off a cliff, and a vague sense he'd had his whole life that the way he would die eventually would be in an elevator. He hoped it was an irrational fear, but when you can accurately see even a glimpse of the future, it becomes more difficult to dismiss premonitions.

With an internal sigh of relief, Preble put the gun back to the president's temple just before the doors opened. A squad of Marines was waiting in a nondescript white hallway with a giant presidential seal in front of the elevators. They were impressed enough for another standoff.

Thirty seconds hadn't been enough for anyone to freeze the elevator, but they'd been enough for the president to clear his thoughts. He turned to the shortest of the Secret Service bodyguards, the only woman, and tried again. "Kris, put your gun down. That's an order. All of you, put your guns down."

Kris didn't like it. She was the head of his security detail. "I'm sorry, Mr. President, but—"

Not just the Secret Service agents, but the entire squad of Marines hung off her every word, looking for a direction, trying to determine whether they should be shooting Preble or backing off. This was a situation nobody had ever prepared for, and for a second, she was the most powerful person in the room.

"No buts. This is a strategic decision for the national security of the United States, and as much as I appreciate what you're trying to do, if you can't obey my orders I will have you removed right now. When Teddy Roosevelt charged that hill in Cuba at the head of his troops and caught two bullets, he was acting as the commander-in-chief not as a Secret Service package. We are in a war here, and you will not interfere with how I run that war, is that clear?"

Preble put his gun back in his belt.

"Yes, sir," Kris said.

"Now, everyone under my authority in this room, put your guns away."

The four agents put their pistols away, though not without hesitation. The squad of Marines lowered theirs.

The president turned back to Kris. "What time is it?"

"Uh, ten to six, sir."

"Good enough for a drink. Let's go find a place to sit."

Unlike the White House proper, the bunker underneath it was one set of vault-sized doors after another. Preble stuck close to President Grape as they walked into a command-and-control area that seemed modeled on NASA's control centre in Houston. But unlike Houston, which satisfied itself with one wall holding a giant split-screen, this room covered three sides with twenty-foot-tall data walls made up of projection cubes lined up in a seamless array, nearly a hundred million pixels of resolution. One ad-hoc section showed the world, one the United States, and the rest, over 80 percent, were focused on Washington D.C. and the attack on the White House—a unified threat board interspersed with charts, graphs, troop numbers, dozens of dimensions of military, economic, informational and diplomatic data, with hi-res pictorializations of military, political, economic, infrastructure, social, and information instrumentalities, matrices, forms and programs. Information about every corner of the world cross-linked with decisions that were disaggregated into a series of systems, then plugged back into a matrix to show their interrelations, then turned into human interfaces, pretty charts with arrows going up and arrows going down. Preble noticed one graph labelled "SS Act HumAss"—short, he'd be told if he were to ask, for "Secret Service actionable human assets"—had a sharp down arrow next to it.

"Fish is right," he mumbled as they continued through a door in one of the walls. Right about humanity becoming mechanized, digitized, almost mineralized. This here was "the system," or at least a glimpse of it. This is The Man, who is not human. People see it as a problem of technology, but it isn't technology. It's the way people restructure their own thinking to match that of computers. Because humans are the more adaptable of the two. The door led to a meeting room that, except for another giant presidential seal standing in place of windows, could have been in any large corporation.

A secretary or waitress ran up to them, hesitating only slightly at the sight of the armed Marines who'd followed the president.

"It's Stacey, right?"

"Uh, yes, sir, Mr. President."

"Who else is down here? Is Ham here, or Garland? Anybody?"

"No, sir. Just regular staff. The chairman of the joint chiefs has a subcommittee meeting on the Hill, so he's close. The vice president is on Air Force Two."

"Good. Get me a gin tonic. And call Ham. He's probably on his way here anyway. Tell him and tell whoever is running security now that I do not want an assault team trying to storm this place or doing anything stupid without my express orders. Mr. Jefferson, what would you like?"

"If you're having a gin tonic and Ham, I'd like a beer and Fish." Turning to Stacey, he added, "Something bitter and dark...please."

"What kind of fish would you like?" Stacey asked.

"Sorry. Robert Legmegbetegedettebbeknek. He's my attorney. Your security guys have his cell, I'm sure, since they tortured him for three months. I'd like him down here as soon as possible."

"You want your attorney?" the president asked, openly incredulous as he took his suit jacket off and pulled up a chair. "You turning yourself in? After shooting all my—"

Preble shook his head. "I already tried that. And got shot in the ass for it."

"So it is possible? To shoot you, I mean."

"Only if I'm trying not to kill anyone. We're past that stage now."

The president blinked, then decided to roll with whatever Preble said. "Shall we wait for your attorney, then?"

"Let's wait for our drinks." Preble sat heavily next to the president, legs apart, with his chair a couple of feet away from the table. Kris, after a long stare at Preble, took a chair as well, on the other side of Preble. She swivelled hers sideways, facing Preble, obviously uncomfortable by the lack of white space between her VIP and the killer. The Russian stood awkwardly in the doorway, and one of the other agents stood behind him. The other two went back into the command-and-control room. So did the Marines, looking uncertainly over their shoulders.

The president turned to the Russian. "What's your name, son?"

"Ivan." He pointed at a chair.

"Of course." Grape nodded, and Ivan sat. "We may ask you to leave the room at any time, in which case I hope you won't be offended." He gestured at the press pass hanging around Ivan's neck. "Your pass says Alex Novinar. The Atlanta Constitution, huh?"

"I am representing Russia at this table. So you may call me Ivan. Also, it's my real name."

"In that case, you'll have a vodka."

"I will have water."

"You will have a vodka," the president insisted. He felt out of control, as though the situation had gotten much bigger than him, but as he insisted that Ivan drink vodka he realized that the control from which he'd shaken free wasn't his own. The situation had freed him from a role in which he was "the package," protected, sheltered, and put on a pedestal, but oddly powerless to do something as simple as go to the toilet when he felt like it, because his timing might offend some schedule or security protocol. Ivan's visible irritation at being told what to drink made him feel better.

Jefferson had killed nearly his entire bodyguard. Men and women who had dedicated their lives to protecting him, who had given their lives for him. And yet, suddenly, with most of them gone, he felt like he could breathe again—it was a horrible thought, he was ashamed the moment he had it. He looked at Kris, sitting at the table with him, and realized he'd never really talked to her. Or to any of the agents who were now dead. They weren't allowed to talk to him, not like that, and he'd just obeyed the protocol. He was the president, he could have changed the rules, but he hadn't.

Stacey brought the gin tonic, vodka and a bottle of Pete's Wicked Ale, unopened. She handed Preble the bottle, an opener and an empty beer mug. Preble opened the beer and poured it into the mug. "Thank you," Preble said to her.

She gave him a long look, weighing what to say to a man who'd just killed several dozen of her friends. Her professionalism won the choice of words she used, but not the tone. "Let me know if you need anything else."

"Just one thing. I noticed you thoughtfully left it unopened for me, but still, if I fall asleep, I'll shoot the president before I do. And you as well."

She smiled now. "How charming."

John Grape put down his gin tonic and reached for Preble's mug. "Stacey, I order you to tell me now if there is anything unusual about the beer."

"The beer is normal, sir."

The president took a sip, while Kris glared at the spectacle of the president acting as food tester to a terrorist, then handed it back to Preble and picked up his gin tonic again. "Okay, I'm going to treat this as a peace negotiation and try to build some trust."

"That's the first good news I've heard in a long time, Mr. President. Though I thought the United States doesn't negotiate with nonstate actors." Then, because he didn't want to come across as confrontational, he added, "I want to make sure our agreements stick."

"That's just a polite way of saying we don't negotiate with the weak. You're not weak, Mr. Jefferson, so you get treated as a state. Good enough?"

Preble remembered his conversation with Fish about Mr. Potato Head. This was the negotiating position he'd been aiming for. "Good enough. At least until someone like Bigman thinks he spots a moment of weakness. You know what I want, I think."

The president nodded. "Your family."

"Yes. After that, an island. Ronald Stone suggested putting my family on South Sandwich protected by the Brits from both of you." He glanced from Grape to Ivan and back. "And I want nukes. Five from each of you."

Grape guffawed. "You're not getting nukes."

Ivan flexed his jaw muscles.

"I already have them. But I want it to be obvious so that some idiot who doesn't quite understand won't start seeing weaknesses where there aren't any."

The president looked left and right, as though the nukes were somewhere in the room. "What do you mean you have them?"

Preble leaned in. "I could go on a computer next door and start World War III right now. I know every code. And if you change them, I'll still know them. But I wouldn't even have to do that. I could extort the decisions I want from any world leader, and if I couldn't, I could instigate the regime change necessary to get leaders who would listen. Surely you've thought of all this.

Bigman certainly has. What Bigman doesn't know is that my precognition window fluctuates, and sometimes I can see months and even years ahead, so there is no way to change the system to be demon-proof." Though his window had been expanding lately, it had done so by a matter of a few seconds. The months and years were a bluff, a lie.

Fish had told him that to get any permanent peace he would need to transcend the role of an individual, and now the president was telling him he had the power of a state. But nothing had really changed except his willingness to pay the price. Who was it that said the only real power is the power to take life? He remembered talking with Jane about this idea, about real power being the power to *not* take life, and only now understood why she'd seen it as horrible. In Churchill, he'd seen it as a comment on mercy. But its evil was in assuming that power and life-taking were so tied together that an effort of will was necessary to stay it. The nuclear deterrence game assumed death was the default. He had thought he was turning into a monster, but maybe that was just him accepting the mirror side of power. Maybe all nations—all Mr. Potato Head collective entities with this sort of power—were monsters.

The president leaned in hard as well now, so that he and Preble looked something like Kennedy and Kruschev, except nobody was banging a shoe. "I'm not going down in history as the president who gave nuclear weapons to a madman, and neither is anyone who succeeds me."

Preble backed off a bit. "I'm not a madman. I want nukes for the exact same reason you want them. As a deterrent to protect my family. If that's mad, it's only in the Cold War sense. You leave us be, we'll leave you be."

"No, there's a fundamental difference. In a nation there are safeguards, protocols, sanity checks. I couldn't even launch a nuclear strike on my own."

"You have as many safeguards up to ensure a nuclear war as you have to prevent it. What do the computers do if they think they recognize a first strike from the Russians?"

"They go up the DEFCON chain, yes, but they can be overridden."

"But the default is death."

"What?"

"It's all a chess game, isn't it?" Preble said, almost through his teeth. "All a very tightly played chess game. The way a computer plays, though at least for a nuclear war you allow for a human override. How's Pakistan's nuclear arsenal set up? Israel's? China's? China had a deliberate policy for twenty years of giving nuclear technology to as many third-world countries as possible, with the conscious strategy that it was in the best position to come out on top in the aftermath of a nonapocalyptic nuclear war."

"I don't answer for China. But what's to stop us from giving you a bomb that would just go off?" The president changed tacks. "Take you and your island away."

"Before that would happen, whoever gave me the bad bomb would lose their ten most heavily populated metropolitan areas."

"So you don't need the bombs."

"I've told you I don't." Preble stared into President Grape's brown eyes. He trusted the president. It was strange—this was the man for whom all those assholes who had taken Kasper and Jane worked, directly or indirectly following his orders, and yet him Preble trusted. Up to a point. "What I need is for your side to give up on killing me. You understand mutually assured destruction. You do not understand the idea that you can't fight me, whether with guns or software. I'm not scared of your soldiers, but I am terrified of your stupidity. Of someone convincing themselves that they've found a way to lock me out." He paused. "There is, of course, one way that you could lock me out of your nuclear arsenal."

The president's eyebrows shot up. "Oh, what's that?"

"Disarm. If there are no nukes left on the planet, then I can't hack into them. If there are no chemical or biological weapons, I can't use them against you."

"That's insane."

Preble snorted a cut-off laugh. "Okay. After I have my family safe on our nuclear-armed island, then we can engage in disarmament talks. Maybe we can even talk about things like pollution, poverty, and a cure for cancer. All sorts of things. But the first step is to get my family back here. Can you please arrange for that now?"

"And what? You set yourself up as a world dictator? Someone doesn't sign a climate treaty, you nuke one of their cities?"

"Not at all. Ever since that stupid subway, I have only responded in kind, proportionally to what I was attacked with. But there are certain advantages to seeing the future that I've never let myself explore because I was trying to keep a low profile. Medical research, for example. Most research today is a matter of cracking nature's codes, choosing the right option out of a near-infinite set of possibilities." He swallowed hard, realizing he was repeating Jane's arguments from long ago. It brought a flash from the past that stretched from their early days dating to their winter in Canada. Their months within the warm cabin huddled in the frozen north seemed idyllic now and as distant as any biblical Garden of Eden. "Give me an island and a research lab, and I'll give you the cure for cancer if you cut your particle emissions by 50 percent. That sort of thing."

"If you had the cure for cancer you wouldn't just share it with the world for free?"

"Do you? You could use eminent domain to expropriate any drug patent from one of your pharmaceutical companies."

"We have laws, a whole economic system to—."

"You make the system. But, yes, of course I'd share the cure anyway. Fish will be here any minute. You can debate systems with him. I've had enough—I want my family now."

"All right." The president leaned back, blinking intently. "As the man said, let's make a deal. The full peace, islands, nukes, all that can wait. If you can really reprogram our nuclear arsenal, then there's no risk to you waiting. Right now, I get you your family back here and give you a full presidential pardon, and you stop killing people. A ceasefire and a sign of good faith. Deal?"

"Deal." *Get you your family back.* Those words popped Preble into the present. He'd rarely had a happy emotion close his window, but this was overwhelming, a lake pushing a mountain out of the way, forcing it to slide off its foundations, not like a burst dam but an entire massive lake emptying at once, a tidal wave that floods through hundreds of miles of valleys, insisting on finding a way to the sea, taking all of man's carefully erected structures with it. "You get my family back. You put Kasper sitting on my lap, and everything else is negotiable. Everything else is secondary."

The president turned to Stacey, who was just walking into the room with Fish and another Secret Service agent. "Get me Bigman."

Fish seemed in awe of the room he'd just come from, looking over his shoulder at the screens on the walls until the last second, seeming disappointed to be forced to leave it in favour of a conference room.

"Yes, sir," Stacey answered. "And, Mr. President, the chairman of the joint chiefs is on his way down. Also, this is Mr. Jefferson's attorney."

Preble nodded silently to Fish, who sat down wide-eyed, finally shifting his attention to Preble and the president as Stacey dialled a number from memory into the speakerphone in the centre of the desk—it looked like a black octopus that had been flattened into the table. A full five rings before Thaddeus Bigman picked up his phone. "Mr. Bigman," Stacey said. "I have the president on the line for you."

Fish jumped and sprawled himself onto the table. From his end, it was the only way he could reach the octopus phone and press mute. The Secret Service twitched, worried he was attacking the president, but didn't draw down. Stacey jumped back, for the first time momentarily frightened.

"Wait," Fish said.

"What for?" Preble asked.

"Wait for the chairman of the joint chiefs to be in the room."

Two minutes later Hammond de Koek, the chairman of the joint chiefs, entered the room. He was past mandatory retirement age in the military (as the CJC you get an extension), but still built like a barrel. He had the Marine-cut grey hair and square shoulders that one expected in generals, but wire-rimmed glasses broke the pattern. He gave Preble only a quick glance, then a longer one to Kris. He ignored Fish, Stacey and Ivan. Then he turned back to his boss. "Mr. President. If I may ask, what the hell is going on?"

"Mr. Jefferson and I have just negotiated a ceasefire. We will give him back his family, and he'll stop killing people."

"We don't negotiate with terrorists, Mr. President." His tone was abrupt, borderline bark-at-a-second-lieutenant. And not a particularly swift second lieutenant.

"Let's leave categories out of this, shall we, and focus on solving the problem here. We've decided to give Mr. Jefferson the status of a head of state. He may have his own island nation at the end of this."

"What he should have at the end of this is a lethal injection." De Koek looked straight at Preble, locking gazes.

"Nevertheless, we are signing a ceasefire today." He pointed at the phone. "Mr. Fish, I assume you don't mind?"

De Koek snorted. President Grape unmuted the phone and clicked it over to speaker, with a glance to make sure Preble understood that this was for his benefit. Thaddeus Bigman's low voice boomed through the room. "Mr. President."

"Assistant Director Bigman. Where are you?"

"I understand your press junket didn't go well, Mr. President. I'm really sorry to hear that."

"I asked you a question."

"Unfortunately, sir, you asked it over a speakerphone, after suddenly muting a phone call. Which makes me think Mr. Preble Jefferson is in the room with you."

"He is. We just negotiated a ceasefire to all hostilities. I understand you're the only one who knows where his family is."

"Yes."

"We're going to bring them here. Where are they?"

"I'm sorry, sir, but that information is on a need-to-know basis."

The president slapped the table. "I'm your commander-in-chief, Assistant Director Yagbig. You will tell me now where they are or you will be relieved of duty."

"I'm sorry, sir, but you've so much as admitted that you've been compromised. The Principals' Committee prepared for this contingency. None of us are indispensable. Not even you, Mr. President."

"Your little politburo idea was never approved!"

"No sir, not officially. But contingency plans had to be made. It was decided that in the event you were taken as a de facto hostage, it would be treated as incapacity under the 25th Amendment. A hostage, after all, does not have the capacity to make independent decisions."

"You need a cabinet vote for invoking the 25th!"

"Normally, yes. But this is not a full invocation of the amendment. Just a partial one, until you are no longer a hostage."

"This is treason!"

"Since you don't have the capacity to make any decisions, we will not treat your betrayal of the Office of the President as treasonous. It wouldn't do for the American public to think of their president as a coward. But you are henceforth out of the chain-of-command loop."

"For God's sakes, don't do this! We have to stop before this escalates any more."

"Escalates to what? More than a lone renegade gaining control over the president of the United States? More than the president becoming a puppet for a would-be world dictator who may not even be the same species as us? How does it escalate any more than that?"

"He has control over our nukes."

"No, he doesn't. Sure, he can get the codes, but the codes aren't enough to launch. Haven't you been reading your nuclear protocols, Mr. President?"

Fish cut in. "Mr. Bigman, this is Robert Legmegbetegedettebbeknek speaking. Mr. Jefferson's attorney. We met in New York. I just wanted to let you know that both the president and the chairman of the joint chiefs are in the room with us."

There was a long pause on both ends, broken by de Koek, "Sumbitch!"

"Alright," the president said. "What did I miss by not reading the three-hundred-page nuke rules that I got along with all my other homework when I took office?"

Chapter 24

"MR. PRESIDENT," THE CHAIRMAN OF THE JOINT CHIEFS SAID, forming each word carefully, making sure each one ended, crisply, neatly, folded and tucked away, before he started the next. "A first strike requires not just authentication codes but also retinal identification of you and another person from a 'qualified' list. People who are qualified to co-launch with you. It's a very short list, but I am on it." The chairman of the joint chiefs turned to Preble, "But there's no way on God's green Earth that I am participating in a nuclear launch."

"The launch computer and retinal scanner are next door, right?" Preble turned to Stacey, who was standing awkwardly next to the speakerphone, listening to the conversation. "Stacey, could you please bring me a spoon."

"Uh, yes," she turned to leave, then turned back to look at Preble as her face turned white. "What do you want the spoon for?"

"For my beer."

Ivan shared a derisive snort.

De Koek looked from Preble to Stacey and back, his face made of stone. "While you're getting Mr. Jefferson his spoon, would you please get me a fork?"

"And so nuclear war, perhaps the fate of the human race, depends on a battle between a spoon and a fork," Fish said.

"No, it doesn't," Preble said, turning back to the speakerphone.

But Fish kept going, half-giggling nervously and unable to stop. "Sort of like that joke about the guy caught by cannibals, sees all his friends getting skinned, eaten, and stretched into canoes. His last wish is for a fork, so he can stab himself over and over screaming, 'You won't make a canoe out of me!'"

Stacey and Kris looked at Fish like they were sure he was speaking in code. The whole conversation had turned giddy with stress and knocked the normally sharp Stacey off balance, unsure what to do. "So, should I get, uh, anything?"

"No, Stacey," de Koek said. "Mr. Jefferson is just trying to make a point but doesn't want to explicitly face the fact that he's threatening me. Which is a little odd given that he's talking about launching nuclear weapons."

"This could all be stopped by giving back my family!" Preble continued into the speakerphone. "I don't understand why you can't do that."

"Because then there would be nothing to restrain you." Bigman's voice was usually deep and smooth, like a jazz player or a radio DJ, a voice that commanded attention far more than his physical presence. But what came out of the speakerphone now was cold, clipped, and nearly breaking in places. Like everyone in the White House bunker, his saliva glands must have stopped working properly. He was feeling the strain. "Right now, you don't know where they are. Any city you destroy, you take a risk that that city is exactly where I put them. You would then be their executioner. But there's also the principle of it. No man is above the law. We live in a society, we are social animals. And the reason we've survived as a species is because it's hard-wired in us to punish antisocial behaviour. You, Mr. Preble Jefferson, are a freak. In the past, we ostracized physical and mental freaks to protect the gene pool, though their impact is minimal in an age when all humanity is devolving, when the weak no longer die out. That will be a problem in a thousand years, perhaps. You, on the other hand, are an imminent threat to the fabric of humanity. A man who can see the future can never be part of society. What the social contract gives to the individual, its 'consideration,' is protection from the unexpected. The essence of any contract is protection from the unforeseen future. Fear. Fear that the price will fluctuate, that the goods won't be up to par, that the business partner may not be as good a friend as I thought. Fear that without the protection of the group, you wouldn't survive. So we give up our rights to the group in exchange for its protection. Protection that's not necessary for a man who can see the future. So your social contract is without consideration. It's void. No matter how much you tried to conform to the rules, your compliance would be a gift, one that you could stop giving at any moment. You wouldn't be bound by the contract. And that makes you a permanent threat. No matter what you do, you are the enemy. The only part of you that's human is your wife and son, and through them, I can force you to be a little bit human, to feel fear like the rest of us."

Fish spoke first. "Mr. Bigman, your fear of monsters is turning you into one as well."

"Mr. Fish, wasn't it one of your anarchist friends who said, 'In times of radical crisis, everything depends on the individual who says no, who, acting out of the courageous impulses of human solitude, refuses to assent to a power that would be totalizing.' Without the restraint of his wife and son, Mr. Jefferson's power would be totalizing—"

Fish nearly choked. "Did you notice the human solitude part of what you just quoted?"

"—if you don't give me back Kasper and Jane right now," Preble interrupted, "I will turn Cheyenne Mountain into a slag pit."

"Cheyenne Mountain can take a nuke. That's what it was built for."

"Can it take a hundred?"

"And what if Kasper and Jane are somewhere in Colorado?"

"I don't think they are," Preble said through clenched teeth. "You didn't have them with you at the NSA, or when you flew away. I'm guessing you have them in some black CIA facility, and to save your own skin, you'll finally tell me where they are. But only then."

There was a long pause on the other end, while everyone in the room from the president down to Stacey stared intently at the speakerphone. Finally, Bigman said, "What if they're in Washington D.C.?"

"Tell me where, and this will...Oh."

A pause. "You missed my point. You nuke me, and I'll nuke you."

Stacey mumbled something about boys, nukes, and Jesus Christ. Everyone exhaled or coughed or wheezed, even the Secret Service.

"Thad, you'd kill Washington D.C.," the president said in a barely audible voice.

"Mutually assured destruction. To save the country."

"Including Fifi and Kiki?" Like most politicians, Grape had a remarkable memory for names, and he'd met Fifi Kennedy Yagbig several times. And even if he hadn't, Bigman's wife and daughter were famous in the Washington cocktail circuit just because of their names.

Bigman's voice turned a touch more metallic. "This is bigger than all of us. And I had them moved."

"All right, Bigman," Preble said grimly, "Let's play chicken."

Fish looked at Preble, clearly distressed, then reached over to hit the mute button on the phone. "This isn't going right. The guy's a machine. You can't play chicken with a computer."

"You want to play chicken with a computer?" Ivan cut in, unexpectedly, without changing his conflicted expression. From the neck down he seemed to slouch in hangdog misery, but his pop-out eyes looked like he was ready to scream at any moment. "You throw the steering wheel out the window."

"Ivan's right," Preble said. "So long as they see that we're throwing it out."

"Ivan's hoping to trigger a civil war," Fish said. "It's too many people, Preble. You can't do this. It's not worth it."

Preble's anger at Bigman wanted to refocus on someone present, someone whom he could punch, and he had to struggle to prevent that target from being his friend. "Not worth it for what, Fish? Not worth it for your new society? I agree: not worth it. Not worth it for Kasper and Jane? I'll be Attila the Hun if that's what it takes."

"And when do you stop?"

"When I have them back."

"And if they're dead?" Fish swallowed hard but forced himself to continue. "If their helicopter crashed? What if the reason Bigman isn't compromising is because he can't. Because they're dead and he's terrified of what you'll do if you find out?"

"Please don't go there, Fish. You thought this would be easy? You can't go back to your armchair. You can see this through to the end, or you can go to prison for life."

Fish glared. "Don't be rude. I want to come to the right answer here. To build a better world and avoid killing millions. Whether I spend my last few years playing chess in jail or in the Flea House is hardly on the same scale, so please don't insult me."

"I'm sorry. But this is the moment you were waiting for, the sliver of present time where the future gets shaped. The dark tea-time of the soul, or whatever you called it once."

"Midnight. Midnight of the soul."

"Whatever." Preble shrugged. "This is the disconnect between the particular and the general that you always talk about. This is when you take on your original sin. Knowledge of evil. Real knowledge of it. I'm a monster, but you want to be a moral man, don't you Fish? You really really do. You always have, more than anything, even while you were telling me to embrace my inner monster."

"Ethical, not moral. There's a difference."

"Ok, ethical. I do understand the difference. Well, to truly be an ethical man you need that knowledge of what it is to be a monster, and you need to be in the midnight-of-the-soul situation, nobody to ask for guidance. You can't just ride the monster in a big fat armchair and pretend you're untouched. Look at how Bigman sees the world. It's him and a few others prowling through a sea of babies who don't ever have to face the knowledge and choices that can make them either evil or ethical or both."

"Bigman calculates and reacts. You're a monster from a fucking fairy tale, Preble. Grendel, or Grendel's mother. He's monstrous in a different way. He doesn't think about ethics any more than a machine would."

"No, but you do. And if you want to be an ethical man, Fish, you can't ride that armchair. You launch that nuke. Or stop me from launching it. But don't sit there and moan. You wanted to build a society around a kernel of destruction—."

Fish slumped. "I guess it didn't really hit me that destruction means killing people who are totally God-damned innocent."

"Really?" Preble deflated a little. "You want your revolution to be a Hollywood movie? The system you hate is built of human beings. All the cops and soldiers and people too poor to pay for college without signing up for the military. You think the Brits in 1776 were all bad guys?

"No," Fish sighed. "It was brother killing brother."

"I know you get it in the abstract, but this is real. If it goes bad, we're going to kill innocent people, real people, just like I've been doing every day lately. Now, are we still on the same side here?"

Fish looked around as though he suddenly realized everyone else had a drink except for him. Without asking, he took Preble's beer, barely touched, and drank several swallows. It calmed him. "That was the least inspirational call to arms I've ever heard. Next time rent Braveheart or something before you try to convince me to go to war."

"I know why I'm doing this. How about you?"

"Let's get it over with." Fish looked so pale Preble thought he might pass out. "Just try not to fucking nuke anyone."

Preble turned to the president and the CJC. "Okay, let's go next door."

Hammond de Koek shook his bald head. "I'm not going to help you launch a nuclear strike."

"I don't need your help. I only need your eye. Now move."

The president raised his hands. "Mr. Jefferson, we had a peace negotiation here. This is hardly in the spirit of—"

"Unfortunately, it seems that you've lost the power to negotiate on behalf of the United States."

"Mr. President," Fish cut in. "I doubt they can reprogram the White House nuclear protocols from outside, but they can get their own silos to run independently. And I think there really is a risk of Bigman nuking us. At this point, he pretty much has to take out not only Preble but you and all other witnesses to your exchange."

"But he can't do any of this alone."

"He's probably got the vice president working with him."

"Garland? Garland and I have never had a great relationship, beyond getting me Ohio. But he'd never—"

"The vice president knows that if he doesn't cooperate, he'll be deemed 'compromised' as well. There's probably a small group that see this as an opportunity, and if any one of them tries to change direction they'd be deemed compromised. That's how these things usually work, anyway."

"A politburo," the president said softly. "They called it a 'board of directors,' but described a politburo."

"And that didn't set off alarm bells?"

"It was a conversation, in passing. And I said no."

Preble gestured for the president and CJC to precede him. Like having his own nukes, it was to dissuade more than because it made any difference. Kris, Stacey, Ivan, and Fish all followed as they entered the huge room full of computers and wall-screens. He walked up to the first terminal, where a spectacled young analyst was staring up at him and the president.

"Which computer— Oh." He had expected that there'd be one special computer that would handle the nukes, in a vault somewhere. But now he saw that he could use any of the computers in this room. He looked down at the analyst. "Can I have your seat, please?"

The young soldier stood up awkwardly, looking at the president to see what he should do. He only moved out of the way when the president gave him a curt nod.

"But stay close," Preble said, then suggested the president pull up a chair and that the CJC sit at the next terminal.

The soldier had had the presence of mind to log out when he saw them walking up, but it actually helped. Preble typed in the president's personal password, and the screen read, "Welcome, President Grape," and presented a list of options. It was all very user-friendly. Click on nuclear arsenal, click on status, and he was about to click on Defcon 1 when he saw that NORAD and several silos in Nevada suddenly jumped to Defcon 1 on their own. Then the whole U.S. military shot up to Defcon 2.

"He's fast," Preble said.

"Jesus Christ," de Koek swore.

The president stared slack-jawed at Preble, then de Koek. "You weren't in on it?"

De Koek shook his head, eyes wide. "Not this."

"What were you in on?"

"Just...just a contingency plan. The committee realized that you would be Jefferson's natural target, so they set up a contingency plan. I wasn't part of it. I didn't want to be."

"But who exactly is on this committee?"

"Garland and Bigman and probably a bunch of people too afraid to say no, who just said they didn't want to hear about it but didn't stop it."

"Like you."

"It violated the chain of command, so I couldn't be a part of it. But it made sense." De Koek gestured towards Preble by way of justification. "And nobody thought it would end up like this!"

Preble selected all of Strategic Air Command and bumped it up to Defcon 1. The computer requested an authorization code. Interesting. It wasn't the launching itself that required the nuclear codes, but bringing SAC up to Defcon 1. From Defcon 1, you could do anything, which was why even during the Cuban Missile Crisis SAC had only gone to Defcon 2. He entered the president's code. It was long, 12 digits, but not time constrained. They could have Preble-proofed it by simply adding a ten-second delay to all codes. If he waited to act, in a few years every important code would have a time delay on it. He was surprised that they hadn't already done so while he was in Canada, but maybe he'd escalated too far too fast, beyond the government's ability to adapt. The machine might be all-consuming, but it was slow.

Code Authenticated – President of the United States, John E. Grape. Please look at the screen. Hit Enter when ready. Preble gestured at the president to put his face in front of the webcam above the computer.

Preble pointed the gun at de Koek's head. "Shh."

"What?"

"You were about to yell for someone to do something. All it would mean is a lot of people dead in here."

He turned the gun to point at Kris. "I don't want to shoot you, but I will." Then he turned back to Grape. "Now, Mr. President, as you can see I'm playing chicken with Mr. Bigman. He needs to know that if he launches at Washington, he will get hurt as well. If you're thinking about protecting the American people, the affected Washington D.C. area will be around five million, while if for some reason my threat to nuke Cheyenne Mountain turned real, you'd lose about thirty to fifty thousand, including the surrounding towns."

"This is just crazy. Totally crazy. Playing chicken with nuclear weapons?"

"You did it with Russia for sixty years. At any rate, I am increasingly convinced Bigman actually wants to nuke Washington. He brought local control over NORAD silos to Defcon 1, and there's only one reason to do that. That phone call was probably recorded, which means I've probably given him the excuse he needed, and he has most of the deputies on the Principals' Committee behind him. He'll be a hero for preventing all-out Armageddon and for stopping me, and the vice president will become not just president, but a wartime president with no Congress or Supreme Court or other limitations on his power."

"He'll be the messiah," Fish said. "And you'll be the Antichrist. The first scientific reference everyone who looks at the idea will find, every reporter, will have the word demon in it. Laplace's Demon. The Bible Belt will lose its mind. And even without all that, if Bigman nukes Washington, then people will have to turn him into a hero. It's too big a disaster. People will need the relief of knowing it prevented a much greater evil, saved everyone still alive. People need a forward-moving narrative, not despair. In the meantime, he'll have wiped out anyone who would still oppose his new regime."

"Whose regime? Bigman's or Garland's?"

"I don't know. Does it matter? Maybe Bigman will remain as the vice president's eminence grise until he sees how this plays out. He seems to thrive in chaos. You go short. He goes long. You see the future. He surfs it."

Preble turned to the president, who looked like he was near overload, listening while he scratched his left elbow furiously through his white dress shirt. Everything was spiralling into complexity at an exponential rate, and the more confused it became the more Grape just wanted to find a fix, a solution that cut to the chase. What was it H. L. Mencken once said, For every complex problem, there is a simple solution. And it's always wrong. Grape felt nauseous.

"Mr. President, none of that will be possible if you live through this," Preble said. "But if you and the Supreme Court and

Congress are all gone, there'll be nothing stopping him and whoever else is on this new politburo."

"I...I can't just put my face there and wipe out fifty thousand people."

"But you can choose to not put your face there and wipe out five million?"

The president stared at Preble for a few seconds, then slowly moved in front of the webcam. In the end, he moved because it was an action. Any action was better than sitting there helpless. Preble hit Enter.

Retinal scan match. Enter secondary authorization.

Preble entered another 12-digit code that led the computer to flash Code Authenticated – Chairman of the Joint Chiefs William de Koek. Please look at the screen. Hit Enter when ready. He turned to de Koek. "Well, what's your choice."

De Koek had been thinking furiously, staring down while his jaw muscles twitched hard, mirroring Ivan, while the president had gone through his own hesitation.

"Ham, do it," the president said.

"Is that an order, sir?"

The president nodded silently.

"I need you to say it, sir."

"Yes," Grape whispered. "It's an order."

De Koek stood, nearly told Preble to move out of the chair, thought better of it, and put his face in front of the webcam.

Retinal scan match. The page changed to a tactical display, showing ICBM silos and target coordinates. Again, it was all very user-friendly. He didn't need to know the latitude and longitude of a target, just click on the map, and the computer offered choices for him to select. In the process, it gave him the corresponding numeric coordinates in case he cared or perhaps as a gentle chastisement that he hadn't done this the old-fashioned way.

Preble selected a silo in North Dakota and clicked four nukes onto Cheyenne Mountain.

Invalid target coordinates. You are not authorized to target within United States territory. Please select another target.

De Koek exhaled audibly. That's why he'd been willing to put his face in front of the camera. That, and he didn't want to die just yet.

But Preble wasn't looking at de Koek. Like half the staff in the command room, he was staring at the wall screens. They showed massive activity by the various United States armed forces along the entire Eastern Seaboard. After watching the screen for a while, Preble asked, "Is Bigman going to have the same problems launching at Washington from Cheyenne?"

"Initially, yes," de Koek answered without a smile or any other acknowledgement of his little victory. "But if he has the Pentagon on his side, SAC can override. Or he can just use tactical nukes from bombers. But that expands the number of people who can put the decision to a sanity test."

"Can you call the Pentagon and tell them to hold off?"

"I would. I hate nukes. It's a weapon for politicians and terrorists. But I'll get the same reaction as the president got. Compromised, out of the loop. There are some personal friendships I could call on that might work, but then we're talking civil war."

"Who will the military follow?"

De Koek shrugged. "Given how this has been set up? Whoever forms the majority of the Principals' Committee. Everyone's heard rumours about you. Everyone's talked from the beginning about how you could turn any asset. The minute someone is in a room with you, they're presumed to have gone zombie. That includes the president and myself. We inoculated the system."

"Are they scared enough to go nuclear?"

"It depends on the tensions between the deputies and the generals. The generals will want to storm this bunker using conventional troops. And the deputies, the Principals' Committee, will have to be careful about pissing off the generals, at least for a while. They're the only power base left. On the other hand, the last thing the generals want is a military government. They'll be desperate to lay the responsibility at the feet of a civilian political committee."

"This bunker's becoming a trap," Preble sighed.

"Command centres are always traps. All that sense of command and control is always an illusion. Every wartime general learns that eventually."

"How long before we lose our eyes and ears?"

"That will take a while. This place was made to prevent just that sort of thing. You have eyes, ears and a very ambivalent set of soldiers, including myself, who still want to follow the orders of the president of the United States, compromised or not. Maybe it helps to know that if those who are doing their duty outside this bunker succeed, then we will all most likely die. And, although I will not help you get the ability to nuke American cities, I actually believe you that if we give you your family and a shitty little island you may just go away. So I really hope you have some plan to get us all out of this without killing millions of Americans in the process. Do I make myself clear?"

Preble didn't answer, seeing that Fish was about to interrupt him anyway.

"General, all our lives are tied together in here. Whatever happens to Preble, probably happens to you and me and the president and all the other people here. Between the existing bunker defences and Preble's precognitive skills, I can't imagine anyone getting in. They'll end up plugging the entrance either with bodies or rubble, depending on what they use. The best conventional bunker buster you have is Deep Throat, right? The GBU-28? And that will only penetrate thirty meters of earth or six meters of concrete. They can't even starve us out. They could 'contain' Preble down here for ten years, but they don't have the patience for that. It would drive them out of their minds, and it assumes they want to minimize casualties. If this really is Bigman's big play at becoming king, is it reasonable to estimate he'll nuke within an hour?"

The CJC nodded grimly. "If he's really that...insane. Then yes, tactically I'd say that's a reasonable estimate." He turned to Preble. "You have a plan?"

Preble nodded, then turned to Kris. "Keep Ivan back a bit. I don't want him to see this information."

Ivan looked like he was trying to think of an argument for staying. They must have all sounded hollow even to him, because he shrugged and walked back towards the meeting room, then stood in the doorway with his shoulders hunkered in like a troll blocking a bridge.

While everyone was watching Ivan, Preble turned back to the computer, mumbling, "Steering wheel out." He clicked back, went to launch options, found the Navy's boomer submarines, selected two in the Arctic Ocean and two in the South China Sea—they didn't have specific locations, just general areas—and sent ten nukes at Moscow and—

"—what are you doing?" de Koek asked, a tinge of panic in his voice, as he looked back at the screen.

—ten at Beijing.

"Preble, are you—" Fish didn't finish his sentence.

Enter time of launch in EST.

Preble looked at the clock. It was 8 PM already. He chose 8 AM Eastern Standard Time from a scroll-down menu.

Select mode.

There were various options. Preble chose Silent.

Select cancellation options.

Preble chose By password.

Enter cancellation password.

Preble covered the keypad as he typed in *badbear*.

Select secondary cancellation options.

Now the menu included a new option: None. Preble clicked on it.

Confirm strategic thermonuclear strikes on Moscow (55 45 N 37 36 E) and Beijing (39 55 N 116 25 E) from nuclear submarines Houston, Nashville, Charlotte, and Fargo; Silent; Cancellation by password only.

De Koek tried to grab the keyboard just as Preble hit him in the side of the head with the butt of the gun while clicking enter with his left hand. De Koek slid to the floor.

Strategic thermonuclear strikes on Moscow (55 45 N 37 36 E) and Beijing (39 55 N 116 25 E) from nuclear submarines Houston, Nashville, Charlotte, and Fargo, Silent, Cancellation by password only, confirmed for 8:00 (8AM) EST, 13:00 (1PM) Zulu.

"Preble," Fish asked in a low voice. "Why are you nuking Moscow and Beijing?"

"What?" Ivan jumped forward, stopped by a hard arm from Kris.

Meanwhile, the computer was asking whether he wanted to Launch More, Return to Main Menu, or Return to Windows.

Chapter 25

Fabio Viscusi sat in the attack room eating a
cucumber-and-mayo sandwich and drinking a coffee as Lieutenant Kowalski brought the USS Fargo to VLF depth, twenty
meters below the surface. They'd been laying low as only boomer
submarines can lay low, 200 meters down, at the edge of the
Arctic continental shelf off the coast of Murmansk, patrolling in
circles to make sure nobody was following. Driving a boomer was
the most boring job in the world, even he had to admit it—when
Viscusi had started, you still had to watch a depth gage and course
indicator; now you had to keep a white dot in a small white circle,
and that was it, you were on course. And the kids who were doing
this for six hours at a stretch had grown up with Xbox and Play-
Station: they could do circus tricks with the white dot and circle if
he let them. Sometimes he let them—not this close to Russia, of
course—just to stop the jokes that they were still in port, since the
only time you felt like you were moving was when someone hot-
dogged.

It was the most boring job in the world, except when it
became the most exciting job in the world. His sister, Mary, was a
detective in the LAPD, and she claimed it was similar. Hours and
hours of nothing, and then suddenly a ping and you wonder
whether a Russian sonar heard you drop a wrench. And all of it

overwhelmed with paperwork, which, at least, on a submarine was never on paper anymore. It was all touch screens now—still backed up by mechanicals, thank God—and the most common submariner injury was near-point stress. He doubted Mary could really understand what it was like to sit at the bottom of the sea, rising up just under the surface every eight hours to get new orders if there were any, and sink back down. For one hundred days at a time. The routine sometimes seemed like it was designed to drive them all nuts. Yeah, insanity was exactly what you wanted from the crew of Ohio-class SSBN with twenty-four nuclear Trident II missiles.

Maybe he'd been at this too long. They only gave you a boomer after you'd already captained an attack boat, after you'd proven you weren't a risk-taker. That you were mature in a way that only someone with the ability to end the world needed to be mature. Plus something like 120 psychological exams over the course of his career. The United States Navy had a very odd relationship with its boomer captains. They hated the fact that a boomer was independent, but that independence was the key to maintaining nuclear deterrence and a credible second-strike capacity. If the Russians cut off the head in Washington, if they turned all of America into nuclear slag and prevented an ICBM counter-launch, the boomer subs out there had enough SSBMs to ensure that the price was too high. It was called a "fail-deadly." Like fail-safe, but everybody dies.

Captaining a sub was the last macho job in the military, with the possible exception of a few Navy Seal-type ops guys. When you were down, nobody told you what to do, nobody helped you make decisions. You came up, got your orders, and then you decided how to implement them. When Viscusi had gone to Annapolis, they'd still taught that that's what made the United States military superior to the Russians. America pushed responsibility down to the lowest levels, and that made it unpredictable. During a now near-mythical military exchange that became a teaching point from Annapolis to West Point, a Soviet general, after drinking too much with an American general, had slammed his glass down on the table and said in disgust that American officers don't read their own textbooks. If you could see 10 percent of a Soviet formation, you found the right page, and you knew where everyone else would be. Not so for the Americans.

That was then. After the Cold War ended, the politicians and generals wanted war to be a chess game with a single unified brass mind controlling every piece. Independence was risky. Security became everything. No accidents, no jocks. Virtual paper-shuffling trumped gut instincts and soldiers finalized their transformation from warriors to tools. This became painfully obvious to everyone when Joint Forces Command staged the largest war games in American history and chose Paul Van Ripper—an old friend of Viscusi's—to play the op force. Van Ripper's chaotic, messy, gut-instinct approach to running his small rebel force did the impossible and defeated the entire U.S. military, with its total informational control. But instead of learning from this, the brass replaced Van Ripper and replayed the war game, this time making sure the op-force followed a script. Then they declared victory. Since then, the Blue Team mindset had permeated every last nook and cranny of the U.S. military, to the point where now a sergeant couldn't shit without permission from at least a full-bird colonel.

"VLF requests packet, sir," Kowalski reported, bringing Viscusi out of his reverie.

"All right. Stick it out. ESM depth."

"ESM clear, Captain," Kowalski reported a minute later. "I got three land-based radar, looks like Morzhovets Island, Kanin, and Belomorsk, and one ship-based. Sierra, Lima and India bands. No Juliet. No aircraft, nothing that can pick us up."

"Periscope up. Let's take a look." He didn't strictly need visual, but he liked to look, even though it was all digital now and he was looking at a screen. It showed about four miles of open water. No activity. Peace on the sea. "Send the packet, when ready."

"Transmitting," Kowalski answered. "Uh, sir, we have a priority one Flash coming in from Atlantic Six." Atlantic SSIX was the submarine satellite for Atlantic Fleet Communications. "On your screen now, captain."

"Priority one?" Viscusi raised an eyebrow. Something was happening. Something more than a position change. But what popped up on his screen nearly made him spill his coffee.

Z130000ZTOP SECRETFROM: COMSUBLANTTO:

SUBLANTFLEETSTATUS CHANGE: DEFCON ONE
REPEAT DEFCON ONE
SUPPLANT Z125300Z STATUS CHANGE
REPEAT CHANGE FROM DEFCON THREE TO
DEFCON ONE
ALL CODES

"Holy fuck!" Kowalski said. "Is this a drill?"

Viscusi was so shocked himself that he didn't reprimand Kowalski. Last time they'd checked, the world was at Defcon Five. Not Three. On 9/11 they'd briefly gone to Three. And it had never been to One. Never. One basically meant they were already shedding nukes. He put his coffee down—he was suddenly not sleepy at all—checking the liquid to see if his hands shook, they didn't, then walked the five steps to his attack-room safe and used the key around his neck to open the safe. For this they still used paper, even on a sub. He opened the envelope that he'd never expected to open. Hoped and prayed that he'd never have to open. The U.S. military changed all codes at Defcon Three, but how in God's name could something have escalated from total peace to World War III? That just couldn't happen, could it? Whoever was attacking would have to mobilize, and that took time, time to spot it and slowly ratchet up the war footing. It must have been a surprise attack, something far worse than 9/11.

With the new codes he walked back to his communications computer.

The computer then gave him the rest of the message. He wished it hadn't. His ex-wife was still in Hoboken. Their son at NYU. Maybe. He almost stumbled as the thought froze him—they might all be dead within twenty-four hours. They might already be dead, if this really was a response. It had to be a response, didn't it? They were second strike. Jesus Christ. But then why was the sea quiet? This channel between the Barents and White Seas was called "The Throat" for a reason. It should be plugged with ship- and plane-based sonar and radar if the Russians were expecting a second strike.

"Kowalski, lower all masts. Take her to two hundred."

"Aye aye, sir."

In the background, an electrician reported that UHF and ESM antennae were lowered, a diving officer repeated two hundred and down angles on the planes, and Kowalksi announced that they were moving her, all ahead two-thirds. The boat ran itself. The crew ran itself. They'd been doing the routine for so long, both gold and blue shifts were an extension of the submarine, or she was an extension of them.

When the boat was driving herself back down to the edge of the continental shelf, Kowalski came up to his captain. "Are we shooting, sir?"

"You know I can't answer that."

"I know I can't call my wife or anything, but, just, in my head—"

"We have a job to do. That job is what keeps our families safe."

It had to be a response, didn't it? The good guys didn't shoot first. Not with nukes. But why the quiet. And the delay? It was more than ten hours before they were to launch. That didn't make sense for a second strike. The only thing that made sense was that someone was playing a hell of a game of chicken and they intended to cut it closer than the Cuban Missile Crisis. He wondered what it was about. If the Russians launched a massive conventional attack on Europe or, say, Alaska, then this sort of thing might make sense, but nothing like that could happen overnight. You can't hide that kind of buildup. And the White Sea would not be quiet. However he parsed it, Viscusi couldn't make it make sense.

But then it wasn't his job to make it make sense. All he had to know was that if this was a game of chicken, then the bad guys would soon know what he was about to do. Deterrence only worked if the bad guys knew. Which meant the entire Russian navy and air force would be hunting for him. Which meant it was time to get out of the throat, into the belly, and hide as only a boomer can hide. Until it was time to come back up and end the world.

━━━

"What does Russia have to do with this?" Ivan shouted. "You want to blow each other up, have a nice day." With an effort that visibly shook him, he restrained himself and lowered his voice as he glared at Preble. "Okay, I understand the Americans are afraid that if they leave you alone Russia will try to capture you, and you want to be free from everybody. But why bomb Moscow?"

"I think you should call your president." Preble said by way of answer, then turned to Grape. "And the Chinese president or general secretary or whatever title he goes by."

Ivan's voice was under control now, but his eyes still bulged. "I...I can't just pick up the phone and call President Peskov."

"Mr. President, you have a red phone or something to call President Peskov?"

John Grape still looked like he'd been hit in the head. "Uh, yes, of course."

"Call him, please. If we still have the threat board up, then we still have the phone. Stacey?"

Stacey dialled a number, talked to someone, then handed the phone to Grape. "President Peskov, this is John Grape calling from Washington."

Although in public appearances Peskov always insisted on a translator, he spoke perfect English, and this was no time to indulge his distaste at the linguistic imbalance. "President Grape, I was just about to call. Why have your forces gone to Defcon One?"

"I'm afraid it's not good news, President Peskov."

"Obvious."

"I have a Russian FSB agent here with me, in the strategic nuclear bunker below the White House. His name is Ivan uh—"

"Ivan Grigorovich Adamov."

"Ivan Adamov, his cover is Alexei Novinar, reports to your Mikhail Klurglur. I understand —"

"Mr. President, you have never been to Defcon One. To go there for no reason is the action of a lunatic."

"Yes. Please just listen, Mr. President. This is very awkward. Are you familiar with our problems with Mr. Preble Jefferson?"

"Of course."

"Mr. Jefferson is in the bunker with us. He would like to talk to you. If you would like to talk to Mr. Adamov afterwards to assure yourself that this is not some monstrous joke..."

"Of course, it is a monstrous joke. But as you say, I am

listening first. If talking to Mr. Jefferson explains why you put the human race at risk, then I will do so."

John Grape handed the phone to Preble. As he did so, he covered the mouthpiece and said, "Please don't kill us all."

"President Peskov, this is Preble Jefferson speaking."

"Yes."

"I'm going to put you on speaker phone, so the president, the chairman of the joint chiefs, Ivan, and Fish, my attorney, can all understand." Preble clicked over the phone.

"You have brought your attorney?" Peskov's voice finally dropped its matter-of-fact tone, seeming almost awed at the strangeness of the thought.

"President Peskov, I have just ordered the launch of multiple nuclear missiles from multiple submarines. Boomers. They will launch in twelve hours simultaneously at Moscow—"

"Cunt with ears!"

"—and Beijing. I presume from what I've read on ballistic submarines that there is no way you would be able to stop all of these missiles even if you know they are coming."

There was a very long pause. "Is this a joke? Some sort of radio station prank?"

"No, sir. I suggest you hang up the phone and call the White House red phone. It should reroute to the bunker. Or I could let you speak to Ivan."

"Why would you do such a thing? You know that our only response can be a full nuclear counterstrike. Our people would accept no less. We are talking about the end of the world."

"I'm sorry, Mr. President. Though I am no fan of either your country or China, you have done nothing here to justify being pulled into this situation. Moscow and Beijing are, as you say, collateral damage. Much as my family has been in my own little war with the United States. Now I am going to tell you how to save your cities. The only way to do so is to help me save my family. I am the only person capable of stopping those nuclear strikes. If I die, those strikes will take place. Just so we're clear, if I personally do not take affirmative steps, those strikes will take place. In order for me to take those steps, I need my family back. Afterwards, if we are left alone, I will guarantee not to do this sort of thing again."

"How noble of you. I will phone back in ten minutes. I have been briefed on your situation only in passing. My adviser on this issue is here with me."

"Very well. But let me give you the whole picture first, because time is of the essence. If your security services know where my family is, then simply telling me quickly where they are will be sufficient. Assuming they really are there. If you do not know where they are, then the course of action is more difficult. The man who does know is Thaddeus Bigman. Yagbig. He's currently underground in Cheyenne Mountain, Colorado. It is highly likely that he will launch a nuclear strike against Washington within the hour—"

"What—"

"If he does, we will all die in here, and if we die, there is no way to recall those submarines. Which means Moscow is toast. Mr. Bigman and I are having a disagreement about whether or not he should tell me where my wife and son are. I feel that with a sufficient threat to his own personal safety, he would release their location. Before starting the clock on Moscow, I tried to send missiles at Cheyenne Mountain, but the computer system here will not let me select a domestic target. So, if you do not have the correct information as to my family's whereabouts, then the course of action by which you will save Moscow will be to send whatever it takes to destroy the bunker at Cheyenne Mountain. As the headquarters of NORAD, I'm sure you've worked out the combination of nukes required to take it out. Send only missiles that can be de-activated en route so that this remains a negotiation and does not turn into a war. And it would be nice if they're low radiation, just in case, so we don't poison the whole planet."

There was another long pause, during which they could all hear Peskov breathing into his phone. "Mr. Jefferson. I am Russian. I am not environmentalist. But I do know that even without radiation a nuclear exchange, even small one, will release enough soot to lower planet's temperature for decades, destroying the crop yields and starving hundreds of millions worldwide."

Fish interrupted here, his information-maven mode triggered. "Actually, Mr. President, the best estimates are that an exchange of fifty Hiroshima-sized bombs would blast five million tons of soot into the air, which would lower temperatures by about three degrees for up to a decade. That would just about balance out global warming."

"Who is speaking?"

"Fish. Mr. Jefferson's, uh, lawyer."

"Hiroshima was fifteen kilotons. To break through Cheyenne you need at least a megaton, which is seventy Hiroshimas."

"No, it's not, Mr. President. The soot comes mostly from the surface, and a megaton bomb would vaporize most of it. The tonnage of the bomb doesn't make nearly as big a difference to the soot ratio as the number of separate bombs—"

"Enough. I do not speak with lawyers. Only a lazy man would not piss on your face. Mr. Jefferson, are you telling me that to stop strike on Moscow I need to destroy the Colorado?"

"I will request the same thing of the Chinese."

There was a pause, and Preble imagined he could almost see Peskov rubbing his face. When he spoke, his voice was both lower and slower, and he'd mostly regained control over his articles. "You will ask for ten and the Chinese will send a hundred and then apologize afterward. In Russia, we learned that the Chinese have only three military tactics: the Great Offensive, the Small Retreat, and Infiltration by Small Groups of Two to Three Million Across the Border. The last they tried for decades across our border in Siberia. I suspect when they find out you have launched nuclear missiles at Beijing, they will choose the Great Offensive. Mr. Jefferson, during the Cold War we learned not to play games with nuclear weapons. There has always been a significant faction of the Chinese military that, like you, has not learned this yet. And you have just given them power."

"Mr. President—"

"Wait. I will end this with one warning. If we know where your family is, we will tell you. A gift from Mother Russia to world peace. Russian peace. But if one missile hits Moscow, we will launch a full nuclear counterstrike. I assume you have some reason to believe your family is not in Colorado. Fine. But if they are anywhere in the United States, our counterstrike will kill them. And then presumably the retaliation from what's left of the United States will make the rest of the world uninhabitable. If one nuclear bomb lands on Moscow. One single bomb...If you are doing all this to save your family, you had better hope your Big Man put them on the Moon."

Everybody in the situation room stared at the phone while Peskov spoke. Then, almost as one, they looked up at Preble. He looked disconnected.

"I repeat. To save Moscow, you must either tell me the location of my family or destroy Cheyenne Mountain. I look forward to your phone call soon."

He hung up. Everyone in the ready room had stopped everything, including breathing. Grape had listened to the whole thing with a grotesque, involuntary tinge of pleasure. He'd had to deal with Peskov a number of times, and he hated trying to negotiate with the ex-KGB hybrid between human, shark and poison spider. And despite the fact that Peskov had ended with a threat, Grape could tell that Preble Jefferson had completely rattled him. Hell, he should be rattled. The whole world should be rattled.

It was Stacey that finally broke the silence: "Just how far into the future can you see?"

Preble looked up at her, suddenly tired. "Far enough," he lied. "Now get me the Chinese, please."

⊏⊐

President Ilya Peskov hung up the phone and looked at his Information Minister. "You did not warn me of this, Mikhail Alexandrovich."

Klurglur shifted in the overstuffed red chair facing Peskov's massive desk and pinched his nose repeatedly. "It is difficult to predict the behaviour of madmen."

"But that is your job."

"In this case, it was an impossible job. The Americans themselves didn't predict that Jefferson could not only get to President Grape but get control over the White House nuclear command center."

"Except it seems that the vice president and Mr. Bigman did predict just that."

"I think they had a contingency plan. If an opportunity opened up."

"And why did we not have a contingency plan?"

Klurglur swallowed hard. He was old friends with Peskov, their friendship as stable as any friendship in Russian politics could be. But suddenly nothing in the world felt stable. "We do. It is almost exactly what you described to Mr. Jefferson. One bomb on Moscow, and we respond overwhelmingly. The only difference is that the standard 'massive retaliation' doctrine is a tenfold increase. They send one nuke, we send ten. They send ten, we send one hundred. But the problem is that this contingency assumes state action. We punish America for the decisions of its leaders. This is more like a terrorist strike, except there is no network to break, no harbouring country to destroy."

"America?"

Klurglur lifted his palms up in a gesture that looked almost Italian. "They are hardly harbouring him. They are doing everything they can to kill him. In fact, they have been remarkably prescient about this. They almost caught him in Manitoba."

"At which we expressed outrage. Have you revised your estimate of how far he can see into the future?"

"We're still assuming a matter of seconds. But he's certainly acting now like a man who can see days."

"Jesus, Mary and Joseph, Mikhail, how do we bring this back to—"

"Sir?" Peskov's personal secretary interrupted, peeking her head in. Despite having worked for Peskov for nearly two years, she still avoided the room if she could. Far more than, say, the Oval Office in the White House, this still-mahogany-and-red-velvet room held all the power in Russia. No matter how many times she went in, it was never comfortable. "There's a call from a Thaddeus Bigman out of Cheyenne Mountain for you, calling on behalf of American Vice President Garland O'Reilly. But he is calling him President O'Reilly."

Peskov and Klurglur exchanged a look. "Civil war?" Peskov asked.

Klurglur shrugged. "If not, perhaps it could be turned into one."

"Do we want that?"

"As long as it doesn't go nuclear, yes."

"Our banks would collapse."

"And oil would go through the roof. Gazprom will be our bank."

"As long as it doesn't go nuclear." Peskov lifted the phone. "Peskov speaking."

"Mr. President. This is Thaddeus Bigman—"

"So you are the Big Man?"

"—calling on behalf of President Garland O'Reilly."

"What happened to President John Grape?"

"We've had an incident that you're probably aware of."

"Yes. Actually, I just spoke with...John Grape."

The pause was nearly imperceptible. "Yes. Unfortunately, he has been captured by a terrorist named Preble Jefferson. We've had some trouble with this individual."

"I spoke with Mr. Jefferson as well."

Another tiny pause. A worthy opponent, Peskov thought with a grim smile, as Bigman asked, "May I ask what he said?"

"You may ask, but I would first like to know why you called."

"Yes. You may have noticed that our forces have gone to Defcon Two."

"We do tend to notice that sort of thing, yes. And your submarine fleet is apparently on Defcon One."

"Yes, but that has nothing to do with you. I am simply calling to assure you that in the event that any of our forces actually go nuclear, it is in response to a domestic terrorist threat, not anything focused outside our borders."

"I do wish that were true, Mr. Big Man."

"Excuse me?"

Now it was Peskov's turn to pause, as he ran through his options and settled on an unusual one. The truth. "Apparently your terrorist has access to some of your submarine-based strategic assets, and has triggered them to launch at Moscow and Beijing. And he seems to be backed by President John Grape and your chairman of the joint chiefs."

"That...that's insane." For the first time in the phone call, Thaddeus Bigman's voice wobbled. "They're bluffing."

"You don't get into my position in Russia by being easily fooled. Mr. Jefferson might be able to see future, but I am the human lie detector. Whether he is insane or not, I do not know. But when he says those submarines are on the clock, I believe him.

And I suggest you believe me, because these are not the little feather games."

"Jesus Christ."

"I think this is more a question of Lucifer than of Jesus Christ. Mr. Jefferson has given me two options. Tell him where his family is or destroy you. If that means destroying Colorado, that's okay. I get a, what's your word, a freebie. And as much as I dislike being extorted, as much as he will pay for it eventually, right now those seem my only options for defending my capital city."

"Do you know...where the family is?"

Peskov frowned at this question. "I think it is your responsibility to tell him."

"So you don't know."

"You give them back to him, or I will do what he wishes."

"If you nuke Colorado, we will consider that an unprovoked first-strike on the United States and will respond with the full nuclear might of the United States."

"President Grape—"

"Is no longer the president. President O'Reilly is the president now."

"Not President Bigman?"

Bigman ignored the jab. "President O'Reilly has the backing of the Pentagon. You attack Colorado, and it's war." There was a pause, as Bigman changed tones. "Here's what you do. You take those missiles, and send them to Washington D.C. I'm sure you've always wanted to nuke Washington. Well, here's your chance. No consequences. No hard feelings."

"For a people who have no aesthetic sense for the absurd, you have made a remarkably absurd situation out of this. And if I bomb Washington, how do we stop the Trident missiles coming to Moscow?"

"We'll take them out with our own attack subs. We have their signatures, we know what to look for better than you."

Peskov looked at Klurglur, who was shaking his head. Then back to Bigman, he said, "We've been war gaming this for fifty years. We know how difficult it is to take out your boomers. Even if you know which subs are compromised and roughly where they are, there is no guarantee you would get them. If you want to bomb your own cities, you do it yourselves. Leave

Russia out of it. But if one nuclear weapon lands on the Russian soil, we will launch a full nuclear counterstrike against all American assets worldwide. You will have started the World War III. So if you destroy Washington now, if you kill Mr. Jefferson before he stops those subs, you will be guaranteeing the end of our species. To me it seems easier to tell Mr. Jefferson where his family is."

"I'm offering a trade, Washington at 100 percent for, say, a 50 percent risk of Moscow."

It took Peskov a second to figure out what Bigman meant. "The chance of you catching both those boomer submarines is more like 10 percent."

"You're still getting 100 percent for 90. It's a better deal."

"Moscow has a population of over ten million. The Washington metropolitan area is half that at best."

"God damn it, spread it out a bit if you want to go all Turkish Bazaar on me!" Bigman's voice cracked for a high-pitched second. Enough to make Peskov wonder whether the American used voice training to lower it. "Take a whole chain along the coast, make sure you include Baltimore, bump it up to fifteen million so you feel like you really got a good deal, and let's not end the world today. But keep it close to Washington so we can spin it, and don't even think about sending one to Cheyenne. And if you have any neutron bombs prepped, it would be nice to be able to keep the infrastructure."

Peskov paused for a long time before answering, so long that Bigman started to wonder if he was still there. Peskov didn't care about how he looked anymore. He needed to make sense of the situation. Desperately. "Have you killed them, Mr. Bigman?" he finally asked. "If you have, tell him and stop this. If you haven't, give them back."

"That woman and child are the only thing keeping the world from ending, Mr. President."

"Are you not paying attention? Jefferson has made destruction the default, probably because of this idea of yours. Doing nothing now means we all die." Peskov said and almost hung up the phone, before a second thought made him add, "Don't do anything stupid before I call back."

Then he hung up and turned to Klurglur. "Find that family,

Mikhail. Or find out what happened to them. I don't care what it takes. Burn all our assets if necessary, but find them."

"Could this be a massive trick by the Americans?"

"No. This is a war between two monsters, and I just decided which one I prefer. And one more thing. Get my daughters to my dacha. I suggest you get your family out as well."

Chapter 26

THADDEUS BIGMAN SAT AT A COMPUTER PANEL SURROUNDED by threat boards in a bunker that was almost identical to the one under the White House—complete with continuously welded low-carbon steel plates, reinforced concrete bulkheads, and baffled steel—except that at six hundred meters, it was twice as deep. His bunker could take a lot more pounding than the one in which Preble Jefferson was hiding. But anything over a megaton, even if it didn't kill him, would melt the surface rock shut and probably sever all communications, no matter how hardened they were. They had equipment to dig their way back out, but he'd be stuck here for months, unable to shape how the information war played out. He might climb out of his hole only to be dragged to a lethal injection.

Even now he could tell that some generals and deputies around him were sobering up. Automatic protocols were established precisely because most people couldn't think clearly and efficiently in high-stress situations, and yet there was nothing like the threat of death to undo all the carefully planned protocols. The world looked different when you were about to die—duty, rules, and protocols be damned.

He walked over to a conference room that was also a near-replica of the one under the White House, except that there was no massive presidential seal. There was a pot of hot coffee ready on a service stand by the wall. Bigman poured himself a cup, black, then sat alone at the conference table. Halfway through his coffee he reached across the table to the flat black phone, and made two calls. The first was to Agent Lebowski, the agent he always used to shadow Fifi or Kiki, and told him to remove both of them from any urban areas within the United States. "Take them shopping at an outlet mall in the middle of nowhere. Even better, take them on a road trip to Canada."

The second call was to the White House bunker, where he was put through to Preble. "Mr. Jefferson," he said. "Preble. May I call you Preble?"

Preble listened.

"This time you can't duck, Preble," Bigman said when he realized he wasn't going to get an answer.

"This time nobody can duck."

Bigman took another sip of coffee. "You know, I once read that every man has a devil who haunts him. When we first talked in that NYPD precinct house, when I first figured out what you were, I knew I was your personal devil. It really was bad luck for you that I saw that video. Very few people would have jumped to the crazy idea that you could see the future. They would have jammed the situation into some rational, conventional explanation. I am your personal devil, but you are also mine."

"Fuck off, Thad. You have my family. I want them back. I have made the consequences of your refusal as horrendous as I possibly could, and yet you still refuse. I will repeat my promise, on my word of honour: if you give them back, I will go away. I will hurt nobody else. I will dedicate my life to searching for a cure for any other disease you wish. Or solving any problem you wish. Medicine, weapons, good, evil, I don't care. You choose the problem, and I will take it on as my mission in life. A life I wish to live with Kasper and Jane."

"Your word of honour means nothing to me."

"Because you have none."

"Honour is a tool for convincing grunts to risk their lives in service of a cause."

"Like I said. Why are you calling?"

"To tell you my realization that we are devils to each other.

Tied together. And if the world is going to end, then I think we should be together."

"And here I thought I was the one going crazy."

Bigman laughed. He actually laughed. "It's not possible to stay sane when you have your finger on the button."

"You don't want to find a way out?"

"Yes," Bigman said. A tired sigh. "Here it is. You leave. Go away. We never chase you again. You can even have your island. But your family stays. I'll give you my word that they will not be hurt. No experiments on Kasper. Just a family living on a base under permanent house arrest, moved periodically, always in secret locations but always comfortable. You will never know where they are, and if you try to find out, the deal is off, and we start experiments."

Preble closed his eyes. "Why?"

"Insurance. Didn't your lawyer tell you? The answer is always insurance."

"I'll think about it."

"Turn the clock off on the subs."

"No. I'll think on the clock. That much, my lawyer did tell me."

⊏⊐

The entire Russian navy and air force were going fishing. Every reservist with a rowboat was being called up. But while those subs stayed at the bottom of the sea—probably somewhere around Murmansk or Arkhangelsk—there was little chance of spotting them. The navy would have a minute, at best, to spot and destroy them when they came to the surface to launch. Not nearly enough, and a full minute was more wishful thinking than rational military planning.

Those subs had been a thorn in Russia's side for over half a century, and now they just might chop off its head. Without American boomers, the Soviet Union would likely still be alive and well, spanning from the Sea of Japan to Normandy. Throughout the sixties and seventies, the USSR had an overwhelming conventional advantage over NATO. All the plans said unequivocally that they could take all Europe ex-UK in five days.

And during all that time, the Americans had had only one trump card: they said if the USSR tried a conventional war in Europe, they'd respond with nuclear strikes from their boomers. No proportionality, no warrior ethic, just straight-out nuclear black-mail. While Hollywood made movies about Mother Russia starting nuclear war, in private negotiations American presidents, one after the other, insisted that they would go nuclear first. And it had worked because of those subs. Despite every effort, Russia had never found a way to neutralize them. There was no way. If those subs launched, Moscow's layers and layers of missile defence might take out a few Tridents with lucky hits, but not multiple Tridents from multiple Ohio-class subs.

Unless a way was found for the Americans to contact their subs, or Preble Jefferson countermanded the order, Moscow would die. It could take the world with it, it could punish anyone it chose in its death, but it would die. Moscow wasn't just the capi-tal. It wasn't Washington. In practical terms, it was Washington and New York wrapped up in one, but emotionally it was far more than that. Washington and New York were just cities in a country, but Mother Russia herself had grown out of the Duchy of Muscovy. In the end, every inch of Russian land outside Moscow was just a glorified colony.

It had been sacked by the Mongols twice in the 1200s, by the Mongol-Tatars in the 1300s, by the Crimean Tatars in the 1500s, three times in the 1600s—by the Swedes, then the Polish-Lithua-nians, and then the plague—and finally by the Moscovites them-selves in the 1800s in order to starve out Napoleon. Moscow always survived, rebuilt and grew. Could it survive nukes? It might take two hundred years before people could live there again. But then, in its youth Moscow had paid tribute to the Golden Horde for over two hundred years. It had bowed, so that it could rise again. Maybe he was wrong. Maybe she could survive even this.

There was a knock on the door. "Come."

"Mr. President," Klurglur said, walking up to Peskov's huge old desk. It was at this desk that Stalin had decided to kill 60 million of his own people. It was at this desk that Alexander I had decided to burn Moscow, and with it Napoleon's reign over Europe. People focused on Waterloo, but Napoleon was outnumbered two to one at Waterloo. He'd had no chance, and it was only because he was Napoleon that the battle had been so close. No, Napoleon's defeat came from Alexander's single, excruciating decision to burn Moscow. That decision had frozen, starved and ultimately destroyed the unstoppable Grande Armée of a million men. A Russian sacrifice that had saved Europe.

"Mr. President," Klurglur interrupted Peskov's thoughts, "as you know we have no satellite imagery of what happened in Hudson's Bay, but I had my analysts search all satellite images for the icebreaker that kidnapped Jefferson's family." He put two sets of pictures on the desk. "The USS Polar Star. This one is an image from just prior to the kidnapping. And this one is an image taken five days after the kidnapping, when the icebreaker came within range of one of our satellites."

"No helicopter," Peskov said.

"No helicopter."

"Does that mean they're dead?"

"It increases the odds substantially."

"But that should be easy enough. Find out who was on that helicopter and check for funerals, insurance procedures." Peskov cut himself off with a frown, sure that Klurglur would know this already.

"This was an NSA operation, and they have some all-black teams. Those men would have been officially dead years ago, for exactly this reason. A team like that disappears and nobody knows it except for whichever cell organized it, in this case Mr. Bigman. And any of the people who worked with them."

"The icebreaker. Where is it now?"

"Exactly what I wanted to ask approval for. It's currently in the Hudson Straight. We could have a team there from Severnaya Zemlya in four hours. But it might be seen as an act of war."

Peskov slapped the desk. Stalin's desk. "An act of war? Hah. If there was ever a military action that could be labelled an act of peace, this is it." He turned to his secretary, who was always by his side now. "Tatiana, call Thaddeus Bigman and relay the following message: 'If we see any American nuclear launch targeting Washingon D.C., we will respond immediately with sufficient tonnage to destroy Cheyenne Mountain.' End of message, no discussions. Just relay the message. But first, get me Jefferson again. Maybe we can make those boomers bob."

"Ilya, one thing. What if they are dead? Do you really want to tell the one man who must act that he has nothing to live for."

"Cunt with ears..." Peskov mumbled as he took the phone. It took less than thirty seconds to reach Jefferson. Peskov explained that they'd found the icebreaker and would send a team to extract information from the crew. And he asked for time.

"You have nine hours and counting."

"It will take that long just to get to the ship!"

"I'm not changing the launch time. Before the boomers launch, they'll come close to the surface to check if the orders have been changed. You know that is your best time to catch them. If they do it once, you have almost no chance. But if they do it two times, three times, you just might get them."

"We are doing our best to save the world here."

"Must feel unnatural for you."

Peskov gritted his teeth. "Russia might not buy into American moralistic hypocrisy. But when the world really needs saving, who is there? Who broke Napoleon? Who broke Hitler? And now again, it is Russia who will save the world. If you give us the time to do so."

"Work fast."

"Mr. Jefferson, I will personally ensure that at least one megaton is targeted at that icebreaker. It seems quite possible that your family, if they are still alive, are on that ship. If you launch before we find out, you will never know."

⸺

Captain Grigori Asimov, no relation to the writer, ran out on his static line into the frigid Arctic air. Even though it was summer, this high up it was minus 30 and with the wind-chill from the moving Antonov An-74, even at just above stall speed, was a cold minus 70. Only for a minute, but a minute was enough to lose body parts at 70 below. Very few countries even had paratroops trained to jump into such cold, but Russia maintained a certain pride in its Icemen, and actually geared them up properly. They also maintained a 5 percent mortality rate in training. Five percent or less, during peacetime, and his lieutenants didn't need to write up a report.

But even for Asimov, parachuting onto an icebreaker in the Arctic Ocean seemed like what the Americans called Russian roulette. If you missed the ship, you froze to death almost instantly. Whoever had planned this mission cared about getting enough men onto the icebreaker far more than they cared about avoiding casualties. Most of all, they cared about speed. They'd sent all four Antonovs from Ostrov Greem Bell airbase in Franz Joseph Land, and all three from Rogachevo in Novaya Zemlya. Unfortunately, both bases were primarily for forward staging of bombers and for early warning radar, with only limited numbers of paratroop transports. At 22 paratroops per transport, with a few extra squeezed in, there were 170 Russian commandos now jumping onto the USS Polar Star. The 10th Air Army at PVO Arkangelsk was also sending four times that number, but whoever was running the mission clearly didn't think using overwhelming numbers justified the three-hour delay from Arkhangelsk. So the 10th Air Army became simply a second wave in case the first failed.

Asimov was actually relieved about this. Without its helicopter, the USS Polar Star was unlikely to have its assault team on board, and he liked the odds of 170 commandos against 138 sailors, cooks and sonar technicians. He liked them much better than trying to land nearly a thousand men simultaneously onto a moving icebreaker with unpredictable Arctic downdrafts. And he had no doubt that the wise leaders in Moscow would rather dump a thousand men onto the ship and have five hundred land than throw 170 and end with 170 on board.

As it was, 152 landed on the ship, eight with broken ankles, legs, or wrists, he'd find out later, and eighteen landed in the below-freezing Arctic water. Eighteen deaths caused by too many people trying to land on too small a target. Even if they still had a few minutes, these were minutes that mattered only to them. There was simply no way to rescue them in time, and landing in the sleet grey water they might as well have gone through a black hole. Asimov didn't have the exact number, but he watched and calculated by force of habit. It looked like over ten percent—above ten percent even he would have to write a report, not just his lieutenants. If this were a training mission.

But it wasn't. Their mission was to find out what happened to the family of Preble Jefferson, and, in a move that was highly unusual for the Russian military, they were told the true stakes of their mission: failure could mean the end of the human race.

The crew of the USS Polar Star were used to complaints by the Canadian government over incursions into its Arctic territorial waters, a convention of international law that they were under strict orders to periodically violate in order to protect the freedom of maritime passage—and carve out a long-term claim on those waters if oil should ever be discovered there. But they were not used to anything more aggressive than repeated polite requests to leave. On one single occasion a Canadian icebreaker had physically pushed them back into international waters, for which the Canadian captain had been court-martialled by his own government for starting an international incident.

The Defcon One status had been conveyed to the U.S. Coast Guard, but they'd been given no additional information. The standard Coast Guard protocol above Defcon Three for its icebreakers was to go to live ammunition, aid U.S. ships through icefields and defend against enemy submarines. But the protocols assumed either mission orders, or that they'd be in U.S. coastal waters with a set patrol area. Instead, they were in Canada with no instructions whatsoever.

When it started snowing Arctic Russian commandos, the Coast Guard first assumed it was an exercise. It was always an exercise, and the Defcon One thing made no sense. There were no significant international tensions outside the Middle East and nobody had told them to look out for a Russian invasion. When the Russians landed, they managed to get a few shots off, three different pockets of soldiers barricaded themselves in defensible positions, but for all intents and purposes the Russian commandos secured the icebreaker in less than ten minutes, losing only nine men to actual fighting.

Chapter 27

"ILYA!" KLURGLUR RAN INTO PRESIDENT PESKOV'S OFFICE without knocking. "We have word."

Peskov nodded wearily. He'd just finished a conversation with his defence minister. "No family."

Captain Asimov's interview techniques had been crude but efficient. There were only three NSA agents on the ship when the team landed, all radio and communications people. Asimov chose a boatswain at random and put a bullet between his eyes—so that the boatswain would really learn, as the grim joke went—and the NSA people started to talk. Knowing that everybody eventually breaks under torture made giving in early much easier, especially if you had proof the interviewer wasn't bluffing. And it didn't feel like they were revealing national security secrets when they admitted that a helicopter had been sent to take Jefferson's family. He'd shot at it and punctured its gas tank. Unable to make it back to the ship, the chopper had landed on a huge tabular iceberg, basically a floating plateau more than two miles across. Too big to flip. They'd radioed in, they had the packages, everyone was safe, would the Polar Star please come pick them up.

But the Polar Star, like all icebreakers, was made for riding on top of thin ice shelves and crushing them down. It couldn't break through the massive multi-mile floating tabs that were often taller than the ship itself. They had to weave and had to do it carefully because the icebergs moved, even the giant ones, and if the ship got caught between two huge tabs its chances would be about the same as a bicyclist between two delivery trucks on a Manhattan bridge. So they'd radioed back to the chopper that the heavy ice was delaying them. They would be there in the morning. The helicopter had plenty of cold weather gear to camp overnight on the ice.

At less than ten nautical miles long, the helicopter's improvised landing-pad iceberg didn't warrant a name, but it looked like a moving wall on the ship's radar. Even with other moving walls in the way, the ship had no trouble tracking it, but somehow they lost communication after the second "be there in the morning" message. There was no reason for losing radio. When they'd arrived, they found no one.

The two-mile floating ice table was still there. The chopper wasn't. The pilot had chosen a good berg on which to land, but he might have landed too close to the edge. A chunk, any size, might have calved and the calved portion might have flipped. Icebergs were almost surreal in their placidity, their serene calm that suddenly and without warning could turn jarringly violent, rip, calve, flip, and then return to calm.

At any rate, they'd found nothing. They'd waited for a day, but the helicopter had landed on the eastern end of the floating island and the prevailing currents and winds were pushing the tab eastward, covering the area where the helicopter would have been earlier. There was no way to search under water that first day. The second day they were able to get above the last known GPS coordinates, but with the depth and the frigid waters the best they could do is bounce a sonar and see if there was metal down there. There was. That was all they knew. They'd never be able to spot bodies, let alone recover them.

"So Mr. Jefferson's family is dead," Peskov said in a tone that was begging to be disputed.

"It's overwhelmingly likely."

"Not certain?"

"I lost a brother in Ukraine, Ilya. I know he's dead, but they never found his body, so I do not know it with certainty. If you love someone, there is a part that is never certain."

"You think that's how Jefferson will see it?"

Klurglur shook his head. By an unspoken shift, they were just old friends now, friends who had watched each other's backs for three decades, figuring out a problem together. A big problem. "I have no idea how he will see it. But he has made it quite clear that they are now the only things he lives for, his only anchors to the world. I think I understand now why Bigman would bring the world to the edge of destruction rather than tell him."

"To protect himself. From revenge?"

"Perhaps. But consider. This man can destroy the world. What happens when you tell him that he has nothing to live for?"

"But the alternative. We are headed there anyway."

"Maybe it is time to reconsider our response. Moscow can rebuild. Beijing can rebuild. Washington can rebuild. So long as the human race survives."

"I do not think our military would accept— "

Klurglur scratched his beard. "This is not the Americans bombing Moscow, Ilya. This is an individual, a terrorist destroying the capitals of the three big players. No, not a terrorist. A demon. An alien mutation from another planet with strange science-fiction powers. And we, working in cooperation, stopped him. Perhaps it is time to focus the countries of the Earth on an external threat, one that we can all believe in, regardless of nationality, regardless of religion. Each can use the name that works for his belief system, but whatever his name, the enemy will be a single focused person who could be anyone at any time. It would have worked with Al Qaeda or ISIS if they weren't tied to one religion that belongs to a billion people. This will work better. Eternal vigilance against freaks hidden among us who have the power to kill millions. To end the world. Because if there was one, there will surely be more. Perhaps like my brother, perhaps little Kasper Jaspers Jefferson is alive, out there somewhere, with the same powers as his monstrous father. Powers that would drive anyone mad. He or his kind could be anywhere, from the fence until lunchtime, as they used to say. It will make all three countries stronger in the end, not relative to each other, perhaps, but relative to destabilizing internal forces. Remember, the USSR fell from the inside, not the outside."

Peskov rubbed his face, trying to bring some blood back to the surface. "Tatiana, please get me another coffee. And the defence minister. And then Mr. Thaddeus Bigman at Cheyenne Mountain, Colorado."

⊏⊐

A cell phone number suddenly popped into Preble Jefferson's mind. Waiting for the world to end was still waiting, and despite the threat board and all the other electronics in the bunker, Preble felt tied down. The millions of possible futures in which he normally lived had been narrowed down by the confines of the room, but the bunker had a telephone and that linked him to possibilities. Preble periodically opened his mind to all the possible numbers in the world that would give him answers in English. He wasn't trying to crack a code, there was no specific answer to grab and pull backwards, but some combination of his window and subconscious continued to work the phones as he sat in the bunker.

Once when he had explained how it worked to Fish, Fish had told him about the game in which Bobby Fischer defeated Byrne, described by chess commentators as "more witchcraft than chess."

Preble's witchcraft had given him nothing all night, and then suddenly it got him a U.S. Coast Guard engineer screaming while trying to keep his voice low that Russians had taken over the USS Polar Star. He dialled the number. "Is this Ensign First Class John MacKenzie?"

"Yes! You need to get word to the Pentagon that Russian commandos have taken over the USS Polar Star!"

"What is the location of the Polar Star, ensign?"

"Ah, ten miles north of Ivujivik, passing Digges Island. I've been hiding in a—"

Preble hesitated, but try though he might, he couldn't stop himself from hearing an answer to a potential question. He could jump ahead. It was all fast enough and without his nose he could see far enough. Too far. What happened to the helicopter?

I don't know. The iceberg must have calved. It wasn't there when we got there. Sonar showed metal....

Six seconds. Maybe seven.

"Are you still there?" the ensign asked.

Preble had never before used up his whole window thinking. Thinking so slowly that the ensign had waited for a response, waited and began to wonder whether he was still there. And he'd never asked the question. He'd spent his entire life forcing himself to learn to ask his questions out loud, to get answers he's already heard five seconds hence, a constant echo to which he had sentenced himself for life in order to appear normal, to function in a society that lived out of alignment with his own personal space-time. A lifetime of driving behind Honda CRVs with soccer moms doing the speed limit in the passing lane, thinking he was the menace because he wanted to go five seconds faster.

And they—they, the sum total of his neighbours—had killed Kasper and Jane simply because they were afraid. It always came back to fear. He hated fear, hated it the way Fish hated communism or a Sunday school teacher hated Satan, perhaps the only thing he truly hated in the world. It was repulsive—how little the world religions knew to not include fear in their list of deadly sins. Or perhaps they knew a lot. Vampires lived off fear: institutions, governments, religions, everyone who ever wanted to shrink and control humanity in order to better feed off it used fear. For decades now, Americans had been subjected to careful social engineering designed to make them fearful. Because without fear a man might stand up, claim his divine spark, steal fire from the gods, and slug it out with the angels. Like Bigman had said, fearlessness made men difficult to govern.

Fear turned people into either slaves or monsters or both.

Seeing the future took one form of fear away, but he still felt it. He felt it second-hand, but his fear of losing Kasper and Jane had been enough to turn him into a killer. How much worse fear for one's own safety? A sad, small emotion unworthy of our species. And yet our world nurtured it, told others to respect it so that we might not feel bad about being fearful. The fearful deserved what they feared, and if they were afraid of nuclear annihilation then that's what he would give them.

What had Kasper ever done to anyone?

"Hello?" the ensign begged, a loud whisper. "Please, answer! Are you still there?"

"You're going to hell, ensign."

Preble hung up the phone. He turned to the computer, clicked through to new launch options, and only stopped when Fish had forcibly turned his whole chair around, away from the computer.

"Preble, stop!"

Preble looked up at Fish. "Don't get in my way."

"What happened?"

"It's time to start over."

Suddenly everyone in the room was silent. Freakishly silent. Afraid. The president, the technicians, the analysts, the soldiers, even Kris of the Secret Service was listening in fear. Even Ivan, with his lightbulb eyes. The only person in the room who was not afraid was Fish. He may have been paranoid, but he wasn't afraid.

Preble kept his eyes locked on those of his friend, but his voice might have come from a computer. "The helicopter had to land on an iceberg. Because I shot a hole in the gas tank. It disappeared. No trace. The sonar guys on the USS Polar Star tried searching for it on the sea bed. They found metal. No survivors. They're dead, Fish."

"You don't know that. Unless you've seen the bodies, you don't know for sure." Fish's face and hands had gone completely pale as he stood unnaturally rigid above the sitting Preble, a weird replay of how all this had started, with Officer L. Paskalakki looming above him in the subway. "But let's stipulate for a second that they are. Are you going to kill everybody in revenge? A little girl in Maine or wherever asking her Mommy if she can paint her toenails just like her and suddenly boom, you kill her?"

"Our world is sick."

"So fix it. Don't end it."

Preble didn't answer. He saw that Kris was about to pull out her gun and try to shoot him, which would prompt every other soldier in the room to try as well. Preble shoved his chair on its wheels backwards into her, hard, then followed after it. He side-stepped the gun coming up, hit Kris in the knee and twisted the gun out of her hand at the same time. He shot Ivan as the Russian dove at him, then three Marines who were about to fire at him. The rest put their guns down on the floor. Afraid. With the right combination of fear and timing, you could break anyone. De Koek, who'd regained consciousness seconds after the hit to the head— that now felt like a lifetime ago, though it was only minutes— hadn't even tried to reach for his sidearm.

Kris was on her knees on the ground, but she tried to roll and launch herself at Preble's legs. Preble hit her on the head with the butt of the gun, knocking her out. She would keep trying. If he left her alive, Kris wouldn't stop trying to stop Preble. Exactly for that reason, Preble didn't want to shoot her. He wanted to shoot the Marines who'd put their guns down. He wanted to shoot de Koek. He'd never wanted to shoot someone before.

He lifted his gun and pointed it at de Koek's ugly square face.

He couldn't do it. He had known he wouldn't be able to, but somehow he had blocked it out.

Preble looked at Fish. He didn't know his friend anymore. "What happened, Fish? We were going to save Kasper and Jane, and then change the world."

"I'm sorry, Preble. I'm so sorry about Kasper and Jane. But whether we change the world or not is still up to you. You're not the only one with a family he loves. Please, don't destroy the world."

"It's not my world. They destroyed my world already."

"You are the one who shot that hole in the gas tank. You are the reason they landed on an iceberg. And it's not your fucking decision whether the world ends or not, or it shouldn't be, anymore than it should be that of any politician. And if there is anything that your very existence proves is that time doesn't really exist. It's just a pattern that we can't see, like we can't see or hear microwaves. We can only see the residue of that pattern as the change in the microwave popcorn. And if time doesn't exist, then Kasper and Jane are still alive in some way. Live, lived, will live, they all overlap."

"All my life I lived in the future. Now I'm going to live in the past?"

"There is no past or future!"

"If that's true, then I'm not skilled enough. I see seconds, not infinities. I can't see far enough to be with Kasper and Jane. And even if I could, if I went and sat in a cave and concentrated really hard, there'd still be no fifth birthday. In all your physics, where is Kasper's fifth birthday? It was taken from him and no shift in my ability to see patterns in the universe will give it back to him. I'll —" Preble's voice broke, and he stopped. He couldn't control himself, he was sobbing, watching blind as Fish took two steps to

De Koek, took his service revolver from him and pointed it at Preble.

Preble had never hidden anything from his friend. Fish was the only one in the room who knew that when flooded with emotion, Preble's window disappeared. He could shoot him now, and Preble wouldn't be able to duck or weave. He would just die, and the world might live. Maybe with Grape and de Koek's eyeballs they could get some sort of override for the boomer orders. At the very least, Fish could make sure no new nukes were launched. If he pulled the trigger. "Give me your word now you won't launch more."

"Shoot, Fish. I don't care. I don't care about—" Preble gasped and nearly fell out of his chair.

"What?"

Preble had died an infinite number of times in potential futures. He was used to it. But a wave, a ripple of horror like he'd never felt before, came to him, and it came from much further than he'd ever experienced. The death of millions and millions.

He could be in so many different locations by then. He could experience the death an infinite number of different ways, standing side by side with a thousand different individuals. The cumulative effect was synergistic and overwhelming. He'd just seen the world end. In a dead loud whisper, he said, "They've launched at Washington. And Moscow. And Beijing."

"Who has? When?"

He could barely talk. "I don't know when. Maybe forty-five minutes from now. America, Russia and China have all launched missiles at all three cities."

"You can't see that far."

"I can see through the cracks. I can't see you shooting me, but I can see that I'm going to die soon. Millions and millions...my God..."

Fish hesitated, wondering whether this was a trick. Preble didn't play chess this way, but he was hardly the same person he'd played in the Flea House every Thursday night. "So stop it!"

"I...I don't think I can... Fish, get out of here. Go start your new society."

"Without you my new society will be in prison."

"Take the president, then. Work something out."

"President Grape is a dead man walking if he steps out of this bunker."

"In a day or two. But he can get you out of Washington. And who knows? He's a politician, good at surviving. Fish, I can see again, so you can't shoot me, but I'll try to stop this. I'll do everything I can to stop this."

Fish still hesitated, still holding the gun pointed at his best friend's forehead.

"You have my word. If you saw what I just saw...What have I done?"

⊏⊐

Viscusi hadn't slept at all. Who could sleep, knowing the world was about to end. Wondering whether it might have already. They were in complete darkness at the bottom of the White Sea, blind to what had happened to their world. He and Kowalski were the only ones on the ship who knew what they were about to do, but they didn't talk to each other. They couldn't bear to. Each forced himself onto autopilot, with the only disturbing moments when they passed by each other. You couldn't pass someone on a sub, anywhere on a sub, without both of you turning sideways, and the look Kowalski gave him every time scared the shit out of him. It probably went both ways.

There were procedures, mechanisms. A machine didn't freak out and screw things up. Viscusi became a ghost, prowling every corner of his ship—from the Star Trek control room to the racks in the torpedo room, men sleeping on top of three-ton explosive fish in the equivalent of a closet shelf with a curtain instead of a door—watching, observing, and saying nothing. And he could smell the submarine. It's the first thing that hits you the moment you get on the ladder, exhaust, sweat, lube oil, old electricity, smoke, salt water, grease, trash and sanitation, but really more than all that. It's a pea-soup-thick "submarine smell," every Bubblehead's wife knows it by name. They all forbid their husbands from taking civvy clothes on board unless they're wrapped in airtight plastic. You don't smell it after the first week, the port is what smells funny when you get back home. But Viscusi was smelling it now like he'd just gotten on board.

Kowalski didn't prowl. He drove the electronics techs to the verge of fragging him by having them manually plot and replot their bearings so many times they figured out that something was seriously wrong, and whispers spread. There was a half-joke Bubbleheads used to explain their duties on a sub to outsiders: install 300 additional oil temperature gauges in your car, then sit in the driver's seat with your hands on the wheel and the motor running for six hours every day, but don't go anywhere. Take notes on all indicators and gauges every thirty minutes in a log. And now Kowalski was insisting that they note every five minutes.

A boomer submarine was always a sort of neurotic ghost ship, but now it was in overdrive.

"Up EMS!" Nearly time.

Kowalski whistled, back in duty-and-action mode. "They know we're here, Captain. I've never seen so much radar. In every band. I read nearly three-dozen transmitters. Ship, land, air, you name it, they're searching. Somebody told them. No way this is a general alert. I've got four, scratch that, five Juliet bands. We stick our periscope up, they'll cut it off for us. And with the light we have minutes before they get a visual. We need to launch and get back down, sir!"

"Commence Trident launch sequence."

"Sir?" The weapons tech's eyes nearly popped out of his head.

"You heard me, sailor. Commence Trident launch sequence."

"Incoming VLF package," Kowalski announced.

"Launch sequence initiated," the weapons tech announced, voice shaking. "On your keys, sirs."

Once their launch coordinates were properly established—which is why Kowalski had been driving the techs crazy—the computer did everything else. Viscusi and Kowalski just had to turn their keys. They walked up to the board, inserted their keys, and waited for the comm tech to send Viscusi the decoded packet.

"Torpedo in the water! Torpedo in the water!" the sonar tech screamed. "Two, three, four birds, bearing 210 degrees, four clicks. They fired too soon, but it will be here in thirty seconds, sir!"

"We need to launch, sir!" Kowalski shouted.

"On your screen now, sir," the com tech said.

Viscusi's eyes scanned the VLF package on the screen too fast, then stopped dead: Abort. "Abort launch! Dive, planes down full, bring her about to ninety degrees, release decoys!"

"More birds in the water sir!" the sonar tech screamed again. "Bearing 170 degrees, two clicks." He continued to shout out new torpedo bearings as the Russian air and naval armada in the White Sea found their ghost ship, his voice steady. If he'd thought about it, he'd know they had no chance, but his job was to yell out torpedo locations, and he kept yelling as the boomer dove, turned, sent out decoys, cavitated, hoped that some of the bubbles would attract torpedoes, and finally blew up. The other three American boomers were luckier. They received their abort orders and sunk back into their depths, but the USS Fargo went down with all hands. Right before it did, Viscusi and Kowalski exchanged a look of relief. If the Russians were still at sea, if they'd been expecting them, if they received abort orders, then maybe their families were still alive. Maybe.

Preble Jefferson tried to reach Peskov, Secretary Xu, and Thaddeus Bigman for nearly 30 minutes, without success. Finally, he phoned Klurglur—Fish had given him the number before running out of the bunker. Klurglur picked up, then handed the phone to Peskov.

Preble could barely hear either of them over the sound of a helicopter. They were probably already dozens of miles from Moscow. Preble struggled to keep his mind clear: he could feel the idea of the helicopter as a giant hand, trying to push him over a cliff.

"Are you crazy, not picking up the phone?"

"Your Thaddeus Bigman warned me that one of your skills is foreseeing what our answer would be in any circumstance. It's hard to keep a secret from you."

"You can always lie, for God's sakes. Listen, I aborted the boomer launches."

Peskov laughed, sounding like it was through a clenched jaw. "You mean we sunk the submarine."

"I sent the abort order to all four submarines. Two in the

White Sea, two in the South China Sea. So now you stop your launch."

"Cunt with ears! Jesus, Mary and Joseph!"

"You have only minutes."

"You fucking lunatic, it's not that simple! I can't abort without Chairman Xu and Thaddeus Bigman also aborting. We're each bombing all three capitals."

"If you and Xu abort, it's two thirds less damage."

"And then it's an act of war by the United States and we are forced to respond with 'massive retaliation.' And then they'll respond with their second-strike capability. The only way to prevent this from turning into war is...it must be proportional. It's the only way to save the world. All three of us bomb all three cities with the exact same number of bombs. Or all three of us to stop."

"So stop—"

Needles shredded Preble's body, every joint, every inch of his skin, his vision doubled, tunnelled, his lungs exploded, pain spreading from just below his sternum like a massive hit in the chest, tearing bits as all the air forced itself out, forced his mouth open. He couldn't inhale. He'd died a million times over the course of his life—the excruciating fire of burnt airways, the sudden thirst of a severed aorta, the chest-ripping feel of drowning, the cooking of the brain as the skull heats from very high voltage electrocution, the exploding heart of long falls, the sheer weirdness of a decapitation. But he'd never gone past the nearly euphoric firing of synapses as the brain fought in futility for oxygen. Every one of the deaths he'd ever experienced, including the guillotine, hanging, crushing—his window had never been long enough to bridge the few seconds' worth of residual life stored in the brain, or perhaps it had just refused to go there all the way. He'd never really died before, and especially not like this, in a vacuum. He was swelling. The water in his cells was vaporizing, but remained contained by his skin. He was a colony, a colony of cells with each individual cell exploding. What a strange way to die. Funny, not in an elevator. He'd been so sure it would be in an elevator. The bunker must have stopped the shock wave and the fire. But the nukes got far enough down to vaporize the air system. For a few seconds, everything above was vacuum. It sucked out all the air from the entire bunker. If it hadn't, the air itself would have caught fire and burned them alive, like heretics and witches. But it hadn't. It had just gone away. Leaving them to explode from within. Amazing he could bloat this much and still be conscious. Kasper had been such a brave boy with that bear. That moment of hugging him in his orange lifejacket, with no window, no future, that had been significant. That had been his life.

He saw all of it at once. Not in succession, but all in one point, with lines made up of multiple points, each a different reality, different choices, a multiverse of lives, many with Kasper growing old. But even in this one, he couldn't tell for sure, they all blurred together, but even in this one Kasper was alive, if he still understood what now meant, then Kasper was still alive.

"Cunt with ears! You can't start something like this and then say you changed your fucking mind. You imbecile! I'm calling Bigman—"

The phone went dead.

Epilogue

Watching Preble run after the helicopter, gradually getting smaller and further, had been wrenching for Jane, but it had nearly broken Kasper. He'd tried to jump down to his father, and she'd gone from hating the soldier for how tightly and roughly he gripped her son to being momentarily grateful. Kasper had screamed "Daddy!" the entire time as they flew away from their cabin, out over Hudson's Bay, as the pilot decided that he couldn't make it to the USS Polar Star, and even after they'd landed heavily on a relatively flat part of the giant floating ice table. It was such a hard landing that she'd been knocked to the floor—not only were they completely out of gas, but the thermals above iceberg-ocean-iceberg changes were difficult.

As soon as they were on the ice, however, the soldier gave Kasper back to her. He was still repeating, "I want to go with Daddy!"

She carried Kasper out of the helicopter, wanting to get as far away as possible from the thing that had broken their family, but scared to go too far on the crevassed surface of the iceberg. There were ten of them. Eight soldiers and two pilots. The one in charge was a hard-looking man in his mid-thirties whom everybody called "major," with a nose that looked like it had been broken over and over again and had then developed some sort of melanoma on top of all the breaks, or maybe he'd had skin grafted onto half his nose.

The team of eight actually seemed like two teams. There were two radio guys, two guys with extra large guns, two of everything. One of the radio guys called the ship and handed the radio to the major, though the pilot had been doing all the talking before.

Jane didn't hear the start of the conversation, but she came back in time to hear the pilot say, "Look at this wind. I say we just wait in the chopper."

"Too near the edge," the major answered. "We'll set up camp thirty meters in-berg from the LZ."

The pilot bristled at the criticism of his landing but joined the rest of the team in setting up tents, sleeping bags, and other survival gear on the ice. The guard who had held Kasper was detailed to watch them. He looked a bit like a hard version of Tiger Woods, which made him seem almost familiar, and was the friendliest of the group. He gave both of them cold weather gear, including a jacket Kasper's size—meaning this whole thing had been well planned in advance—but his eyes were as cold as the rest of the team. The only ones with any life in their eyes were the two pilots.

Kasper went to the camp and started to investigate all the gear, the sleeping bags, everything. Jane wanted to stop him, just to keep him close, but she was relieved he'd stopped screaming, was almost surprised at how quickly he got distracted by the gear, and so she let him. The soldiers also seemed relieved at the end of the screaming, and since they didn't leave guns lying around, saw no reason to stop him.

"Momma, I need to poop!" Kasper yelled suddenly.

Jane looked at Kasper. "Ah, okay, honey, you can go right here. I'll go find you some paper."

"No, I don't want the bad man to see me poop. Come. Come." He grabbed her hand and pulled. "You can wipe my butt with snow, but I don't want the bad man to see my butt."

Tiger Woods hesitated, looked around at the empty expanse of ice, shrugged and said, "Just don't fall into a hole."

Kasper kept pulling Jane, looking back at the man, and saying, "The bad man can see my butt."

When they were about twenty meters from the soldier, he yelled, "Okay, that's enough."

Kasper continued to pull Jane's hand insistently.

She said, "That's enough. It's dangerous to go too far."

"No, Momma," he said in a low voice, "The ice is broken. Run. Carry me! Carry me! Run!"

Jane froze for a moment, then picked up Kasper and ran as fast as she could away from the helicopter, camp, and the soldier. He started to run after them. And then there was an immense roar, like the world was ripping apart, followed by a small splash. She turned back, and the iceberg which had extended thirty meters to the makeshift camp, thirty more to the helicopter, and another twenty past the helicopter, ended less than ten meters out. Beyond, separated now by a large gap, was a far smaller iceberg that seemed jagged, with a series of tapered teeth like merlons in a crenellated battlement. The edge of the two-mile tabular iceberg had clearly been much shallower, and when it calved the portion that was left visible above the water was less than a quarter the size of the shelf that had been there before. There was no sign of the helicopter, the soldiers, or of anything else.

"Oh my god," Jane whispered.

"We'll be okay, Momma. Our friend will come. But we have to wait first."

"When?"

Kasper paused. "After two times sleepie pie. It's going to be so cold."

Jane looked at her son, terrified. "When did you start seeing the future, Kasper?"

"What's 'future,' Momma?"

"Never mind."

"Tell me! What's 'future'?"

Then she realized that Preble had never been able to see what happens "after two times sleepie pie." Not by a long shot. But then Preble's abilities had only come with puberty. They'd talked about the possibility of Kasper inheriting it but assumed it wouldn't be an issue for another ten years. They'd just locked themselves into that assumption. "Future is tomorrow, and the day after tomorrow, and the day after that."

"Momma, I'm sad."

"I am too, honey. But we shouldn't be."

Kasper looked at her, almost angry. "I have to be sad!"

"Why's that, Kasper?"

"Because Daddy's stuck. When I see Daddy, he can't go."

"What do you mean, when you see Daddy?"

"When I see him."

"In the future?"

"What's 'future'? You didn't tell me, Momma!"

"Just tell me where you see Daddy?"

"In New York. And Bali. And when he was like me, in...Abbacookie."

"Abbacookie? You mean Albuquerque? New Mexico?"

"Yeah, Albacookie."

"But...your Daddy left Albuquerque when he was ten or so."

"He was there when he was little, like me."

"You see him there?"

"Yes. He's stuck there.'"

They spent the night huddled in a half-igloo they made on the ice. With only an hour or so of darkness, the snow as insulation, and the cold-weather gear, it didn't get dangerously cold, but it was still miserable. Kasper told her he had a radio and showed it to her. He'd taken it from the camp. It relieved and frightened her at the same time.

If a storm came, they'd be dead. So when the USS Polar Star came along the next morning, searching without putting any men on the berg, she nearly radioed them. She would have, to keep them from freezing to death, or starving, except that Kasper had known. He was like Preble and that meant two things. They had hope off the iceberg. He said tomorrow a friend would come. And if she called out to the ship, they'd take him. The simple fact that they were alive would be proof enough that Kasper shared Preble's gift. So she let the ship go.

When it left, she tried to think like Preble. Oddly enough, she'd been almost bored by his talent. Oh, not when he'd first told her, to be sure, but after years and years together it had become just the thing that took his time away. Still, she knew how Preble's window worked better than anyone. Better even than Fish. "Kasper, pumpkin, if you turn the radio button in your mind, can you tell which station will reach our friend? The friend you said would help us?"

Without hesitation or testing Kasper turned the dial and said, "Hello!"

"Hello," a voice bounced off the Iridium satellite above the Arctic Ocean. "Shiatie Taget. Who is this?"

"Hello. My momma and I need a boat. Lat 58.924499, long -94.237976. Please."

Jane took the radio from Kasper. "Mr. Taget? We're friends. We need your help very urgently."

There was a long pause, as though the satellite was extra far. "I know someone who will be very happy to see you. It will take me some time to get through. Ice. Can you repeat your coordinates?"

"Um, hold on, my son knows them."

"Your little boy?" Shiatie sounded puzzled.

Jane held the radio to Kasper and he repeated the numbers. Then they got off, to preserve the battery, just in case. "How did you know those numbers, Kasper?"

Kasper shrugged. "Other numbers make us cold."

Jane was tempted to radio Churchill to find out about Preble, but she knew she needed to avoid unnecessary radio traffic. Or using any of their names. Shiatie wouldn't talk—the Inuit were the most discrete people on the planet—but Churchill was full of southerners. Churchill had a government, police, all of it. Preble would have to suffer one more day, then they'd be together.

Shiatie picked them up that night—hungry, cold and thirsty (the ice was salty!)—and took them to Churchill. He wanted to take them to the hospital, but Jane insisted they were okay. As they pulled into Churchill harbour, however, she put a hand on his shoulder and asked him to stop the boat. And explained that the American military was after them. He listened without a word, shrugged, then took them to his house, a simple shack twenty miles outside Churchill on the river with polar bear skins stretched over doors made of plasterboard, depressing government-issue plasticized-wood furniture, and gallons of fuel and kerosene. When he went into town to ask about Preble, Shiatie's wife gave them raw caribou meat and narwhal to eat. The narwhal was so tough that Kasper couldn't eat it without his mother's help.

Shiatie came back four hours later with news Preble had gone south. Then said they could stay as long as they wished. The next day, the Americans bombed Manitoba, and a week later the White House, Capitol, Library of Congress, Supreme Court, Lincoln and Washington Memorials, Union Station, National Archives, Smithsonian Institute, National Gallery, the Kremlin, Red Square, Dzerzhinksky Square, Gorky Park, Ivan's Wall, Church of Saint Simeon the Stylite, monuments to Marshal Zhukov, Peter the Great and Lenin, the Tomb of the Unknown Soldier, the yellow-tiled roofs of the Forbidden City, the 485 lions on the Marco Polo bridge, the Summer Palace, Temple of Heaven, Great Hall of the People, Bird's Nest Olympic stadium, as well as skyscrapers, slums, factories, projects, apartment blocks, stores, avenues and playgrounds all skipped the liquid state as they went from solid to gas. Three capitals and nearly forty million people disappeared in boiling cauldrons of fire that burst skywards through the atmosphere, giant wounds in the Earth, dirty yellow gas pushing itself like infected pus towards outer space.

Jane stared at Shiatie's television set for nearly an hour before slowly realizing that Kasper was sitting beside her on the faded lime-green sofa, watching, just as silent. She was crying for her husband, without a sound or tears or movement, and for the millions of people in Washington and Moscow and Beijing who'd lost husbands and wives and children, but most of all she cried for the knowledge that Kasper would one day enter the world: a world that, when it realized what he was, would be his enemy.

"Shiatie," she asked that evening, "is there a village somewhere we can hide for a long time. Years?"

Shiatie gave her that long look of his, like he saw through everything, like he saw the future and the past and the present and none of it fazed him enough to move except perhaps the request of a friend. He left very early the next morning, and returned mid-day. "I've found you a village. It's very small and the men still follow the hunt. They are family."

"If you see Preble, tell him. Otherwise, don't ever tell anyone."

Shiatie looked at her and Kasper again, then threw a newspaper onto the 1970s plastic-and-laminate dining table, the sort that was now hip again in Williamsburg, Brooklyn, where they'd been a family and had a life. Preble's face stared out of the front page with second-coming font headlines declaring him The Demon. Jane stared at the upside-down paper and knew that the day would come when Kasper would ask her whether his father was really the most evil monster who had ever lived and she would say, no, he was just a man who made a mistake.

At that moment Kasper turned to her and said, "Don't worry, Momma. When I'm big like Daddy, when I'm seventeen, I'll beat the bad men. I'll beat them all."

Acknowledgments

There's an easy part to the acknowledgments: Thank you Christoph Paul, Leza Cantoral, Kaitlyn Kessinger, Joel Amat Güell, and the whole team at CLASH Books! What you do for writers and writing is truly extraordinary. I feel very lucky that this book found a home with publishers who care about books the way you do, beyond labels and boundaries, who focus on the two things that truly matter: the people and the art.

I also want to thank Catherine Adams, the best developmental editor out there, who easily hops with me across genres to identify the core of my stories and sharpen them. And Holly Watson, my amazing publicist. And my early readers, Emma Payne, Joe Pan, Martin Ott, Mark Powell, Outi Korhonen, Pete Duval, Mike Spencer Bown, Andrew Case, Ben Swire, Kevin Winchester, Marc Marins, Galen Backwater, Aaron Haspel, and Sgt. JD McLeod, who generously shared their time, suggestions and improvements. And blurbs. There's nothing more fun than bouncing ideas.

Closer to home, my parents, Paul and Darina Boldizar. I'm lucky to be one of those people who can say without hesitation that there's no one in life who will always have your back the way your mom and dad will. In small things and big, I always knew they'd be there for me in a way that transcends any other considerations. That knowledge was a tremendous source of security growing up, though unlike Preble the only dead body they ever needed to help me bury was my law career. When they read SECONDS, they said, "Finally, you wrote something that's not confusing!" But they always supported me, even through the confusing ones.

Much of this book comes out of that protective family energy. I dislike biographical decoding of literature. It's a simplistic lens that flattens multiple dimensions into a shadow. But certain ignition energies do come from the author's own life—in this case, it was my son's brief abduction when he was very young. It all turned out well, and that's one of the best things about being a writer. Ten years later you can be grateful for events that melt your teeth with stress while they're happening—because they give you a story and a fire.

Give me ten more and I'll write a novel where the monster is cancer. My beautiful wife, Tania Xenis, died of colon cancer while I was finalizing this one. She was the kindest person I've ever known, that anyone who knew her has ever known. She lived by the idea that it's always sunny if you go high enough, and she kept that even through her cancer. She called it the "garden growing inside me." She didn't like how SECONDS ended, because it felt dark and she was never dark. But it couldn't end any other way—at least in a novel you can keep your family alive.

For me, the crack of light was everything I learned about the nature of time. I believe Einstein in his letter to the family of his lifelong friend: "People like us, who believe in physics, know that the distinction between past, present, and future is only a stubbornly persistent illusion."

Time is not a river where some depart ahead of others. Those waves are always interacting and the angels on the head of the pin are always dancing together.

About the Author

Alexander Boldizar was the first post-independence Slovak citizen to graduate with a *Juris Doctor* degree from Harvard Law School. Since then, he has been an art gallery director in Bali, an attorney in San Francisco and Prague, a pseudo-geisha in Japan, a hermit in Tennessee, a paleontologist in the Sahara, a porter in the High Arctic, a consultant on Wall Street, an art critic out of Jakarta and Singapore, and a police-abuse watchdog and Times Square billboard writer in New York City. He now lives in Vancouver, Canada.

Boldizar's writing has won the PEN/Nob Hill prize, a Somerset Award for literary fiction, and other awards, including a *Best New American Voices* nomination. His novel, *The Ugly*, was a best-seller among small presses in the United States with several "Best Book of 2016" awards and lists. He has a black belt in Brazilian jiu-jitsu, is a founding director of a charity that brings circus to youth in at-risk communities, and was once challenged to a leg-wrestling contest by the founder of *The Onion*.

Also by Alexander Boldizar

THE UGLY

Also by CLASH Books

BAD FOUNDATIONS
Brian Allen Carr

THE KING OF VIDEO POKER
Paolo Iacovelli

VIOLENT FACULTIES
Charlene Elsby

THE RACHEL CONDITION
Nicholas Rombles

DEATH ROW RESTAURANT
Daniel Gonzalez

I, CARAVAGGIO
Eugenio Volpe

DARRYL
Jackie Ess

EVERYTHING THE DARKNESS EATS
Eric LaRocca

ANYBODY HOME?
Michael J. Seidlinger

THE LOGOS
Mark de Silva

WE PUT THE LIT IN LITERARY

CLASHBOOKS.COM

FOLLOW US

TWITTER

IG

FB

@clashbooks